Praise for *New*

Best Laid Plans

"Amazing . . . The interconnectivity of Brennan's books allows her ensemble of characters to evolve, adding a rich flavor to the intense suspense. Hang on tight, for this incredible tale will keep readers guessing while providing some heart-stopping thrills!"
—*RT Book Reviews* (4½ stars, Top Pick!)

Notorious

"Packs in the thrills as investigative reporter Max confronts new murders and old family secrets in a suspense novel guaranteed to keep you up late at night!"
—Lisa Gardner

"Brennan introduces readers to a new and fascinating heroine worth rooting for. She's an investigative reporter who's not afraid to kick butt, climb a tree, or go to jail in pursuit of her story. She's savvy and smart and takes no prisoners. Buckle up and brace yourself for Maxine Revere."
—Sandra Brown

"Explosive suspense ratchets up with every turn of the page . . . will leave people clamoring for more stories of Max Revere. I know I will be!"
—James Rollins

Dead Heat

"Gut-wrenching and chilling, this is a story you won't soon forget!"
—*RT Book Reviews* (4½ stars)

heart-stopping thriller . . . From first to last, this story grabs hold and never lets go."

"An excellent addition to the Lucy Kincaid series. Lucy and Sean continue to develop as complex, imperfect characters with a passion for justice . . . The suspense was can't-put-it-down exciting."

Also by Allison Brennan

Best Laid Plans
Compulsion
Notorious
Dead Heat
Cold Snap
Stolen
Stalked
Silenced
If I Should Die
Kiss Me, Kill Me
Love Me to Death
Carnal Sin
Original Sin
Cutting Edge
Fatal Secrets
Sudden Death
Playing Dead
Tempting Evil
Killing Fear
Fear No Evil
See No Evil
Speak No Evil
The Kill
The Hunt
The Prey

NO
GOOD
DEED

Allison Brennan

St. Martin's Paperbacks

NO GOOD DEED

Copyright © 2015 by Allison Brennan.
Excerpt from *Poisonous* copyright © 2015 by Allison Brennan.

All rights reserved.

For information address St. Martin's Press, 175 Fifth Avenue, New York, NY 10010.

ISBN: 978-1-250-06433-2

Printed in the United States of America

St. Martin's Paperbacks edition / November 2015

St. Martin's Paperbacks are published by St. Martin's Press, 175 Fifth Avenue, New York, NY 10010.

10 9 8 7 6 5 4 3 2 1

CHAPTER ONE

Nicole Rollins had always been a meticulous planner. She had contingencies for almost every possible scenario, which was why she'd been able to deceive the DEA for fifteen years. People were mostly predictable, and mostly fools.

Even though being arrested wasn't in her master plan, she had a contingency, and the minute she was arraigned the clock started ticking. Her people knew what to do and when to do it. The time line, by necessity, had to be fluid, but when she was ready, she gave the signal and the countdown began. Nothing was left to chance, because she only had one shot at escaping and she had to get it right.

And if she got it wrong? She'd go out big and take as many of those motherfuckers with her as possible.

But she wasn't going to get it wrong.

Today marked the end of her old life. Cliché, but true. Nicole sat patiently in the back of the federal prisoner transport van, her face blank. Bored. Defeated.

Boredom and defeat were the farthest things from her mind. Anticipation flowed hot through her veins.

Her feet were shackled and locked to a bolt on the floor. Her hands were cuffed in front of her and attached to a chain around her waist. She wore an orange jumpsuit—she despised orange, it made her skin appear sallow—and her blond hair was now cut short, without concern for style.

Nicole liked her new, short hair. After a trim, it would be fun and sassy. She needed a little fun in her life after being in jail for nearly three months. She'd have to dye it darker, maybe add a few highlights, enough of an appearance change to get by until she could hook up with a plastic surgeon she knew in Monterrey, Mexico. He was good; he'd be able to change the shape of her face and eyes so the feds would be hard-pressed to identify her.

Two armed guards sat with her in the back—one with his back to the front of the truck, the other directly across from her. Another guard drove, and a fourth was in the passenger seat. A steel-reinforced door with a bulletproof window separated the cab from the back. Closed-circuit cameras showed the rear compartment to the guards up front. They were being recorded, but there was no live camera feed. She didn't care—within thirty minutes she'd be dead or gone. How it happened would be irrelevant.

Two federal SUVs escorted the van, front and back. This was the third time Nicole had been transported from the jail to the federal courthouse. The first two times were uneventful but necessary so her team could adjust last-minute details. Last Monday she went to the courthouse to give the assistant US attorney a juicy morsel to exploit. On Thursday it was to review documentation and sign the plea agreement. After the explosion at the DEA's evidence locker ten days ago, the AUSA was more than happy to use Nicole as a source of information.

The angry, defeated look on Brad Donnelly's face as he watched her in the courtroom that day had thrilled her to no end. She won, he lost.

He had far, far more to lose before she was done with him and the people he worked for.

Today the guards were taking her to the courthouse to spill her guts. She'd already agreed to the plea deal. She'd promised to tell everything she knew about Tobias, his operation, the drug and gun pipelines from Mexico into the US, how they laundered money. All in exchange for the federal prison of her choice.

She was a damn good actress—good enough to convince the AUSA and the judge that she was remorseful. Good enough to convince them she would talk.

Nicole was used to stakeouts and long periods of waiting; she remained calm. Very calm. An alert dream state.

Waiting.

Waiting.

Nicole smiled deep inside, so deep that her blue eyes remained blank and her mouth a thin, straight line. Her plan was nearly foolproof. She had contingencies on top of her contingencies, which was why the DEA had never known she was the most dangerous fox in their henhouse.

The transport van slowed as they approached a red light. The lead SUV had already driven through the intersection. The lead car had a sensor that turned red lights green so they wouldn't even have to slow down. Except now the light was red. They stopped. They had no choice.

A school bus had entered the intersection.

Nicole couldn't see the bus from the back of the van, but she knew it was there.

She didn't smile. She didn't react at all.

Her heart pounded in her chest, adrenaline surging in anticipation. And still, she remained motionless.

Nicole had taken the gamble when she planned her escape that the AUSA would follow standard protocols for a cooperating prisoner, but she also knew that there were some factors that she couldn't control. Would her former partner Brad Donnelly convince the AUSA to change routes? Would Samantha Archer tell Brad about the transport in the first place? If Brad were in charge, he'd have brought the AUSA to the prison—but Sam always played according to the rules. She was predictable, and so far, Nicole had never been wrong about what her former boss would do.

She wasn't wrong today, either.

It also helped that she'd stacked the deck, so to speak, by having someone on the inside to ensure that the transport didn't deviate from protocol. And if they did deviate? She had another plan, though that would have resulted in a higher body count.

This time she didn't need it.

The guard sitting directly in front of her spoke into his radio. "Report."

The passenger said, "Traffic stop."

The guard was suspicious. Too smart for his own good. He said, "It's supposed to be green all the way."

"The lead car is holding up across the intersection, we have the tail car, nothing out of the ordinary."

The guard said, "Run it."

"Can't. Traffic—a school bus."

Nicole smiled and closed her eyes.

The school bus full of children stopped in the middle of the intersection.

"Shit," the driver said. He radioed immediately. "Alpha-One, we have a situation. Code Yellow."

The lead SUV responded. "Back up, re-route parallel to the north."

"Negative," Alpha-Two responded. "No way to turn around without exiting the vehicle and directing traffic."

Alpha-One said, "Code Red, be alert. Backup en route."

The school bus didn't move. Three masked men emerged with fully automatic weapons and opened fire on the front of the transport van.

The windshield was bulletproof, but enough pressure

from high-caliber weapons and even bulletproof glass breaks.

In less than ten seconds both cops in the cab were dead.

It had been Nicole's idea to use the school bus. No cop would return fire when the shooters were shielded by children.

The guards in the back of the transport van had their guns out—one aimed at Nicole, one aimed at the door. The smart guard who'd sensed a problem before the problem occurred reported through the open mike, "Two officers down! We're under attack. Three shooters minimum, possible fourth in the bus, multiple hostages."

There was no response.

"Alpha-One, this is Zeta-One. I repeat, officers down. Under attack. Hostages in bus. Confirm."

Silence.

"Alpha-Two! Are you there?"

Silence.

One of the two masked men climbed up the front of the truck, through the broken glass, and extracted keys from one of the dead guards.

"You'll never get away with this," the smart guard told Nicole. "They'll hunt you down like a rabid dog."

She didn't say a word, just stared at him.

He turned his gun on her. "I die, you die."

"And then all those children die," she whispered.

His face fell. She smiled. Just a small smile, but her excitement was growing and she couldn't contain her glee.

Sirens roared from seemingly every direction, coming closer.

"Open the door," Nicole said.

The armored van had to be unlocked from the outside, but opened from the inside. Her team could get in because they had the right tools, but it would take longer.

Time was critical.

"Officer, if you do not open the door in ten seconds, my people will start killing those children, one by one, until you do."

"Don't do it, Isaac," the second guard said.

"Seven seconds. I'm not bluffing."

The smart guard, Isaac, was torn. She saw it in his eyes. This was the type of dilemma they'd been trained for, even when the threat was rare. Did you let a prisoner go to save innocent lives? It was a fair trade, as far as Nicole was concerned. But in training, you never gave in to terrorists. In the textbooks, there were hard-and-fast rules. All criminals were terrorists. Do not negotiate. Wait for the hostage rescue team.

"Four seconds."

Isaac glanced out the front and saw a gunman emerge from the bus holding a child in front of him.

Children . . . that was a wild card. You could train for it, but until you were in a situation with the barrel of a gun at the back of a child's head, you really didn't know what you would do.

Isaac got up and turned the knob. The click told her it was open.

"Put the gun down and you'll be spared," she said.

"Don't do it! They'll kill us both!"

She looked Isaac in the eye. "I'm not lying."

The door opened and Isaac put his gun down and his hands up.

The other guard didn't. He didn't get a shot off before a bullet pierced his skull.

One of the masked men quickly unlocked Nicole's shackles. She picked up the gun that Isaac had dropped. "No one may believe it, Isaac, but sleep well because you will save those kids."

"Will?" he said through clenched teeth.

"Time?" she asked one of her men.

"Eight fifty-four and thirty seconds. Thirty-one, thirty-two—"

Nicole cut him off and turned back to Isaac. "You have five minutes, twenty-ish seconds to get those kids off the bus before the bomb goes off. And if you are wondering, there really is a bomb. It *will* explode at nine a.m."

Nicole sprinted alongside her rescuers. The police would be closing in fast, but they had an escape route already in place. A car idled in the alleyway off the main street and Nicole and two of her men jumped in. Those who'd stayed with the bus had their own escape route.

The driver glanced at Nicole. "You cut your hair."

She touched Joseph's face. How she'd missed him! "It'll grow back."

"I like it."

She smiled as Joseph sped away. "Do we have Santiago locked down?"

"Tight. Dover is running the operation."

"That means there can be no witnesses. We can't risk exposing him right now."

"He knows the drill. Everything is on schedule."

She pulled a gun, watch, and cell phone from the glove compartment. They listened to the police band as Joseph traversed downtown San Antonio. It didn't take long for Isaac the smart guard to alert authorities to the bomb threat.

It was no idle threat.

She glanced at her watch, her stomach tingling with anticipation. She stripped off the jumpsuit and pulled on the simple black dress that Joseph tossed her.

They were almost to Amistad Park when she heard the explosion in the distance.

Distractions always worked.

The explosion was the cue for the helicopter to land. It

had been painted to look like a news chopper. She and Joseph got out of the car and ran across the soccer field to where the chopper had set down. The men in the back jumped into the front seats and drove off to dump the vehicle. Less than three minutes after the explosion, Nicole and Joseph were strapped into the helicopter and lifting off from the grass.

Joseph leaned over and kissed her hard on the lips, then held her face in his hands and looked at her. He didn't have to say anything—couldn't over the sound of the engine and the blades whirling above them—but his eyes said everything.

She was loved. And she was free.

CHAPTER TWO

Lucy Kincaid walked into FBI headquarters Monday morning, late for the first time since she'd started working in the San Antonio field office six months ago. Surprisingly, she didn't feel guilty.

She'd had the best weekend of her life. A weekend that had changed her in a deep, fundamental way because what Sean had done—what he'd said, what he'd confessed, what he'd shown her—removed the invisible weight that had held her back for years. She walked lighter. She felt *happy*. In the eighteen months she'd known and loved Sean, he'd made her happy—ice skating in DC, a weekend in New York City, feeding her chocolate-covered strawberries, taking her to a kids' movie: These were all wonderful and romantic gestures. She laughed with Sean when laughter had been elusive for years.

She'd had happy times before, but she'd never truly felt happiness, deep down inside. Until now.

It certainly wasn't only because of the exquisite engagement ring on her finger, or the three lazy days at the beach house in San Diego, or the birth of her beautiful, perfect nephew. She, Lucy Kincaid, finally accepted—and liked— who she was.

For years she'd thought that she was irrevocably damaged, that the horrific kidnapping and rape that had destroyed her at eighteen would haunt her for the rest of her life. She wanted desperately to be normal; she wanted to be like everyone else. And she recognized that while she would never forget what happened, and while it had in fact changed her life, the cruel acts didn't define her. Accepting that part of her past and who she had become washed away the lingering doubts and numbing pain. She wasn't normal, and that was okay. Accepting her differences, accepting that it was *okay* not to be like everyone else, had been difficult. Even Sean's love couldn't get her out of the rut of believing she didn't deserve love and affection. She realized this last weekend that only she held herself back, only she lived with one foot in the past, fearing it would come back and destroy her.

Now her past no longer taunted her. For the first time in years, she'd had a full week of restful sleep. Maybe the nightmares would come back, but she'd deal with them rather than ignore them. Because the nightmares showed her problems that needed fixing, rather than flaws that were permanent.

"Look who just floated in." Kenzie Malone leaned back in her chair.

"What?" Lucy said, momentarily confused. "Oh, I'm late. Sorry. We flew back this morning and Sean dropped me off. We didn't even go home first."

"You're like only thirty minutes late. Juan isn't even in yet." Kenzie rolled her chair over to Lucy's cubicle and grinned, her eyes sparkling. "Tell me *everything*."

Kenzie's nickname was the Energizer Bunny. She never stopped. Once a month she trained with the National Guard; she'd served six years in the army before going to college. Lucy hadn't yet worked any cases with Kenzie, but they'd become friends. Maybe because the only other female agent on their squad was just a few years from retirement and didn't socialize with anyone.

"It was fun," Lucy said. "Relaxing. I needed it."

"And—holy shit, that's a ring." Kenzie grabbed Lucy's hand. "A *ring*. You're getting married."

Lucy blushed.

"Now I know why your feet aren't on the ground."

"Is it that obvious?"

"First, you're late—you're never late, Kincaid. And you were smiling. Honestly, you don't smile enough." Kenzie leaned over and hugged her. "I'm so, so happy for you. You and Sean are made for each other."

Lucy smiled. "He's pretty great."

"When are you going to introduce me to his brother?"

"*Kane?*" Lucy laughed. "Oh, Kenzie, Kane is nothing like Sean." That wasn't completely true. Kane and Sean were two sides of the same coin, but Kane was dark and Sean was light.

Lucy had become worried about Kane, especially his obsession with Tobias, the elusive gunrunner he'd been hunting for nearly three months. But Sean told her Kane was fine. That Kane was just being Kane. Lucy wasn't as confident, but she didn't know Kane as well as Sean did.

"I might not need an introduction." Kenzie winked and leaned in. "I met a guy a couple of months ago."

"And you didn't tell me?"

"I didn't want to say anything until we had at least three dates. You know how it is . . . you like someone, then find out he snores like your grandpa or picks his nose when he thinks you're not looking."

"Kenzie!"

She laughed. "Eric does neither. He's a cop with SAPD, SWAT-trained, all-around *hot*. I think you worked with him on Operation Heatwave. Eric Butcher. Ryan introduced us—seems Eric had been interested in me for a while and wanted to make sure I didn't have a boyfriend."

"I remember Butcher. Definitely your type."

Kenzie leaned back. "Maybe we can make it a foursome this weekend?"

Lucy wasn't as social as Sean, but Sean would probably enjoy it. "I'll ask Sean. He loves having people over to the house."

"That would be fun."

"Must be serious, if you're introducing Eric to your friends and colleagues."

"We'll see—" She nodded at the ring. "So, when's the big day?"

"We're not doing anything big, and I don't know when. I suggested eloping, but Sean thinks my father will draw and quarter him if we don't get married in the church." That had been a big concession on Sean's part. Lucy went to church semi-regularly, but Sean detested organized religion. "Sean's been working on the boys' home with the pastor at Saint Catherine's, so we'll ask him to marry us. Sean respects him."

"So I'll get to meet your entire family—very cool. And what about your sister? Did she have the baby?"

"Last Thursday. He's perfect." Lucy held out her phone, which had a picture of John Patrick Thomas set as the wallpaper.

"God, I love babies. I feel my biological clock ticking. I'm thirty-four, Lucy! Maybe that's why I want it to work out with Eric. He's the first guy I've really liked in . . . well, years. At least you have a few years before you have to worry about that."

Lucy felt the twinge in her hollow stomach. It was the one truth that still bothered her, that she couldn't have children of her own with Sean. She'd accepted that Sean was okay with it, and that when and if they wanted children they would adopt. There were so many children who needed homes—not newborns, who were easier to place, but older kids who'd been lost or forgotten by the system. Still, Lucy grieved that she couldn't have a child of her own.

But Kenzie didn't know, and she didn't mean anything by her comment. Lucy said, "Thirty-four isn't old. Carina is thirty-eight. Nora, Sean's sister-in-law, was forty when she had her baby."

"And that's only six years away for me."

Zach Charles, the analyst assigned to the Violent Crimes Squad, jumped up from his cubicle and bellowed across the room, "There's been a prison break—conference room, stat."

Half the Violent Crimes Squad was present, and they rushed to the conference room where they were joined immediately by Special Agent in Charge Ritz Naygrow. Twenty agents filled the room, with more trickling in as Naygrow spoke. Lucy's cell phone vibrated in her pocket. She glanced at the number—it was Brad Donnelly with the DEA. She didn't take it, but she had a bad feeling she knew who had escaped.

"People, I don't have many details but will tell you what I know. A federal prisoner transport unit taking former DEA agent Nicole Rollins to the courthouse was hit minutes ago."

The conference room television was on and muted. A news helicopter was circling a yellow school bus that was stopped in the middle of an intersection. The armored van could be seen on the bottom of the screen as the helicopter shifted perspective, but there was no movement in the van.

"Multiple shots have been fired. We don't know if the shooters are targeting her because she cut a plea deal, or if this is an escape attempt. SWAT team leader Leo

Proctor just left with his team to assist the DEA and the US Marshals. As you can see on the television, a school bus of hostages is in play, possibly as a distraction. Be alert and ready to go in the field. We'll be assisting in any way we can."

Kenzie said, "Kids are running out of the bus."

They all turned to the television, faces grim. A guard and several civilians were helping the children, but everyone appeared frantic. This wasn't a typical rescue operation. A guard was seen carrying a small child as he ran out of the bus.

Only seconds later the bus exploded.

A chorus of curses and gasps filled the room.

Naygrow told ASAC Abigail Durant to take over the meeting and he quickly left the room.

Durant stepped up and looked around the room. "Agent Figueroa, put together a team of agents with medical training and get on-scene stat. Agent Proctor is our lead in the field, connect with him as soon as you arrive. The marshals' office has point on this, but since there's extenuating circumstances, the DEA will be all over it."

"Yes, ma'am," Emilio Figueroa said.

Emilio had been a paramedic for eight years before joining the FBI. Lucy didn't know him well because he'd been cross-training weekly with all first responders in the area.

Lucy stepped up. "Emilio, I'm an EMT and search-and-rescue-certified."

"Okay. You, Kenzie, Ryan—oh, wait, he and Nate are with Proctor's SWAT unit. Nelson—" Emilio looked around.

"I'll go," an older agent said.

"Thanks, Pete. Grab your go-bags and firearms and meet in the garage in three minutes."

For emergencies, they had prepared medical kits

secured in the locker room. It had been a project Emilio had worked on when he first joined the San Antonio FBI office eight years ago. He worked closely with the SWAT team on training to ensure members of Proctor's team were up-to-date on triage and other medical protocols.

"Wear your vests," Abigail ordered as they started out. "We don't know what we're walking into."

Five minutes later Lucy was in a tactical SUV with Kenzie and Emilio while the other two agents followed in a pool car. Lucy immediately returned Brad's call—he'd texted her *urgent* multiple times.

He answered immediately. "Did you hear?"

"I'm on my way with a medical team."

"It was a bomb," Brad said. "She's gone."

"Nicole's dead?"

"Gone. It was a fucking escape. At least two guards are dead, possibly more—it's a clusterfuck."

"The children?"

"I don't know. I'm getting reports—one indicated that one of the guards got all the kids out, but we don't have confirmation. There were eight people assigned to transport her in three vehicles. *Eight.* Two were DEA. No one has checked in."

"We're only a few minutes out."

"I just got here. Find me when you arrive." He hung up.

Lucy told the others what Brad had said.

Emilio said, "I have a report from Proctor that there are at least three confirmed dead, guards who were in the transport van."

"Any word on Rollins?" Lucy asked.

"Nothing. But SAPD put up roadblocks and helicopters. Border patrol is on alert. It's not going to be easy for her to disappear."

"She planned this escape while sitting in solitary

confinement for nearly three months," Lucy said. "She will have planned it all the way through."

If it were her, she'd immediately head for the border, but not on any major thoroughfares. Rollins had friends in Mexico—criminals she'd worked with or helped while she was a DEA agent. Those were likely the ones involved in her escape. Staying local would increase her chances of being caught. The closest border was a two-and-a-half-hour drive away. But the fastest route wouldn't necessarily be the safest. Nicole had a head start, but not a big one.

Lucy sent Sean a text message.

Rollins escaped. Alert Kane.

If there was any chatter about the escape, Kane would uncover it. Not only did he have moles in key places, but his instincts were borderline psychic. His knowledge of the drug cartels and travel routes and heavy hitters in the criminal underworld could help them find Rollins before she disappeared permanently.

Traffic was a mess as Emilio navigated through roadblocks and detours until they finally reached the crime scene. They were ordered to park a full block away. SAPD had cordoned off two square blocks and was still in the process of evacuating civilians. All that remained of the bus was smoke. The firefighters were doing their job to ensure that the fire was fully out before their investigation team went to work. Lucy stepped out of the SUV and was hit with a wave of humidity even though it was only nine twenty in the morning.

The scene was controlled chaos. Dozens of cops, EMTs, paramedics, firefighters all doing their jobs. Emilio's team pulled their medic bags from the back of the SUV. Most of the injuries appeared to be from glass and flying debris.

As a group, the five of them approached the staging area. Immediately SWAT team leader Leo Proctor flagged Lucy. "Kincaid, we need a psychologist."

"What happened?"

"The officer who survived the transport attack—he's the one who saved the kids on the bus. He won't put down one of the kids. He seems to be coherent, but I think he has to be in shock." He shook his head. "Dammit, Lucy, the gunmen killed the bus driver in front of the children. Shot the two guards driving the van."

"School's out for the summer," Lucy said. "Was it a camp?"

"A summer program at Saint Catherine's."

"Oh my God," Lucy said, automatically crossing herself. "That's where I go to church."

"If you want me to bring in someone else—"

"No, I'll do it."

"We need intel. Officer Harris gave a statement, but we still don't know what the fuck happened. All he's clearly said was that he had five minutes to get the kids out of the bus."

"Harris—SAPD?"

"Corrections. Isaac Harris. He's married and I think he has a kid."

"Where is he?"

Proctor motioned at a pair of US Marshals, introduced Lucy to them. They escorted her down the street to a restaurant that was being used to contain the children. Sitting on a bench outside was a man in uniform, dirty and bloodied, rocking a little girl with long dark braids who couldn't have been more than six.

Lucy asked one of the marshals in a low voice, "Have you contacted the school?"

The marshal said, "Yes. They're sending over staff and

contacting parents. We're setting up a tent to process each family, make sure all children are accounted for and picked up by legal guardians."

"Do you have a roll call?"

"We're working on it. Forty-two children are assigned to the bus, and we have forty here. We don't know if the other two were inside when it exploded."

Lucy glanced inside the restaurant. The staff had served water or juice to all the kids, and several SAPD officers were sitting with them. Some were crying, some were staring blankly, and some were blatantly curious. But all had their innocence stolen today.

"Can you leave me with him?" She motioned toward Isaac Harris.

The marshal nodded and went back to his station.

Lucy assessed the officer. Tall, broad, early thirties. He was sitting like a sentry outside the restaurant, watching everyone who went in with a critical eye. The little girl clung to him, her face buried in his chest, and he cradled her like an infant. Both Harris and the girl were bleeding.

"Officer Harris?" she said as she approached. "I'm FBI Agent Lucy Kincaid. I'm also an EMT. I noticed you and this little girl are bleeding. Can I—"

He cut her off. "We're fine. We're fine."

"I'd like to clean the cut on her face. We don't want it to scar, do we? What's her name?"

"Mary."

"Hi, Mary," Lucy said and sat down.

Harris tensed and stopped rocking. He stared at Lucy with deep suspicion. The girl clung to him even tighter.

"My name is Lucy. May I look at the cut on your head?"

Mary didn't move.

"Isaac," Lucy said, "if I don't clean her wound, it could get infected."

He hesitated, then nodded. In a soft voice, he whispered

to the girl, "Mary, can you turn your head just a little so Ms. Lucy can help?"

The girl immediately obeyed, but didn't open her eyes. Lucy pulled on her gloves, gently pulled back Mary's hair. The wound was superficial—it had bled a lot, but the bleeding had stopped. She might need a couple of stitches. Lucy pulled gauze and a disinfectant from her medical bag.

"Mary, I need to clean the cut on your head. It's going to sting a little bit, but that means the medicine is working."

The girl flinched but didn't cry when Lucy touched the antiseptic to her head.

"You are very brave," Lucy said. She finished cleaning the wound, then bandaged it. "Father Mateo will be so proud of you."

Mary looked at her for the first time, eyes wide, but didn't talk.

Lucy smiled. "Father Mateo is a friend of mine. Would you like to see him?"

Mary gave an almost imperceptible nod. Then she closed her eyes again and settled back into Officer Harris.

"Isaac," Lucy said, "Mary may have a concussion. She needs to be checked out at the hospital."

"I'll take her," he said.

"You can go in the ambulance with her, would that be all right?"

He nodded and kissed the top of Mary's head. He had his own injuries and she wondered if he was more seriously hurt than he'd initially let on.

Lucy figured that once Isaac could leave Mary in a safe environment, like a hospital, he would be able to let go. She didn't understand exactly what he'd gone through—Mary's reaction was normal, but Isaac's wasn't.

"Before you go, I need information, Officer Harris."

"I told the marshals everything I know."

But he wasn't looking at her.

Lucy said, "I know Agent Rollins."

He tensed. Mary whimpered, and he whispered in her ear.

"I know what she's capable of," Lucy continued. "What I don't know is what happened in the van."

He scowled at her. "They killed my partner and the only reason they didn't kill me was because I put my gun down. I could have taken her out. I thought about it . . ." His anger disappeared, and he whispered, "I didn't know about the bomb. I never would have thought about it if I knew."

"How many in the escape?"

"Three that I saw. Probably more. All masked. Plus Rollins. They must have had a car stashed somewhere, but I didn't see it. When she told me I had five minutes—"

"Five minutes?"

"Five minutes, twenty seconds before the bomb went off. They'd already set it before they breached the van. If I hadn't let them in—" He closed his eyes and took a deep breath.

"The bomb would have gone off no matter what."

He nodded. "She said that I could go after her or save the kids."

"You did the right thing." He had to believe that. Lucy didn't know if mistakes were made, but there was no doubt that Nicole would have killed those children. She was playing the odds. And this time, she'd won.

The bomb was a distraction. It diverted attention from Nicole's escape. Isaac Harris didn't see where Nicole and her henchmen had gone or what they were driving because he was focused on getting the kids off the bus.

Tears pooled in the corner of his eyes. "They killed Trevor. He'd just gotten married. He's dead because he did his job. I didn't, and I'm still here."

"Listen to me, Isaac," Lucy said firmly. "You did your job. You saved forty children. Forty kids with parents and grandparents and aunts and uncles and siblings who would all be suffering right now if not for you."

"What do I say to Gina? I was at their wedding . . ." His voice cracked.

"You tell Gina that Trevor died a hero. He died doing his job. Isaac, if you hadn't put down your gun, you would be dead. And so would everyone on that bus."

"I never wanted to be a hero." His voice cracked. "Not like this."

She squeezed his hand. What else could she say?

"I didn't get everyone," he whispered.

"How many?"

"The driver. And—I don't know."

"The driver was already dead."

"You don't know that."

"No, but an autopsy will be done and we'll find out."

"What if I missed someone?"

"They're doing a roll call."

He didn't say anything.

"Isaac, I need more information. Did Nicole say anything, did one of her people say anything, that can help us find her?"

He shook his head. "No. Nothing."

Lucy waited. She didn't talk, just let Isaac remember on his own. Because there was more, there had to be.

"She knew," he suddenly said.

"What did she know?"

"That I had five minutes to get the children off the bus. She asked her partner the time, and then told me I had five minutes and twenty seconds. She knew about the bomb, knew about the timing. She must have planned the entire thing."

"That's good, Isaac. She was in solitary. There weren't

many ways she could have planned and put together this operation. We'll find out how, and then we'll find out where she went." She suspected there was something else in Isaac's head, but she didn't know how to get him to remember.

Out of the corner of her eye Lucy saw Brad Donnelly approaching, but she held up her hand to keep him away.

"How did the men get into the back of the transport?" she asked.

"I opened the door. I had to. She said I had ten seconds or they would start killing the children."

Mary whimpered in his arms and he hugged the girl tightly.

"You did the right thing," Lucy said again.

"And they killed Trevor. I did the right thing but they killed a good man." He closed his eyes.

"Isaac?" Lucy said quietly. "I know a thing or two about survivor's guilt." She slipped her card into his pocket. "Call me anytime you need to talk. But remember this—you did what needed to be done. You'll replay the scene over and over in your head, but in the end, you need to know that had you done anything different, Mary would not be here right now. Do you understand?"

He nodded but didn't look at her.

"I'm going to send over a paramedic. You can go with Mary to the hospital."

He looked up through the window at the rest of the children. "I can't leave them. Someone has to watch over them."

There were a dozen medics and cops in the restaurant tending to the needs of the children. But Isaac didn't see them. Maybe he was blind to everything but the kids.

"Father Mateo is coming," she said. "He'll take care of these kids, I promise."

Lucy got up and walked over to Brad. "It was planned

down to the last detail. They had the bomb set on a timer, multiple gunmen, knew the route, how to breach the van. They left nothing to chance."

"They're gone. Helicopter lifted off from a soccer field two miles from the explosion. We have multiple witnesses—they couldn't identify Nicole from her photo, but agree there was a pilot plus a man and a woman." He squeezed his fists together and said through clenched teeth, "Tobias was behind this."

"Maybe."

He stared at her as if she were speaking in a foreign language. "*Maybe?* Who else?"

"Nicole herself."

"He's in charge. We knew that from the beginning, from when you overheard him three months ago threatening Vasco Trejo. He's the one who orchestrated the slaughter of his rival gang. He ordered the hit on Worthington less than two weeks ago. He bombed the DEA evidence locker. *It's him.*"

"He's involved, but she's important. He wouldn't spring her if she were a nobody."

"She knows too much. He had to get her out."

"Then why not kill her? It was easy enough to kill the guards, to plant a bomb on a church school bus. If Tobias wanted her dead, Brad, she'd be dead."

Lucy didn't know when she'd come to that conclusion— it might have been formulating over the last two weeks, since the explosion at the DEA evidence locker; it might have been even longer, when they first took Nicole down. There was something about her that told Lucy she was a player, not a follower.

"Lucy," Brad said, then stopped as the truth sank in. "You're saying she wasn't just an agent on the take."

"No. She's the ringleader. I'd bet my badge on it."

CHAPTER THREE

Lucy tended to several minor injuries while the paramedics triaged the most serious. Most of the injuries were related to the explosion—cuts, burns, scrapes. Two bystanders who'd been hit by stray bullets during the initial gunfire had already been transported to the hospital before Lucy and her team arrived.

Five people involved with the transport had been killed—three guards in the van, and the two DEA agents in the rear SUV. The lead SUV had two US Marshals; they'd both been incapacitated and were in stable condition at the hospital.

Less than an hour after the explosion, the fire was completely out and arson investigators had begun processing the scene. SWAT were methodically clearing each building. SAPD were retrieving all security cameras from the area so they could piece together a visual of what happened, and the FBI were interviewing witnesses.

Lucy spotted Father Mateo Flannigan as he walked from the staging area to the restaurant where the children were. She caught up to him and put a hand on his arm. "Tell me what you need, Father."

He rested his hand on hers and squeezed. His face was

pale and drawn, his eyes troubled, but he was calm when he said, "I need the children away from here."

"Have their parents been notified?"

"My staff has been working with the police to contact parents. They said forty children came off the bus. I confirmed that two students, brothers, stayed home today."

"Sick?"

"I didn't ask. I spoke to their grandmother and she said their mother dropped them off this morning. Why is it important? We know they weren't on the bus. This should be good news."

It might be nothing, but investigators needed to check out all anomalies. "I need their contact information."

"I gave it to your people. Lucy, I know you're doing your job, but the kids need me now. And I need them."

"Of course." Lucy stepped aside and let Father Mateo console his flock. She'd done all that she could here. She watched as Officer Isaac Harris hugged a petite woman who clutched Mary in her arms. Her mother? That would give Isaac some peace, she hoped.

Lucy walked back to the staging area and found Leo Proctor, who was coordinating all the SWAT teams—FBI, SAPD, and DEA. "I need an agent to check something out," she said. "It might be important."

"DEA is lead on the investigation, marshals are running the manhunt. What's going on?"

"Father Mateo Flannigan, the head pastor at Saint Catherine's, said that two boys who were supposed to be on the bus went to their grandmother's instead."

"And?" He sounded rushed and irritated.

"Gut feeling. They may be sick, but we won't know until we check with their family. Father Flannigan spoke to their grandmother but he may not have asked the right questions."

"Give the intel to the DEA, then report to Casilla."

Lucy couldn't find Brad in the immediate area, so she sent him a text message about the boys. She went back to the restaurant, where parents had started arriving to pick up their children. At a table both SAPD officers and civilian staff were recording everyone's information, verifying identification, and releasing the children. Father Mateo helped facilitate the process.

None of those children would ever be the same. A burning anger filled Lucy. Nicole Rollins had stolen their innocence. She'd set this entire thing up with full knowledge that the kids would be traumatized and possibly killed. Her sole motivation was to escape. Five dead cops and dozens injured.

How could Nicole have ever become a DEA agent? How could she work for more than a decade in a profession she detested? How could she see what violence did to the victims and then perpetuate it herself? When Lucy first met her, while they worked together on Operation Heatwave, she'd thought Nicole was smart, methodical, and a bit cold. A lot of cops—especially those who had high-stress jobs—could be icy. Lucy was herself aloof, especially when processing a crime scene. She saw the scene through the eyes of the killer as well as the victim in order to not only understand the victimology, but to capture the killer.

She could understand Nicole if she wanted to get into her head, but Lucy hesitated. Going so deep into the criminal psyche was unfortunately easy for her, but it took its toll. Still, such analysis was one thing she was particularly good at, and understanding Nicole's plan and why might be the best way for Lucy to help find her.

But what really bothered her, over and above what had happened here today, was how Nicole could spend so many years in law enforcement and yet no one knew her true self. She was able to fool many people for many years. How was she recruited in the first place? What was her background? When did she turn? Was there one incident that had her changing allegiances from the agency that trusted her to a violent criminal organization? Or was it a gradual process?

Lucy walked over to where the fire department had cordoned off the smoldering bus. She overheard the chief report that they had found one body, an adult female. No children had died today.

The death toll could have been so much higher. Lucy would never forget or forgive Nicole. She'd killed an innocent person and five law enforcement officers who were simply doing their job.

She flashed her badge and walked under the crime scene tape to get a closer look at the transport van. The bulletproof glass had been shattered by repetitive, high-velocity firepower. The three dead guards had been removed; they lay on the ground under yellow tarps. The bodies of the two DEA agents from the SUV were down the street under similar tarps. They'd be removed as soon as the coroner arrived. The FBI Evidence Response Team and SAPD were processing the scene; cards with numbers littered the street and vehicles—the highest number she saw was seventy-nine, but there seemed to be over a hundred placards.

Lucy stood next to the driver's door and surveyed the immediate area. The bus had blocked the intersection, separating the lead SUV from the van. This intersection was ideal to set up the trap. They were driving on a narrow two-lane street heading into a four-way intersection. There was no easy way for the large van to turn around. The attack had occurred at approximately eight fifty a.m., a busy commute time.

The two US Marshals had been incapacitated but not killed. Why incapacitate the Marshals but kill the two DEA agents?

Had the transport driver been suspicious? If so, he would have contacted the support teams—but they'd already been taken out.

Lucy saw the scene vividly. The bus stops in the intersection. Gunmen exit, shoot out the window, kill the guards. Fast. Everything happened fast, perfectly timed. No one alerted SAPD or the respective federal agencies prior to the shooting. Blocked communications. No sense of danger until it was too late.

Kill the two guards in the cab. Open the van. Nicole knew what the plan was because she told Isaac he had ten seconds to comply or children would start to die. He complied. Nicole walked free, but to avoid being followed she told Isaac he had five minutes, twenty seconds to get the children to safety.

Giving Nicole and her men enough time to escape.

They could have killed everyone and still had time to escape. Why put the bomb on the bus? Was it more than a distraction? Was there another reason to set off the bomb?

Donnelly reported that only two individuals, a man and woman, boarded a helicopter right after the explosion. Was the bomb also a way to distract first responders from hunting them down? If Isaac had time to alert anyone before he rescued the kids, there was a slim chance Nicole could have been apprehended en route to the helicopter. But she didn't give him the time. And after a disaster—like an explosion—all resources and personnel would rush to the point of origin.

When had the gunmen boarded? They couldn't have been hiding on the bus—there would be no place that the children wouldn't see them. They must have boarded with the last of the children—or hijacked the bus near the end of the route when the missing boys were supposed to be picked up.

She took out her notepad and scribbled her observations. In all likelihood, the lead agents were already following this avenue of investigation, but she didn't want to miss anything. With emotions running high and an escaped felon on the loose, they may not have thought beyond tracking Nicole Rollins's footsteps.

Lucy glanced at her small, neat block letters. While others were running on anger, grief, or determination, she was standing here methodically—coldly—putting together pieces of a puzzle. It had to be done, and she knew she was good at it, but her lack of emotion disturbed her. She blocked out everything except the evidence and the psychology. It bothered her because it was becoming harder and harder for her to connect with people. There seemed to be a wall between her and everyone else. Like Kenzie. She liked Kenzie, but sharing her feelings—like her happiness about her engagement—felt unnatural.

Analyzing the crime scene, getting into Nicole's head, figuring out how all the pieces fit together—that felt natural.

There was something wrong with her.

No. It's not wrong. It's who you are. Accept yourself as you are.

Just this morning she was thinking she had. And then something like this happened and she once again felt disconnected from everyone else.

Only Sean didn't make her feel abnormal. She closed her eyes and remembered their weekend. Remembered that it was okay to be different. That her unique skills would help the FBI and DEA find Nicole Rollins. She breathed deeply and let the calm take over.

"Lucy," Brad said.

She opened her eyes. Brad was both angry and grieving, but keeping his emotions under tight control.

"You said you had something," he said.

She handed him the paper with the names of the two

missing boys and their grandmother's address. "They didn't get on the bus. Father Mateo didn't know why, he thought they might be sick. He spoke briefly with their grandmother when his head count didn't match the number on the bus."

"I'll send someone to check it out later."

"Why didn't they get on the bus?"

"Who cares?" Now Brad's irritability came through. She couldn't blame him.

"What if someone related to them is involved? Nicole knew about the bus, knew the route, knew where and how to get on and how the bus intersected with the prison transport—or how to divert the bus without drawing attention. They could have created the plan by observing the bus routine for a few days, but it would be easier and more reliable to have someone on the inside. How? At the last stop? What if these boys were *supposed* to be at one of the stops but the driver didn't know they wouldn't be and the gunmen hijacked the bus?"

"Shit." Brad ran a hand over his face. "Okay, I see it. We've pulled all the security feeds and our tech people are putting them together, but that takes time and equipment, so it's all going back to headquarters for processing. Debriefing in—" he glanced at his watch "—about ninety minutes. That should give us time to follow-up with these kids."

"I need to report to Casilla."

"I'll ask him if I can use you for the duration."

Lucy would do anything to help, but she also recognized that her boss had only recently begun to trust her again after a series of events that necessitated her violating protocol and engaging in a rescue mission south of the border. Brad had been a part of that. "Are you sure?"

"Lucy, you're the only one I trust. Nicole had someone on the inside—she couldn't have planned and executed this escape without help. The day and time of the transport could have come from her attorney, but the route—you're right, that was limited knowledge and decided at the last minute. She wasn't told."

"She could have guessed."

"Yeah, but there are three preset routes from the jail to the courthouse. She couldn't have known which one we'd choose."

Brad and Lucy walked back toward the staging area where they spotted Juan Casilla talking with Samantha Archer, Juan's counterpart at the DEA, and the SAPD chief of police, Milton Turner. "Stay here," Brad said.

Lucy watched as Brad talked to the group. She couldn't hear what they were saying, but Brad did most of the talking. No one looked at her. Two minutes later he shook Juan's hand, then approached Lucy. "You're with me."

"That was fast."

"I told the truth. We have a mole and I trust you. I didn't need to convince Juan so much as Sam. I don't know why she doesn't see it—I think she's in shock."

"She lost two men today," Lucy said. She needed to talk to Juan to make sure this really was okay with him—their working relationship had been better over the last couple of weeks, but it was still not the same and she feared it would never be.

"We both need to be at the meeting at FBI headquarters later—a multi-jurisdictional clusterfuck if you ask me, but better that we all know who's doing what so we don't miss anything."

"I'm surprised Sam Archer is letting you work this case," Lucy said.

They got into Brad's car and he immediately sped off. "She doesn't have a choice."

"She always has a choice. She's in charge."

"I told Sam and the AUSA that Nicole was playing

them. They didn't believe me, or they thought they could handle her. I told them not to transport Nicole using any method that the DEA has used in the past. They didn't change their methods, only kept her in solitary. Me being right buys me at least a day or two of getting to do whatever the fuck I please. I'm going to find her."

Lucy said, "I understand vendettas better than most people. You have to be smart, Brad—don't go off on your own. Don't be reckless. We need information—not just about what happened today, but about Nicole herself. Who she is now and who she was when she first joined the DEA."

"What's that going to do?"

"I'm a criminal psychologist. I'm going to figure her out. And when I do, I'll know how to find her."

"This isn't magic. We'll find her because of old-fashioned police work. And a limited group of people who have all the information—I was serious that we have a mole."

Lucy agreed about the mole, but Nicole must have thought beyond today, especially with an escape that was so well-planned. She had a place to hide or transportation out of the country. What would she do? Go underground for a week until the manhunt slowed down? Or immediately flee the country? Did she already have a fake passport, money, a final destination?

William Shakespeare wrote, *"The past is prologue."* What was in Nicole's past would tell Lucy exactly what she needed to know to find her.

Ten minutes later Brad and Lucy arrived at the residence of Rosita Nocia, the grandmother of Matthew and Lucas Garcia, the young boys who hadn't boarded the bus. She lived in a small bungalow with a tiny yard of half-dead lawn in a neighborhood filled with small bungalows and half-dead lawns. Most windows had bars and doorways had security screens. The community wasn't severely depressed, but it bordered one of the worst crime areas in southern San Antonio. Brad knocked on the door. A moment later a very old woman opened it. She spoke in Spanish, so Lucy took lead.

After showing their identification and introducing herself and Brad, Lucy said in Spanish, "We're here about Matthew and Lucas. They were supposed to be at summer school today, but weren't at the bus stop."

The elderly woman twisted her apron in her fists. "I don't know."

"You told Father Mateo Flannigan that their mother dropped them off with you."

The grandmother's eyes widened. "*Sí*."

"We need to talk to them."

"They're not here."

"Where are they?"

Mrs. Nocia didn't say anything. She looked at her fingers clutching her apron and dropped it, then stuffed her hands into the pockets.

"Mrs. Nocia, have you been threatened?"

"No, no."

But she was clearly uncomfortable.

"Is there anyone in the house with you?"

"No, I swear on my memaw's grave, I'm alone." She crossed herself, then kissed the crucifix that hung around her neck.

"Were your grandsons here this morning?"

"*Sí*, but just for a minute. They are okay?" It was a question.

Lucy hoped so, but decided to use the woman's worry to her advantage. "That is what we're trying to find out. Were the boys here when Father Mateo called?"

She shook her head.

"Did their mother pick them up?"

Again she shook her head.

Brad was getting angry, and Lucy was afraid that if he lost his temper, Mrs. Nocia would clam up for good.

"Mrs. Nocia, I'm going to call Father Mateo and ask him to come down and speak with you. Maybe you'll feel more comfortable talking to him."

The grandmother shook her head and glanced at Brad, then quickly looked away. Brad tensed beside her. Lucy stepped forward, partly blocking Brad so that Mrs. Nocia would focus solely on her.

"I know you won't lie to Father Mateo."

"Please," Mrs. Nocia begged.

"If you want to make sure that your grandsons are safe, I need to know who took them."

"My daughter told me a man would be by after nine to take them to school. A man came as she said, the boys knew him, they weren't scared, I swear. They left. I—I didn't think anything was wrong until Padre Flannigan called. I didn't mean to do anything wrong. Are they okay? Please, *por favor*, are they okay?"

"Where is your daughter?"

"She works at a hotel. The Star. Good, honest job. She's a good girl."

"Thank you." Lucy handed Mrs. Nocia her card. "Call me if you hear from your daughter or if the boys return. Is their father around?"——

Mrs. Nocia frowned, anger tightening her lips. "No good. He's in jail. He won't divorce her, though Padre says he broke the sacrament of marriage, and that he would support an annulment. My Elena did nothing wrong, but Pedro convinced her that an annulment would send her to Hell, so she won't get an annulment. He was the one who killed a man and he's the one going to Hell." Mrs. Nocia crossed herself again. "I knew he was bad from the beginning, but Elena was sixteen, she didn't listen to her mama."

"Is Pedro's last name also Garcia?"

"*Sí*. The judge said he won't be getting out of prison for twenty years. It should be longer."

In the car Lucy asked Brad, "Do you know the name? Pedro Garcia?"

Brad shook his head as he typed on his phone. "I'm sending the info to our liaison with SAPD. We'll pull his file, see if there's a connection to Nicole or anyone affiliated with Tobias. Let's talk to Elena Garcia and find out what the hell is going on."

Lucy and Brad first checked the Garcia house, a duplex in a neighborhood not far from Mrs. Nocia. No one answered the door. Brad then drove to the Star, a top-rated hotel in downtown San Antonio. After ten minutes of the runaround, they were informed that Elena Garcia had called in sick that morning.

"She's involved up to her eyeballs," Brad said as he sped out of the parking garage.

"She could have been threatened," Lucy said. "She has a mother, two kids."

"Or she could have used her mother."

"Why didn't she just disappear with the boys?" Lucy said. "Mrs. Nocia said a man picked them up."

"If we believe Mrs. Nocia."

Brad was skeptical, but Lucy didn't push her point. She said, "We'll pull her finances, find out if she has other property, relatives, friends. Put someone on both the grandmother's house and Elena's house."

"When I get the details on the dad, I'll have the marshals question him," Brad said. "Get a warrant to search the house."

"I'll talk to Father Mateo."

"Will he cooperate?" Brad said. "In my experience, priests don't like to give up their parishioners."

"He'll talk to me." She didn't add that sometimes, priests and others didn't talk to police because the police hadn't helped when they really needed it. Father Mateo had a sour history with law enforcement after one of his students disappeared—the police thought the kid was a runaway and hadn't done more than a cursory search for him, if that. Michael Rodriguez had been kidnapped and nearly died at the hands of a drug cartel. Father Mateo might be a man of God, but he also had a long memory. Fortunately, Lucy had a good relationship with him, and Sean was instrumental in getting the boys' home running and funded. Considering what had happened today—Father Mateo would help.

Her phone rang. It was Sean.

"Hey," she said. "I only have a minute. Brad and I are on our way back to headquarters for a debriefing. Did you get my message earlier?"

"I've been following the news. Michael called, so I'm heading over to Saint Catherine's. He's scared, though he won't admit it. Says the others are worried and want me to check things out."

Her heart skipped a beat. Michael, even after his kidnapping ordeal, had been instrumental in helping the DEA identify many of the major players in the southern Texas drug trade. Along with Lucy, he'd seen the elusive Tobias who'd orchestrated so much violence over the last few weeks. Nicole knew who Michael was, and it wouldn't be too difficult to find out that he—and the other boys they'd rescued from the cartels—were living at the new boys' home across the street from Saint Catherine's.

"I didn't think that she'd go after Michael."

"Honestly, I don't think she will right now—her goal

is to get away," Sean said. "My guess is she's long gone. But the bus she used was from Saint Catherine's. I doubt that was a coincidence."

She hadn't considered that Nicole planned her escape down to not only using a school bus, but *which* bus.

"It's about fear—these people use fear as a weapon. To scare the boys. To intimidate law enforcement." *And me.*

"You're probably right, but don't go anywhere alone, Lucy. Just in case retribution is in her game plan. I heard she'd escaped in a helicopter, but I'm not taking chances with the boys—or with you. Call me when you know anything. I love you, future Mrs. Rogan."

She smiled. "Love you too." She hung up, and her smile disappeared. "Sean and I have a connection to Saint Catherine's. So does Michael Rodriguez—and Nicole knows that Michael was instrumental in helping us stop Trejo Vasco's operation and uncovering her involvement."

"I'll get a detail on the boys' home as soon as possible. It might be a few hours—everyone is spread thin right now."

"Sean's going there now. He'll stick with them today."

Lucy wanted to believe that Nicole had left town, but she feared there was a bigger, more violent plan in the works.

CHAPTER FOUR

Elise Hansen was counting the days until she would be free.

She had no doubt that she would walk out of the court-room on Wednesday afternoon.

The court might not consider her free. They might expect her to do community service, or live in a group home, or even check in with a probation officer every week. But that didn't matter, because she wouldn't be locked in a cage or in this crazy-loons hospital-prison.

Of course, she'd never do the community service or check in with a probation officer. No one in this city would ever see her again.

She sat in Dr. Oakley's office and stared at her hands. She itched around the edges of the cast that wrapped her right hand. She'd broken her wrist two weeks ago when that bitch fed thought she was saving her life.

"Elise?" Oakley pushed.

The doctor had asked her a difficult question. Not difficult for Elise—she already knew how to answer it—but difficult for the doctor, one of those pivotal questions that would decide if Elise was a victim or a criminal.

Dr. Oakley said in her smooth, calm voice, "We were so close the other day. Don't close me out now."

Elise shook her head and, without looking at the bitch, whispered, "I'm not."

She'd spoken to the doctor every day for almost two weeks. She'd gone through the gamut of emotions: belligerence, rage, fear, sorrow. On Friday she'd broken down completely after the bitch had confronted her about screwing one of the guards—but she didn't explain herself, and she especially didn't explain how she'd set up the entire tryst.

She loved that word. *Tryst*. The guard certainly couldn't talk his way out of it, and Elise had played the it's-only-my-body card perfectly. But she let the uptight, do-gooder doc peel away the "layers" of her personality to get to the root of her feelings of self-worth, and then she lost it.

Oakley put her on suicide watch, which was exactly what Elise needed. Forty-eight hours of round-the-clock observation. She played the part perfectly, and now here they were.

"Elise?" Oakley said.

"It doesn't matter," she said quietly. Resigned. Her fate was sealed, nothing the doctor could do or say would be able to fix it.

"Yes, it matters. *You* matter."

"I'm going to jail forever. That FBI agent said so."

Quiet sigh. "Elise, do you trust me?"

Shrug.

"I know it's difficult for you to trust anyone, but what you tell me is private."

"I don't believe you. You have to tell the judge everything I said."

"It doesn't work like that. I'm a psychiatrist. Yes, I'm appointed by the court, but my opinion matters." Pause. "I've worked with a lot of girls like you."

Of course she had. That's why she'd been appointed Elise's shrink. Because Barbara Oakley worked with underage prostitutes and victims of sex crimes. Elise wondered why. Had little bitchy Barbara been a bad, bad girl? Had she taken it from her daddy? From her uncle? Had she walked the streets and whored herself? Or was she just a do-gooder who learned everything she knew from a book?

A book, Elise decided. Because if Barbara Oakley had spent any serious time on the street, she wouldn't have been so easily manipulated.

Elise almost laughed. She'd never walked a street in her life, unless she had a game to play.

Tobias had told her once that the best lies were based on truth. And Elise could twist any of her life stories as if it were written in stone, and everyone would believe her.

Except maybe that bitch fed. Tobias had said to be extra careful with Lucy Kincaid, but Elise didn't know why. The woman seemed high-strung. She was weak. She had a dark, sick past that Elise could easily exploit. Destroy her with just a few words. But after the hit on the woman failed, Tobias forbade her to engage. Why?

Elise trusted Tobias, and so she would stay away from the fed if she could.

Though she *really* wanted to skewer her.

"You don't know how it is," Elise said.

"Try me."

Silence. Elise fidgeted.

"I want you to know that it was absolutely wrong for Officer Nance to have sex with you."

"I said it was okay. It's not like he raped me or anything."

"You're sixteen."

"So?"

Another sigh. "There are several reasons why it's wrong, not just because you're underage. He's a guard, he's supposed to protect you, not hurt you."

"He didn't hurt me."

"You're sixteen," the do-gooder repeated. "You're a ward of the court. He can't have sex with you, even if it was consensual. Even if you said it was okay. Did you really *want* to have sex with him?"

Of course, Elise thought. *It got me extra time with you, bitch.*

She shrugged. "It's what I do."

"No, it's not."

She frowned.

"Elise, my job is not only to evaluate you, but to help you. You have choices. You're not just a sex toy. You can't think of yourself like that. You're a young woman, a smart young woman, who can choose to respect herself."

"There's nothing wrong with sex."

"No, there isn't—except when it's a form of abuse."

She frowned. Inside, she thought, *Abuse? Really? What's this woman smoking?*

Elise had *never* allowed herself to be abused. Everything she did she did because either she wanted to, or it was part of the plan.

"Last week you told me about your mother."

Elise's mother was dead, so she'd made up a story. It was one she'd worked on for weeks with Mona Hill, the low-life bitch who ran out on her. But Mona was a master at cover stories and had helped falsify the documentation in case anyone went to verify. She'd been paid well for her services, but then she left. Left when Elise needed her. Her fists clenched in her lap. Elise hoped Tobias found her, gutted her, and left her in a ditch to be eaten alive by coyotes. Just rewards for that coward-bitch-whore.

The cover story was brilliant. Elise's "mother" had been a prostitute. She'd been raised with men coming in and out of the apartment to screw her mother for money. It was "no big deal." But her mom got arrested and the system put Elise in foster care.

"I don't want to talk about her," Elise said.

"You already did."

"I don't want to do it again."

"Why?"

"Because she's dead to me."

"Is that because after she was released she didn't get you out of foster care?"

That was the lie that Elise had implied—and the doc was smart enough to pick up on it. Score one for the doc. Or for Elise? It was her idea to be subtle. Tobias was too in-your-face, but Elise understood people. If she gave in too easily, Doc Oakley would be suspicious. So Elise had to let the doc pull every "fact" out of her.

"I don't want to talk about that."

"It's important."

"Why?"

Her voice cracked. She deserved a fucking Academy Award.

"Because *you* are important, Elise."

What the fuck did *that* mean?

"No one cares about me." *Quiet. Keep your voice quiet so she can't hear the excitement.*

"I care."

Silence.

Staying quiet was always a good cue. Up the tension and whatever. Talking too much would only get her in trouble.

"I'm better off alone," she whispered.

"But you're not alone. You found someone else to be a parent. Your brother, Tobias."

Tread carefully here, Elise, she warned herself. *A little truth, a little lie.*

"He's not really your brother, is he?"

She shook her head. "Not by blood or anything," she said.

"But?"

"He looks out for me."

"But you're scared of him."

"No."

Her voice quivered. Just a little.

"Elise, you're safe here."

"I'm not."

"I promise, you are safe."

"I just . . . I just want to make him happy."

"But he's never truly happy, is he?"

"Yes, he is!" Defiant.

"Last week, you told me that Tobias was in one of your foster care homes, but that wasn't completely true, was it?"

"Yes, it was." Whoops. She'd had to backtrack at the time and clam up, because she had some thinking to do. Now she had a better story to go along with the half-truths and outright lies she'd already woven into her past.

"Elise? I need you to be honest with me. I can't help you if you're not honest."

"He wasn't a foster kid, if that's what you mean."

"He's much older than you."

"So?"

"You look up to him. Like a big brother. Like a father."

"Tobias has been more family to me than anyone in my whole entire life!" *Sell it, baby!*

"I see that you believe that."

"Because it's true!"

"Family doesn't hurt family."

"Yes they do."

"Real love doesn't hurt."

Frown. "There's no such thing."

"Tobias took care of you when you needed it. I see that." She sniffed.

"How did Tobias earn your trust, Elise? Why are you protecting him?"

A long silence. Build it up. Make the bitch think she earned the "truth."

Finally, she said, "Tobias was the son of my foster parents. He never once tried to fuck me. All the other guys tried to fuck me, but not Tobias."

Make her believe that he saved you from a fate worse than death. Make her believe that without him, you'd be dead.

"He came over every week for dinner, but I didn't think he liked his parents much. But he treated all of us like family, you know? Played games—I'd never played board games before. Or card games, or anything. He played and we laughed and it felt like—a family, a real family.

"Then his father . . ." Stop. Slow down. Not all at once.

Elise stared at her hands.

"And his father what?"

"He—he told me he knew I'd been arrested for prostitution. And he gave me twenty dollars to suck him off."

"How old were you?"

"Thirteen."

Elise made sure she didn't look at the doc, but she heard the slight intake of breath, subtle, and she knew she had her.

Hook.

Line.

Sinker, sucker.

"And you told Tobias."

Elise shook her head. "I—I didn't want to lose this family. I'd been in six foster homes in two years, I just wanted . . . I don't know."

"Stability. Normalcy."

"I don't know," she repeated. "I guess. Just . . . a place to stay. My own room."

"How did Tobias find out?"

She bit her lip. "His dad stopped paying me, but expected . . . more. And I gave it to him. I mean, it's not a big deal, it's fast, it doesn't hurt, just get it over with and everyone's happy. So I did it. But one day—his wife walked in and she called me a whore. Well, I guess she was right, because it wasn't like I said no or anything. But then she kicked me out, not him, and I didn't want to leave. I didn't want to leave the family. I-I-I broke things. I just wanted to stay, why couldn't she see that? I would have done anything she wanted. I didn't want to be on the streets, I didn't want to screw strangers again. And, and . . ."

She started crying. She let the doc soothe her until she "pulled" herself together. A minute of blubbering was long enough.

Elise blew her nose and took a deep breath. "I'm sorry."

"Don't apologize, Elise. You have nothing to apologize for."

Elise nodded.

"What happened after you broke things? Did your foster mother call child services? The police?"

Elise shrugged. "I-I don't know. I ran out of the house and called Tobias. He saved me then and has always protected me."

"But he also had you do things for him, didn't he?"

"It was just sex. It didn't mean anything."

"You had sex with him?"

Confusion in the doc's voice, and Elise realized she'd gone too far ahead. "No, never! He loves me, like a sister. He just . . . sometimes . . . well, with other men, to, you know, so he could get information or whatever. I don't know, I just did what he told me, and he gave me a place to live, and clothes, and food—"

"He was your pimp."

"No way. He didn't take *any* money. I got to keep it all. And he bought me everything I wanted. He took care of me. He loves me. Like his little sister. He always said he wanted a sister, and now he has m-m-me."

"He used you, Elise."

"No. No, no, you got it wrong." She squeezed out more tears, then wiped her face with the back of her hand. Barb handed her another tissue. Tears always worked with idiots like Barb, but too much and Elise would lose the edge.

"Elise, Tobias gave you a syringe and told you to kill a man."

"No! He said it was drugs, to make him want to fuck me so that we could get pictures and blackmail him. That man wasn't supposed to die. I didn't know, I didn't know and I wish I could go back, I—I—I didn't know what to do. I was so scared and Tobias—" She stopped.

"Tobias what?"

"I didn't want to make him mad. He was counting on me, and I thought I'd screwed up. And I just want to make him happy, because—"

"Because?"

"Nothing."

"Elise, tell me the truth."

"I—I know what happens to people who don't make Tobias happy."

"What happens to those people?"

Quietly. "They die."

That, at least, was the truth.

Before sitting down to talk to Michael, Sean checked the perimeter of the boys' home, the fences and gates and the alarm system. He'd installed it himself, and it was nearly as elaborate as the security he had installed in his and Lucy's house. Everything checked.

He'd tried calling Kane, but as usual was forced to leave a message. Sean didn't doubt his brother would return the call quickly—Kane had become more than a little obsessed with tracking down Tobias. He'd even made the unprecedented move of calling his old friend Rick Stockton, assistant director of the FBI, for information.

"Michael," Sean said, "was there any other reason you called? Did you see or hear something?"

"No," the thirteen-year-old boy said. "But Sister Ruth told us what happened, and where Father Mateo went."

Sister Ruth was a fifty-year-old nun who'd been brought to St. Catherine's to help set up the boys' home. She had extensive experience in the administration of such group homes, and state law required that a licensed adult be on the premises at all times. She ran the house—and the nine boys—like a well-oiled machine. Truth be told, Sean was a little afraid of her.

"Lucy's there, too," Sean said. "None of the kids on the bus was hurt."

"That's what Sister Ruth said."

"Call me anytime, day or night. No matter how silly you think it is. You have good instincts, Michael. I trust them."

Sister Ruth walked into the kitchen where Sean and Michael were talking. "Mr. Rogan—I'm so sorry. He shouldn't have bothered you."

"I don't mind," Sean said. He didn't. He came by the house several times a week. The house was large, but old and in need of repair. It got hot in Texas, so Sean commissioned a pool. The boys had been through hell and then some; he wanted to give them peace. "I'm going to stay for a while, if that's okay."

She frowned. Sean wasn't sure that she liked him, or the arrangement he'd made with Father Mateo over the boys' home. But it was his deal, and he didn't care if the nun approved or not. Sean would do anything in his power to make sure these boys had a sense of normalcy.

"Do you think that's necessary?" she asked.

"Yes," Sean said. "These people are ruthless. I don't think they'll go after the boys, but I'd rather be cautious. I asked Lucy to look into a protection detail on the house, at least for a few days."

"They've been through so much," she said, then seemed to notice that Michael was still in the room. "Michael, would you please help the others with their math homework?"

"Yes, ma'am," Michael said. He nodded to Sean. No smiles. The boy still didn't smile much, if at all. "Thank you, Sean."

Sean squeezed his shoulder, then watched him leave.

"He puts the weight of the world on his back," Sister Ruth said quietly. "I want to help ease his burden, but I can't seem to break through to him. Unlike you."

"I'm not going anywhere," Sean said. "He's slow to trust. But you're good for him."

"I'm trying. I don't know if living here is the right thing for him."

"It's the only right thing," Sean said, tensing. "Michael needs to know that the sacrifices he made, the decisions he made, led to something good. This is good. He needs to see it come to fruition."

"He's a thirteen-year-old boy and acts twice his age."

"You can't force him to be a child, Ruth." Lucy and Mateo called Ruth "Sister" but it didn't roll off of Sean's tongue smoothly. He hadn't been raised in any religion, and he wasn't Catholic. "He needs these boys as much as they need him."

"I hope you're right, because my heart aches for him. He's seen so much violence." She paused, then said in an even lower voice, "I did missionary work in Guatemala, many years ago, when I was much younger. It was both rewarding and extremely heartbreaking. I saw—" She hesitated, then sighed. "I don't need to share the details. But sometimes Michael looks like the boy soldiers who came through the village on occasion. Old. Defeated. Empty."

Sean knew everything about Ruth Baxter because he'd done an extensive background check on her before he allowed her to come to the house, even though Jack Kincaid's old army buddy Padre heartily recommended her. She'd seen a lot more in her missionary work than boy soldiers walking through her village. She'd seen much, much worse. It was because of her empathy and experiences that he, Mateo, and Lucy thought she'd be good for the boys. If it worked, she'd be here a lot longer than the six months the diocese originally had agreed to loan her to Father Mateo.

"Michael is none of that," Sean said. "But he has his own demons to fight, and that's why we're here—why we opened this house. Why you're here helping them. Michael, all of them, are survivors, and we'll make sure they have a future. But to ensure the future, we need to be diligent."

"I understand, Mr. Rogan."

"And please, Ruth—stop calling me that. I'm Sean."

CHAPTER FIVE

Brad and Lucy arrived at FBI headquarters a few minutes after the debriefing started. Every seat in the large conference room was occupied, so they stood in the back of the room while US Marshal Stan Dalton finished his report. Five dead cops—three from the detention center and two from the DEA. The two marshals were both awake but had concussions. They'd given near-identical statements—they'd driven through the intersection on a green light, which immediately changed to red. The transport van couldn't follow because the school bus rolled into the intersection and stopped. They attempted to call in the threat, but their radios were jammed. Their first thought was that the prisoner was in jeopardy since she was turning state's evidence against high-ranking cartel members. Though they were on alert with weapons drawn, they were immediately jumped and incapacitated by two men who seemed to have come out of nowhere.

That meant there were more than three individuals involved. Two or three came off the bus, according to Officer Isaac Harris's statement. Two incapacitated the marshals. That left one or two bad guys who shot and killed the DEA agents. A minimum of five operatives to pull off the escape—and most likely six, counting the getaway driver. The scenario made Lucy wonder if Nicole deliberately spared the marshals while killing DEA agents. If that was true, Nicole had a twisted psychological reason for that decision.

She's at war with the DEA. They turned on her, investigated her, arrested her.

So did the FBI.

But she worked for the DEA.

"We're at three hours, forty minutes since the escape," Dalton said. "Every law enforcement agency has been alerted. We've beefed up security at the border—the marshals' office and the DEA field offices in McAllen and El Paso are heading up the border watch. Where we don't have a station, we've tripled our air patrol and will keep it high for the next seven days at least."

"She'll know that," Brad mumbled. "She'll wait until we pull people back."

Either that or she's already gone, Lucy thought.

Dalton said, "The FBI tech team put together a video of surveillance cameras that has helped us track exactly what happened. If you can, stay after the briefing to watch it. It shows better than I can tell you how violent these bastards are. Here's what we know: two masked and armed men boarded the bus on South Brazos Street where the driver was scheduled to pick up two brothers. The driver was killed immediately. No child was able to give a description of the shooters but all agreed there were two men. This happened only twelve minutes before the attack on the transport van. The timing was impeccable."

Dalton looked around the room, his expression grim but fierce.

"It's clear, based on what Officer Harris had witnessed,"

Dalton continued, "that these men will kill without hesitation. Harris was told that if he put down his gun, he would be spared. His partner fought back and was shot and killed. When Harris put down his gun, Rollins told him that there was a bomb on the bus that would explode in five minutes. He risked his life to bring all the children to safety. Not one child died today. We had losses in our ranks, but no child died and dammit, I will take that victory."

He took a long drink from a water bottle. No one spoke.

"We believe that the explosion had a dual purpose—to give first responders or survivors a distraction, such as the ultimatum given to Officer Harris, and to signal the escape helicopter," Dalton said. "The helicopter was mocked up to look like a media chopper, but we have located it ninety miles east, approximately halfway to Houston. We have people processing the chopper now. Based on where it landed, we don't believe that they could have reached the border yet. However, we can't discount that the location east is a diversion, hoping we'll move our resources toward Houston so they can escape using another route. Every federal and local agency in Houston is going to work the area from the landing site toward their city, while we'll focus west of the landing site."

Lucy was relieved. Nicole would have considered law enforcement protocols and how they would allocate resources, and if she really was heading east she would have landed in a less conspicuous location.

Dalton added, "The Texas Rangers are assisting, their focus in the rural areas. They know back roads and potential hideouts better than anyone. Every law enforcement branch is fully engaged. We will find them. But we all need to keep in mind that they are ruthless and dangerous. They killed five cops today. Every one of you needs to be on full alert at all times. Wear your vests. Go nowhere alone. That is an order, or I will have you removed from this investigation. I want no more dead on my watch."

Samantha Archer stepped forward. "Thank you, Marshal Dalton. I know you all want to get to work. To that end, the FBI and DEA will be working closely with all other agencies. My office has already identified every known associate of Nicole Rollins and is tracking them down. It is clear that Rollins was involved in the planning. She knew about the bomb even though she has been in solitary for nearly three months. She still had access to an attorney, and had been transported twice this past week to the courthouse. She has used moles in the past, and she very well could have one or more now."

Surprised murmurs spread through the group of collected agents, but it didn't surprise either Lucy or Brad.

Archer said, "Agent Donnelly has a report from the field."

Brad spoke from where he stood and heads shifted toward the back of the room. He told the group about the Garcia brothers and what he and Lucy had learned from their grandmother about the father in prison and the unknown man who picked up the boys.

"We need to remember that Nicole Rollins had us fooled for years," Brad continued. "She was my partner on several major drug enforcement investigations. She was privy to years of sensitive information about drug dealers and the cartels. She's been feeding some of them information, yet helping us take down other groups. She subtly steered us to take down the enemies of her boss, Tobias. We don't have a last name. We believe that he is in charge and Nicole is a high-ranking member of his cartel—otherwise he would have had her killed today. My boss and I have spent the last three months compiling a dossier on how she operated in preparation for a trial that was stopped when she agreed to a plea deal—a plea deal she never planned to complete."

Lucy frowned. That wasn't what she and Brad had discussed earlier. But she didn't say anything. Maybe Brad had a reason for the disinformation. Or maybe he didn't agree with her that Nicole was in charge.

Brad walked to the front of the room as he continued. "You all need to understand how these people work. Two weeks ago, immediately prior to Nicole agreeing to the plea deal, Tobias orchestrated a hit against his own people. If it weren't for our partnership with the FBI and the SAPD, we may never have seen the connection. I say this because you might not know what's important when you see it. We need every detail, no matter how small or irrelevant it seems. It took us years to uncover Rollins as a traitor—she slipped up, but her slip was caught only because good agents were doing their jobs well. In addition, Tobias—using information we believe Rollins gave him about our procedures—disguised a bomb in heroin that took out our evidence locker and killed a security guard."

Sam Archer said, "We have a team in Washington poring over Rollins's finances. We had previously uncovered over two million dollars in hidden assets, but to orchestrate an escape like this, she must have had more resources. In addition, Tobias was able to siphon off nearly four million in funds that the late Congresswoman Adeline Reyes-Worthington had laundered for him through her real estate scams. The FBI managed to cut off their money supply, but these people are resourceful and vicious."

Dalton and Archer answered questions from the group, then Abigail Durant, one of the FBI's three ASACs, stood up and said, "Dalton and the marshals' office will be taking the lead on tracking the fugitive Nicole Rollins. I will liaison with the marshals. Any information that directly relates to a sighting or Rollins's whereabouts must be reported to your immediate supervisor or me, anytime of the day or night. Please see your direct supervisor for your assignments." She looked over at Lucy. "Kincaid, I need to see you in my office immediately."

CHAPTER SIX

Lucy stood outside Abigail Durant's door, her stomach doing little flips, but she couldn't think of a reason why she'd be in trouble. For the ten minutes she waited she went through everything she'd done today and during her last investigation into the murder of Harper Worthington and grew increasingly nervous that something was seriously wrong.

Abigail walked briskly down the hall toward Lucy and smiled apologetically as she opened her door. She motioned to one of two chairs opposite her desk. "Thank you for waiting, Agent Kincaid. Please, sit down."

Lucy sat but remained rigid. She admired Abigail, a crisp, professional woman in her forties. But she'd rarely spoken to her directly—assignments came through her direct supervisor, SSA Juan Casilla.

"Juan will be out for the next few days," Abigail said. "Nita, his wife, went into labor this morning."

"Is everything okay?" Lucy liked Juan's family, and regretted that she hadn't spent time with them recently.

"Nita collapsed this morning. They may be performing an emergency C-section. Juan said he would let me know, but I don't expect a call anytime soon. I'm supervising your unit until Barry returns. I left him a message this morning and asked him to call in. We need all hands this week."

When Lucy first worked with Agent Barry Crawford, she thought he not only was too by-the-book, but clocked out at five without any thought to putting in extra time to solve cases and give victims peace. She'd learned that he led a very balanced life, and the time he did put into the job was focused and dedicated. They were certainly quite different in how they approached their jobs, but Lucy had grown to respect Barry's methodology and sharp instincts. That said, they hadn't spoken much since the Harper Worthington murder investigation ended. Lucy trusted Barry as a cop, but not as a friend after she learned he'd called agents in Washington, DC, to investigate her behind her back. She was trying to accept it, and move on, but it still bothered her.

Lucy was curious why Abigail was waiting for Barry when there were other senior agents who could take over temporarily. She didn't say anything, however.

"When Juan and I spoke," Abigail continued, "he said that Brad Donnelly asked for your assistance, a loan to the DEA for the duration. He wants both you and Ryan Quiroz."

"Agent Donnelly has some trust issues right now."

Abigail nodded. "Juan explained. I need you on another part of the task force and I'm not sure you can do both."

Abigail opened a drawer and pulled out a thick folder. She slid it across the desk toward Lucy. "Nicole Rollins's file," Abigail said. "Her initial background check, psych exams, test scores, evaluations. Essentially, an expanded personnel record. Before the debriefing, I contacted headquarters to expedite a profile of Rollins. I spoke with Dr. Hans Vigo, an assistant director whom I understand you know well."

"Dr. Vigo was my mentor at Quantico," Lucy said. That

was the simple version of the truth, which was that Lucy had known Hans for years and he'd been her mentor long before she'd been accepted into the FBI academy. "There's no one better."

"I've never met Dr. Vigo, but his reputation is outstanding, and I was very pleased when he informed me he would be coming here personally to assist. With budget cuts and priorities, headquarters rarely approves BSU going into the field."

"Which was one reason I declined an offer to join the Behavioral Science Unit," Lucy said. "Profiling isn't as effective if criminologists are looking at photos and reports—they need to be in the field, interviewing individuals, viewing the evidence firsthand."

Durant smiled. "That's close to what Dr. Vigo said. He reminded me that you're a criminal psychologist, told me about several cases where you assisted that aren't part of your official record."

Lucy had no idea what Hans had told Abigail, so she remained silent. Abigail waited a beat. Was she expecting Lucy to talk? Her heart raced, and didn't slow even when Abigail did start speaking again.

"Dr. Vigo also has a copy of the Rollins file, but he asked that I bring you in on it as well so that when he arrives tomorrow morning, you'll be up to speed. Will you be able to do that while also assisting Agent Donnelly?"

"I'll make time," Lucy said. "May I be blunt?"

"Please."

"Agent Donnelly is a sharp agent. We both have an understanding of this case that goes beyond Nicole and her escape. This investigation connects to the murder of Congresswoman Reyes-Worthington, the drug runner Tobias, the murdered marines six months ago, and the stolen guns they'd recovered. To bring someone else up to speed would take far too much time, and they wouldn't understand the nuances of the investigation. Except Ryan, of course—he was involved in Operation Heatwave as well, and he's the one who uncovered Rollins's involvement with Tobias."

Abigail raised an eyebrow. "I read Ryan's report. He stated you helped uncover her involvement."

"We both did—using different sources," Lucy said. "But what I'm getting at is that I can work up a profile, but in doing so I would need to involve Brad because he knew Nicole better than anyone else. He'd worked with her for three years. They were partners on Operation Heatwave. He knows things about her that he doesn't realize he knows—so working with him will help me put together a viable analysis. I'll also need to talk to Samantha Archer."

"You have cover from this office, Lucy."

Lucy said, "If I had to guess at this point—based on what we know about Nicole, what happened with Congresswoman Worthington, and the fact that Nicole escaped today instead of being killed so she couldn't testify—Nicole wasn't turned because Tobias caught her killing a drug dealer in cold blood, as the disk we uncovered during Operation Heatwave suggested. I think she made it all up when she realized we had the video. Based on my limited knowledge of her personality and background, I think she was corrupted from the very beginning."

"And you're basing that opinion on what? You haven't read her file yet."

"Because she's smart. She showed no fear at any time. During Operation Heatwave, she behaved exactly as I would have expected a seasoned agent to behave. It was natural. She is so used to playing both sides that it wasn't even a challenge. At most, I would say she was cold—but I know a lot of cops who are cold. Someone of her intelligence—someone who could orchestrate an escape like today—couldn't be blackmailed into it. That makes me think killing the drug dealer five years ago wasn't the first time she'd crossed the line. For Nicole, there was no line to cross because she's never been loyal to the DEA."

Abigail leaned back and steepled her fingers as she looked at Lucy. "That's very interesting. So, essentially, she was a double agent. If this were the Cold War, she would have been an American spy working also for the Soviet Union."

"Uncovering her personal motivation will help us find her," Lucy said.

Abigail made a few notes on a notepad in front of her. "For the time being, work under Agent Donnelly's direction, but report to me daily. That means, by the end of the day—whether that's five, seven, or midnight—I need a report. It doesn't need to be long or formal, but I need something in writing. Copy in Ryan Quiroz, because while I can't give up two agents to the DEA, if I need to reassign you after Dr. Vigo arrives tomorrow, Ryan will step in. Currently he's working with Proctor on security at the jail, our office, and other federal buildings. Any flaw needs to be remedied immediately. We'll meet with Dr. Vigo here at nine a.m. tomorrow."

"Yes, ma'am."

Lucy left Abigail's office a little surprised by the turn of events, but eager to jump into Nicole's file. She went back to her cubicle and sent Brad a message to let her know when he was done.

She also sent an email off to Hans Vigo, offering him a guest room. Her house was certainly big enough, and she hadn't seen him since she graduated from the FBI Academy.

While waiting for Brad, she opened up Nicole's file and started reading.

CHAPTER SEVEN

FBI Supervisory Special Agent Noah Armstrong had just celebrated his fifth anniversary with the FBI. The anniversary came only a week after his thirty-ninth birthday, which itself came a week after his promotion to SSA. The FBI was his second career, after spending more than a decade in the air force, most of it as an Air Force Raven protecting US planes on foreign soil and transporting prisoners internationally. And while he'd planned on being a career air force officer, he'd found a calling in the FBI.

It helped that he was most often assigned special cases by Assistant Director Rick Stockton. Technically, he was a field agent working out of the DC regional office, unassigned to a specific squad, but Noah spent most of his time investigating cases for Stockton. Projects that needed complete discretion. The promotion had no impact on what he did for Stockton, but came with a small pay raise and a private office. Noah found more value in the door than he did in the nominal salary increase.

But even the call he'd received from Stockton's private cell phone thirty minutes ago was odd. The assistant director told him to come to an address in nearby Alexandria, Virginia, and not tell anyone. When Noah arrived, he found waiting for him both Rick Stockton and Dr. Hans Vigo, another assistant director who'd recently returned to duty after being on medical leave for several months.

Hans didn't look like his old self—he'd lost a substantial amount of weight and looked all of his fifty-some years. He could have taken disability since he'd been nearly killed in the line of duty, or retired early because he already had more than twenty years in the Bureau, but he'd chosen to return to work. Hans had no immediate family, no children, no wife—his life was his job. Mandatory retirement was still a few years away.

Noah didn't want that kind of life for himself, but he was nearly forty and hadn't been on a serious date in months. Years. He'd been in love once. So deep in love he'd crossed an ethical line he'd sworn he'd never cross. But instead of losing his soul, he walked away and lost his heart. Only one person had come close to breaking down those barriers, but she was taken, and he wouldn't pursue an unavailable woman—even if he thought he was the better man for her.

A coroner's van was parked on the street at the address Noah had been given, along with several Alexandria police cars, officers standing outside the narrow end-unit town house.

He approached Rich and Hans waiting on the small porch. Someone was dead, and if two assistant directors were here, that meant murder and the victim was a fed. "Who was killed?"

"Logan Dunbar was murdered last night."

"Dunbar?" Noah was one of the few people who knew that Logan Dunbar had been working undercover, gathering evidence against Texas Congresswoman Adeline Reyes-Worthington who'd been suspected of a multitude of political corruption crimes. Noah had been working the DC angle with the other members of Dunbar's small team. Dunbar's assignment was cut short when the congresswoman was murdered. Her crimes were far more severe than bribery—drug running, gunrunning, money laundering, conspiracy to commit murder. Noah had been wading through the documentation that Dunbar had compiled, and they'd planned a huge debriefing later this week. She wasn't the only corrupt official in the middle of the shitstorm. "I just spoke to Dunbar on Friday."

Rick said, "He flew back last night. We don't know if his killer followed him from the airport or was already here. I've called in a forensics team directly from the lab—I want our best people on this."

"You think it's connected to his assignment in San Antonio."

"I don't know," Rick said. "But very few people knew he was coming back last night. My office. His direct supervisor. You. And his next-door neighbor who was watching his place while he was gone. But Dunbar could have told any number of people, both in San Antonio or here. It wasn't like he needed to keep the information secret, now that his assignment was over."

Noah didn't know Dunbar well—most of their conversations had been over the phone or via encrypted email—but Noah knew he was a diligent, dedicated agent.

Hans said, "Dunbar's flight arrived at eight thirty last night. He took a taxi from Dulles; the receipt in his pocket says he paid the driver at nine forty-nine—which would have given him enough time to get his bags, hail a cab, and drive home. He came in through the front door and disengaged the alarm. He didn't reengage it. He put his bag down in the entry at the base of the staircase and went to the kitchen. Took a beer from the refrigerator—it's all that was in there, which isn't surprising since he's been undercover for six months. He opened the beer. Someone shot him twice from behind, once in the back and once in the back of the head, possibly when he was already down."

"No sign of a struggle?"

"None."

"And no one heard anything?"

"It smells professional," Hans said. "Execution."

Rick said, "Logan and I were supposed to meet at one this afternoon. When he didn't show up, I called. No answer. I confirmed his flight, and then I called the Alexandria police for a welfare check. They found the body."

"Anything stolen?"

"Not that any of us can tell. His briefcase is here, but something could have been taken or copied. Noah, I need you to take the lead on this," Rick said. "We need to know if this was connected to San Antonio as soon as possible. If it's not, we'll regroup and look at his old cases and personal life. But it sure as hell wasn't random."

"You heard what happened this morning in San Antonio?" Hans asked Noah.

"The escape? Yes."

"Two dead DEA agents. Dunbar spent the last six months in San Antonio, and there's a tertiary connection between the escaped felon and Logan Dunbar. Nicole Rollins, the escapee, worked for the same gunrunner that Worthington laundered money for," Hans said. "Worthington is dead. Dunbar's murder could be retaliation, payback, or something else."

Rick said, "While we waited for you, I called SAC Naygrow in the San Antonio office to find out where they are on the investigation and who is point. All agencies are working together, and I found out, without explicitly asking, that Lucy is on the task force. But because of Dunbar's murder and the escape, Hans is going to San Antonio. He'll ostensibly profile Nicole Rollins, but he'll be covertly investigating the leak. While logic suggests there is a mole in the DEA who passed on information to Rollins when she was in prison, we also believe there's a mole in the FBI."

"The San Antonio office?"

"Most likely. Kane Rogan contacted me ten days ago and said he believes someone in the FBI is vulnerable, whether because they are the mole or have been compromised in some way we don't know yet. That's why I want Hans down there to assess."

"Rogan," Noah said flatly.

"You don't have a problem with that," Rick said, more as a statement than a question, though the question was there.

"No," Noah said. He still didn't understand Rick Stockton's loyalties to the Rogan family.

Rick clearly didn't believe him; Noah had never told anyone what happened in Europe with Liam and Eden Rogan. It could be that Rick knew what had happened—he had an uncanny way of gathering information—but Rick had never discussed it with Noah.

That was six years ago, and he hadn't seen the Rogan twins since.

But Rick would know that while Noah was in the Air Force, he'd crossed paths with Kane Rogan who, Noah felt, envisioned himself as the Guardian Angel—or Avenging Angel—of innocents south of the border. Kane's team took out guerrilla fighters and cartel leaders, burned cocaine fields, and rescued kidnapped Americans. And on one hand, Noah had a deep respect for what Kane and his ilk did. On the other, he'd seen firsthand in Kane a calm brutality and antipathy for the law that was disturbing. Noah didn't want to believe that the FBI had a corrupt agent, but just because he didn't want to believe didn't mean he wouldn't believe. And though Noah didn't know Kane well, if he had information that he felt was viable enough to share with Rick, there was at least a basis for the suspicion.

Noah realized that Rick was assessing him. "You should tap Lucy to help weed out the traitor," Noah said.

Hans shook his head. "Lucy would not do well in that role."

"I've worked with her, Hans, I know what she's capable of. Lying isn't her strong suit, I grant you, but something like this—when agents are being threatened and killed—she'll rise to the occasion."

"I don't disagree that she could do it, but I don't know the dynamics of the office. I don't know what relationships she's forged and with whom. I don't want to put her in that position of spying on her colleagues, not unless it's absolutely necessary. I would rather use Agent Dunning."

"Dunning?" Noah didn't know him.

"I'll fill you in later," Rick said to Noah. Then to Hans, "You have as much latitude as you need. You speak for me, and I don't doubt that you'll find out the truth. If someone in our house is corrupt, your presence will put the fear of God into them—and may force their hand. No paper trail on this—no email or cell phones. If either of you needs anything, call only though a secure line."

They watched as the coroner's team wheeled Logan Dunbar's body out of his townhouse. They collapsed and lifted the gurney to carry it down the stairs, then raised it and rolled the body to the van. Noah stared at the black bag, a cold anger washing over him. He'd been in the air force for ten years and had never lost a man in his unit. But he'd flown back the bodies of other good soldiers, men and women zipped into body bags, dead simply because they were doing their job.

Noah said, "Dunbar was a good agent. He did his job. Now he's dead. I want to know why and stop these bastards from hurting anyone else."

CHAPTER EIGHT

Lucy scoured Nicole's file, first skimming it, then going back and reading it in greater depth.

Immediately two things became clear: First, Nicole had lied to Lucy about her background. During Operation Heatwave, when Lucy was alone with Nicole, the former fed had said she'd lived in Kansas until she was fourteen and mentioned she had "brothers"—the truth was, she had only one brother, two years older than Nicole and currently in the army. Nicole had only lived in Kansas for fourteen months, when her father had been stationed at Fort Riley, and she'd been five when they moved to Fort Benning in Georgia. When she was nine, her father had left the military after twelve years of service and moved cross-country, to Los Angeles, where he went through the police academy. He'd been killed in the line of duty when Nicole was fifteen.

According to Nicole's application to the DEA, under the question, "Why are you applying to be a federal agent with the Drug Enforcement Administration?" Nicole had written:

> *My father was a veteran in the army and then*
> *served six years as a police officer with the Los*

*Angeles Police Department. He was killed in the
line of duty during a turf war battle. The only way
to stop the violence is to stop these battles, and
that starts at the top—which is why I want to be a
DEA agent.*

Lucy made a note to find out more about the murder of
Nicole's father. Lucy couldn't reconcile Nicole working for
the same sort of people who killed her father. Maybe her
betrayal of the DEA had started with avenging her father—
if a drug dealer was responsible, she may have wanted
access to records that she couldn't get otherwise. But if that
were the case, how did she turn away from revenge to
working with the same type of people who'd killed her dad?

The second truth Lucy learned was that Nicole had
manipulated her way into the San Antonio DEA field office. She wanted to be here for some reason—why, Lucy
had no idea. It took Lucy two passes before she saw the
pattern.

Nicole had been recruited into the DEA right out of college, fifteen years ago. She'd been assigned to the Atlanta
main office for her first year, then to the smaller Savannah
resident office for the second year. After her two-year
rookie probation she'd asked to be transferred to Mexico
City, but had been denied because she didn't speak Spanish
well enough. She'd been transferred to the Chicago Division, where she took night classes to learn Spanish. Over
the next ten years—between the end of her rookie years
until she landed in San Antonio three years ago—she'd
asked for a total of nine transfers. And while she was only
granted two of them, she'd still been moved several
times—no office assignment lasted longer than two years.

Until San Antonio.

It seemed odd to Lucy that Nicole had asked to transfer so many times. In both the DEA and the FBI, rookie agents had little to no influence over their initial two-year assignment. Prior to graduation at Quantico, Lucy was asked to list the three offices she wanted to be assigned to. Nothing guaranteed that she would be assigned to one of the three—it depended on many factors. She'd listed two offices in California—both her family and Sean's family were in California (hers in the south, his in the north)—and Norfolk, because it was in Virginia and only a few hours from where her brothers Dillon and Patrick lived in DC.

They'd given her San Antonio.

It was relatively common that, after a two-year rookie period, federal agents were given the option to move to any available position in another regional office. When Sean bought the house, she'd told him she'd most likely be transferred after two years. He didn't care, he wanted a place that was theirs, and she loved him for it. She loved their home, their neighborhood, and San Antonio had grown on her. She didn't know if she would request a transfer, though she might not have a choice.

Nicole Rollins had spent two years in the Los Angeles DEA office, and her final request was to be transferred to an opening in Houston. She was there for nine months before she was moved laterally into the San Antonio regional office, which was under the Houston umbrella.

She hadn't asked to be moved again since she landed here.

Lucy made a list of Nicole's employment history with the DEA, the names of her direct supervisors in each office, and whether she asked to be transferred to or from any office location. Nicole had never bought a house until arriving in San Antonio.

Three years ago.

Lucy stared at the timeline, her heart racing as she realized that Nicole hadn't been assigned to San Antonio when she killed the drug dealer.

When they DEA recovered the disk three months ago—thanks to Sean's brother Kane—Nicole claimed that the cartel had used that disk as leverage over her for the last five years, implying that she'd been forced into working for them. Yet, it was clear, after this well-orchestrated prison break, that there was much more to the story. Nicole wasn't a timid, fearful federal agent being blackmailed into subservience.

Lucy had assumed the disk had been filmed in San Antonio—Ryan had known about the case—but Nicole was assigned to Los Angeles during that time. If she was in San Antonio five years ago, why? Was she on vacation? On assignment? Who was the man she killed and was there another reason for his murder other than taking his money and drugs?

She closed her eyes and remembered the conversation she'd had with Ryan. It was the disk they'd uncovered that had proven Nicole was a corrupt DEA agent. Ryan said it was from a San Antonio case that was still on the books, unsolved. Nicole had gone into the small electronics repair shop, flashed her badge, and shot the unarmed owner in cold blood. The victim was a known criminal, the shop a link in the chain moving drugs up from Mexico and into the rest of the country.

Lucy needed to see that disk.

"Lucy?"

She jumped up, startled.

Brad stood next to her cubicle. "Sorry—I didn't mean to wake you up."

"I was thinking."

Brad looked over her extensive notes. "You've been busy."

She glanced at her desk. Sticky notes littered Nicole's file and her desk. It was already after two in the afternoon. "ASAC Durant gave me Nicole's file to review."

Brad frowned. "Sam told me. Not to diminish profiling, but we know who we're dealing with."

"We don't know the half of it, Brad." She tapped the file. "Nicole asked to be transferred multiple times over ten years, but once she landed in San Antonio, she requested no more transfers. That tells me she wanted to be here. I need the disk that showed her killing the drug dealer— we need to look deeper into that case. Ryan said it happened in San Antonio, but Nicole worked out of the Los Angeles office during that time period."

"What are you saying? That Ryan lied?"

She was surprised. "No, of course not. I'm saying she was here, that she killed the dealer, and we can confirm through DEA records if she was on duty in LA and if not, what her status was. But was it just the one dealer? Were there more? What was the fallout after his murder? How did the landscape change in San Antonio after he was killed?"

Brad pulled over a chair from another desk and sat down. "I don't understand what you're saying. Nicole claimed that the disk was being used as leverage by Trejo to force her to work for them. Blackmail."

"I don't believe that. Not after today."

"Maybe she became more ruthless as time went on. Once you kill, it's easier to kill again."

"Is it?" she asked, her face blank. Because she had that fear, she'd had it since she first killed a man when she was eighteen, without remorse. The man she'd killed had been a rapist and a murderer—her rapist. But still, she'd killed him in cold blood and felt no guilt.

It wasn't the last time she'd killed. The second time she'd saved the life of an innocent woman. And then, in

Mexico, she'd shot six men. She hadn't counted them at the time, but when it was over, she just knew. She didn't know if they all died, but assumed they had from either the injuries she gave them or the lack of medical attention after.

That darkness inside scared her. Especially now, especially when she'd finally found peace in her life. Because it was still there. The dark threatened her hard-earned peace.

"She had to turn sometime," Brad said. "Five years ago? Longer? Does it matter?"

"Yes," Lucy said without hesitation. "I need to see that video. It'll help me get into her head."

Brad scowled. "I don't want to understand her. I want to find her."

"We'll never find her if we don't understand her," Lucy countered. "She's too smart, too calculating. She's not your average drug dealer. She's ruthless, seasoned, and she knows our playbook. She's been a federal agent for fifteen years, in nine different offices. Why? She knows not only how we do things, but how *you* do things. How Sam does things. That's why I need to see that tape. Was that the first or a repeat? Killing a man in cold blood isn't easy—how did she do it? Did she hesitate? Have a conversation with him first? Was it an accident? An assassination?"

"Assassination," Brad mumbled. "Why would you think that?"

"I don't know, but after the cold-blooded murder of two DEA agents and three guards today, assassination popped into my head. We also need to talk—you, me, Sam Archer."

"I need to get out in the field and find her."

"The marshals are doing everything they can, and they're the best. But even so, they need more information. Were they able to trace Nicole after the helicopter landed?"

Brad shook his head.

"Do we have an ID on any of the men who helped her escape?"

Again, Brad shook his head.

"I also want to talk to her brother, Chris. He's stationed out of Fort Hood. I don't know if he's deployed or on base. I'm going to ask Nate to help—he spent ten years in the army and was stationed at Fort Hood. He'll know people there, who to talk to, to get me to Chris Rollins faster. And I want to go to her house."

"Her house?"

"According to the file, she owned a house in San Antonio that's currently secured by the DEA under asset forfeiture laws. But I don't have any information about her belongings—computer, paperwork, personal effects."

"Well, fuck. All that was destroyed when Tobias planted the bomb in our evidence locker."

Lucy froze. "*All* her personal effects were destroyed?"

"I don't know exactly what was there, but we seized her phones, electronics, date books, anything that was potential evidence."

Lucy stared at the file. "What's the conventional wisdom on why Tobias wanted to destroy the evidence locker?"

"The initial reason still makes sense—that there was something in evidence that implicated him, and we didn't know about it. But another school of thought, which I lean toward, is that he simply wanted to fuck with us—we're scrambling with all the cases we had pending. Evidence is gone. Some bastards are going to get off. The AUSA has already dismissed three cases because we no longer have the evidence—which leads us to the third school of thought. That Tobias wanted someone specific to be released." He narrowed his eyes. "Not Nicole—not only do we have copies of most of the evidence we lost, like the disk, but we have her confession that she was being black-mailed by Vasco Trejo. What we lost was only physical evidence."

"But you had some of the things from her house and desk in that evidence lockup."

"Of course."

She mulled it over. It made sense. It was the only thing that *did* make sense. "During your conversation with her two weeks ago, when she implied that Tobias had set up the hit on his own people, you came away with the thought that she may have known him, but more likely knew him by reputation."

"She was questioned extensively about Tobias and said she'd never seen him."

"She's a liar. We can't believe anything she says."

"She was interrogated by our best people. And her plea agreement was predicated on providing truthful information. If we caught her in a lie, the agreement was null and void."

Lucy clearly saw the truth; why couldn't Brad?

"Brad, she never intended to fulfill her end of the agreement. It didn't matter if she lied, because she was already planning the escape. The only thing that makes sense is that she's been working with Tobias all along. She knew the protocol for drug evidence. She knew that you'd lock it in evidence prior to being sent to the lab for testing, so the risk that anyone would find the bomb was slim. Plant the bomb, wait until the evidence is secure, blow the locker. There was something you had in there that she didn't want us to know about."

"That's a long stretch. And those drugs were worth a million dollars on the street."

"Were they? You did a field test, but didn't test for potency or test all the bricks, correct?"

He hesitated. "I see what you're saying, but—"

"She planned a complex and dangerous escape while in solitary confinement, which meant either her lawyer was helping her or one of the guards. She may have made plans before she was ever captured, in case her duplicity was discovered. The surviving guard, Isaac Harris, said she was privy to information about the escape that she only could have known had she been part of the planning."

"You give her a lot of credit for being smart."

"Nicole Rollins *is* smart. She is willing to do anything necessary to secure her freedom, though what her end-game is, I'm not sure. But I'm positive *she* knows. She does have a plan, and she started the ball rolling the minute she was arrested. I need to get into her house, then talk to her brother."

"When we first arrested Nicole, Chris Rollins was deployed. I don't remember where off the top of my head, but he was overseas. Sam talked to him, then someone from the DOJ. He claims that he and Nicole hadn't spoken in years, that they were estranged."

"But no one was asking about who Nicole was as a kid while they were growing up. What she did, who she socialized with, how she handled setbacks or disappointment. All that is important to develop a reliable profile."

"I still think it's a huge waste of time to dig around in her psyche when that isn't going to guarantee we'll find her."

Brad was getting frustrated, but so was Lucy.

"What is it you want to do now? The marshals are leading the manhunt, so what now?"

"Don't you have to stay here and work on that?" he said with disdain.

Lucy was used to the skepticism of many cops about using psychology as a tool. Not because she had experienced it—she wasn't officially a profiler—but because her older brother Dillon was a forensic psychiatrist and she'd lived with him and his wife, Kate, for seven years. She thought that after years of successful criminal profiling that led to the arrest of killers, more cops would understand it was a valuable tool.

"I can do this while you drive."

That seemed to satisfy him. He said, "I'd really like to wring her attorney's neck, but the marshals are all over the guy. So far, he hasn't given up anything, but we have a lot of latitude. One shred of proof that the lawyer aided and abetted her escape, and he's toast. Disbarment, potential jail time."

Lucy thought back to only two weeks ago, when Tobias's people had held a woman and her children hostage to force a white-collar criminal to transfer funds into their account. If her theory that Tobias and Nicole were truly connected held, that meant that anyone working with Tobias was also connected, in some way, to Nicole.

Elise Hansen. Tobias's much younger sister.

"Brad—I need to talk to Elise."

"She fucked with you last time you went to see her, you can't do that again."

"Don't coddle me," Lucy snapped. "I've faced far more dangerous psychopaths than Elise Hansen. And she *tried* to get under my skin, but failed." *Mostly.* "She must know about Nicole. Elise still claims she's Tobias's little sister." Lucy was skeptical about that. Tobias was in his forties. Elise was sixteen. It was possible they were brother and sister, but it seemed too much of a stretch. Still, Elise knew him, she'd talked to him, she'd seen him. They had substantive proof that she'd acted on Tobias's orders when she killed Congresswoman Worthington's husband. She could very well know something of Nicole Rollins's plans—at least as much as Tobias himself knew.

"I'm not coddling you, Lucy." He ran a hand through his

sandy hair. "Maybe, just a bit. You push yourself to the edge."

"And it's warranted, especially now. Nicole was party to the murder of five cops. She'll kill more if she gets the chance. She has a deep loathing of law enforcement, and the DEA in particular. We need to push ourselves. Find out more about Elise and her relationship with Tobias. More about Nicole and how she hooked up with him. And really—why did Tobias help Nicole escape and not his own sister? It wouldn't be as difficult to free her as this elaborate breakout this morning." She shook her head. "That part doesn't make sense. Yet."

"We don't know that Tobias had a hand in Nicole's escape."

"We might not be able to prove it, but he was part of it. She couldn't do it alone, she had to have someone on the outside with substantial resources. If not Tobias, who?"

Brad didn't have a response.

Nicole needed money and resources. A safe house. The helicopter, the men, the vehicles, the access to Saint Catherine's bus—all that required time and money. Lots of money. The DEA had frozen Nicole's accounts, but she could have had money the DEA hadn't found. Cash in safety deposit boxes, private storage units, under false names and identification. Tobias had a substantial pool of money, even though the FBI had seized the accounts Congresswoman Reyes-Worthington had used to launder Tobias's illegal money.

Was Tobias planning on letting Elise rot? She was sixteen, she could be tried as an adult, particularly since she had been involved in serious felonies. Lucy's partner in the Worthington case, Barry Crawford, had been working closely with the AUSA on Elise's case, because it was a sensitive investigation. So much of the evidence they had against her—for murder, attempted murder, kidnapping, conspiracy, and more—was circumstantial. Last she'd heard, before Barry left on his vacation, the AUSA was working on a plea deal, but Elise wasn't budging. She was holding firm to her statement that she didn't know what was going on, that she only did what she was told because she was scared, and that her brother Tobias would kill her if she said anything.

That last part may have been true—whether or not Tobias was truly her biological brother. But Lucy could see that Elise wasn't scared of anything. She had no fear, no remorse, no thought for anyone. She didn't fear death, and she didn't fear imprisonment. It was a game to her, pure and simple. She looked at the cards each day and made her decisions, with the end goal always to finish ahead of everyone else. She'd change tactics midstream if it benefited her, and if she was caught lying she'd switch tactics again.

Lucy had to find a way to manipulate the game. To manipulate Elise into revealing the game plan, without Elise realizing Lucy was manipulating her. And someone like Elise would be extremely hard to trick. How could someone so young be such an accomplished con artist and liar?

It would also take time to set up. It was midafternoon, and there was no way they could get in to see her today. Lucy would much rather have Hans there as well—if not in the room with her, then observing.

In fact, Lucy suspected that if Hans were in the room, Elise wouldn't talk at all. She didn't respect men. She saw them as a means to an end, weak through sex, easily manipulated.

But observing, Hans might see something Lucy couldn't, because of his experience and distance from the case. She wanted to talk to Barry first. She sent him a text message to call her as soon as he returned from vacation. He would have the most up-to-date information on Elise's case.

"Brad," she said, "I'm going to talk to Elise tomorrow. I'd like you to observe as well."

Brad sighed. "If you really think this is important, fine."

"I appreciate your faith, Brad. I can't do this without you. You know Nicole better than anyone, even Sam."

"Then why couldn't I see her for who she really was?" Brad said quietly.

"Brad, two years ago I was working for a nonprofit company that tracked repeat sex offenders. We'd compile information and evidence for law enforcement, and helped take hundreds of child predators off the streets and put them back in prison. I was obsessed with the program. It was run by a former FBI agent—a woman who'd become something of my mentor. She'd been one of the first female FBI agents, was well respected, and after retirement she committed her life to rooting out these vicious people." Lucy paused, unsure exactly how much she should tell Brad. "I had total faith in her. Blind faith, really, because she was using me to identify parolees for the purpose of killing them."

"A vigilante?"

She nodded. "I identified parolees online, set them up to meet—ostensibly—with a minor, and I assumed that the men were subsequently arrested. I trusted her when she told me they were. I prepared reports and transcripts that I thought were being used in their trials or hearings, even though I was never called on to testify. I didn't think anything of it—because most of these guys were on probation, and there was no trial necessary to put them back in prison for violating parole. I later learned that I was setting them up to be assassinated. The system I believed in had failed by releasing these predators early, but I still believed in it. I thought we were putting them back in prison, where they belonged. Instead they were dead."

"I wouldn't lose sleep over it," he said.

She paused. "She used me, Brad. And because of what this woman did, one of my closest friends was killed. He wasn't a predator, but a cop who thought I was part of the conspiracy. He was investigating it to protect me and he ended up dead. What I'm saying is, I should have seen the truth earlier. I knew all the information, I just didn't put it together fast enough. I saw what I wanted to see—a noble, self-sacrificing retired FBI agent who gave me a cause to believe in, something to work *for*. But when the layers were peeled away, I saw her for who she was: a ruthless businesswoman whose business was murder." Lucy had to stop there. She was still disturbed about what had happened eighteen months ago. Maybe she didn't lose sleep over the dead sex offenders, but the repercussions from that bout of vigilante justice still haunted her.

"And you think that sixteen-year-old prostitute knows something about Nicole?" Brad asked. "What about Mona Hill? The prostitute who was helping her?"

"She's in the wind. Left everything in her apartment and vanished." Lucy paused. "I suspect Tobias had her killed. There's a lot of places to get rid of a body in the desert. She knew too much, he took care of her."

"Then why not kill Elise?"

"I don't know. Except—maybe he knows she won't turn him in. I don't think she'll say a word against him—I'm going to have to twist her around to get her to talk at all, and then I'll need you to help decipher what I know will be an attempt to hurt or deceive me."

He was still skeptical, and Lucy wasn't sure why, but he said, "Fine. I'll talk to Sam and see if we can do it tomorrow morning."

"We *are* doing it," Lucy said. "I don't need Sam Archer's permission."

CHAPTER NINE

Lucy and Brad had to jump through hoops before the US Marshals would give them access to Nicole's house in the hills northwest of San Antonio, but after signing a dozen forms and getting the director's approval, Brad received the lockbox code.

The upscale neighborhood was well established with mature trees and large lots on roads curving up into the hill country, far from the bustle of downtown. The house itself wasn't opulent on the outside, though the location was prime: the end of a cul-de-sac with city views.

"Have you been here before?" Lucy asked Brad.

"A few times," he said. He'd been very quiet on the drive, answering Lucy's questions about Nicole, but not engaging in any further conversation.

Lucy entered in through the front door and stood in the entry, trying to put herself in Nicole's shoes.

The floors were bleached oak. The furnishings ran to the contemporary side, light colors and tasteful modern art. Everything was well placed, as if designed to be right in that spot.

Lucy couldn't picture Nicole living here. She was a single, childless, thirty-eight-year-old female federal agent.

She was also a criminal. That she was able to maintain the act so brilliantly for years told Lucy she was an actress at heart, that she didn't show her true colors, even in her own home.

The house was for show. An infinity pool in the back with views of rolling hills; the city spread away below the front porch. Remote. Beautiful. Peaceful.

Why did she live here? Nicole was single, why wouldn't she live in a smaller place, closer to town—instead of a suburban, family area? Did she need the privacy? Was she seeking something she'd never had growing up?

Like Nicole, Lucy's father had been in the military. Lucy had been a toddler when her dad took a permanent post in San Diego. She didn't remember any of the moves, or the stress on her brothers and sisters—though they still talked about living in cities and places she didn't remember. It connected them, made them closer—and sometimes Lucy had felt like an outsider because she didn't have that same connection with her siblings. Yet she'd also heard about the downside of the constant moving, of changing schools, of not knowing where they were going to be living year-to-year.

The Kincaids had one another—a large, very close Irish Cuban family. It hadn't always been easy, especially with seven kids and one government income. They had little extra. There were times, Lucy remembered, when they lived on soup and vegetables from their garden because the grocery money was needed for shoes or fixing a car. But not once had Lucy felt unloved, unwanted, or lonely.

Lonely. Nicole's house was lonely. It was at the end of the road, the yard looking out into hills, nothing more. Her first thought had been *peaceful*, but under a different lens it was artificial. Airy, generic, empty.

She slowly walked through each room. There were no computers, but cords connected to plugs where computers and printers had once been. The master bedroom was a bit more cluttered, more lived in. Nicole had slept here, but she didn't live here.

"She had another place," Lucy suddenly said.

"Excuse me?"

"She lived here, but she didn't keep anything important here. She had another place. An apartment, a house, I don't know, but that's where she would have kept anything incriminating."

"We found no records of a rental or any other properties in the area," Brad said.

"It wouldn't be under her name. It might be under a partner's name, or a business name, and I suspect it would be closer to the DEA office—might even be a business front, not a house."

"How on earth do you know that?"

"Because the DEA search didn't find anything here. She had to keep her information and files somewhere safe." Lucy hesitated. "But it's probably been cleaned out."

"By who?"

"Tobias? Elise Hansen? I have no idea. *Someone* she was working with. She had six people, at a minimum, helping her escape today."

Brad shook his head. "You're contradicting yourself. First you say that there was something in the evidence locker Nicole didn't want us to see, then you say she kept nothing here, it's all at this fictional location that no longer exists. Do you make this stuff up as you go along?"

Lucy bristled. She stepped away from Brad. "Give me a minute."

He threw his hands in the air and walked out. Fine by her, she needed more than a minute to calm her temper and focus on the house and what was here—and not here.

Her initial impression—expensive, minimalist, sterile—had given her the gut feeling that this house wasn't important to Nicole. She revisited each room. All the food had been emptied from the refrigerator. The cabinets were sparsely filled—place settings for eight, a standard number for most stores' pre-packaged boxes. The plates and glasses were generic as well, bought at a department store but without any personality. The house looked like a model home, everything *just so*. The DEA search had left things jostled and moved, but there wasn't much to jostle and move.

The den where the computer and electronics had been seized was similarly unused. The bookshelves had a collection of books, but none looked to have been read. Most were history, biographies—that they'd been gone through was evident from the uneven placement, but they seemed to be just for show. Knickknacks were sparse. Pictures looked expensive, but again, generic, for decoration and nothing more.

Nicole had used the bedroom more than any other room. There were numerous books stacked on the nightstand—unlike those in the den, these were mostly fiction and true crime. In fact, Lucy had read several of them. She flipped through them, looking for marks or flags; there were none. There was a desk, but it had been cleared out, the papers and anything else now ashes in the DEA evidence locker. Nicole's large walk-in closet was half filled, her drawers filled with jeans and T-shirts and workout clothes. Nicole lived here . . . she just didn't *live* here. It was part of her act. The same act that enabled her to be a DEA agent while simultaneously working with the drug cartels.

Lucy stood in the middle of the bedroom.

Who are you?

Nicole had no remorse for her crimes. She'd shown no remorse during her initial arrest. She'd taunted Brad when he met with her two weeks ago regarding the murders of several drug dealers with ties to Tobias. She faked remorse in court to help get her plea deal—but it was the information she could provide, not the remorse for her actions, that tipped the scales.

Nicole was patient. Was the plan as she'd told Sam Archer, that when she had enough money she was going to skip the country? Or was there something else? And why stay so long? Did she enjoy the double life? Was the double life—access to a constant stream of information—her job?

The money was part of it, but there was more. That her people had killed the DEA agents but not the marshals told Lucy that Nicole had a deep animosity for the DEA. Why? Had something happened in her past that made her hate the DEA? Or were the murders practical, because the regional office was small, and killing DEA agents would limit their resources? Were those agents specifically targeted, or random?

Slowly, Lucy opened the drawers again. One by one, looking for anything out of place. Underwear. Socks. Lingerie. Sexy lingerie, and a lot of it. Nicole had been unmarried, and according to the files hadn't had a regular boyfriend when she was arrested. But what about past boyfriends? A secret boyfriend?

In the bottom right drawer of the dresser were male clothes. T-shirts, running shorts, boxers, socks. Old boyfriend? Current boyfriend? Where was he? Who was he? He didn't live here, but he'd been here.

Lucy walked into the bathroom and went through all the drawers. She found one filled with men's items—deodorant, shampoo, an electric razor, condoms.

Did these items belong to Tobias? Was Nicole sexually involved with the drug lord? That would give more weight to the idea that he would spring her from prison rather than kill her.

Maybe. Maybe.

Lucy walked around again and then it hit her. While the master bedroom was the most lived in, there was still little personal here. According to the records, Nicole had bought this house three years ago, when she first transferred to San Antonio. But there were no photos, no mementos, no personalization of any kind. It was one thing to be a neat, meticulous person; it was quite another to have no human footprint.

Had the DEA taken these things? If so, Lucy could see why Nicole wouldn't want the DEA or the FBI rifling through anything personal. That would give the police an edge, and Nicole didn't want them to have any clues as to where she was or who she was with. Perhaps a photo of her with the owner of the boxers and condoms?

If they had a photo of Tobias, it might change everything.

DEA Agent Adam Dover III had sold his soul to the devil twenty-three years ago and never looked back.

It was impossible to look back when regret would put a bullet in your head.

He looked over at the redhead tied to the straight-backed chair. Her face had swollen from when he'd slammed it into the wall. But the bitch had tried to escape. Feisty little thing. His cock stirred, but he calmed himself down. He had a job to do, and he wouldn't be caught with his pants down.

After he captured Kane Rogan, before he killed the redhead, he might indulge. If it was safe and he had the time.

Safety above all else.

He had no family. He'd been the youngest of four kids, and only son, born and raised in Kern County, California, outside Bakersfield, in a rickety old farmhouse that had once dominated five hundred acres. He'd heard the stories from the time he was a toddler, how his grandfather Adam Dover I had been a successful farmer of alfalfa and cotton. A few bad years had him selling half his land, and then oil. Not on the Dover property—but on the property his grandfather sold. For thirty years, his grandfather and father fought in court as well as paid every cent they had—and money they didn't—to survey their own land for oil.

But it was dry. They were no longer interested in farming when their neighbors had won the oil lottery and they wanted some of the wealth, too.

By the time Adam III was born, they owned the five acres surrounding the farmhouse. His grandfather was long dead, his grandmother a bitchy little woman who complained about everything, his father a drunk who blamed everyone for his problems except his own lazy ass. His mother—God bless her—had run off when Adam was five and never returned.

That was the story, though Adam had always wondered if his father had killed her and buried her under the rosebushes alongside the crumbling barn.

Adam knew the only way out was to go to college. His sisters all married out—two to men just like their father, and both of them had babies before they were out of their teens. One sister was like him—saw college as the answer—and she was now a chemist with some biotech company in Virginia. She never looked back, so Adam did the same. He studied hard, got a scholarship to California State University in Long Beach, and had no idea what he wanted to do with his life. Landing in the DEA had been partly luck of the draw—his roommate dragged him to a career seminar, and the guy putting it on made some great points. Steady income, rewarding work, early retirement, pension—everything that Adam wanted because his father never had it.

The fact that his father hated the government, from

the president on down to street cops, was icing on the cake.

Five years later he killed a man for money—a lot of money—and had been working for the Hunt family ever since.

In two years he'd be able to retire. He didn't look his age—he looked damn good for turning fifty-one last month. But he wanted that pension. He wanted the luxury of a steady check as well as the million-plus dollars he'd saved up doing jobs for the Hunts. He could do what he wanted when he wanted and that was all he cared about. He had no wife, no kids that he knew about, but he didn't particularly like people. He didn't need a wife to get fucked. He was an attractive guy, girls came to him. He took what he could get but didn't much worry about it. He'd seen what happened to men—like Tobias—who let their sick fetishes interfere with their self-preservation.

Adam had more control.

He looked at the redhead again. She glared at him, her pretty blue eyes both scared and defiant. He hoped he had the opportunity to indulge.

Two of his men clomped down into the rectory basement. "He's at the hotel," one said.

"How many?"

"Three—four including Rogan."

Four would be difficult. He knew everything there was to know about Kane Rogan, and Rogan worked in small teams. For a simple missing person Adam hadn't expected Rogan to come down with more than a partner . . . did he suspect a trap?

Dover had four men, but he wasn't alive today because he underestimated his enemy. And Kane Rogan was certainly the enemy. "Call for reinforcements," Dover said. "And don't engage yet. Let's see how fast he traces her steps." He glanced at the redhead and smiled. She continued to glare at him. He just smiled wider.

He was not easily baited.

"And bring me the priest." Dover glanced over at the altar boy he'd taken to ensure the priest would comply. He was tied to a pipe, head down. Defeated. Good. "I need to make sure he understands exactly what he's supposed to do to save his little lamb."

CHAPTER TEN

Nicole fell back onto the sheets, naked, wonderfully sweaty and comfortably sore. She reached over Joseph's naked chest for the water on the nightstand and drank greedily, then stretched and looked down at her lover. "I love you, Joseph."

"I missed you." He kissed her ear, then her neck, caressing her breasts until she considered staying in bed.

"You've done so well without me, I thought you might not need me anymore," she teased.

"Everything is for you, Niki. Everything I do is to make you happy."

"You have made me happy." She brought his hand to her lips and kissed it. "Tobias will be here soon; we should get dressed."

"He can wait," Joseph said. He rolled her over and held her wrists loosely above her head. He kissed her passionately. She'd truly missed his affection while she sat in prison.

"Yes, he can," she said. She returned his kiss, then pulled back. "But he's been reckless and I need to pull him back in line."

Joseph's dark eyes narrowed as he stared at her, his face only inches away. "He had too much freedom. He became arrogant and we lost so much of the ground we gained over the last three years. Longer—all the sacrifices we were forced to make ever since you joined the DEA."

"It's . . . delicate." She moved her body against him, hoping to divert Joseph from this conversation. It was complicated, and while Joseph claimed to understand, he truly didn't. He didn't have family.

"I would have killed him for you," Joseph said.

"He's blood, Joseph." If Tobias didn't yield to her authority, if he continued to make mistakes, she would have to kill him. She'd do it herself, because he *was* blood. She'd never allow anyone else to take him down, not even Joseph. "He knows that he screwed up. Now that I'm out, I will control him. I promise, Joseph."

Joseph didn't say anything. He rolled over to his back. She put her head on his chest, needing him to understand her decision, needing to understand why he was so moody—moodier than usual. "Tell me what's troubling you, baby."

"He's the reason you were found out."

"No, Joseph. That was Trejo and Sanchez. They are dead and their organization has been annihilated."

"Tobias brought Trejo into the operation."

"Yes, but we agreed. At the time, it seemed like the smart decision."

"Perhaps." Joseph sat up and didn't look at her. Nicole didn't move. Sometimes it was best to let her lover work out his problems himself. He would always come around to her viewpoint, he would always support her decisions. They'd been together far too long to let one small disagreement come between them.

"Aside from my arrest, everything else has been moving along according to plan. We had a delay; now we can finish. As soon as we get back the money taken from us, and finish this last big job, we'll have enough resources to disappear and run our operation from anywhere in the world. Without Toby."

When Joseph didn't answer, she said, "Is there another problem?"

"The fed doesn't know anything about our money. If he did, he would have talked."

"Someone does."

"Who?"

"When we get Dunbar's files decoded we'll have our answers. Has Lyle returned?"

"No."

"I should talk to Tobias about it."

She started to get up, but Joseph turned back to her, grabbed her wrist, and pushed her back to the bed. "Make him wait."

Nicole stared into Joseph's dark eyes. This was important to him, she realized, that she choose him and his needs over her cousin.

She smiled and put her hands on the back of his head, kissed him. "He can wait until fucking morning for all I care." She bit his bottom lip and Joseph growled.

"Dear God, I missed you, Niki."

And they made love again.

They'd met in summer school.

Nicole was a sophomore, but she had flunked two classes and to be a junior in the fall, she had to repeat them over the summer. She considered dropping out altogether, but her uncle insisted.

We have big plans for you, Nicole.

Joseph had just turned twenty, and wanted to be in

summer school even less than Nicole. He'd skipped more classes than he took, though he was only a few months away from getting his GED. They were in the same geometry class.

Nicole didn't believe in love at first sight or kindred spirits or soul mates or any of that other crap. Her parents fought constantly until her dad was killed, and her uncle cheated on her aunt practically in front of her. Nicole couldn't wait to get out of the house, to be free.

She missed her dad.

He wasn't perfect, but that was because he missed the army. He became moody and irritable, and really hated being a cop, but he believed in giving 100 percent in everything he did. He could be judgmental and his punishments were severe—but he liked order, what was wrong with that? And her mother was a flake, anyway.

So Nicole didn't believe in love crap, but there was something about Joseph . . . something different. When he looked at her, she got a feeling in her stomach she'd never had before. And he knew. It's like he sensed she was attracted to him, a bee to honey.

It wasn't long before they talked, then went out together, then became inseparable.

Joseph was with her when she found out the truth about her father's murder.

Joseph was with her when her uncle told her what his plans were for her.

And Joseph told her he would stay with her through it all.

Family came with a price, but Joseph's love had no strings.

He even went to college with her. Joseph was smart, he just needed a reason to be smart in school. So he took two years at community college, aced his classes, and was admitted to UCLA as a junior when she entered as a freshman.

And history was made.

Uncle Jimmy didn't like outsiders, but he'd been used to having Joseph around for the last three years. When he told her to lose him so she could clean up yet another mess created by her cousin, though, Nicole put her foot down.

"Joseph is in, or I'm out."

"You can't walk away. We're family. Blood."

"Joseph is in, or I walk. Don't test me." She was terrified. She'd never stood up to her uncle. He was six foot four and 220 pounds. His temper was brutal, almost as brutal as her father's. But he was family. And family stuck together, especially now. Especially after what happened to her father.

Joseph wasn't intimidated. Nicole didn't know how he couldn't be, because Uncle Jimmy had two inches on him and forty pounds. Joseph had had a rough childhood, though he never talked about it. Nicole had never met his parents, didn't even know if they were alive. He was an only child, or so he said.

"Sir, I will be an asset. I will do anything—kill anyone, sacrifice myself—to protect Niki."

Maybe it was his tone, or something in his eyes, but Uncle Jimmy backed down.

"We'll see," he said. "But remember, Nicole, we have bigger plans."

"I'm aware."

Not only was she aware, she'd fixed all the problems with Uncle Jimmy's Big Plan. Uncle Jimmy was smart, but he sometimes forgot that his son was a sick, twisted prick who was going to blow it for all of them.

"Get him, clean up the mess, bring him to me."

Thirty minutes later Nicole and Joseph were standing

in the middle of the whore's bedroom. She was dead, of course.

Tobias was becoming a big fucking problem. Uncle Jimmy had kept him under control for a long time, but over the last year Tobias started disappearing on them for days or weeks at a time. And when he fucked up—like now—he'd call and beg for help and forgiveness.

Tobias was naked, sitting at the end of the bed, smoking a joint. He scowled when he saw them walk in. "Took you fucking long enough."

Tobias was twenty-one, two years younger than Joseph, but a lifetime less mature. He was pudgy around the middle and had ham hocks for fists. How someone so stupid could come from the sperm of Uncle Jimmy was beyond Nicole's comprehension.

Maybe it was the mix of Uncle Jimmy's brutality and Aunt Maggie's idiot IQ.

Nicole put on latex gloves and looked at the girl. This wasn't the first dead girl she'd seen, but her stomach still twisted in knots. She didn't know if it would ever get easier.

The girl had been gagged so she couldn't scream while Tobias tortured her. Her flesh had been burned, cut, and bruised, as if he couldn't decide what to do. His sperm had dried all over her body. Reluctantly, Nicole pressed two fingers against her neck, just to make sure she was dead.

She was very dead.

"Why didn't you call sooner?" she snapped, turning away from the mess.

"I didn't know she couldn't take it."

Nicole dry-heaved and ran to the bathroom, where she puked into the toilet. Tobias was sick, she'd always known it, but this . . . this was worse than anything before. Uncle Jimmy was going to have to stop him, and if that meant killing him or sending him away, so be it. He couldn't go off and kill hookers whenever he wanted—he would eventually be caught. It would come back on the family. Their plan would be in jeopardy.

"Niki," Joseph said quietly, standing behind her.

"I'm fine."

"His prints are everywhere. He's probably in the system already, from one of the others."

This wasn't the first girl Tobias had killed, but they'd always taken care of potential evidence. Uncle Jimmy taught her how to clean up the scene, but this was . . . worse than usual.

"He'll grow out of it," Uncle Jimmy had always said.

Nicole pretended to believe it, but now she couldn't. She wanted Tobias caught and locked up.

But he knew too much about Uncle Jimmy. About her plans for after college. About the family. If Tobias went to prison, she would never be who she was supposed to be.

And she would never have the chance to lead the family.

"We do what Uncle Jimmy wants."

"Damn straight," Tobias said. He stood up, his dick half hard, and glanced over at the dead girl, consideration on his face.

Joseph turned and hit him. "If you were my family, you would already be dead."

"I will kill you!" Tobias said and lunged for Joseph.

Tobias was not only weak, but stoned, and Joseph sidestepped him and then tripped him. Tobias landed on the floor with a grunt.

"Stop," Nicole said. "Stop it!"

Tobias pulled himself up and glared at Joseph but he didn't make a move.

That was when Nicole realized who had the real power in the family. And it wasn't Tobias.

"This is beyond a standard cleanup," she said. "Ideas?"

"Fire," Joseph said. "It's the only way to ensure every-thing is destroyed."

"Done." She looked at Joseph, felt that rush that only he gave her. Together, they were stronger. Together, she could do anything.

She said to Tobias, "Get dressed. Go to my car. Stay until I get there."

"You've always been a bitch."

"And I've never had to have anyone clean up my mistakes!"

Tobias made a move toward her, then glanced at Joseph and backed off. He picked up his clothes and left.

"We should let him go to prison," Joseph said.

"He's family," she said, as if that answered everything.

Joseph didn't say anything, but she knew exactly what he was thinking.

"I can't," she said, answering his unspoken suggestion.

"I can."

She shook her head. "We'll deal with Tobias later."

She looked back at the body, but had to turn away. What had happened to her family? How could Uncle Jimmy have let this happen? "I don't know where to begin."

Joseph said, "This is an old apartment." He led her from the bedroom to the living room. The heating unit was in the wall. "Gas."

"Will that work?"

"We'll make sure it does. Go to the bathroom. Look for nail polish remover, rubbing alcohol, anything like that."

Nicole did as Joseph said. She tried not to look at the girl's pictures taped to the mirror. Maybe she hadn't been a hooker. But she looked like one. Where had Tobias found her? It was a one-bedroom apartment and it didn't look *like she had a roommate, but would someone be looking for her?*

Except it was after midnight. No one would be coming around now.

She found one half bottle and one full bottle of nail polish remover under the sink. No rubbing alcohol, but she found a large bottle of hydrogen peroxide. Once, when she was ten or eleven, she and her best friend had tried to lighten their hair with the stuff. It smelled awful, and made Nicole's naturally blond hair an odd streaky white, and Jenny's brownish hair an ugly red.

She brought the material to Joseph, who was pouring vegetable oil into a pot on the stove. "Will this work?" she asked him.

He glanced over and nodded. "Grab all the loose blankets and sheets you can find and bunch them up under the curtains in her bedroom. Douse them with the nail polish. Then grab some clothes and whatever and put those under the window in the living room. Pour the hydrogen peroxide on them."

"When do we light them?"

"We don't—we're going to be long gone."

She didn't know what the plan was, but she trusted Joseph. She had to. She did what he said. When she was done, he was on his hands and knees in front of the heater, the front panel on the floor. She watched him blow out the pilot light.

"I don't know how long it'll take for the apartment to fill with gas, but it shouldn't be too long. The flames from the stove will cause an explosion, and the bedding will keep the fire burning."

"Shouldn't we put it on the body?"

He shook his head. "This will work. Even if they recover her body, there won't be any physical evidence tying her to Tobias."

"But they'll know this wasn't an accident."

"Tobias swore to Jimmy that no one saw him with the girl. If he lied, that's on him, not us."

She nodded. They could only do so much. *"Okay. We should go."*

They left. Nicole wished she knew how long this would take, but they couldn't wait around. Joseph had wisely parked two blocks away. There were no security cameras or anyone around who could identify them leaving the apartment in Van Nuys. By the time they reached the car, Tobias was asleep in the back.

"We should have left him there," she mumbled.

But of course she couldn't. Tobias was family.

She had to protect her family.

Two days later, Joseph handed her a copy of the LA Times *after her chemistry class. She read it and began to shake.*

"Joseph—I didn't think—"

"I did. There was no other choice. It was either let Tobias rot or solve the problem." He touched her chin, forced her to look at him. *"I love you, Niki. I will always protect you."*

For a minute, she wanted to run away. Her and Joseph, leave the family, let Uncle Jimmy move his own damn drugs, let her flaky mother get taken by the next con artist, let Tobias rot in prison for murder, just disappear and never look back. She and Joseph, alone together.

As if he could read her mind, Joseph said, *"Just say the word, Niki."*

She wanted to. Desperately.

But they were family. And only the family cared about retribution for her father's murder.

"I can't. I love you, Joseph, I love you so much . . . but they're my family. I can't walk away. I have to follow

through. It's my legacy." Her bottom lip quivered. *"I don't want to lose you."*

He hugged her tight. *"You will never lose me. I will be with you always. I will protect you from everyone—from your family, from your enemies, from the government. I am your protector, your lover, your soul mate."*

She squeezed her eyes shut. There was no going back.

VAN NUYS—A six-unit apartment building on Archwood Street near Saticoy and Sepulveda burned to the ground Saturday night. Four people died in the blaze, which started at approximately 2:30 a.m. The fire began in an upstairs unit rented by 19-year-old Maria Lopez, a student at a local community college. Witnesses report that they first heard an explosion. One of the complex renters, 69-year-old Hap Tomas, said the explosion woke him and he immediately ran outside. The upper floors were already on fire. He woke up the residents in the other downstairs units and they all were uninjured, treated for smoke inhalation and minor burns. Four of the six upstairs unit residents were killed. The other two weren't at home.

The Los Angeles Fire Department released an unconfirmed report that a gas leak contributed to the fire. Arson has not been ruled out. A full investigation is under way.

Joseph watched Niki sleep. He hated that she'd spent three months in prison. They had been apart for much longer than three months over the twenty-three years he'd known her, but prison was different.

For five years he'd worked for Congresswoman Adeline Reyes-Worthington. Five miserable years. And in the end, she'd screwed up everything. It had been a pleasure to break her neck. When Niki finally was transferred to San Antonio, they saw each other when they could, which wasn't often enough for Joseph. But now . . . now he wouldn't leave her side. She needed him, more than she knew.

She may have kept Tobias on a short leash, but her incarceration had broken his chains, and she didn't know the half of what he'd done. But Joseph knew Niki . . . she had to learn of his screwups on her own. She had to come to the decision herself to take him out.

He knew she would. He just prayed it wouldn't be too late.

His phone vibrated. He reached over and looked at the screen.

A photo of their enemy, with a brief message from Dover.

Green light?

"Who is it?" Niki asked with a yawn.

He showed her the message.

"How did you set the trap? He's never fallen for it before."

"Patience, Niki. You have to know the enemy to defeat the enemy. I assume you want the plan to move forward?"

"Absolutely. I don't care what they do to him, as long as they don't kill him. I need information."

"Understood."

Joseph responded.

It's a go.

CHAPTER ELEVEN

For twenty-six years, Kane Rogan had been a soldier. He'd only spent six years in the marines, but those six years had taught him a lifetime of skills and forged friendships that were stronger than blood.

Twenty years as a freelance soldier/mercenary/hostage negotiator—whatever you wanted to call it—only honed his skills. Kane had a sixth sense that only the most elite special forces units had. Mental muscle, spidey sense, whatever they called it, Kane had it—and as soon as he saw Siobhan's cell phone on the charger in her hotel room, he knew she was in danger. Or dead.

He searched the room. Her clothes were there—just a few things, but she traveled light. A couple of changes, toiletries, her backpack.

And her camera.

Siobhan Walsh went nowhere without that damn camera, and she certainly wouldn't leave it in a hotel overnight. He'd tracked down the taxi that had picked her up for breakfast, but instead of a restaurant, it had dropped her outside a church, Our Lady of Light. That made sense—Siobhan was Catholic, and yesterday was Sunday.

But she'd never come back to the hotel.

He grabbed her camera and cell phone and stored them in his jeep.

Kane checked out the church. The evening Mass would be starting in fifteen minutes, and he found the priest in the room behind the altar making preparations. The young priest handed one of the two altar boys the gifts and the other a large, heavy book covered in red leather. He saw Kane in the narrow entry when he looked up. Fear filled his eyes.

Kane didn't say anything as he stepped aside to let the two boys pass. Then he said, "I'm looking for a woman who was here yesterday," he said in Spanish. "This high"— he put his hand under his chin—"long curly red hair. Looks Irish. She would stand out."

The priest shook his head. "Sorry, señor."

"Sorry you didn't see her?"

Again, he shook his head. He was nervous. He was lying.

"*Sí*," he said.

"She is a photojournalist who's been working with the Sisters of Mercy."

His eyes widened in surprise. The Sisters of Mercy were well known and respected in this part of Mexico. "I don't know. I didn't see her."

But he didn't look at Kane.

"You're lying, Padre."

"No, señor. I don't want trouble. Please. You need to go. Mass is starting."

One of the altar servers returned and the priest looked torn. He said quietly, "Return after Mass. Please."

Kane looked out. About a dozen people were in the church; more were coming in.

"One hour," Kane said and left.

* * *

Two days ago Siobhan had called her half-sister and said she thought she was being followed. Lieutenant Colonel Andrea Walsh immediately called Kane, hoping he was within a hundred miles of Siobhan. He hadn't been, but he called Andie back immediately.

"What the hell is she up to now?"

"Relax, Kane. Siobhan returned from a three-month trip with the Sisters of Mercy in Oaxaca. Part of her Children of Mexico series. She was taking some R and R in Santiago when she called me."

"And?"

"And now I can't reach her. Her phone rings, I get voice mail. She always calls me back right away because she knows I worry. When she didn't call back by this morning, I contacted the hotel she's at and they said she didn't come in last night—she left yesterday morning, Sunday, and hasn't returned."

"I'm in Juarez. It'll take me a few hours to get a team together and get down there."

"I'm sure it's nothing."

"You wouldn't have called me if it was nothing, Andie."

"She's the only family I have."

He wanted to say, Then why do you let her travel to the most dangerous places south of the border? Why didn't you keep her in DC, which was a damn sight safer than Oaxaca, Mexico? *But he didn't, because he knew the answer: Siobhan would do whatever she damn well pleased.*

"I'll find her. But I'm dragging her sorry ass back to the States and you need to lay down the law with your sister because I don't have time for this."

Andie Walsh was career military. She and Kane had been in the same basic training program, but she'd been an officer candidate because she had a four-year degree and wanted to make the marines her career. Her dad had been a marine, her brother had been a marine. It was in her blood. She was now the number-two-ranked officer at the Officer Candidates School at Quantico.

How Siobhan had even half the same blood in her veins as Andie eluded Kane.

Kane rendezvoused with his men at a small bar not far from the hotel. He had three men with him—a standard foursome that he took on most operations. Ranger was following up on a lead about Tobias, something Kane had planned to do himself until Andie called him.

He'd brought in one of his regulars, Blitz, as well as two new recruits, Dyson and Gomez, former marines who'd recently signed on with RCK for a two-year contract. Dyson was quiet with sharp recon skills, and Gomez was a wily chameleon who could fly anything. Kane had been using Sean far too much lately, and while he trusted his brother explicitly, Sean was needed elsewhere. Sean had someone else to live for, and Kane wasn't going to repeatedly risk his brother's life. He didn't want to face Lucy and tell her the man she loved was dead.

Sometimes, Kane was surprised they'd lived as long as they had.

"The priest was lying," Kane said.

"Fuck," Gomez muttered. "What's the world coming to when you can't trust a fucking priest?"

Kane didn't know whether he was being sarcastic or serious.

"The target has been missing for thirty-three hours. Stay alert." He ran through the plan he'd formulated on his way back to the bar. He looked at his watch. "You have twenty minutes downtime, but stay alert. Be outside at twenty hundred hours."

Kane stepped outside. He couldn't put his finger on *why* he felt they were in danger, but the feeling was as thick as the humidity that hung in the air like a hot, wet blanket. He felt eyes on him and walked around to the side, where no one could get a direct hit on him but where he had a good field of vision. Didn't help his nerves. Someone was watching them. Someone had followed him from the hotel. Was this the same feeling Siobhan had when she called Andie? Siobhan would never ask for help, not unless there was a serious situation. Andie had told her to change her routine, leave early, not tell anyone where she was going.

Yet she'd stayed.

What did you get yourself into, Siobhan?

Why couldn't Andie's little sister just stay in the States—didn't the US have enough problems to photograph? Why come down here? Why risk her life? This wasn't the first time he'd been sent to bail the photojournalist out of hot water.

Third time's a charm, sugar. Next time you're on your own.

Next time? Hell no. He'd get Rick Stockton to flag Siobhan Walsh's fucking passport to prevent her from ever leaving the United States again. Then she could be Jack Kincaid's problem instead of his.

Not that lack of a passport would stop the girl from doing whatever she damn well pleased.

Kane wasn't surprised when Blitz followed him out.

"Someone's watching us," Kane said.

"Yep," Blitz said.

"Were you followed from the airport?"

"Yep. Couldn't get eyes on them. They were there, then gone. They're good."

"Military?"

Blitz shrugged. "Experienced."

"How many?"

"Pair."

"Same here."

Again, it was a feeling, not because Kane had seen two people tracking him. But he trusted his gut.

"Four—same as us," Blitz said.

"Odds in our favor." Kane would put his men up against twice the number and be confident they'd come away unscathed.

Siobhan, of course, was the wild card. Anytime there was a hostage, that changed the game.

"Santiago is pretty tame," Blitz said.

"She was targeted," Kane said. "Siobhan and her damn camera."

Because what else could it be? Criminals, particularly the cartels and the corrupt cops, were nervous around journalists.

And having her targeted because she was a photojournalist was much better than having Siobhan targeted because she was a woman.

Or because of him.

If anyone had hurt her, they would soon be dead.

Kane pulled out his sat phone and called Jack Kincaid. His partner answered immediately.

"Kincaid."

"She left everything in her hotel room and hasn't been seen for thirty-three hours. Disappeared at a church." He gave him the name and location.

"And?"

"We're being followed. Two teams of two. I'm going dark. If you don't hear from me in eight hours, notify Ranger."

"Nicole Rollins escaped this morning during a transport. Sean, Lucy, and Stockton all want to talk to you."

Rollins. Well, fuck.

"This morning?"

"Yes."

"Did she flee the country?"

"Negative. Padre had his ear to the ground in Hidalgo, and I called in some favors in El Paso. She's definitely in hiding, but we believe—and so does the FBI—that she's still in Texas. Lucy called me herself—she thinks you're at the top of her hit list."

"I'm aware of Lucy's theories."

"You disagree?"

"No." Kane just didn't think he was the only one on the list. "As soon as I grab Siobhan, I'll head to San Antonio." Several thoughts, none of them good, twisted around his head. "Find out who knew Siobhan was in Santiago. According to Andie Walsh, this was an unscheduled vacation."

"You don't think this was random."

"No."

"A trap?"

"She's bait, Jack. I feel it in my bones. And if I don't bite, they'll kill her."

"I can get you backup by morning."

"Only if you don't hear from me. Out." He hung up. "Blitz," Kane said, "as soon as we secure the target, get her out. Don't look back."

"Someone knows she's important to you."

"She's no more important than anyone else," Kane snapped. Shit, this is why he didn't have attachments. He wasn't attached to Siobhan Walsh in any way, but he'd known her for ten, twelve years now. Longer. And he'd known her sister since he was an eighteen-year-old recruit. It wouldn't have been difficult to connect Kane to Andie Walsh, then Andie to Siobhan, and Siobhan to her dangerous life.

Blitz cleared his throat. "Meaning, they know she's connected. That you've come for her before."

That, he could believe. Because Siobhan was bait. If they were dealing with terrorists, Andie was a high-value target. And while Kane viewed every member of every cartel as a terrorist, they wouldn't give a shit about a lieutenant colonel in the marines stationed at Quantico.

Which meant that Siobhan, a civilian, was bait for Kane.

He didn't have to think about why. He knew damn well *why*. The only thing he'd been working on for three months was finding Tobias. His only attachments were his family, but his family was protected—Sean and Lucy could watch out for each other; Duke was well trained to protect his wife and baby daughter (and Kane had already talked to Jack about keeping an eye on them); and Liam and Eden were in Europe, far from his enemies' reach.

Two weeks ago he'd lost a source of information, and that's when he realized that he was a specific target. It had been a trap; he'd survived, his snitch had not. And until Siobhan's disappearance yesterday, he'd kept a very low profile.

Shit, shit, shit.

Gomez and Dyson stepped out of the bar. "Sarge?" Gomez said.

Kane hated being called Sarge, which was his last rank before he left the marines, but marines were creatures of order, and it would take a few jobs before Gomez and Dyson changed.

"She's bait," Kane said.

"Tobias," Blitz said, his face dark. He'd been there when they rescued the boys who ran drugs for Trejo, who worked for Tobias.

"Nicole Rollins escaped from custody today. She's still in Texas. I've created a shitstorm for them, and they need to use me as an example. No matter what, get Siobhan out."

"Safe house in Arteaga?" Blitz asked. That had been the original plan. Regroup in Arteaga, accessible on foot in a day, an hour by vehicle, or twenty minutes by plane. Kane had contacts there. But he didn't know who had been compromised.

"Last resort. Get her to the safe house in Hidalgo, across the border, and contact Jack."

"What about you?"

He didn't respond, because Blitz and the others couldn't be distracted from getting Siobhan to safety.

These bastards thought they could use a friend of his to bait him? They didn't know who they were fucking with. He would turn the tables and find out exactly where Tobias was hiding. He'd get every piece of information from these scumbags. And if any of them so much as touched a hair on Siobhan . . .

Blitz cleared his throat. "Boss, we'll get Tobias another day."

"This ends now," Kane said.

He didn't need to acknowledge Blitz's loyalty. Blitz would die for Kane, or any one of their team. He and Ranger were the most loyal men Kane could have hoped for. Dyson and Gomez had potential, but they didn't have the experience.

"Understood."

They made their way separately to the church, Dyson pairing off with Kane, Gomez with Blitz. It didn't take long; Santiago wasn't a big town. He nodded to his men, and they split up. They had his back while Kane tracked down the priest.

Kane walked into the back of the church. As soon as the door closed, the priest saw him. His eyes were scared, but he didn't falter from his closing prayer.

Kane scanned the room. Three dozen parishioners. He didn't know if that was good or bad for a weeknight. Most of them were older women. He didn't see anyone who looked suspicious, and he didn't see Siobhan.

He didn't expect to.

He was acutely aware of his surroundings. The church wasn't large, a long narrow hall with about thirty rows of pews and an aisle down the middle. A small room to the right was probably for prayers or baptisms or whatever. Kane respected the churches, but he didn't believe or disbelieve. What was the point? Some on his team, like Ranger, were true believers. Others, like Blitz, were nonbelievers. But when push came to shove, he trusted both of them with his life.

The two altar boys followed the priest down the aisle when Mass was over. The priest was looking at Kane, his young face a hard line. How old was this guy? Certainly no older than Sean. And he was scared.

Someone had threatened him. It took a lot of balls to threaten a man of God.

The priest turned to him. "I am truly sorry. I had no choice."

The priest had set him up, but Kane had expected it. So he waited where he stood, ready to shoot or fight.

He said into his com, "Stay sharp. Sound off."

"Beta here." Blitz.

"Charlie here." Gomez.

"Delta here." Dyson.

He kept his com open because his men needed to know what was happening. People filed out, glancing at him, scurrying. Did they suspect violence was about to break out? Or did he just have that effect on people?

The last of the parishioners exited. The church was stifling, not air-conditioned, the layers of human sweat and humidity and perfume and incense clogging his senses.

The main door opened and the priest came back in.

"I can't do this," he said quietly to Kane. "They took one of my altar boys. They would have killed him, and your friend, if I didn't tell you to return."

Leverage. "Leave," Kane said.

"I need to fix this. I am sorry, so sorry."

"Where are they?"

"The rectory basement."

Kane said in his com, "Blitz?"

"We're on it; Dyson has your six."

"They took them yesterday, after the morning Mass," the priest continued. "I was to notify them when someone showed up asking about the redheaded girl. They promised to release both of them if I convinced you to return here."

"When?"

He paused. "Now."

"Go, Padre. You're in danger."

"You're the one they want. When I showed them your picture they said there's a reward for your capture."

Kane stepped to the side and pushed the priest out the door, then closed it again. During his recon, he'd noticed only one rear entrance to the church. The small rectory was behind it. Best way to keep the priest in line was to threaten one of his own.

Over the com, Blitz said, "Movement in the back. Two shooters, with the boy."

"Copy."

Kane took six steps to the right and stood just inside the small sanctuary off the vestibule. These people had threatened a priest, kidnapped a child and a woman. Reward for his capture—they wanted him alive. But that didn't mean they wouldn't kill everyone else.

Two shooters with the boy, which meant at least two shooters with Siobhan. He said, "Get eyes on her now."

"Roger."

He heard a door open in the back before he saw anyone. There was some fumbling, something got knocked over, and he saw movement from the room behind the altar. Kane peered through the slit in the doorway. A boy, not more than eight years of age, still dressed in his black altar boy attire, was gagged and his hands were tied in front of him. His face was dirty and stained with tears. He had a cut on the side of his head.

They'd hit a child.

The rage pouring through Kane veins calmed him.

One man had a handgun held to the back of the boy's head. The other had an AK-47 strapped over one shoulder, and a large handgun in his left hand. Looked like a .45-caliber, but Kane couldn't tell from the angle. Powerful gun. Did he know how to use it? How well trained were these men? Former military? Former Mexican police? Or had they been trained by the cartels? Were they part of Tobias's gang or freelancers?

Didn't matter. They knew something, and if they didn't know, they would still be dead.

The asshole with the AK-47 started walking along the perimeter of the church, looking up and down each pew. "We know you're in here, Rogan." He spoke perfect English. This man might live in Mexico, but he was an American. Ten more feet and he'd see Kane.

"Throw out your weapons, come peacefully, and we'll let the boy go."

Siobhan. They wouldn't let her go. Her imprisonment was the only thing that would keep Kane compliant. They knew that. They'd done this sort of thing before.

But they'd never tried this stunt with Kane.

"If you don't come out, we'll kill the boy."

In his ear, Kane heard Blitz. "Eyes on the target. Two guards. One roaming."

He tapped his com twice so Blitz would know he'd heard him.

There was noise outside the main doors. It distracted the men just enough for Kane to step out.

The doors opened and the priest ran in.

The left-handed man aimed at the priest, but hesitated just a second. Kane fired two shots, aiming center mass, then one slightly higher.

All three hit and the bad guy went down without getting off a shot.

He turned to the man at the altar who had his gun on the boy. This bad guy wasn't as confident or cocky. He was shaking, which was problematic.

The priest said, "Let him go, señor. Let the boy go. Don't shed any more blood in God's house."

Kane walked fast toward the altar. He read the gunman's eyes. He wasn't a child killer. He was conflicted.

But he still had the gun on the back of the boy's head with his right hand, and his left hand gripped the gown and the boy's shoulder.

"Let him go and you live," Kane said. "Five. Four."

The priest said, "Please, señor. He's a boy."

"Three. Two. One."

The gunman pushed the boy to the ground and aimed his gun at Kane.

He was dead before he could fire.

"Get the boy out of here," Kane ordered the priest and ran toward the back.

He'd heard nothing from Blitz, and the other shooters must have heard the gunshots.

He stopped, just before he exited. He realized he'd almost made a fatal mistake—never run blind out of a building.

Because this was Siobhan. He'd almost been reckless because of Siobhan.

"Report," he said.

Silence.

"Dyson," he said.

"The priest just left with the boy."

"I'm coming out the back."

"Roger, I'll be there in ten."

Ten beats. Kane counted them, not liking that his patience was slipping. He took a long, deep breath.

On the eleventh beat, he cautiously opened the door, but didn't step out. Gunfire erupted, right in front of him. Dyson had turned the corner of the church, and the gunman unleashed a modified AK-47. Dyson retreated, but he might have been hit.

Kane jumped out of the doorway and tackled the shooter. The spray of bullets went high. Kane disarmed him and knocked him out with the butt of his own gun.

"Dyson," he said into his com.

"I'm okay."

"Hit?"

"Flesh wound."

Blitz burst out of the rectory half carrying Siobhan.

Time stopped, just for a second.

She was in a long, dirty white sundress, not the jeans she lived in. Blood, both old and fresh, stained the cotton. A bruise, purple and black, enlarged her right cheek.

They'd hurt her. Those fucking bastards had hit her.

Blitz was bleeding from his arm. "Knives. Gomez." He shook his head. "I got one, one escaped, but he's seriously hurt."

"Recon, get Gomez, meet in the church in five."

Blitz nodded to Dyson and passed Siobhan off to Kane.

Kane picked her up. "I can walk," she said, her voice scratchy.

Kane carried her into the church and set her down on the pew. He took a bottle of water from his pack and handed it to her. She drank. "Thanks," she said.

"Where are you injured?"

"It's fine."

He glared at her and inspected her dress, looking for bullet holes or knife marks.

"The blood is mostly from your friend," she said. "Kane—I'm sorry. I knew someone was following me, I should have left town. I planned to leave right after church, and then . . ." Her voice trailed off.

"This time it wasn't your fault."

She tensed. "This time? And the other times were? You're a piece of work, Rogan." She tried to stand, then winced.

He pushed her back down. One of her crystal-clear blue eyes was swollen. Her silky red hair was tangled and matted. "Where. Are. You. Injured."

"Last night I tried to escape with Diego," she said. "Is he okay?"

"Yes," Kane said.

"They just . . . they just hit me. I'm sore."

He applied pressure on her stomach and she winced. He unbuttoned her dress, tried to ignore her lacy white bra, and looked at the bruising. "Cracked or broken ribs."

"I don't think—"

"No, you don't."

He buttoned her back up and tried to ignore the tears that welled in her eyes.

This was why he didn't form attachments. They could be used against him. He didn't even have an attachment to Siobhan, but he wanted to hunt down and kill the last man left standing.

But he couldn't. He needed that man alive because he needed information.

Blitz and Dyson came in. "The priest took the boy to his mother," Blitz said. "We secured Gomez's body in the jeep. The priest told me to give you this." He handed Kane a slip of paper. There was a local address. "I asked him where someone would go for stitches or surgery, other than a hospital. The fifth guy isn't going to get much farther than that without medical attention."

"Take her to Hidalgo."

"Rogan," Blitz said, "I never question your orders, but this time—it's you they want."

"I know."

Siobhan said, "Don't be foolish, Kane. They were willing to kill a priest and a little boy and—and me to get you." Her voice cracked, her concern digging around in his hardened heart.

"But they didn't," he said. "You don't know what's going on here, stay out of it."

"You think I'm deaf? They work for a man named Joseph. They don't want you dead; Joseph thinks you know something about money that was stolen from them."

"Does the name Tobias mean anything to you?" Kane asked.

"No. Should it?"

Joseph. The FBI was looking for a man named Joseph Contreras who was suspected of killing Congresswoman Adeline Reyes-Worthington. Broke her neck and disappeared. There was nothing on Contreras, but Kane hadn't looked too deep—his focus was Tobias. If Worthington was working for Tobias, though, then it stood to reason that when she was going to turn state's evidence, Tobias had ordered Joseph to kill her. Tobias's other front man, Jay, had been killed by SWAT during a hostage standoff two weeks ago; he would need a new one. Perhaps Joseph had been promoted? Or had he been part of Tobias's operation all along.

"Kane," Siobhan continued, "the man who got away— he's American. He's not like the others, though he spoke decent Spanish. He was in charge. He was the one making the calls, making the decisions. He seems to think he knows what you'll do, but he was surprised that you came with a team of four."

Kane didn't quite know what to make of that information. "Description?"

Blitz said, "Six feet tall, light-brown hair gray on the sides, probably close to forty-five, fifty."

"He was in good shape," Siobhan added. "Lean and muscular. Nice looking. Clean, articulate. He had a faded scar on his right forearm about this long." She put her fingers about three inches apart.

Not Tobias. Same age, but Tobias was balding and rounded. "Did you get a name?" Kane asked.

She shook her head. "They all called him 'sir' or 'boss.' He called in reinforcements, I know that they hadn't arrived before you did."

"Blitz, Dyson, get Siobhan and Gomez to Hidalgo." He looked at his watch. With Gomez dead, Kane was the only one who could fly the plane. "It's a three-hour drive to Hidalgo. Be alert, stay on the main road. Watch for patrols. When you get near Hidalgo, call Padre and he'll get you across the border. Tell him she needs medical attention. She has a cracked rib. Take care of your injuries on the road."

"We'll come back for you."

"Negative. I have the damn plane, I'll fly myself out."

"Kane—"

"I need information. Go, before the Mexican police swarm this place. I'll be in Hidalgo before dawn."

He didn't want to look at Siobhan again, but he did. She looked worried, and not about herself.

"I packed up your things, they're in the jeep. I'll be fine, kid."

She bristled and he almost smiled. He knew she hated to be called "kid."

Before she could open her mouth, he said, "And call your sister." Then he left.

He had a man to find.

CHAPTER TWELVE

It was after nine that night by the time Sean left St. Catherine's Boys' Home. Lucy had called an hour ago to say she was bringing Brad Donnelly over to talk about the Rollins escape. Normally Sean wouldn't mind, but right now he was tired and worried and wanted to hold Lucy. He'd had a long talk with Father Mateo Flannigan and the boys about security and ended up hiring a private security company for the next couple of days, until he had a better sense whether St. Catherine's—or Michael in particular—was in danger. He called his brother Duke, hoping to get an urgent message to Kane.

"You're in contact with Kane more than I am," Duke said.

"But he still works under the RCK umbrella. You know where he is."

"I don't, but Jack would. Call him."

Sean didn't tell Duke that he'd already left a message for Jack Kincaid, Lucy's brother, who was one of the principals at Rogan-Caruso-Kincaid. Now that Jack was married and living in Sacramento with his wife, an FBI agent, he didn't work beyond US borders. But Jack still worked closely with Kane on planning and scheduling operations south of the border. It used to be Jack's life, when he lived in Hidalgo, Texas, and most of Jack's team had moved over to work with Kane when Jack gave up international ops.

"I'll do that," Sean said. "How're Nora and Molly?"

"Amazing. Nora went back to work last week. It was bittersweet. Nora missed her job, but now she misses the time with Molly."

"Are you taking her to work with you?"

"I pretty much work from home," Duke said. "I take her with me when I go into the office, but when I need to go on-site to install or test a system, we have a terrific nanny."

"Mister Mom," Sean said. "I never thought I'd see the day."

"Babies are a lot easier than genius teenagers," Duke said.

Duke had raised Sean from the time Sean was fourteen. Duke hadn't been much older—he'd been twenty-three when their parents were killed in a small plane crash. Sean, the youngest Rogan and the only minor at the time, needed a guardian, and Duke was the only one willing to do it. Kane was fighting wars and the twins, Liam and Eden, were in college in Europe. Sean loved his brother for sacrificing so much to raise him, but it hadn't been easy for either of them. As a teenager, Sean had been angry, resentful, and far too smart for his own good. Duke was a borderline dictator, trying to control Sean without understanding the root of Sean's anger. They'd had ups and downs over the years, but even after Sean fought his way into the family business—as a respected member of RCK—Duke still treated him like the black sheep, the screwup, the problem kid.

Sean had had to leave RCK, or he would never have been able to save his relationship with his brother. Or his own self-respect.

"I suppose they are," Sean said.

"I didn't mean it as a jab."

Maybe not consciously. "I know." Duke still couldn't see that Sean needed to forge his own path. It didn't help that Duke—and the other principals of RCK—kept sending him jobs. He didn't want to be tethered forever to his brother. He turned down more jobs than he took, but some were interesting or challenging, and Sean loved a challenge.

"Give my best to Nora," Sean said and hung up before he or Duke said something they'd regret.

Sean pulled into his garage, noting Brad's truck parked in front of the house. Lucy had sent him a slew of messages over the course of the day, the last of which was that she and Brad were bringing Tex-Mex home at eight thirty. Sean liked Brad, but he wanted Lucy to himself. They'd had three perfect, carefree days in San Diego, where Lucy had completely relaxed and had fun, something she didn't do often enough. They'd swum in the ocean, surfed, run on the beach at dawn, made love several times a day, and still managed to touch bases with everyone in Lucy's large Irish Cuban family—including the newest addition, her nephew John Patrick Thomas.

And then their first day back in San Antonio, Lucy was pulled into a major case.

He walked in through the side door and found Lucy and Brad eating takeout while sitting at the island in the center of the kitchen.

Lucy smiled at him, but her eyes were troubled. "How are the boys? Father Mateo?"

"Safe," he said. He kissed his fiancée, maybe a bit longer than he normally would have in front of company. He felt a pang of jealousy that had no place in his relationship with Lucy—she loved him, he knew it. He'd mostly gotten over his insecurity that he wasn't good enough for her, but Brad Donnelly reminded him too much of Noah Armstrong—another competent, alpha-male federal agent who had befriended Lucy and was attracted to her. Sean and Noah had settled their differences and Sean now considered him a friend, but it had taken a year before Sean stopped feeling threatened by the fed.

He started to walk to the refrigerator for a beer, but Lucy put her hand on his forearm. She didn't need to say anything; he saw the worry. He didn't want to add to her stress. Not after today and five dead cops.

One of whom could have been Lucy.

He put it out of his mind. He had to, or he wouldn't be able to function. The idea of tossing Lucy back on his plane and returning to the beach house in San Diego had crossed his mind more than once today.

"It's been a long day," he said, touching her cheek. "For all of us."

"So you're getting married," Brad said. "Congratulations."

"Thanks," Sean said, pleased that Brad acknowledged it. How petty was that? But he nodded to the bottle in front of him. "Another?"

Brad drained it and nodded. "Thanks."

He extracted two beers, handed one to Brad, then drank half of his in one long gulp. He dished up a small plate. "You're not sick, are you?" Lucy said, motioning to his modest serving.

"I ate dinner with the boys. But I can't resist these tamales." He sat next to Lucy. "What don't I know?"

"Not much," Lucy said. "There're so many agencies and people involved, it's controlled chaos at both the FBI and the DEA. The marshals seem to be on top of things, but so far no sightings after the helicopter left the park this morning. After the debriefing, and my meeting with the

ASAC—" She paused when her cell phone vibrated on the table.

"It's Noah," she said to Sean. She answered the phone. "Hello, Noah. This is a surprise."

"Lucy. Good to hear your voice."

Lucy hadn't spoken to Noah since she graduated from Quantico six months before. He'd been one of her training agents, but he'd also become a friend. She should have made more of an effort to keep in touch. She'd emailed him a few times, sharing some of her experiences as a rookie, but it wasn't the same as face-to-face.

"I wish I was calling to say hello," Noah continued. "Special Agent Logan Dunbar was murdered last night, only minutes after he arrived home from San Antonio."

Her heart dropped. Another dead agent? "What happened?" Her voice sounded calmer than she felt.

"We believe the killer was waiting outside Dunbar's town house for him to return, but I'm waiting for the ERT report. No sign of forced entry, but Dunbar wasn't expecting the attack. Two bullets to the back, one in the head. Rick Stockton asked me to work the case because I was privy to Dunbar's undercover work in San Antonio."

"I didn't know that."

She realized she sounded angry. Why? Because she'd been out of the loop? Or because Dunbar's undercover work had indirectly led an innocent man to his death? She wouldn't soon forget her last investigation, or the fact that Dunbar had kept too much information to himself when it would have been useful if the San Antonio field office had known about his assignment.

"I was his liaison with Rick."

It would have been a million times easier two weeks ago if Noah had simply called her and explained what was going on after Dunbar was forced to come forward. She trusted Noah, and it would have saved time and sour feelings if Noah smoothed things over.

"You think it's connected to his undercover assignment in San Antonio."

"I can't prove it, but yes, I think it is. We have the best crime techs going through his house. Nothing appears missing, but because we don't know what he came home with we can't be positive. He supposedly shipped all his files back to headquarters, but we haven't received them yet. The cyber lab is going through his electronics to see if they've been accessed. I just debriefed Rick and Hans, and we all concur that Dunbar was killed because of something that happened in San Antonio."

"Maybe, but his investigation wrapped up nearly two weeks ago, after Adeline Worthington was killed."

"Dunbar was working with the AUSA on indictments of individuals who profited from her corruption. Not just in Texas, but staff here in DC—in Congress, at the EPA, at the Bureau of Land Management. All she needed was one well-placed person in each organization."

"But you already ID'd them, correct?"

"Yes—but maybe we missed someone. Maybe Dunbar had additional information that was worth killing for, or he knew something that he hadn't put in his reports. I'll be going through the paperwork myself and review each report. Rick told me you were part of that investigation."

"I worked Harper Worthington's murder, not his wife's crimes." Then she remembered Barry. "My partner on the case, Barry Crawford, worked with Dunbar on the followup. It was a complex financial situation, and I'll admit I had a hard time grasping the nuances of the illegal land transactions. I can give you Barry's contact information. He's out of town, but our boss called him back in." Her instincts twitched. She'd also sent him a message, but he'd never returned her call. Barry was a by-the-book agent. He would have responded. Maybe he was still traveling.

She had a bad feeling.

"I read your reports, Lucy. Two of the three primary people involved in the money laundering scheme were murdered—the congresswoman and her campaign manager. The finance guy, James Everett, turned state's evidence, correct?"

"Yes. He's in witness protection with his family. That's all I know about it—if you need to talk to Everett, you'll have to go through the US Marshals' office."

"I've spent most of today going over the financials of anyone who might have had a reason to take a hit out on Dunbar, because the scene reads like a hit. I was hoping you might have some ideas."

"You'll have to talk to Barry. He's a meticulous agent."

"I'll contact your SAC and make sure Barry contacts me as soon as possible. Watch your back, Lucy—if Dunbar was targeted because of the Worthington investigation, you and your partner need to be alert." Noah paused, then said, "Dunbar was killed last night when he came in from the airport. Nicole Rollins escaped this morning. What if, after the escape, he realized he knew something important about who might have helped her? Something that would lead to her location?"

"Tobias is connected to both Congresswoman Reyes-Worthington and to Nicole. Did Rick fill you in on Tobias? And my theory that he and Nicole are partners?"

"Yes," Noah said. "I'm up to speed. The timing is too coincidental, there is most likely a connection. Dunbar has an apartment in San Antonio—I'm sending you the location. He wasn't supposed to leave anything related to the case—"

"But you want us to verify. Absolutely. Call me if you need anything, Noah. I'm sorry about Agent Dunbar."

"Thank you, Lucy. Please be careful out there."

Lucy ended the call and Brad immediately said, "Logan Dunbar was killed?"

"Last night, when he returned to DC." She glanced at Sean. He had a dark expression on his face and looked more like his older brother Kane than she'd ever thought before.

"Noah thinks that bitch is involved."

Lucy was about to argue with Sean, try to convince him that Dunbar's murder and Nicole's escape were unconnected. But she didn't believe it, and Sean would be furious if she tried to pretend there was nothing to be concerned about.

"He doesn't think it's a coincidence," Lucy said carefully. "Noah doesn't know why, but his current theory is that Dunbar knew something that might have hindered Nicole's escape. He and Barry had been working nonstop putting together cases against those involved with the congresswoman. And Noah hasn't discounted that it may have been one of the lobbyists Dunbar was going after connected to the Worthington case."

Sean wasn't buying it. "She killed five cops. Six isn't stretching it."

"Sean—" Lucy began.

"You two," Sean said, cutting her off, "started this. With Ryan. You have to warn him."

"She's on the run," Brad said. "Why come back here? Every cop in Texas is looking for her."

"She didn't pull the trigger on Dunbar, but that doesn't mean she wasn't involved. Nicole is connected to Tobias. Tobias has extensive connections. Call Ryan. And then call Barry."

Lucy felt physically ill. Would Nicole go after them out of spite? Revenge? Anger? There had to be a reason—because Nicole Rollins did nothing without a reason.

But she pulled up her phone and dialed Ryan Quiroz.

"It's nearly eleven," Ryan answered.

"Agent Logan Dunbar was murdered last night in DC. There may be a connection with his undercover work in San Antonio." She hesitated, then added, "There may be a connection to Nicole Rollins."

"That's fucked."

"You said it." She hesitated. "Where are your boys?"

"Austin, with my ex. I drove them back up yesterday."

"Do you have a friend who can check on them?"

"Yes. You don't think—"

"I don't know what to think, but it doesn't hurt to be cautious."

"I'll call my ex-brother-in-law. He's a cop in Austin."

She hung up and called Barry. His phone went directly to voice mail. "Barry, it's Lucy Kincaid. Call me as soon as you get this message, any time of the day or night." She didn't want to say too much over the phone, but she felt she didn't have a choice under the circumstances. "Logan Dunbar was murdered last night. So please, call me." She hung up.

"Why isn't he answering?" Brad asked.

Lucy was now very worried about Barry. She'd texted him earlier, left a message earlier, she'd just called him . . . why hadn't he at least reached out? She sent an email message to Abigail Durant.

Have you spoken to Agent Crawford? I haven't been able to reach him all day.

"You need to have Juan send someone to check on him," Sean said.

"I emailed Durant, the ASAC. Nita went into labor today. Juan's going to be gone for the rest of the week." She scanned emails, but didn't see a baby announcement.

Sean glanced at Brad. "You're welcome to stay here tonight. Our house is a fortress."

"I'll be okay," Brad said, stretching. "But thanks anyway."

Lucy walked him to the door. "Headquarters, nine a.m.," she said.

Brad hesitated. "Are you sure about this? I don't think you should talk to her. I doubt she knows anything."

"We'll find out."

She closed the door and turned, surprised to find Sean standing behind her. "Who?" he asked.

"Elise Hansen."

"Why do you need to talk to her?"

"You know why."

"Her connection to Tobias."

"And Nicole. We need information. Hans will be here in the morning, I'm not doing this alone."

Sean touched her cheek. "I won't ask you not to do this."

"Thank you."

"But Lucy—do *not* let her get to you."

She stepped forward and wrapped her arms around his waist and rested her head on his chest. She didn't have a response. All she could do was shut down her emotions, focus on the facts. She hugged him for a long minute. "I should clean up the kitchen," she whispered.

"Tomorrow," he said and picked her up.

Her hand rested over his heart, which was beating rapidly. "Don't worry about me," she said. "Please, Sean."

"Asking me not to worry is like asking me to stop breathing." He held her tight as he walked up the stairs and turned into their bedroom. "I love you, Lucy." He dropped her onto the bed and fell down beside her. He took her hand, the one with the engagement ring, and kissed it. "I couldn't survive if anything happened to you."

His voice cracked and she grabbed his face and brought his lips to hers. "Nothing," she murmured, "will happen to me."

"Don't," he said, staring at her. His dark-blue eyes darkened, deepened, and she couldn't look away. "Don't say it. Don't jinx it. Just be here now, just tell me you love me."

"I love you, Sean," she whispered.

Sean leaned in to kiss her when his cell phone vibrated in his pocket. "Dammit," he whispered. He pulled it out, planning on sending the caller to voice mail, but it was eleven at night and it could be . . . "Kane," he said.

They sat at the end of the bed. "When I say it's important, I mean it," Sean answered.

"Tobias's people kidnapped Andrea Walsh's sister in Santiago to use as bait to lure me in. We took out four of the five goons, lost one of my men, and Blitz is taking Siobhan to Jack's place as we speak."

"Shit, Kane. Where are you?"

Lucy leaned in to listen, her hand entwined with Sean's.

"Tracking the fifth man. I'm calling to give you and Lucy a heads-up. Siobhan said a man named Joseph put the bounty on my head. They want me alive because they think I have their money."

"What?" Sean wasn't easily confused, but this one stumped him.

"They will soon figure out I'm not the one with the skill," he said pointedly.

Lucy squeezed his hand hard. Very hard.

"The FBI has their money, good luck getting it out of them. Pass it along."

"I don't think that's their point," Kane said. "I spoke to Jack, he told me about Rollins. Her escape coupled with the bounty on me—plus their desire to retrieve the money the FBI seized—makes you a target. I'll be there as soon as I can. Watch your ass, Sean. And Lucy."

"Watch your own," Sean began, but the line went dead. "Damn him." Sean stood and ran his hands through his hair. "He has a fucking *bounty* on his head and he's in

Santiago tracking one of the men who tried to grab him?"

"Sean—they're going to figure out it was you."

"They can't. My name isn't on anything. No one even knows I was there, and ASAC Dean Hooper is the name on the docs."

"We should warn him, too. Do these people really think they can target federal agents and get away with it?"

"These people think they can get away with anything, and they will—until they're stopped." Sean pulled Lucy into a hug, but he was thinking about Kane. And the threat to Lucy. Unspoken, but it was there. "Joseph—why does that name sound familiar?"

"Joseph Contreras worked for Adeline Worthington. We believe he'd been working for Tobias as well, and that he killed Adeline when she agreed to turn state's evidence."

"Tobias killed Garza and Contreras killed Worthington, and they both disappeared." Sean stared at Lucy. "Promise me, Lucy—"

"Don't say it. Promise me the same."

He held her close. His life would be over if anything happened to her.

CHAPTER THIRTEEN

Brad knocked on Sam's door. It was late, but she'd be up.

She answered with a gun in her hand.

"What are you doing here?"

"Can I come in?"

She hesitated, then sighed and opened the door. "I'm tired, but I can't sleep," she said. She bolted the door behind him. "I'm lost, Brad."

"This wasn't your fault."

"Of course it was!" Sam exclaimed. "You warned me. I knew she was dangerous, I knew she was a liar, but I thought—hell, I don't know *what* I thought."

Her eyes were red, and though she wasn't drunk she was well on her way. Not good. After the call Lucy got from DC about the FBI agent who'd been killed, they all needed to be on alert. No way was he leaving her alone, vulnerable.

"This wasn't your call," he said. "The AUSA and the DOJ made the decision to negotiate that plea deal. I made my opinion well known, but no one cared. Except *you*. You did everything you could to minimize her chance of escape."

Sam picked up a drink that looked like it was more vodka than cranberry juice. She drained it.

Brad took the glass from her and walked to the kitchen, rinsed it out and put it in the sink.

"Don't be a dick," Sam said.

He turned to face her. "Sammie—"

"Don't call me that." But she averted her eyes.

He stepped forward. "Agent Kincaid wants to talk to you tomorrow about Nicole. She's profiling the bitch, with some high-ranking shrink from DC."

"I know. She sent me a message. I'll be in a meeting with Moody all morning. If I still *have* a job when they're done with me, I told Lucy I'd talk to her after lunch."

"You've got to get it together, Sam."

"She killed five cops. Two were *mine*."

"They were my friends, too, Sam."

"But they worked *for me*. I should have protected them. Done . . . *something* different."

"Dammit, Sam, what could you have done? The AUSA ordered the transfer from the jail to the courthouse so Nicole could talk . . . she had no intention of doing or saying anything that would help us. This was planned from the beginning. Yeah, I'm pissed. I'm furious. But they had inside information, otherwise they'd never have been able to pull this off. They have money and resources. A helicopter. Access to information. A fucking *plan*. But the plan can't be mapped out forever. She doesn't have enough money to hide forever. We *will* find her."

"God, I hope you're right."

"Hope has nothing to do with it, Sammie," he said, ignoring her previous admonition. "We're better than she is. We'll pursue every lead, look under every rock, we will not stop until she is in prison or dead." *Dead*, he thought. He wanted Nicole Rollins dead in the worst way, and that made him uncomfortable. Not because she didn't deserve it, but because he felt no guilt.

He didn't want to test his character. He hoped someone else—someone stronger than him—found and arrested her before Brad had to make that decision.

Brad touched her hair, her face, her neck. "Sammie—"

"We shouldn't be doing this, Brad. I told you last week—"

"Shh." He kissed her.

Yeah, this was wrong. Sam was his boss. They'd had an affair years ago, when they were colleagues but equals. That hadn't worked well, but now they were both older. Smarter. More disciplined. They'd kept their distance because Sam was his boss and he didn't want to be forced to transfer, but the night after Nicole's plea agreement was signed off by the court, they'd had dinner and one thing led to another and reminded Brad that he still cared for Sam. That she needed him.

And now she needed him even more.

"Brad—" she said, breathless.

"You talk too much," he said and kissed her again.

Her resistance was short-lived. In a blink she turned the tables and pushed him against the kitchen counter, her long, lean body pressed hard against his.

Life was too short to live with regrets.

Joseph reached over Niki's naked body and grabbed his cell phone. She ran her hands over his bare chest. "Who is it?" she asked, her voice husky from sex and sleep.

"The guy sitting on Archer's house."

"Don't let him touch her."

"I know, sweetheart." Joseph answered the call. "What?"

"Donnelly showed up here about an hour ago. Hasn't left. Lights just went off."

"Interesting," Joseph said.

Nicole sat up. "Did he say Donnelly was there?"

Joseph put his finger to her lips. "Let me know when he leaves," he said.

"I can take them both."

"No. Stay where you are. Report any change of status."

"Yes, boss."

Joseph hung up and rolled on top of Niki. "I know what you're thinking."

"It will fuck him up. I want to do it."

"It's too dangerous. We need to wait."

"It's my risk to take."

Joseph used his knee to spread her legs apart. "I'm not going to lose you, Niki." He slowly entered her. With Niki, he was always ready, always craving her. He would do anything for her. He had killed for her. He would die for her.

She sighed and closed her eyes. "You won't lose me," she whispered.

He didn't talk. Instead, he showed her how much he loved her. He made love slowly, meticulously, until he felt the switch inside her flip, the one where she turned from being in control to giving it up. Her body heated and sweat glistened on her skin in the dim lights. It was late, they were exhausted from the escape and then spending all afternoon and evening in bed. But he would never be too tired to bring the woman he loved the simple pleasure of orgasm.

They'd been apart too long. Stolen hours for three years. Before San Antonio, they didn't have to be as discreet, but he'd had work to do south of the border and there were times when they'd been apart for months.

Joseph brought Niki over the top, and he followed her. He kissed her, held her, whispered his love in her ear.

"Take me to her," Niki said. "I want her to see me when she dies."

He didn't want to. He wanted to run far away, him and Niki, and disappear. Let Tobias try to run the operation without them. He would be dead or in jail within a month.

"Anything for you," he said.

She smiled and kissed him.

"On one condition," he added.

She raised an eyebrow. "Conditions?"

"One. I'm going with you. You do exactly what I say. If I say we leave, we leave. Trust my instincts, Niki. The one time you didn't, you ended up in jail."

Her body stiffened, and he almost felt bad for saying it. Except she had to see that this was where he served her best. Protecting her.

Then she sighed and relaxed. "I became too arrogant."

"It wasn't you. It was Sanchez and Trejo. You were juggling many things. You were simply trying to fix their mistakes.

"I could have stopped them, but I liked the plan. Donnelly was becoming bolder. Getting close. But he didn't realize how close he was, and it was foolish of me to sanction the hit on him. I should have found another way to take him out."

"Don't." He kissed her again. "Don't beat yourself up. You are the smartest woman I know. Brad Donnelly has never played by the rules, and he was already causing problems in our organization. Sanchez and Trejo simply had no talent for planning."

"It was Kane Rogan," she said with a scowl. "He's fucked us over more times than I can count. That little bitch Kincaid would never have found Trejo if Rogan didn't lead her there by the nose. They will both be dead when this is over."

"We need to kill Rogan now. Allowing him to live is dangerous."

"It's the plan to interrogate him, and you agreed."

"Yes, but—" How did he explain to her that the last two weeks had put him on edge? He'd never felt so vulnerable. Maybe because in the past, no one knew that Niki was part of the operation. Now she was America's Most Wanted. And . . . he wasn't confident that Rogan would give them anything. The man had been a marine, had gone up against some of the biggest cartels. He'd been a one-man wrecking crew in some regions, and the loyalty of his men was admirable. There were rumors about what he'd done, about what he'd suffered . . . but Joseph didn't know how much was true and how much was grandstanding. Still, a marine wouldn't break easily under torture.

Instead of arguing with Niki, he said, "We have a big enough nest egg to disappear."

"We've talked about this. It's not only about the money. We made promises, and we have to keep them or we'll never be safe, or free." She paused. "And what we have won't last. A couple of years, and then what? We need the money that was stolen from us, rebuild our operation, and *then* we go."

He dropped the subject. He would bring it up, again, when this stage was over.

It *was* partly about the money. When Adeline Worthington cut ties with Tobias and hid their money, they couldn't retrieve it all.

Because of Kane Rogan. But it wasn't solely the mercenary who stopped them—it was that fed, Lucy Kincaid, a bitch with a bone, digging and digging until they had to cut and run.

The bigger plan was to take their money and set up an empire in South America. With Tobias as the figurehead and Nicole and Joseph running the operation from behind the scenes—and far away—they would control the lion's share of the drug trade into the United States. Once they put Kane Rogan's head on a stick and paraded him around for the cartels to see, the cartels would bow down to *them*. Everyone wanted Kane Rogan dead, but only Nicole would deliver his corpse.

He said, "I won't stop you from killing Samantha Archer yourself, but remember the original plan."

She scowled. "That bastard Kane Rogan has screwed up more of our plans than anyone. And I will kill him. Slowly. He thinks he's tough, but he'll beg to die. I'll make sure of it." She sat up, beautiful in the nude, completely unmindful of her nakedness. Joseph could stare at her for hours. "And we still don't know how he drained our money. He's not exactly a computer mastermind. Are we getting the computer forensics report?"

"It's sensitive right now. Everyone is looking at everyone else. My contact is being extra cautious."

"Tell him caution will get him dead."

Joseph didn't say anything. Niki would come around. She always did. Which was why they had survived for so long in the most dangerous business on the planet.

His phone beeped. He picked it up. "It's Lyle. He has the documents from DC."

"It's about fucking time." She pulled on jeans and a tank top. She'd never looked sexier. "He's here, right? He's not going to make me wait, is he?"

"He's here."

They left the bedroom and went downstairs. The house was in the middle of the property and well-guarded. They had multiple routes to escape *if* the feds tracked them down.

Lyle was drinking Scotch at the bar in the large gathering room. Tobias was standing behind the bar, playing the bartender. Joseph stared at him, keeping his antipathy hidden.

Tobias. He would be at the bottom of a lake if Joseph had his way. His sick fetishes disgusted Joseph. He was a stupid, self-centered, pompous ass. He acted as if he really was the head of their organization, instead of the figurehead. And then he'd gone and killed Garza. In fucking *public*. Caught on camera at the airport. Why couldn't he have just thought for *five seconds* that there would be cameras all over the fucking airport?

Tobias had grown fat and lazy. He had ostensibly been in charge for three months and it had gone to his head. He was their biggest problem, bigger than Kane Rogan. Joseph had verbally put the blame on Trejo and Sanchez, because Niki would never see that Tobias was the root of all their problems. He always had been, from the moment they'd set the fire in Van Nuys twenty years ago and killed three people in order to destroy the remains of the woman Tobias strangled to death.

Joseph should have killed him and not said a word. He knew how to make a body disappear. Niki would never have figured out it was him.

But he didn't lie to the woman he loved.

Tobias glared at them. "We were supposed to meet hours ago, but you two were upstairs fucking all day."

Niki walked behind the bar and kissed Tobias on the cheek. "Shut up," she said, but with a smile. "I've been in jail for nearly three months, I deserved one day for myself."

Tobias grunted.

She turned to Lyle. "Joseph said you had something."

"I did exactly what you said," Lyle said. "But it took our guys a while to crack the code."

She said, "Give it to me."

He handed her a flash drive.

"Don't you care about what happened with Kane Rogan?" Tobias said.

Niki frowned and looked from Tobias to Joseph. "He was captured in Santiago," she said.

Sean rubbed his temples. Lucy hated the fear that clouded his eyes. "You heard Kane last night on the phone. Tobias and his people are behind this. Nicole Rollins is out there, somewhere, with a plan—and that plan so far has killed five cops. Six, including Dunbar. I don't want to leave you. Come with me."

"To Hidalgo?"

"To Mexico, if I have to go. You'd be an asset. My Spanish is okay, but yours is perfect."

"Sean—you're worried about me, I get it. But I'm aware of the threat, I'll be on alert. I have work to do here—Hans is coming in, I'm working on the profile of Rollins, I'm talking to Elise Hansen today. We need more information so we can find both Rollins and Tobias."

He looked pained.

"Sean—you have to go. Jack would only call you if he was truly concerned."

"I know, but—dammit!" He slammed his fist on the desk. "This is the worst time to leave you alone. Jack would do it, but it would take him a day to get down there."

"I'm not alone. I can ask Kenzie to come over. Or Nate. I'm not scared, Sean, but if it would make you feel better, I'll ask the whole damn squad to spend the night. We certainly have the room."

That brought a marginal grin to his face. "I told you we needed the space." He leaned over and touched her hair. "I would feel better if you weren't alone." He kissed her lightly. "Though no one is as good as me."

She took his hand and squeezed it. "That's why you need to find Kane."

"I'll talk to Nate. I trust him."

"Because he was army, like Jack."

"Because he was special forces. I trust him with you, and with your life."

She wrinkled her nose. "I don't get it."

Tobias snorted but didn't say anything.

Joseph lost his temper. He crossed the room and jumped over the bar. His hand was around Tobias's thick, ugly neck. He pushed him against the wall. Glasses fell to the floor and shattered.

Niki said, "Joseph!"

Joseph hated this man. Hated him with a passion that had him squeezing harder. It would be so easy to kill him right now.

"Please, Joseph," Niki said. Joseph could barely hear her.

He stared into Tobias's arrogant, scared, beady eyes. They watered, reddened, and Tobias was shaking. He grabbed Joseph's wrists but had no strength to push him off. He was a pathetic, weak coward. Tobias knew exactly what Joseph wanted to do to him, and better, he feared him.

Good. He *should* be afraid. If Joseph had the opportunity to kill him without it coming back to hurt Niki, he'd do it. Without hesitation and certainly without remorse. Tobias deserved worse than a bullet in the brain.

Joseph let go and stepped back. Tobias sputtered and coughed.

Niki took a step toward Tobias, but Joseph caught her eye. She stopped, straightened her spine, and said in a calm voice, "What happened with Kane Rogan?"

Tobias didn't answer right away. He stood up, poured a glass of Scotch with shaking hands, and drained it. Then he said, "We don't have him."

"What do you mean, we don't have him?" she asked. Niki sounded as angry as Joseph felt. Good. She needed to be angry.

"The priest," Tobias said. "He fucked it all up. He must have told Rogan where we had the girl, because he brought enough men to take out everyone. Dover got away, he's hurt pretty bad, but he took out one of theirs."

"Did he have a fucking *army*?" Niki asked. "How could Rogan take out a dozen men?"

Tobias didn't look at her. "We had five. Five is usually enough."

"Five against Rogan?"

"Rogan had three men."

"Five. Five idiots against four trained US soldiers." Niki picked up a glass and threw it toward Tobias. It hit the wall behind him. "Didn't the fiasco at Trejo's compound teach you anything? There were four then, too, against twenty!"

Tobias stepped toward Niki. Joseph resisted every urge to push him back against the wall. Niki was going to have to learn that her cousin was out of control.

"You got arrested, Nicole."

"How did Trejo get that disk?" she countered.

"How do I know?"

"You're lucky the DEA hasn't figured out what really happened five years ago, otherwise they never would have pled, and my escape would have been that much harder."

"That FBI bitch didn't need the disk to figure it out."

Niki reddened and Joseph stepped back. Finally. Tobias was showing his true colors.

"You, Toby, are a fool if you think you have the power here. You are a figurehead, nothing more. Your games have gotten us into far more hot water than anything I have done. What you did with Elise was inexcusable."

"Leave her out of this."

"I can't! She's in jail because of you."

"She's exactly where she needs to be. You always do this, Nicole. You treat me like *I'm* the idiot. Like *I* don't know how to run this operation."

"Elise is in *jail*," Niki repeated.

"She'll be out by Wednesday afternoon."

"You're delusional," Joseph said. "No way will the feds let her go."

"Don't underestimate her. Our contact at the juvenile detention center told me that the shrink they assigned wants Elise transferred to a minimum-security facility for minors, and possibly a group home. I'm watching the situation closely. You've always underestimated her, Nicole."

"She's a loose cannon," Niki said. "She doesn't follow orders."

Except, Joseph thought, from Tobias. They were both sick.

"We're family," he said. "We stick together. You can't leave her behind."

Niki sighed and rubbed her eyes. "I never planned on leaving her. I just wish you'd left her in DC where she was gathering information, and doing a damn good job of it. Now she's been compromised. The feds have her DNA and prints. She's been burned."

"Elise is meant for better things," Tobias said. "She's smart. And if you'd work with her, you'd know that."

"She's sixteen! Reckless. A know-it-all. I'm still reeling over the fact that Jimmy gave her to you at thirteen. She wasn't ready."

"She was ready, and I'll prove to you that she can do anything."

"First, let's see if she can get herself out—and *not* lead the feds to us. Then we'll talk."

"Fine," Tobias said, frowning.

Niki turned to Joseph. She looked so tired, so . . . worn out. She shouldn't feel that way, not now when she was free.

Joseph said, "I'll reach out to Dover, find out what happened with Rogan, and we'll regroup. We should take them all out, no more games."

Tobias snorted. "Games? What's that *game* of yours in the basement?"

Niki looked at him. "What's in the basement?" she asked.

"Someone I thought would be more help than he was," Joseph replied. "I'll explain later." He glared at Tobias. Damn him, Joseph wanted to tell Niki himself. He wanted information first—but now he'd have to confess he jumped the gun a bit while she was still in prison. But he wasn't going to do it around Tobias.

She rubbed her eyes. "Toby, stop trying to divide us. We're united—a family. Joseph is family, as much as you and me. Don't forget it."

"Never," he said, and Joseph knew he was mocking them. "He's not blood."

"Stop," Niki said. "Fighting now only gives the feds more power. United, we will win. Remember that. It's been true for years, it's true now. We need our money," she repeated. "And if Rogan saw Dover, he's burned. It won't take long for the feds to trace Dover back to Los Angeles."

"Maggie will take care of it," Joseph said. "You're not the only one in the family, Niki. Others need to carry their weight." He glared at Tobias. He was either too dense or too arrogant to see Joseph's rage.

Good. Then you won't see me coming with the knife when I gut you and leave you to die slowly in the middle of a remote desert. Scorpions will sting you. Snakes will bite you. Coyotes will eat you alive and then the vultures will pick your bones clean.

"Take me to Samantha Archer," Niki said. "I need to regain control."

"Are you sure?" Joseph asked, enjoying the image of Tobias screaming in pain.

She nodded. "Toby, contact Dover and tell him the bounty on Kane Rogan just doubled. Dead or alive. He's too much trouble."

Tobias sneered. "Happily."

* * *

Tobias watched Nicole leave the room with that asshole Joseph. God, he hated that man. Joseph thought he was better than him—*him*. Joseph was turning Nicole against him. Joseph had worked on her for years, and every little mistake—even things that weren't his fault—Joseph used against him.

Lyle had watched the entire thing from his seat in the corner. Tobias would have forgotten he was there, except he spoke up after Nicole left. "Hey! Nicole! You forgot—"

The flash drive. It was sitting on the bar, next to the computer. Tobias caught his eye and shook his head. Lyle stared at him and Tobias didn't know who he was siding with.

Nicole walked back into the room. "What?"

"Do you need a driver? Because I have the Lincoln."

"Give the keys to me. Joseph will drive. You stay here and get some rest; tomorrow will be a long day."

He tossed her the keys and turned to Tobias after she left.

"What the hell?"

Tobias picked up the flash drive and stuck it in the computer. "We're going to figure this out. Nicole's going to realize that she needs me. I'm not just a *figurehead*."

"Sure, buddy, anything you want."

Inside, Tobias was smiling. That was one thing that Nicole had forgotten. Tobias was very good at making friends.

Much better than either her or her fuck-buddy Joseph.

Kane Rogan found and lost the bastard's trail twice that night. The priest's idea of a medical center hadn't panned out, but Kane bribed a hooker who ended up having a wealth of information. Could be because she didn't have to spread her legs for him and he paid her far more than her weekly rate. He hated that so many women down here felt they had no choice but prostitution, but he'd learned that people were resilient and they did what was necessary to survive.

What was necessary to survive also included betraying him, so he trusted very few people. But this time, his hunch had paid off, and the intel was solid. The man he was tracking was heading to Juarez territory southeast of Santiago—the one place Kane hesitated to go. He'd made a mortal enemy of Felipe Juarez, and it was personal. If it was just business, Kane wouldn't care, and Juarez probably wouldn't have held a grudge. But as it was, Kane got Juarez's thirteen-year-old daughter out of an arranged marriage to the slimy thirty-year-old son of a cartel leader, and smuggled her into the States. He bought her false documentation, and a friend of his in Immigration placed her in a home. Her identity was a closely guarded secret—Kane didn't even know what her new name was, and he didn't want to know. His Immigration contact kept tabs on her and now, eight years later, she was in college and studying to be a doctor.

Kane wondered if Juarez had been the one to give Tobias's people the information about Siobhan. Siobhan was the one who had alerted Kane to the situation with the arranged marriage. Normally he would have nothing to do with the personal workings of families. If it wasn't directly related to drug or human trafficking, he steered clear, and Juarez was a criminal gangster, not an international drug trafficker. There were too many problems and Kane couldn't fix every damn one of them.

But Siobhan said if he didn't help her, she'd rescue the girl herself. Essentially blackmailing him into it because he knew Siobhan was ill prepared to do something of that magnitude.

Kane's past, coming back to bite him in the ass. He wasn't surprised.

Kane stole a truck and picked up the trail of Tobias's man near the border of Juarez territory. The bastard was driving a military jeep, just like the prostitute had said, with a missing taillight. He'd pulled over to rest, and that was his one mistake. He should have driven straight through.

But pain did that to people.

Kane found the jeep half hidden on the edge of a side road off the main highway. *Main* and *highway* being subjective terms because traffic was sparse, especially at night, on this side of Santiago. He waited, watching, to make sure it wasn't an ambush.

They were miles from anywhere, and the closest town was small, less than five hundred people. Juarez owned everyone in the area, so Kane would find no safe haven. His map told him he'd already crossed into Juarez territory. Was that why the kidnapper had stopped? Did he think that Kane wouldn't pursue him? Kane had to make a decision: Turn back now or follow through with his plan.

Kane did not shirk from his duty. And his duty was to find Tobias. His life—Sean's life, Lucy's life—depended on it.

In fact, there was no doubt in Kane's mind that Tobias would go after everyone in Kane's life, starting with his brothers and sister, then moving to everyone who worked for RCK.

Kane was going to end this war before anyone else got hurt.

There were no streetlights in the area. A flashlight would be visible to anyone on the road. The land was a mix of desert and farmland, with scraggly trees and bushes. To the south and west there were mountains, but here was a flat, dry valley. Easy to track someone. Easy to be tracked.

After fifteen minutes of silence, Kane moved over to the jeep and shone a dim red light inside. Blood had pooled under the gas pedal. This man's right leg was bleeding, though there wasn't enough blood loss to kill him. Not yet. But there was also blood on the back of the seat and on the gearshift. Blitz had said it was serious, but Kane had been seriously injured in the past and able to patch himself up sufficiently until he could get medical attention.

Kane had to assume that the man he was tracking had the skills to take care of himself. He also had to assume that he knew the area better than Kane. Because he'd tried to stay away from Juarez, all that Kane knew was what was on his map.

He paralleled the trail the kidnapper had walked, uphill and into increasingly dense foliage. Two hundred yards in, Kane came upon a one-room shack. There was no electricity going to the building, no sign that anyone was inside.

It was darker here than on the road. Kane didn't see any booby traps, but he needed to be cautious as he approached. He listened, waiting for sounds that he was surrounded. Waiting for an ambush.

Silence. Then he heard a grunt from the cabin. Faint. He listened again, heard a faint *fuck*.

Sounded just like him when he was stitching himself up.

Still, he waited. He saw a brief flash of light from the cabin, a yellowy glow that might have been from a flashlight. Then it went out. Could have been a signal, so he waited even longer.

Still, nothing.

He approached the cabin. Gun in hand he inspected the door. No lock, nothing to keep him out. No wires along the edges. The wood was warped and splintery. He walked around the perimeter. A lone, uncovered window in the back gave him a visual. A man lay on a sleeping bag in the corner, propped up by the walls, the door in his line of vision. He had bandages all around him, and his pants were cut open. A very faint glow from a flashlight under a rag illuminated the area. It looked like a gunshot wound to the leg, and a knife wound to his right arm. But he was sweating and that suggested he was battling an infection or another complication.

He had a gun within reach to his right, but that was the only weapon Kane could see.

Kane silently moved back to the door. Did he wait until the kidnapper tried to leave? Or had he called someone for a rescue?

A voice came from the inside. Kane hadn't heard a phone ring, but it was clear that the kidnapper was talking to someone.

"I need extraction," the kidnapper said.

It might have been a sat phone, because Kane was getting no cellular signal out here.

"Off Eighty-Five, near Pino Suarez. A nothing dot on the map right over the Tamaulipas border." Silence. Kane heard the voice on the other end but couldn't make out any words.

"Joseph, sir. The plan was solid. We should have had more men or the kill order . . . Yes, he gave it now, but before it was alive only . . . I'm good for a day, but that bastard shot me and . . . yes, I appreciate it. I can make it easily, it's only five or six miles and I have a vehicle . . . of course. That is the goal, sir. Thank you."

Movement and shuffling. Kane moved out of sight, toward the jeep. It seemed as if the bastard kidnapper was meeting up with someone. Five or six miles . . . probably Mainero. Juarez had a presence there and it was six miles southeast. Nothing else was that close.

Kane had to assume that Joseph had already called in reinforcements. Siobhan had said he had, but Kane hadn't seen or sensed anyone, and his instincts were sharp, especially when he was on full alert. Yet . . . they could be waiting for him. Waiting for him to come to them, in Juarez-controlled territory. Kane could defend himself against one, two, even more . . . but not against a virtual army. He didn't have a death wish, he had no backup, and he needed to get out alive—with information that would help find Tobias.

He was going to end this now.

Kane listened as the door opened on rusty hinges. The kidnapper stepped out. Looked around. Winced at the pain in his leg. He had a backpack over his shoulder, and a gun in his hand.

Kane didn't even need to step out of his hiding spot. He shot the kidnapper in his already injured leg. The man collapsed in the dirt. He still held his gun, fired in the direction Kane had been, but Kane had already moved away. He rushed the kidnapper before the bastard could get his bearings and kicked the gun out of his hand.

The bastard laughed. "You won't get out of Mexico alive."

"So I've been told many times."

"You're a dead man. Juarez has already sealed off the border."

Bluff? Kane had crossed into Juarez territory more than an hour ago. Maybe he'd spent too much time being cautious. Waiting.

"Kill me," he said. "Joseph will kill me anyway because your little redheaded bitch saw me and lived."

"I'm not going to kill you," Kane said. "You're going to tell me what I need to know."

He laughed. "I'm not scared of you."

The bastard was in pain. Kane stepped on his shot-up leg and the asshole screamed.

"Fuck you!"

"Why was the order originally a capture-alive order?"

"Probably to torture you," he hissed. "Many people want to take a crack at your skull."

"What did Tobias and Joseph think I would tell you?"

He was silent. Kane applied more pressure to his leg. To his credit, he didn't cry out this time. He grunted instead.

Kane hit him in the jaw. "That's for touching the red-head."

Kane wanted to kill him. He also wanted to take him into custody and interrogate him—or turn him over to the feds. And—he wanted to leave him and let Tobias clean up his own mess.

Kane rolled the kidnapper over. He tried to crawl away, but Kane put his boot on his back and held him down. He searched his pockets. Located a knife, wallet, US passport, keys. He flipped over the passport.

Adam Duncan Dover III.

He opened the wallet. Inside he found another ID. A federal ID.

"You fucking traitor."

Kane was torn. He couldn't get out of Juarez territory dragging an injured, uncooperative prisoner. But he couldn't just let this traitor go.

A sound registered in his subconscious. From down on the road.

If Dover was right and Juarez had sealed the border, they were going to sweep until they caught his scent.

Kane picked up Dover's gun, his backpack, and kept his ID. Dover pushed himself up and leaned against the shack. "The war on drugs was lost before it started, Rogan. You're fucking Don Quixote, and you remember what happened to him—he was beaten and died."

Kane didn't say anything. If this was only about the war on drugs, Kane would have quit years ago. It might have started out that way, but it was more than that now. Kane didn't consider himself a hero, and he certainly wasn't a saint. He didn't believe in God and he didn't believe in Hell. The only thing he believed in was evil, and it was rooted in bastards like Adam Dover and Joseph Contreras and Nicole Rollins and Tobias.

Kane left Dover alive but immobile, not going down the path toward the road because that was the direction of the sound. But he needed a vehicle. He'd have to hoof it to Mainero, where he could hot-wire a car. Or maybe he could reach Dover's jeep and use it to get to Mainero. He'd have to head through the mountains to escape because every major road in this area would have a Juarez sentry. His plane was forty miles to the northwest. Not impossible to get to on foot, but it would take time. It would be dangerous, but he didn't have a choice.

He moved out.

Ten minutes later he heard a single gunshot behind him. *Good-bye, traitor.*

CHAPTER FOURTEEN

Samantha Archer fell back into bed and closed her eyes. Why had she let Brad stay?

Because you're still in love with him.

She'd tried to tell herself she wasn't. They'd been involved years ago, when they were both in Phoenix. She'd moved to the Houston office first, then she'd been promoted to lead the DEA's San Antonio Resident Agency. When Brad had transferred here, as her subordinate, she remembered all the reasons she'd loved him before . . . and all the reasons it hadn't worked out. Because she was his direct supervisor, it was easy to maintain the emotional distance. There had been a couple of times when they'd almost fallen in bed together, but she'd always put an end to it. And Brad finally stopped pushing.

Until last week.

Brad Donnelly was the kind of guy who was both very good and very bad for her. Gorgeous and alpha and brave. Cocky and hotheaded. Smart, and a smart-ass. He took too many risks, but he was usually right. He broke too many rules, but he also saved lives. He believed in their mission. He was loyal.

But one day he would cross a line they couldn't come back from. One day he would end up fired or dead. And she, as his boss, didn't want to be his lover when that day inevitably came.

Maybe in her next life.

She stretched and wished she could go back to sleep, but her brain wouldn't stop thinking. For a few blissful hours she'd slept dreamlessly curled next to Brad, able to block the pain of yesterday, from seeing her dead agents to telling their families they were dead. It had been hell. Worse. She'd sell her soul if that meant she could turn the clock back twenty-four hours and stop the violence that defined June 15 and would forever be a day of mourning for the DEA.

"It's five," she mumbled as she dragged herself out of bed. She had a full day ahead of her. The ASAC of the Houston DEA office was coming in this morning for a big briefing at the FBI—but he wanted to meet with her first. Nine a.m., her office, even though she'd spent an hour on a video conference call with her boss, the AUSA, and higher-ups in the DOJ late yesterday afternoon.

Her headache was already returning.

She stretched, padded down the long hall to her kitchen to start the coffee, then back to her bedroom for a shower. She liked her house. She'd bought into a new subdivision shortly after taking the position in San Antonio. It was the smallest model in the area, though at over twenty-four hundred square feet it was more than enough for her. She'd been tired of renting apartments, and the one condo she'd bought, when she lived and worked in Phoenix, hadn't retained its value. It was basically like renting, with more headaches.

But she'd had this house for four years, and she didn't plan on moving anytime soon. She liked her job, liked her position, and if she got promoted into DC? Well, she'd cross that bridge when she came to it. She'd probably keep the house because she loved San Antonio and planned to retire here.

She'd washed her hair last night when she and Brad showered together. But she needed a quick, cold rinse to wake up. Two minutes later she stepped out and grabbed the towel off the hook.

Out of the corner of her eye she saw movement in the long, steamed mirror.

But it was too late to do anything. She had no gun in the bathroom, no phone, and she'd sent Brad packing thirty minutes ago. The fleeting thought that he'd returned disappeared when Nicole Rollins stepped into the doorway.

Nicole fired the gun. The bullet hit Sam in the right knee, shattering it. Blinding pain rushed every nerve and she collapsed to the tile floor.

Sam wanted to tell Nicole that she wouldn't get away with this, that they would track her down and find her, that she'd go to prison for the rest of her miserable life. Sam wanted to tell Nicole to go to hell, that she wasn't afraid of her.

But Sam was afraid. She didn't want to die. She didn't want to die naked in her bathroom. She didn't want to die at the age of forty-two when she had so much she still wanted to do.

Nicole smiled.

"You should consider yourself honored that I wanted to kill you myself," she said.

"What the fuck do you want?" Her voice was weak, the pain in her leg making her nauseous. She'd never been shot before. Seventeen years in the DEA and she'd never once been shot.

"I want many things, Samantha. And I will get them all, because I always win."

Nicole stepped into the bathroom and looked around

with a smirk on her face. "I heard Brad was here last night. Let me clue you in on a little secret about Brad."

Sam looked around in vain for anything she could use as a weapon. There was nothing. Even her can of hair spray was on the far side of the counter.

A gun trumped hair spray any day.

Nicole was going to kill her.

And there was nothing Sam could do about it.

Her bottom lip involuntarily quivered.

Nicole said, "Never mind."

"What?"

"I don't have time, and it doesn't matter anyway. Brad will die this week. And Tom, down in McAllen, who figured out I used the money from the evidence locker to set up that hooker. My fault, really—but he's going to die for it anyway. He's on my list." She looked at her watch. "Hmm, well, he's already dead by now. And then I have a list of FBI agents who irritate me—at the top of it is that bitch who fucked with me. You did surprise me, though, letting her go down to Mexico in direct violation of every FBI protocol on the books. And didn't even tell her boss about it. I was surprised, because I've never known you to bend let alone break the rules."

"I don't know what you're talking about. Nicole, let me help you. Please. Don't—don't kill me."

Sam didn't want to beg—God, she didn't want to beg—but she didn't want to die. She grabbed the counter and pulled herself up. Her knee was bleeding, pooling with the water on the damp tiles. It throbbed, alternately numb and hot.

Nicole looked at her quizzically. "You really didn't know that Lucy Kincaid went down to Mexico with Kane Rogan to rescue Brad?"

Sam blinked. Now things began to make sense. Brad's complete trust in Lucy, why he wanted to work with her all the time, why he was spending more time at FBI head-quarters than in the DEA office. Sam had thought Brad had the hots for Lucy, until she found out the agent was living with a guy. But she'd saved his life, which explained his complete trust.

Sam had followed the rules when Brad was kidnapped. She'd gone through the proper channels, knowing that the longer they delayed, the greater the chances he would be dead. But she couldn't do it any other way.

"Nicole—"

"I don't want you to feel *too* bad. You were marginally competent. I had to be careful, especially around Brad. But I fooled you, and I fooled him, for *years*. Took me a long time to build up his trust, but then he trusted me more than anyone. And just for the record? You were dead as soon as I transferred into your office three years ago."

Sam felt the bullet pierce her chest. She toppled over, facedown on the tile, vainly trying to grab the counter. The pain was worse than anything she could have imagined. Worse than the knee. She couldn't breathe.

"I'd wanted to shoot you in the gut and let you die slowly, but Joseph reminded me that you might live long enough to drag your sorry ass to the phone. Not that you know anything, but it's better this way."

Sam didn't feel the last bullet as it exploded in her brain.

Nicole fired twice more just because she felt like it.

Joseph drove Nicole the long way back to their hideout west of San Antonio. He stayed off the interstate as well as the state highways. The police had roadblocks earlier, but not on every road and they focused on highways head-ing toward the border. They couldn't stop all cars leaving San Antonio all day, every day, and once they found the helicopter a hundred miles away, they pulled much of their local resources into the expanded zone.

Which had been Nicole's plan all along. She understood how her former colleagues thought, how they operated, how they divided resources. And so far, she'd been right about everything. Another reason he loved her.

Joseph knew southern Texas better than any native, knew every road, mapped and unmapped. He'd picked the property years ago, when he moved to San Antonio ahead of Nicole. It would take the feds—even the best of them—time and resources to track the ownership, and that would presuppose that they would even know where to start looking. The remote property could access three different state highways within ten minutes, and he had seven different escape routes. Now, because it was a dry summer, he had an extra route—a dry creek bed where he'd hidden a four-wheel drive. If the feds got close, they couldn't cut off all passages, and they wouldn't even consider the creek bed. And if there was an early-summer storm or they found the jeep? He had a plane.

Tobias didn't know about the plane, or the hidden jeep. Joseph hadn't told Nicole, either, but he hadn't lied to her. He was in charge of protecting her; that meant he needed to get her out of danger if it approached.

He was not responsible for Tobias.

"Do you feel better?" he asked her.

"Yes," she said, but she didn't look happy.

"I did some damage control in Santiago."

"Damage control," she said with disdain. "I wanted Kane Rogan."

"And you will still have him, Niki. Paul is a smart operative. He called in reinforcements. One of the men Rogan killed was his brother-in-law, he wants him dead but he's willing to turn him over to us to prove his loyalty."

"You're right," she said. "I should never have tried to capture him alive. I wanted to hurt him for what he did to us. But I want his execution recorded, remind him of that. We need proof."

He'd already told Paul the exact same thing. "He knows," he said. "At least Rogan's death should give you some satisfaction."

"It might. But first Paul has to find him."

"Rogan is alone. He sent his men back to the States with the girl."

"Why did he stay?"

"My guess? To track Dover. But Paul took care of that situation. He also has an advantage—he knows the area better than Rogan. Rogan is alone, he doesn't have a base of operations in Santiago, and now he's in Juarez territory. Rogan's men are spread thin, thanks to the operations we've put in play over the last three months. Paul has called in a small army, and they are surrounding him as we speak. They'll squeeze, and he'll have to come up for air. It's only a matter of time."

"I can be very patient, if I know I will win."

He took her hand and kissed it.

"Shit," she mumbled. "The flash drive. Tobias distracted me, and Lyle said his people were able to decode Agent Dunbar's files."

"We'll be back in less than an hour."

"Good. Because I want my money back. None of this means shit if we don't have that money."

But when they arrived at the compound, Tobias and Lyle were gone—and so was the flash drive.

CHAPTER FIFTEEN

When Lucy woke up early Tuesday morning, Sean wasn't in bed. It was barely dawn, but she couldn't sleep anymore, knowing she had to be up in an hour anyway. They'd be pulling sixteen-hour days until Nicole Rollins was apprehended.

She found Sean on the phone in his downstairs office. He didn't look at her when she walked in, instead stared straight ahead, his expression hard. She turned to leave but he cleared his throat and waved her in. She sat on the chair across from him, curling her legs under her. A male voice was on the other end, but Lucy couldn't make it out.

Sean said, "It would be faster if I didn't have to stop in Hidalgo."

Again, Sean listened, then said, "Fine. I'll be there in two hours, but Blitz had better have good intel when I get there or this side trip will cost us time." He hung up. He looked at Lucy, but his mind was far away. "Kane's missing."

"Is this unusual?"

"If Jack's worried, I'm worried."

"How long?"

"Last night, when we talked to him, he didn't tell me

that he had sent his entire team with Siobhan to Hidalgo, leaving him alone to track the lone Tobias operative."

"Siobhan—who?"

"Siobhan Walsh. She's a freelance photojournalist. Her sister is some big lieutenant colonel at Quantico. Officer school. Kane has known Andie since he enlisted." He paused. "Remember when I snuck into the FBI academy to see you last fall?"

She almost smiled. "How could I forget?"

"Andie was my buddy who got me through the gate. Anyway, Siobhan travels to impoverished areas and takes pictures that tell a story. I'll show you some of her work, it's really good. She mostly works in Mexico and Central America, and she runs into trouble on occasion. Kane gets her out of it. This time, Kane told Jack that someone took Siobhan as bait for him. Kane got her out—but he stayed behind to find out more. He told Blitz—you met him when we rescued the boys—"

"I remember." She still had nightmares about it, though they were finally few and far apart.

"He said he'd be in Hidalgo by dawn. It's dawn. He's not there, and neither Blitz nor Jack can reach him. Jack pinged his plane, and it's still at a landing strip outside Santiago." He paused. "It could be that nothing happened, equipment failed and Kane couldn't check in to say why he was delayed."

"Jack wouldn't call you if he wasn't concerned," Lucy said. "You don't have to sugarcoat it for me."

"Kane has been in and out of more jams than anyone I know."

"But you're going."

Sean ran a hand through his hair. "I'm going to fly to Hidalgo. I'm hoping by the time I arrive Kane will have contacted someone. But it's only an hour flight to Santiago from there—if I need to go."

"If? Of course you need to find Kane."

"Of course you don't." He kissed her nose, then rested his forehead against hers. "Lucy—do you remember the Cinderella Strangler in New York?"

"I won't forget."

"And how when you walked into the killer's apartment, you . . . disconnected?"

"Sean—"

"There is no one who gets into the heads of these people better than you. But it affects you, and you shut down. You completely turn off. You put yourself in their shoes. You understand them. And you'll do the same with Elise, with Nicole. With Tobias. I want to be here for you, because I know it tears you up inside."

"Sean—don't—"

He rubbed his hands up and down her back. "I would never leave for anything or anyone. But Kane—"

"Stop. Find your brother. It's a day or two. I'll have Nate. I'll have Hans. I'm a lot stronger now than I was in New York."

"I know, but—"

She silenced him with a kiss.

"Be careful, Sean."

"Always, princess." He smiled, but it didn't reach his eyes. He was already thinking about his brother and what he might find down in Santiago. She didn't want his attention divided because he always worried about her.

She said, "If you don't check in every six hours, I'm going to follow you."

That snapped him to attention. "No."

"Yes. You love me? Well, I love you more. And I'm not going to have you disappear on me when we haven't even set a wedding date."

He opened his mouth, then closed it. "I'll have my sat phone with me. I'll call you, I promise."

She kissed him, long and hard. "Go find Kane."

*   *   *

Sean drove Lucy to work on his way to the small private airport where he housed his plane. He was on the phone most of the time, talking to Blitz in Hidalgo, a small border town where her brother Jack had lived for years when he'd been a soldier-for-hire, before he signed on with RCK. But he hung up as soon as he pulled into the secure FBI parking lot.

"I could have driven myself," Lucy said.

"We talked about this. These people got to your car once before," Sean said. He didn't have to remind her—three months ago during Operation Heatwave a bomb had been placed under her car. It didn't detonate, and they couldn't prove Nicole had ordered it planted, but that's most likely what had happened. "Humor me. Please."

She did, because he was worried—about her and about his brother. "I will be extra cautious," she said. "You too."

"You have the secure phone I gave you?"

"Of course."

Nate walked out of the main doors. "I don't need an escort into the building," Lucy said, exasperated. "The parking lot is gated with a guard.

Sean kissed her. "Love you."

"Love you too."

She got out and approached Nate. Sean peeled out of the parking lot, going much faster than the posted speed.

"Sorry about this," she told her friend.

He waved it off. She noticed he was wearing his Kevlar vest and had an extra gun strapped to his belt. He looked more like a soldier than a federal agent. Nate was tall and slender, all muscle, and reminded her of her brother Patrick. Except for the military part. She thought Sean and Nate had hit it off immediately because Nate's personality was more like Patrick, but his training was more like Jack. Best of both worlds, as far as security-conscious Sean Rogan was concerned.

"Ryan left to pick up Assistant Director Vigo from the airport."

She was looking forward to seeing Hans again. "Have you heard from Juan?"

"They had a boy, an hour or so ago. Nita had a rough time of it. There were complications and they had to do an emergency C-section. I don't know the details, Zach's at the hospital now. Ostensibly to give Juan a briefing, but he promised he'd find out what happened."

"Poor Nita."

"We don't even know the name—I don't think they picked one out." He paused. "I'm not having kids."

"Why?"

"You have to ask?"

"If I could, I'd have kids," she said. "The world is a dangerous place, but why else do what we do if not to make it better? If not to raise good kids in a troubled world?"

He shrugged. "I wouldn't make a good dad."

"I think you're wrong."

"If I had a kid, I'd be like Sarah Connor in *T-2*, training him or her to fight a war."

Lucy didn't see it. Then she looked at Nate again, assessing him impartially. It was there, that edginess that both Kane and Jack had. The eyes that had seen evil, the hands that had killed, the soul that had mourned. Nate might have the happy-go-lucky exterior when he relaxed, he might be able to enjoy playing video games all night with Sean or laughing over beers in the kitchen, but she suspected that was just it, an exterior. A remnant of who he was before he became a soldier. Could he ever go back? Or was there no going back, just moving forward? Jack had adjusted to a more domestic life once he married Megan, but he still had the edge. He still had the instincts of a career soldier. Yet—he had found a peace he hadn't had before Megan, and for that reason alone she loved her sister-in-law.

She squeezed Nate's hand, spontaneously. "Thank you. Really."

"I'd do anything for you and Sean."

She wondered why that was. They'd known Nate for six months, but he and Sean had bonded immediately. She hadn't really asked why. Maybe she should have. Was there more to their friendship than she knew? If so, why hadn't they told her? Or maybe she was reading more into it than was there. She could have simply asked Sean. Maybe she would, when he returned.

"Briefing in ten minutes," Nate said, then slipped past Lucy into his own cubicle.

Kenzie leaned over to Lucy. "What was that all about?"

"What was what?" Lucy asked. She dumped her files on her desk.

"That thing with you and Nate?"

"Nothing."

"Did you and Sean have a fight?"

"No!" Lucy stared at her, eyes wide. "Why on earth would you think that?"

Kenzie tilted her head. "I guess—I don't know. You were holding hands."

"Not like that. Sean had to go out of town and Nate's going to keep an eye on the place." Lucy didn't know how much she should say. Because if she said it out loud, it made both her and Sean seem paranoid. And maybe they were, but after what they'd been through they had reason to be paranoid. "Agent Logan Dunbar was murdered when he returned to DC two nights ago. It may be connected to Nicole Rollins's escape. But Sean had an emergency to take care of out of town, so until we know more he wants Nate to stay at the house. As a precaution."

Kenzie shook her head. "I couldn't live your life. Do you always walk around with a target on your back?" Her eyes widened. "Oh shit, I'm sorry."

Two weeks ago, Lucy had been shot in the back. If not for her vest, she would have been seriously injured or killed. "Don't apologize. It's apropos."

"Is Sean okay? Is it family?"

She nodded, but didn't say anything else. Kenzie's phone buzzed and Lucy was relieved. She smiled at her friend, then turned back to her own desk while Kenzie grabbed her phone.

Lucy booted up her computer and downloaded the notes she'd emailed to herself. She had a preliminary profile of Nicole Rollins. It was incomplete, but a good beginning—and she was looking forward to discussing it with Hans. He probably already had his profile written, and then it was a matter of interviews with Elise and Nicole's brother, Chris. Those were the two people Lucy felt would add immensely to the profile.

She'd also begun thinking that maybe the key to finding Nicole was to find Tobias. It was counterintuitive—Tobias could walk freely because they had no solid description of him. Lucy would recognize him, but she hadn't been satisfied with any of the sketches. They had a partial image of him from the Dallas airport after he poisoned Rob Garza, but it was clear that he'd altered his appearance substantially—whether temporarily or permanently, they couldn't know. They'd been looking for him for three months—not only the FBI and the DEA, but Kane Rogan had put the full force of RCK into searching for him. He was a ghost, frustrating everyone involved in tracking him.

Nicole was a virtual prisoner. She might be able to change her looks, but she was on the radar of every law enforcement agency in the country. Unless she was already out of the country with a fake ID. If Lucy were Nicole, that's what she would have done. Driven into Canada on a US passport, then used a Canadian passport to fly to Europe. Obtain another false passport and fly to a temporary safe haven, a place without extradition. Wait out the manhunt for a few months. Build up a profile with a name and background, and move again, into whatever country she planned to live out her years as a fugitive. For Nicole, it would be someplace in South America, Lucy suspected. She would have contacts from her years as a double agent, along with money and resources, and though she wasn't a native Spanish speaker, she would be able to get by. New name, new background, new everything. Maybe even a new face.

Lucy wouldn't have been able to come up with that plan a few years ago, but after being with Sean for the last eighteen months she'd learned a lot about the system—and how to get around it. The only wrench in Nicole's plans was money—she'd need millions of dollars to pull off an elaborate transformation.

Her email beeped and a message came in from Sam Archer's chief analyst.

Nate walked by. "The debriefing starts in five minutes," he said.

"Yeah, I just want to read this message. I'll be right there."

"Five minutes," he repeated and left.

Lucy opened the message.

Here's the video you requested. I'm sorry I didn't send it last night, I didn't receive the approval before I left for the day. ASAC Archer said to assist you with whatever you need, so please do not hesitate to contact me. Below are my direct office line and my cell phone if you need to contact me after hours.

—Sarah Reynosa Martin

Lucy viewed the video of Nicole killing the drug dealer. She watched it twice. There was a familiarity between the drug dealer—Ramon Ramos—and Nicole. The way she killed him was both impulsive . . . yet not. That couldn't be. She started to watch it a third time, wishing the tape was clearer so she could read their lips. There was more to this even than could be seen on this recording. Nicole acted impulsively, first drawing her gun and shooting him in the knee without hesitation—not even a minute after she entered. In fact, she shot him as soon as she determined they were alone.

Then Nicole had a conversation with him. It lasted nearly two minutes—one minute, forty-nine seconds according to the time stamp. Then she shot him in the gut. He keeled over. She said something as she walked over directly above him and shot him three times in the head.

Her face was impassive. Somewhat irritated. It wasn't the first time Nicole had killed.

"Lucy!" Nate snapped from the head of the aisle. "Everyone is in the conference room. The debriefing started ten minutes ago. Durant told me to find you."

She grabbed her file and walked briskly behind Nate, still disturbed by what she'd watched on that video. She wanted to watch it again. She was fluent in American Sign Language and could also translate via lip-reading if she could improve the quality of the video.

She stood in the back of the conference room. Brad was near the front, listening to the US Marshal tell the group, essentially, that they hadn't found Nicole.

"However," he said, "we located one of the suspected shooters yesterday. He's not talking, he's lawyered up, but we have physical evidence that he was on the bus. Our best interrogator is working on him now. First person to cooperate won't get the death penalty."

There was some discussion about what to do with the

information this suspect gave them, how they were going to approach Nicole's safe house for example, but Lucy knew in her gut that this guy knew next to nothing.

"Excuse me," she said. "Marshal?"

It took a moment before he spotted her in the back. "And you are?"

"Lucy Kincaid, FBI. With all due respect, this guy doesn't know where Nicole Rollins is. No one does, except Nicole and the man she flew away with at Amistad Park."

"You can't know that."

"Sir, Rollins has been a corrupt agent from the moment she entered the DEA. During her fifteen-year career, no one suspected her duplicity. This tells me that she's extremely cunning and distrustful. Everyone who participated in her escape was a hired gun. They've been paid and she doesn't care if we know that she paid them, because she's free. The most he'll be able to give you is who else he worked with, what gang he's affiliated with, and how he was paid. You might be able to parlay that into additional information and stifle her ability to hire people to help her. But he's far more terrified about what Nicole's people will do to him in prison than what we'll do to him."

"Agent Kincaid, I appreciate your input, but it's a rare criminal who has that much power."

"Consider Nicole Rollins a rare criminal."

No one spoke, and Lucy stood in the back of the room, rigid, all eyes on her. She wished she could disappear, but she stood firm. Not only did she believe she was right about Nicole, but there was so much more they needed to learn. Time was against them.

She noticed that Brad kept looking at his phone. The subliminal power of suggestion had her looking at the clock. It was after nine. Was something supposed to happen at nine?

Suddenly Brad broke the silence. "Marshal, I need to call my office. Excuse me."

Brad rushed out of the conference room.

Abigail Durant said, "Marshal, please keep us informed and if you need our assistance in any way, let me know. Everyone knows what they need to do—let's do it. Let's find Rollins before anyone else is hurt." She caught Lucy's eye and motioned for her to come forward as the rest of the staff filed out.

"No one has been able to reach Agent Crawford," Durant said. "He didn't contact you?"

There was faint hope in her voice.

"No, ma'am."

"I've already sent Agents Malone and Figueroa to his house. Zach is tracking his flight status and credit cards. We confirmed with a neighbor that he left his house at three thirty Friday afternoon and no one has seen anything suspicious."

"You think—"

"I don't think anything," Durant interrupted. "I'm worried, because it isn't like Barry not to check in when we're trying to reach him. After what happened in DC with Agent Dunbar I'd rather be embarrassed when we find him than not looking at all."

"Let me know what I can do."

"You have your plate full right now." She looked at her watch. "I'll call you when Ryan gets back with AD Vigo."

Lucy walked slowly out of the conference room.

Barry would have called. He was too good an agent, too meticulous, too by-the-book, not to check in after hearing the news about Nicole—even if there was a legitimate reason he wasn't getting his messages.

Something had happened. And it wasn't going to be good news.

CHAPTER SIXTEEN

Lucy found Brad using an empty desk down the hall from the Violent Crimes Squad. He finished sending a message on his phone. "Is everything okay?" she asked.

"Tom Saldana was killed last night," Brad said.

"The SSA in McAllen?"

"Yes. I just got off the phone with Clark—the agent still on medical leave from the shootout in McAllen—and he's broken up but is going into the office. I just left a message for Sam. She's probably already dealing with the fallout, but we need to know if this is connected to Nicole Rollins."

"What happened?"

"Tom was meeting with an informant yesterday at approximately eleven p.m. Both Tom and the informant were found dead early this morning in an alley by local police. Each was shot twice in the chest. From the evidence, it looks like they were killed where they were found. We just don't have anything else to go on, and Tom had been on edge since Operation Heatwave. Pushing boundaries, trying to find Tobias. He wasn't working with anyone. After Kane lost one of his informants two weeks ago, I told Tom to keep a low profile—I thought he was, but now this?"

"Barry Crawford is missing."

"Well, fuck. Dunbar, Crawford, Saldana—does she plan on killing every federal agent in Texas? Taking out our people one by one? Some sort of vendetta against the DEA and the FBI?"

"You need to tell Durant. Everyone needs to be on full alert," Lucy said. "Especially you, Brad."

Nate approached. "Durant wants you in her office," he said to Lucy.

"Come with me." Lucy motioned for Brad to follow.

"What happened?" Nate said.

"A DEA agent was killed last night, along with his informant," Lucy said.

"Houston is coming in—the SAC himself, Edward Moody. Probably an entourage as well." Brad paused, glanced at Nate, then kept talking. "After I left you and Sean, I went to see her. She's lost agents before, but not like this. Tom's murder is like rubbing salt in the wound."

Not just for Sam Archer, but for Brad, Lucy thought. For all of them.

Nate said quietly to Lucy, "Let me know if you leave."

She nodded, and Nate walked back to the Violent Crimes Squad wing. She didn't like this protective detail, and Nate couldn't put aside his own work to watch her back. She didn't think Sean had thought this through well enough. Brad gave her an odd look. "I'll explain later," she said.

As soon as they walked into Abigail Durant's office, Lucy smiled. "Hans," she said.

He walked over and took her hands into both of his. She noticed he still had a slight limp, even though he'd been back from his medical leave for two months. "Lucy, it is so good to see you." He looked at the ring on her left hand, and his grin widened. "Congratulations. When?"

"Sean proposed last weekend. We haven't set a date yet."

"He's a good man. And lucky." Hans kissed her on the cheek. It made her feel awkward, in front of her boss and Brad, but she was thrilled to see Hans again.

He stepped back and extended his hand to Brad. "You must be Agent Donnelly. I'm Hans Vigo, with the FBI." Hans motioned toward the small conference table in the corner of Durant's office. "We have a lot of work to do, and not a lot of time."

Brad glanced at Durant. "Ma'am, I came in because we have a situation. One of our agents was murdered last night in McAllen. He was connected to Operation Heatwave—he's the one who uncovered the missing money from the evidence locker that helped lead us to uncover Rollins's duplicity."

"Do you think his murder is connected to her escape?" Durant asked.

"I don't know, but after Agent Dunbar was killed the other night, we need to assume it's connected. In the last decade, only a dozen DEA agents have been killed in the line of duty, and half of them were outside of our borders. In the last two days? Three."

Lucy said, "After talking to Agent Armstrong in DC last night, he believes Agent Dunbar's murder is related to his work here, but we have no proof yet."

"Dr. Vigo, thoughts?" Durant asked.

"Ms. Rollins is perfectly capable of orchestrating the hits, and I would suggest that all your agents be extra diligent until she's back in prison. In particularly, anyone who worked on Operation Heatwave or the Worthington case."

Durant frowned but didn't comment. "I'll speak with Ritz and we'll issue a memo this morning. But we've already told every agent, here and at the DEA, that no one is to work alone. That was partly because of Agent Donnelly's concern that Rollins has someone inside."

She turned to Brad. "Brad, if it's true that Rollins is targeting individuals who had a direct hand in her capture and imprisonment, my guess is that you're at the top of her list."

"I'm well aware."

"If you need a protective detail, let me know. We're in this together, there're no interagency problems. Ritz has spoken with your SAC Moody several times in the last two days. San Antonio DEA is a small, regional office and we have the staff and resources to cover anything you need." She picked up her briefcase and walked to the door. "I'm going to leave you three in here while I talk to Ritz, then I'll call Sam and we'll work out the details. Dr. Vigo, thank you again for coming out so quickly. Feel free to use my desk." She left, closing the door behind her.

Hans instead sat at the small round table in the corner. Lucy and Brad sat across from him. "Lucy, I read your reports—everything from Operation Heatwave through the Worthington investigation and your memos to Abigail. You want to interview a prostitute named Elise Hansen, the girl who may have killed Harper Worthington?"

"She killed him," Lucy said. "I have no doubt that she knew exactly what she was doing."

Hans flipped through the reports. "She claims she was threatened and coerced."

"Perhaps that's how it started," Lucy said, carefully picking her words, "but Elise Hansen is a sociopath. Her statements are designed to elicit sympathy. If she is in fact related to Tobias, I would say that she's part of the inner circle." She paused. "I talked to her face-to-face, Hans. She's manipulative and cagey. She knows exactly what she's doing and why. More, she enjoys it. Everything is a game to her. I've never met anyone like her before. She's not afraid of prison, she's not afraid of dying, she's not afraid of getting hurt."

"You've gotten into her head," Hans said.

"Not fast enough," Lucy said. "She had me and Tia— Detective Tia Mancini with SAPD—fooled for a while. Because of that, Tia nearly died. She won't be back on duty for at least two months."

"I don't think Hansen fooled you," Hans said. "I read everything you wrote, Lucy, and while you left some things out, I read between the lines."

She frowned. "I didn't leave anything out."

"You were diligent, but you left out your opinion—until the memo last night to Abigail where you shared some of your opinion under the guise of profiling."

Lucy wasn't sure she understood Hans. She said, "At first I believed what she wanted me to believe when I walked into the crime scene. That Harper Worthington was a pervert who liked to screw teenage girls. I sympathized with her, expecting her to be a typical underage prostitute—abused as a child, used by a boyfriend or pimp, angry and scared of the failed system."

"Like the girls you helped in DC last summer."

She nodded. "After I talked to her, I thought she was hiding things, but I also knew that I had to build trust. I believed she was using her anger and fear to cover up the pain of her past. But evidence doesn't lie. Too many things didn't make sense. Her reactions were right on . . . yet they didn't feel right. Almost . . . as if her reactions weren't quite natural. I didn't figure it out in time."

"But you caught on before anyone else," Hans said.

"I don't know—"

"I read all the reports on this matter. It's clear that Elise Hansen is a sociopath, surprisingly mature considering her age." He looked at his watch. "It's well after nine, what time can we talk to her?"

Brad said, "I talked to Sam last night—ASAC Samantha Archer, my boss—and she said Lucy is on the short list of who's allowed to speak to her. The AUSA may want to observe."

"They'll get in the way," Hans said. "Their interest in this case may not perfectly align with our interest. I'll take any heat from the DOJ, if it comes to that."

Lucy said, "I should talk to her alone. Elise doesn't respect men. I don't know that I can get her to slip up— she's far too shrewd to let me manipulate her—but the information I want may seem innocuous. So I'm going to give her information. She'll like that, and she'll be giddy if she thinks that I'm frustrated or let something slip out. But I have to play this very carefully, because she *is* extremely astute."

Brad had been looking at his phone on and off while Lucy spoke. Now she asked, "Is something wrong?"

"I don't know," he said. He put his phone down. "I told Lucy last night that I don't think it's a good idea for her to have a sit-down with Elise."

"Why?" Hans asked.

"Because Brad thinks that Elise got under my skin last time I saw her."

"She did," Brad said.

Lucy bristled. "Not as much as you think. But I'm better prepared now. Ten days ago? I wasn't. I went in still thinking there might be hope to save her. I was disturbed, more than anything. And she played off one of my fears— that she would be able to manipulate her way out of serious jail time. That's her plan, and maybe she can—I don't know anything about her court-appointed psychiatrist. But Elise won't get out without me fighting every step of the way to give her the maximum sentence."

Hans looked down. "Barbara Oakley. I don't know her." He flipped a page. "Elise Hansen hasn't been charged with anything."

"The AUSA is an asshole," Lucy said. Then she blushed. "I shouldn't have said that."

"Hansen's under a fourteen-day psych hold," Hans said.

"Which expires tomorrow," Brad said.

"That's why Tobias didn't break her out—he doesn't have to," Lucy said. "Why didn't I see this last night?"

"But there are going to be charges," Hans said.

"Are there?"

Hans frowned. "I don't have any more information on this than you do, but there appears to be ample evidence."

"If you listen to her side of the story, she was threatened into killing Harper Worthington. If they put her in a group home or juvie, it's only a matter of days before she slips away." Hours, Lucy thought.

"Let's talk to her, then the AUSA," Hans said. "There's precedence for keeping her up to thirty days in a psych facility. And if that doesn't work, we'll arrange for protective custody."

"Tobias doesn't want her dead," Brad said, again looking at his phone.

"But we can make an argument that he does," Hans countered.

Brad rose. "I want to go with you, but I have to check in at my office."

"Is something wrong?"

"Sam had a meeting with Moody thirty minutes ago. She texted me before nine saying she was going to be late. I just texted her to find out where she was, but she hasn't gotten back to me or returned any of the calls from her admin. I need to cover for her."

"Go," Lucy said. "But take someone with you. Durant

has already cleared it, and she's right about one thing—you've pissed off Nicole more than anyone."

"She's wrong about that," Brad said.

"Now is not the time to play hero. Take the help, Brad."

"I will, but you and your future brother-in-law are the two who should really watch out. Nicole might hate me, but she knows that it was you and Kane Rogan who took her down." Suddenly he stopped talking. "Oh shit, Lucy."

She closed her eyes. "It's okay."

"I'm sorry—"

"It's okay. Really." She glanced at Hans. "I'll explain."

"Explain in the car," Hans said.

Brad left, and Lucy tapped Nate to drive them to the county jail. Though Elise was a minor, the county jail had one of the few secure psychiatric facilities in the area that also included a juvenile wing. And since she hadn't been charged—officially—with a crime, it was the only place they could secure Elise until the fourteen-day observation period was over.

Lucy was in the backseat while Nate drove. She said, "Nate—I need to tell Hans something off the record."

"My ears are sealed."

Lucy suspected Nate already knew what she was about to say. If not because Sean had told him, then because he'd figured it out on his own.

She said, "Three months ago, when Brad Donnelly was kidnapped, I—"

Hans interrupted her. "Don't tell me."

"But—"

"I don't know what Agent Donnelly meant by his comment, and I don't care."

She frowned. She realized that she'd created this mess. She'd gone to Mexico as part of the rescue operation, she'd put herself in danger. She wanted to come clean.

"I recognize that Rollins has a particular reason to put you in her sights," Hans continued. "I'm not, however, going to let you destroy your career." He paused. "I'm fairly certain that Rick Stockton is intimately familiar with every RCK operation that crosses paths with the FBI."

She didn't know whether to be relieved or worried.

"Lucy," Hans said, changing the subject, "I heard that Sean is funding a group home for the boys rescued from Trejo's cartel."

"Yes, with Saint Catherine's, my church."

"It's an extremely generous contribution."

"Sean wanted to. Those boys were broken. They needed peace. A home. Father Mateo has been great with them."

"I also heard that some of the boys didn't make it."

A flash of the dead clouded her vision for a moment. She blinked, putting the image of boys tossed away like garbage out of her mind. She didn't want a nightmare tonight, especially with Sean out of town. "They were murdered," she said. "Shot and killed in front of the others to force compliance. Left to rot in the same building where the boys were locked up."

"One of the problems with . . . vague reports," Hans said cryptically, "is that those who witnessed such violence may not seek out the help they need."

"I know what you're saying," she said. "The boys have counseling, and they have Sean. He's good with them."

"I wasn't talking about the boys."

She bit her lip. "I had a problem with nightmares for a while, but it's over. And I have Sean."

"And he has you."

Spontaneously, she said, "Stay at our house. Sean is out of town and we have plenty of room. More than enough."

"Sean left you alone? With Rollins on the loose?"

"No, sir," Nate said, "Sean left her with me."

"Nate—Dunning, right?"

"Yes, sir."

"I read your file."

"Sir?"

Hans laughed. "I was the assistant director at Quantico when you went through the academy."

Nate almost blushed. "I didn't make the connection. I apologize."

"Now they've stuck me in headquarters. I wish I could go back to Quantico."

"If you really wanted to, you'd make it happen," Lucy said.

"Perhaps you're right," he said. "Where is Sean? It's not like him to leave during a situation like this."

"There may be some trouble with Kane. It could be nothing—communications failure. Or he might be in real trouble."

"Rollins," Hans said.

"She won't kill him quietly. She'll be bold about it. She'll want everyone to know that she took him out." But Lucy's gut churned. What was Sean getting himself into?

"You already have a profile on her."

"A beginning. That's why I want to talk to Elise, then to Chris, Nicole's brother."

Nate said, "On that, I spoke to my former commanding officer at Fort Hood. Chris Rollins is deployed in Afghanistan. He's a lieutenant, has a spotless service record. Career military—he was ROTC in college, and has been an active service member for sixteen years. He volunteered to do another tour in Afghanistan. It's a hard life, but for some people it's exactly what they need."

"Can we talk to him?"

"Not a problem. His commander is already aware we want to speak to him. They're ten hours ahead of us where he's stationed."

"Anytime he can talk, I'll make myself available."

"Good call, Lucy," Hans said. "You're trying to figure out what their childhood was like."

"I want to know why she lied to me."

"Excuse me?"

"She told me—this was during Operation Heatwave, when she had no reason to lie—that she lived in Kansas until she was fourteen with her brothers. It was a nothing conversation, about tornadoes or something innocuous. Yet she has only one brother, and she lived in Kansas for only fourteen *months*, when she was much younger. So there was some truth, but it was twisted."

"That's interesting. Is she a pathological liar?"

"No, I don't think so."

"Why not?"

"It was more like . . . a game. Just like Elise. And if the truth came out, she could say she misspoke, or that I misheard, or that the conversation never took place. It wasn't anything I would need or care to verify."

"That kind of lying suggests a compulsion."

"In hindsight, I think that she was trying to build a rapport with me of some sort. She knew I came from a large family, but she didn't realize that—except for me—my brothers and sisters were raised like she was, in a military family moving base-to-base. Had she known that, it might have changed what she said. Her father left the military when she was still young, became a cop. He was killed in the line of duty when she was fifteen. I've sent a request to the LA field office to find out more about his death."

"Hmm," Hans said. Lucy didn't know what he meant by that, and he didn't elaborate.

Nate showed his badge to the security guard outside the jail, and was directed to the opposite end of the facility. He parked, they went through security and relinquished their weapons, then were escorted to a holding room. The guard told them it would be at least ten minutes while they moved the prisoner to an interview room.

Hans turned to Nate. "Agent Dunning, would you mind giving Lucy and me a minute?"

"Of course." He stepped outside.

"Is something wrong?" Lucy asked.

"No. You trust him."

"Yes. Nate is Sean's closest friend here."

"I didn't know that, but I suppose it's obvious."

"Obvious?"

"Sean would never have left town if he didn't think you were safe."

"Nate was special forces."

"I know. I wasn't lying when I said I read his file."

"Oh." She bit her lip. "Hans—why do I think you're trying to tell me something? Can you just spill it?"

"I read your report last night, the one you sent to Abigail Durant. It was good. Brief, to the point, and like I said earlier, you shared some of your opinion—I want more."

"It's nothing I can prove."

"In profiling, proving something is an art, not a science. We're talking about human beings. No humans can be put into a neat box."

She didn't know what he wanted from her.

Hans continued, "I don't see the connection between Nicole Rollins and Elise Hansen, and why you believe you'll gain anything from this conversation."

"It's a theory."

"I want your theory."

"I think . . ." She hesitated. For years she'd hedged and second-guessed herself, not trusting her own instincts, always deferring to those with more experience. And she still did that. But when it came to predators—of any kind—she had a sixth sense that she couldn't ignore.

She said, "Nicole Rollins is in charge. I wrote that she

was working with Tobias and was possibly his lover, someone he trusted. But after watching the video of her killing a low-life drug dealer, I think she's too arrogant and too smart to take orders. At the *minimum*, she and Tobias are equal partners. He must have orchestrated her escape—or implemented a plan she came up with as a contingency. She couldn't do it on her own, and the marshals haven't found any record that her lawyer was passing information—though I think he certainly was the go-between, whether or not he knew it."

"Go on," Hans said when she paused for a minute.

"Kane called us last night, said a man named Joseph put a bounty on Kane's head. Joseph must be Joseph Contreras, the man we suspect of killing Congresswoman Reyes-Worthington, the man we suspect was working for Tobias to keep her in line. There's almost *nothing* on him. Maybe he falsified his records, or used a different name and Social, or *something*, but it's like he doesn't exist except as a tax record. We're looking out of state, but it's going to take time."

"Nicole moved to LA when she was young."

"Yes."

"Look there. You're already looking into her father's murder, we should look deeper—broader—than that."

She should have seen that. Dammit, she'd missed the background. "Of course."

"I have a contact in LA, she used to work out of BSU until budget cuts. Now she's one of the two SSAs of Violent Crimes out of the main LA headquarters."

"That would be very helpful." One thing Lucy detested about working for the federal government was the bureaucracy. She could request all the information and help she wanted, but getting people to act on it quickly was hit or miss. Having an internal contact in the right office could save them days of waiting.

"How does Elise Hansen fit in?" Hans asked.

"That's the question I've been asking myself for two weeks. Tobias is no younger than forty. Elise is sixteen. Brother and sister? Possible, but unlikely. Father and daughter? Maybe. But that doesn't feel right to me. How Elise talked about him as a brother fits better. Could be they're cousins or related in another way, or perhaps Elise is the daughter of someone Tobias is close to. Elise has prostituted herself, but she's not a traditional hooker. For her, sex is a tool, a means to an end. Elise didn't talk about Tobias in a sexual way. It could be that Tobias took Elise under his wing, in some sort of crude protective brotherly way, honing her already psychopathic tendencies to serve his needs. Elise has no respect for men, and I can't exclude Tobias from that assessment. Yet . . . she has a nonsexual affection for him, even though I don't see her bonding with anyone. If we shut down Tobias, found Nicole and took out their entire operation, Elise would survive without any sense of loss." She rubbed her temples, feeling a headache building. "I need to figure it out. This doesn't make sense yet. I'm missing information, but it's critical information."

"And we have no information about where Elise was prior to DC?"

Lucy shook her head. "She had several identification cards from Nevada and the Las Vegas office determined that they were all fake. And after her story of being in foster care, we pulled her name and all her aliases—nothing matches."

Lucy feared that Elise would win in the end. There was little evidence that refuted her statement that she was terrified and threatened and thought she had no choice. Just because there was no record of her in Nevada or elsewhere wasn't proof that she was lying. Lucy didn't know much of what Elise had said to the shrinks, but her hearing was tomorrow and if she played the psychiatrist like Lucy thought she would, Dr. Oakley would say anything that Elise wanted her to.

Because of the circumstances, Elise would never be released without some sort of monitoring, but she wouldn't be hindered by rules or threats. She was used to disappearing, and she would walk away without hesitation. If Tobias was truly involved—if he was her family, blood or not—then he had the money to help her disappear.

"She refuses to tell us her real name and where she was born. There should be a record of her in foster care, but we can't check if she keeps lying."

"Refuses out of fear?"

"No. She's not scared, Hans. She's sixteen years old and a cold-blooded killer. I *know* it."

CHAPTER SEVENTEEN

Sean landed his Cessna on the small, rough airstrip at Jack Kincaid's expansive property outside Hidalgo, Texas. It was a nearly four-hour drive from San Antonio, but only fifty-three minutes from takeoff to landing in Sean's plane. By the time he'd taxied into the barn that was used primarily as hangar, Blitz had driven out to meet him. The airstrip was nearly a mile from Jack's house, which sat in the middle of two hundred acres of flat desert.

Sean shook Blitz's hand, then jumped into the truck. "Any word?"

Blitz shook his head. "I shouldn't have left him."

"You followed orders. I know Kane; he didn't give you an option."

"I was about to go back to Santiago when Jack called and said you were on your way. I'm going with you."

"Good. I don't know that area well."

"None of us does. We don't have any contacts there, our closest safe house is an hour away, outside Saltillo. That's where Kane would go if he was injured or lost communication."

If he was able, Sean thought.

"Jack said you lost a man."

"Gomez. New guy. Didn't see the knife. None of us did before it was too late." He paused. "First we've lost in four years."

"Do you have a plan?"

"Jack and I have been working it out." He stopped under the carport next to Jack's small ranch house. "Jack's on his way to San Antonio, told me to tell you."

"I didn't leave Lucy without backup."

"I know, but, well, you know."

Lucy was Jack's little sister. Of course Sean understood. He hadn't wanted to leave her, either. And while he trusted Nate, he was relieved Jack was coming down.

"What's the plan?"

"Fly to the closest safe house. Its cover is legit—Sisters of Mercy. They'll know what we're dealing with, give us a direction to start."

"I know how to find him. I'm not going to waste time going an hour out of our way." Blitz looked at him, skeptical, so Sean explained. "After we took out Trejo's compound three months ago, I reprogrammed Kane's watch as a quasi-GPS."

"How the hell? He never takes it off."

"He didn't have to. Once I got the serial number, I was able to hack in remotely. There's a downside—the watch synchronizes automatically every twelve hours, midnight and noon Central Time. I won't know where he is until noon. And it'll just give me a snapshot; if he moves after that, I won't be able to track him on the fly." Yet. He was working on it, but it meant hacking a satellite instead of a simple computerized watch. Extremely illegal, and while within his skill set, there was a greater chance of being caught. He was working on the not getting caught part.

Blitz said, "We have ninety-six minutes."

"It'll take us an hour to get to Santiago, maybe a little longer depending on if I have to elude radar. The Nicole

Rollins escape increased border patrols, both surface and air."

"Then let's go. I'll just grab my equipment."

Sean followed Blitz into the house. The last time he'd been here had been with the boys they'd rescued—he still ached inside. Though he'd hired private security to watch the boys' home, he wished he could be there himself. He wished he could be at Lucy's side. Too many things were happening all at once.

But now, finding Kane was the priority.

Siobhan Walsh was sitting on the couch drinking tea. She wore a tank top, and bruises covered her fair skin. An ugly bruise blackened one eye. They'd beaten her. No wonder Kane stayed to track the survivor. Not only for information, but for retribution.

"Oh my God, it's Sean!" She jumped up, then winced.

"Sit down," a familiar voice said.

Father Frances Cardenas—known as Padre—was Jack Kincaid's closest friend and former army buddy. He crossed the room and eased Siobhan back onto the couch.

"Two cracked ribs," Padre said. "I had a doctor in to tape her up, but she doesn't sit still." He gave her a stern but affectionate look.

Sean walked over and kissed Siobhan on her good cheek. "It's good to see you again, Sunshine."

She rolled her eyes. "You and your damn nicknames."

"It fits you."

Last time Sean had seen Siobhan had been three years ago. Kane had picked her up when she got mixed up with a violent human trafficking organization. She'd been doing a piece tracking a family who'd lost everything when the cartels seized their land and pressed the men of the family into working for them. The women had been sold to human traffickers, but the Sisters of Mercy, a group Siobhan worked with, had rescued them. One of the rescued women trusted the wrong person, however, and they were all imprisoned—including Siobhan.

Sean hadn't been part of the rescue operation, he'd stayed with the plane for three days waiting for Kane to show up with the hostages. Kane had stayed behind. Later, Sean learned he'd rescued the boys who'd been pressed into field-work for the cartels, then reunited them with their families which he also relocated so the cartel couldn't find them. The patriarch of the family had been murdered in front of his sons when he refused to cooperate. Sean suspected Kane had done more than rescue the large extended family, but he'd never asked and Kane had never spoken of it.

"This isn't my fault," she said.

"No one thinks it is."

"Kane does. He's so . . . frustrating. I was on vacation. I spent three months in the outskirts of Oaxaca. It was . . . tough." She didn't say anything else. Sean could imagine the conditions down there.

"I look forward to seeing your spread."

She smiled. "Thanks—it's going to be good. The sisters need some positive PR, they've lost nearly half of their do-nations, but the need is even greater. The sucky economy really messes with charitable giving. I'm hoping this piece will help turn it around."

"I'm sure it will. So why were you in Santiago?"

"I needed a break. I heard about a great little spa there and I like going to new places. I'd never been there be-fore, other than passing through. Someone was following me, almost from the minute I arrived."

"Who knew you were going to be there?"

She shrugged. "Andie, of course. The sisters. I didn't keep it a secret."

"Can I see your phone?"

She frowned, then handed it to Sean. "Blitz told me to turn it off."

"Smart." Sean turned it on, but immediately disabled the cellular service. Then he hacked into the operating system. No one had hacked her GPS. Then he went into the emails and there it was. Simple.

"You found something," Siobhan said.

"Very old school, which is why it works. There's a bcc on every email you send. It's going to a blind account. I might be able to trace it."

"Are you serious? Someone is reading *all* my emails?"

"Where were you on Friday morning? Around ten a.m.?"

"Friday? That's when I left Oaxaca. The airport. Or the plane. The Xoxocotlán International Airport."

"Don't use this phone for email. It's not bugged, you can call your sister."

"Can't you disable it?"

"Yes—but I don't know that I want to." He glanced at Padre. "I'll only have one shot—they may not have thought to disable the blind account, and I can trace it, but I don't have the time to do it now. Padre, if anything happens, call Patrick Kincaid. He'll know what to do."

Blitz said, "We need to go, if we want to land before noon."

Siobhan said, "Be careful."

Sean winked at her. "Always." He glanced at Padre, and the priest nodded. Padre would keep an eye on Siobhan until they figured out if she was still in danger.

The other new guy, Dyson, drove them back to the plane. "I should go with you," he said.

Blitz said, "We need two people on Siobhan until we get back. Understood?"

"Yes, sir."

"Knock it off with the sir. I haven't been in the army in fifteen years." He tossed Sean one of the bags. "Let's get your brother, Little Rogan."

Through clenched teeth Sean said, "Don't call me that."

CHAPTER EIGHTEEN

Lucy and Hans had to wait more than fifteen minutes before the guard returned to tell them Elise Hansen was ready to talk to them. He led the way through the maze of corridors. "I was required to notify her psychiatrist," the guard said. "Dr. Oakley is not in yet, but I left a message." The guard paused, then said softly, "I'm not supposed to let anyone speak to Hansen without Dr. Oakley's approval."

"That's new," Lucy said. And odd. Her attorney, maybe—but she'd already put in the record that she wasn't here to discuss Elise's case.

"You think she knows something about the escape yesterday."

"Possibly, but—"

"I knew one of the guards who was killed. And between you and me, her shrink won't let you talk to her. Dr. Oakley thinks you could damage her psyche." He rolled his eyes. "But there's nothing in the official file prohibiting you from seeing her."

"She's a piece of work," he added. "I'll leave it at that."

Piece of work pretty much summed up Elise Hansen.

Lucy recognized that they were walking a fine line. While she technically had clearance to talk to Elise, there could be an issue because Elise was under psychiatric observation.

The guard said, "Ms. Hansen is in the interview room. I'll be right outside."

"I'll be observing," Hans said.

The guard opened the door to a small observation room that adjoined the interview room. "Dr. Vigo, you can use this room. You'll be able to watch and listen. A recording is made of all interviews with psychiatric hold inmates, though they're restricted without a warrant."

"Thank you," Hans said. "I'd like a moment alone with Agent Kincaid."

"Watch yourself with her," the guard said to Lucy and stepped into the hall.

Lucy wondered what the guard knew—or suspected.

Lucy looked through the one-way mirror. Elise sat at the table, her left arm restrained to a bar in front of her. Her right arm was still in a sling from when she'd been shot two weeks ago, and her forearm was in a cast. If Lucy was right, then Elise had set the whole thing up. Elise had tried to get Lucy killed. She hadn't planned the attack, but she'd played her part perfectly.

"Are you ready?" Hans asked her.

"Hans—I know what you're thinking, but I'm fine. I can handle her."

He nodded. "It's harder when you're dealing with a true sociopath. You have great compassion, Lucy."

She didn't see that. Sometimes, she felt as cold as Elise Hansen. Emotionless. Yet, it broke her heart that she didn't believe a sixteen-year-old was redeemable. She'd always believed that criminals were more a product of their environment than of birth. She couldn't believe that God would be so cruel as to predispose an innocent young baby to grow into a psychopathic killer. She and her older brother Dillon had argued about it many times.

"Some people are born evil," Dillon had said. *"They know what they're doing is wrong and they do it anyway without any remorse."*

Looking into Elise's eyes, Lucy knew without a doubt that she had been born bad and she'd grown up in an environment that encouraged her natural—her *sociopathic*—tendencies. She had no remorse and more, she enjoyed every minute of her life.

"I'm okay, Hans. I know exactly who she is."

Lucy stepped out. The guard at the door told her the rules—don't give the prisoner anything, don't take anything from her, don't touch her.

Lucy hesitated, just a minute, to mentally shield herself from whatever games Elise wanted to play. She had to remember that Elise would exploit any weakness she saw.

"I get a trial by jury. My brother and I always win."

When Elise said that two weeks ago, it had unnerved Lucy and she hadn't been able to hide her reaction. Lucy couldn't let Elise know if she hit another sensitive spot.

Her face impassive, with just a touch of disdain, Lucy entered the interview room.

"Elise Hansen," she said with a small smile. She sat down across from the teenager and made a point of looking her over and nodding. "You look well."

She looked much younger without all the makeup. Her bleached-blond hair had started to grow out, revealing dark-blond roots. She looked almost innocent.

This girl didn't have an innocent bone in her body.

"So do you," Elise said with a half smile. "I knew you'd be back, Agent Kincaid. Lucy, right? Lucy Kincaid." She had a sparkle in her eye. She was already enjoying the conversation, in the *I have a secret you don't* kind of way. "Where's my lawyer?"

"I'm not here about your case. I have some questions relating to another matter and was hoping you'd answer them."

"Why?"

"Why not?"

Elise shrugged. Curiosity shone in her eyes, but she wasn't going to ask. It was a game, Lucy reminded herself. A game Lucy would have to play if she wanted to get anything useful from Elise.

"There's really nothing in it for me to help you, is there?"

"I didn't say I wanted your help. But if you'd like to think of it as helping me, that's fine."

Elise leaned forward and spoke very softly. "You know I'm getting out tomorrow."

"Maybe you will," Lucy said openly and without anger.

Elise glanced at Lucy's hands. "You didn't have that ring on last time you were here. So you're getting married."

Lucy mentally hit herself that she hadn't taken off her engagement ring. Though why would it matter? What could Elise do with the information? Why was Lucy fearful that she knew?

Because, Lucy thought, any personal information Elise had could be used against her.

"I wanted to share some information," Lucy said, ignoring the comment about her ring.

Elise grinned. "Really? Out of the kindness of your heart? You think I'm that naive?"

"I don't think you're naive at all, Elise."

"So spill."

"Tobias helped a former DEA agent escape from custody yesterday," Lucy said.

"Huh." No other reaction. Not even curiosity. "What's it to me?"

"Why not you?"

"Me?"

"He left you here."

She laughed. "I'm not going to be here much longer. I'm getting out tomorrow."

"Maybe."

"Definitely."

"Do you know Nicole Rollins?"

There was a sparkle in her eye. She *wanted* Lucy to know that she knew Nicole. "Nicole *who*?"

Lucy said quietly, "You know exactly who I'm talking about. She works with Tobias. In fact, I think she's in charge of the entire operation and your brother—if Tobias really is your brother—works for her."

Elise smiled. "Girls *are* smarter than boys. Most of them, anyway."

Lucy didn't say anything. She watched Elise, waiting for her to continue.

Elise didn't feel the need to fill the silence with chatter. She stared back at Lucy, not intimidated in the least. Lucy didn't expect her to be and let the silence hang.

Lucy was very good at the cold facade. She could sit here all day. And she'd given Elise enough to make her curious. If Elise wasn't curious, she, too, would have sat there and stared all day. But curiosity . . . it might be Elise's only weakness.

Elise spoke first, her lips curved into a half-smile.

"I've learned a lot in the last two weeks, Agent Kincaid. I learned that my behavior is a result of abuse I suffered as a child. Abuse I barely remember. I learned that I sell my body as a way to gain the love and affection I never had as a little girl. There's hope for me, Lucy."

She was lying. Sitting there regurgitating whatever her

shrink had told her. She didn't believe a word of it, but there was no doubt that she could play the role for a judge and jury.

"Elise, you're not getting out. You'll be locked up for a long, long time."

Elise leaned forward and dipped her head slightly, so her hair fell in front of her face. She whispered so quietly that Lucy doubted the recording could pick up the words, though Lucy heard them very clearly. "You are wrong, Lucy. Very, very wrong."

Then tears slipped out of her eyes, completely unexpectedly, and for a split second Lucy was surprised. She had interviewed suspects who could fake emotion, who could force themselves to cry, but not so spontaneously.

"Why would you say that to me?" Elise said.

"What do you think I said?"

"That you want to lock me away forever and ever."

"I didn't say that, Elise." She kept her voice calm, reminding herself that Elise was acting for the camera.

"You hate me. Why are you so mean?" Her voice rose. "What did I ever do to you?"

Voices outside the door distracted Lucy, and then the door opened.

Dr. Barbara Oakley stormed in. "Agent Kincaid! I did not give you permission to speak with my patient."

"She has information regarding an ongoing investigation."

Oakley walked over to Elise and squatted next to her. "Elise, I'm going to take you back to your room, okay?"

Elise sobbed and nodded. "I'm sorry, Dr. Oakley. I wanted to help, really, b-b-but I don't know what she wants from me! I don't want to be locked up. I don't want to die in jail. I didn't mean to do anything wrong!"

Her voice was pained, in anguish, a complete reversal from five minutes ago. Certainly, when Lucy showed

Dr. Oakley the recording, she'd see that Elise was manipulating her and the system.

"You didn't do anything wrong, Elise. This is not your fault. We'll talk about this later."

"I'm sorry, I'm sorry," Elise repeated.

Dr. Oakley ordered the guard to unlock the restraints and take Elise to her office. As soon as Elise left, Oakley turned to Lucy. "I'm filing a complaint with your superiors."

"That was an act," Lucy said. "She's manipulating you."

Oakley stared at Lucy, her eyes wide and full of rage. "I've been a psychiatrist for longer than you've been alive, and have worked with juvenile criminals for the past decade. You have no idea what Elise Hansen has suffered. Yes, she's manipulative. She's had to be in order to survive. Do you even understand what girls like Elise have lived through? The abuse, the rapes, the complete devaluing as a human being? I've worked daily, for two weeks, to get her to open up to me, and we've made great progress based on mutual trust and understanding. You set us back. She's terrified of being locked up."

"That girl is scared of nothing," Lucy snapped.

Hans Vigo walked in and said, "Dr. Oakley, I'm Dr. Hans Vigo with the FBI."

"And you're responsible for this? Who do you think you are? Have you ever worked with abused children? I'll be taking this up with your superior as well, Dr. Vigo. Let me make this perfectly clear: Elise Hansen is under my care, as a patient and as a ward of the court. Neither of you is allowed to speak with her again unless both myself and her lawyer are present. Your actions show complete disdain for the plight of victims and is on its face a gross abuse of power."

Lucy rarely lost her temper, but the control she'd exhibited during her brief conversation with Elise disappeared.

"Elise Hansen is a cold-blooded killer who is not afraid of anything or anyone. You should have your license revoked if you can't even see the sociopath right in front of you."

She was shaking. Why had she said anything? She should have walked out.

Lucy glanced at Hans and saw that he was just as surprised by her outburst as she was. She opened her mouth to apologize to Oakley, but the doctor said, "Elise will get the care she needs to help her cope with the trauma that has been her life for the past sixteen years. Your lack of compassion is terrifying, Agent Kincaid."

Hans handed Oakley his card. "Please call me, Dr. Oakley, and I'll straighten this matter out."

She took his card but didn't look at it. She slipped it into her pocket. "There is nothing to straighten out," she said and left.

"Lucy," Hans began.

"I screwed up." So much for her icy exterior. When had she become such a hothead? It wasn't like her.

"You handled Elise just right. We'll talk about Dr. Oakley later—you should have let me handle her, but it's done." He held out her cell phone. "It's been vibrating nonstop for the last fifteen minutes."

She took her phone. There were numerous missed calls and messages from Brad, Ryan, Zach, and one from ASAC Abigail Durant.

She called Durant first. "Ma'am, I'm sorry, I was interviewing Elise Hansen at the jail."

"Samantha Archer was shot to death in her house. Zach Charles will send you the address—Agent Quiroz is already en route with Agent Donnelly. Our office is handling the investigation."

Her stomach twisted. "Rollins."

"Be careful, Agent Kincaid. Put Dr. Vigo on the phone."

Lucy handed the phone to Hans. He didn't say anything for a minute, then said, "I understand. I'll call you back." He handed the phone back to Lucy. "She wants me to take lead as the highest-ranking agent. SAC Ritz Naygrow is on his way—he's in McAllen and won't be back until later this afternoon. How well did you know Samantha Archer?"

"I worked with her during Operation Heatwave, but I didn't know her well."

"Then you'll be okay walking through the scene?"

"Yes," she replied. Why had Nicole killed Sam Archer? As a threat? As payback? She was bold, vindictive, brazen. Nothing seemed to faze her—just like Elise.

"Even the smartest criminals are caught," Hans said, as if reading her mind.

But when? Her sister-in-law Kate had been after Trask, the man who had killed Kate's partner, for over five years. He'd continued raping and murdering women for not only his own pleasure, but also the pleasure of the sickos who paid to watch the violence. He'd killed his first woman when he was eighteen, and he hadn't stopped until Lucy killed him twenty years later. Trask had been smart and ruthless and evil.

Just like Nicole Rollins.

What if they couldn't find her? What if she eluded their manhunt? Lucy would never have peace, not knowing when Nicole would go after her—or someone she loved.

She turned to Hans. "And some get away with murder for years."

CHAPTER NINETEEN

Lucy, Nate, and Hans arrived at Sam Archer's quasi-suburban house only fifteen minutes after Lucy spoke to Durant. The street was blocked off at both ends. Security was tight and all identification scrutinized.

Brad and Ryan stood next to the tactical van talking to a short, grim man in a pale-gray suit that matched his hair. Though Lucy had never met him before, she recognized the DEA Special-Agent-in-Charge Edward Moody from his photos.

"I'll handle Moody and keep Agent Donnelly outside," Hans said. "You walk through the scene."

"Is ERT here yet?" Lucy asked. Protocol dictated that ERT process the evidence once the crime scene was secured.

"Before this place becomes a zoo, I want your initial assessment. Get into their heads, Lucy. The victim and the killer."

She nodded, but inside her gut twisted.

What did Nicole want? Why act so smart, plan a brilliant escape, then risk exposure in order to kill one person? Of course—just because Sam was dead didn't mean Nicole pulled the trigger herself. She could have sent Joseph

Contreras to do it—the man they suspected had broken Congresswoman Worthington's neck.

After the two cops cleared them, Lucy and Nate approached the threshold of Sam Archer's house. Lucy slipped on gloves and handed Nate a pair. "Don't touch anything," she said. "But just in case."

Steeling herself against death, Lucy stepped inside.

Sam's house was neat. Cluttered, but not messy. A wide entry. A living and dining room that were scarcely used. A generic house in a generic neighborhood, but Sam had added a few personal touches. Color on the walls, art that didn't quite fit with the decor but was fun, as if she'd picked it because she liked it, not because it matched her furniture. Straight ahead was a great room, with the kitchen, eating nook, and family room flowing into large windows that looked out at a small, peanut-shaped swimming pool. Trees shielded most of Sam's yard from her neighbors, but the surrounding houses could be seen through the leaves.

It was a spacious, comfortable house for a single, professional woman.

Sam clearly lived in the great room. Pictures of family and friends on the walls; books and papers scattered on all available surfaces; dishes rinsed but not washed, stacked in the sink. A collection of whimsical salt- and pepper shakers lined three shelves on a narrow wall that separated the kitchen from the eating area. A full pot of coffee had been brewed—the carafe was still full—but at least two hours had passed since it had been made and the light was off. Lucy felt the side of the pot with the back of her gloved hand. Room temperature, maybe a bit warmer. It had been off for at least an hour, if not longer. It was ten thirty in the morning. Sam started the pot before seven thirty but hadn't poured a cup.

Hadn't Sam sent Brad a text message at nine telling him

she was running late? Where was her phone? Was she already dead?

She had a meeting at nine at the office. She wouldn't be late for it—not with the SAC himself coming into town.

She was already dead.

The family room was comfortable and well lived-in with a fireplace on one end and a large-screen television on another wall. A billiard table fit comfortably between the sectional sofa and the wall of windows. Cushions were scattered around the room—and so were clothes. Women's clothes, including a bra and panties.

Sam had a man here last night.

Nate saw the same thing Lucy saw, but he didn't comment.

A large, wide hall separated the front of the house from the back. Lucy walked down the middle, Nate three feet ahead of her, checking doorways though the house had already been cleared by responding officers. He was silent, listening as she listened to the sounds of cops outside, trucks and cars and the occasional whirl of a siren cutting through the idyllic middle-class development. There was a den on the right—with a computer and files. "Whoever killed her could have had time to access anything in here," Lucy said, mostly to herself.

She was glad when Nate didn't talk. She didn't want a conversation. She was absorbing the scene, the setting, the house. Picturing Sam Archer, a forty-something professional. A woman as well as a federal agent.

Two large bedrooms were unused—one had been converted into a weight room, the other was a guest room. Both had their own bathrooms. Neither appeared disturbed, but that would be up to ERT to determine.

The master suite was at the end of the wide hall. Lucy paused for a minute outside the open door. Her heart was racing because she knew that Sam Archer was dead inside. .

She grounded herself. Yes, she knew Sam Archer; she liked the woman. But Sam was a victim now. Sam needed Lucy to give her justice.

Lucy opened her eyes and stepped over the threshold.

The first thing she saw was a king-sized bed. The comforter was on the floor. The sheets were tangled at the foot, and all pillows had been used. Sam could simply be a restless sleeper, but more likely the man who removed her clothing in the family room was the same man who slept in this bed.

Sam could very well have been killed by someone she knew.

She walked over to the bed.

"Lucy," Nate said quietly.

She ignored him. There was something familiar in the air—a scent. She smelled blood but didn't see any in here. She focused on the scent of perfume.

Not perfume. Cologne. Distinctive.

She knew who'd spent the night with Sam Archer.

"Lucy—" Nate began.

"Shh," she said. Conversation would distract her.

She crossed the master bedroom and stopped at the doorway to the bathroom.

Sam was dead on the stone tile floor just outside the shower. A green towel, stained dark with blood, lay on the tile next to her. She was naked.

She'd been surprised by her killer.

Didn't she have a security system? If so, had she neglected to turn it on? Had the killer disabled it? Or did the killer know the code?

Sam's blood snaked through the grout for several feet. Soaking in, staining the porous material.

Sam's right knee was a bloody mess. She'd been shot in the stomach, then the head.

Lucy turned abruptly and bumped into Nate.

"Are you okay?"

"Nicole Rollins killed her."

"That's what we think, but—"

"I know. Nicole came herself to kill her—and she wants us to know it was her." She turned back to face the bathroom. She looked at the blood spatter patterns. She wasn't a blood spatter expert, but she knew enough about patterns as well as human physiology to know that Sam had been shot in the knee first.

"Nicole stood here and waited for Sam to be done in the shower. Sam stepped out—reached for the towel—maybe she saw something, or maybe Nicole spoke. But Nicole faced her naked. Sam had no place to go. Trapped. Nicole had a silencer."

"How do you know?"

"Because no one called about hearing gunshots. She was killed hours ago, people would have been home. This is a family neighborhood, the lots aren't large. Someone would have heard something."

Lucy continued. "Nicole shot Sam in the knee as soon as Sam saw her." Lucy gestured to a bloody handprint on the bathtub, a pool on the floor several feet from where Sam's body now lay. "Sam fell to the floor. Touched her knee, or the ground, tried to pull herself up on the bathtub."

"How—"

She put up her hand to silence him. She couldn't have doubts now, not now. This was what she did. This was what she was good at, why Hans wanted her to see the scene fresh.

"Sam's lover left and she made coffee. He didn't stay for coffee; it was dark. He wanted to get home, shower, change into new clothes before going to work. He doesn't have anything of his in this house, because the relationship just started. Or, I should say, resumed sometime after

Nicole was arrested." How did she know that Sam and Brad had been lovers in the past? Had Brad told her? Or had she picked up on it by watching them together? She didn't remember but was confident it was true.

"Sam showers, gets out, Nicole is here, right where we are. She shoots Sam in the knee, then she talks to her. She'll need to talk to her. To gloat. To brag. To tell Sam that she's better, that she's going to win because she's smarter than Sam, smarter than the whole DEA. She doesn't need information, because she still has someone inside. But Nicole is better than Sam, and she'll want Sam to know it. Rub salt in the wound, because Nicole likes to feel smarter than everyone else. Ha, ha, you didn't even know you had a fox in the henhouse, Sam, did you?" Lucy said, mimicking Nicole gloating.

"Sam pulled herself up, because she wanted to appear strong, but she knew as soon as she saw Nicole that she was dead. What would Sam have said or done? She might have pleaded for her life. Sam didn't want to die. She limped forward several feet—" Lucy stared at the blood behind Sam, at the distinct pools, the smears.

Nicole knew that Brad had been here. She'd been watching. Lucy would need to talk to Brad to confirm the time line. *Brad leaves, Sam makes coffee, gets in the shower, gets out,* bang! *Knee blown out. Thirty minutes, tops. Probably less.*

"Nicole could have killed Brad, but she doesn't want to yet. She wants to make him suffer, but she also considers him a worthy adversary. Worthy, but not as good as she is. When Brad gets angry and emotional, he makes mistakes. She enjoys watching Brad make mistakes."

"Brad?" Nate said.

"He was here last night."

"Did he tell you that?"

She shook her head. "I just know." Except he'd men-

tioned in passing that he'd talked to Sam after leaving
Sean and Lucy last night. He just hadn't said he'd stayed
all night.

"Brad will be pulled from the investigation. He could
be suspended."

Lucy ignored Nate. The last person she wanted to hurt
was Brad, but he had to come clean about his affair with
Sam. It established a time line, and his DNA would be all
over the place. The ERT would process every inch of Sam's
house, and if he lied he would be fired.

What did Nicole *really* want to accomplish by killing
Sam Archer? Had this always been her plan? Payback
for having her arrested? Or was it something more? Did
this vendetta go back only three months . . . or longer? Did
Nicole hate Sam, or was this murder a psychological
attack on Brad? If so, why Brad? Was this personal . . . or
professional? Did Nicole stay in town for some practical
reason before she could disappear, or was she here solely
for a personal vendetta?

Lucy shook her head. She didn't see it. Not yet. Neither
reason stood out as being right. Nicole was too smart, too
methodical, to remain in San Antonio just to seek revenge
on people she didn't like—people she thought betrayed or
hurt her, or those who destroyed her criminal enterprise.
Yet . . . there *was* something personal about this murder.
A gloating. A *you can't catch me, I'm smarter than you
all* vibe. She enjoyed it—there was no doubt in Lucy's
mind that Nicole found a thrill in killing Sam Archer—
but she didn't kill indiscriminately. There was a purpose
to Sam's murder. A reason for every crime Nicole committed.

She needed Brad's files. All of them. And every case
Nicole worked on. There was an overlap somewhere in the
past. Brad might not even know. But smart killers like
Nicole didn't wantonly kill people. They had a reason. Tom

in McAllen was killed because he found the evidence against her, and Nicole needed to use him as an example.

Go after me, I'll end you.

Yet Nicole didn't take him out personally. She would have been hard-pressed to be in McAllen late last night and here early this morning. Besides, the security was tighter closer to the border. Most likely, Nicole sent one of her minions to kill Tom. Same for Logan Dunbar, who was killed before she escaped. Those may have been simple revenge kills.

You mess with my operation, I kill you. But you're not worth my time. I have people. I have power. See? Snap my fingers and you're dead.

Sam Archer wasn't a simple revenge kill. Sam's death was a calculated move.

Elise's comments from two weeks ago came back to Lucy.

My brother and I always win.

What did that have to do with Nicole? That Nicole, too, always wins?

"She shot her in the knee and gloated," Lucy repeated, getting back into the scene in front of her. "Then stomach. Sam was on the ground, unable to move. Nicole could have left her there, to bleed to death, but that would be foolish. There's no guarantee that someone will die from a gut wound, and Nicole may have said something that she couldn't risk Sam living long enough to repeat. Because that wouldn't be in the plan. She has to keep the endgame to herself, but she had to tell *someone* because she's egotistical that way. Proud of herself. So she walked in—"

Nate put his hand on Lucy's shoulder as she was about to step into the bathroom. She shook her head, clearing her mind. She'd been in Nicole's shoes, had felt that sick pride oozing through her veins.

"She crossed the floor. Shot her in the head. Made sure Sam couldn't talk."

She couldn't tell from here how many times Sam had been shot in the head. But she knew.

"Three times. She shot her three times in the head."

Just like the drug dealer Ramos.

Ha, ha, you can't catch me.

Lucy turned to Nate. She looked into his dark eyes and was relieved that she didn't see worry or pity there.

Then she noticed Hans Vigo on the other side of the master bedroom. How long had he been there? Why hadn't she sensed him watching her?

"Nicole killed Sam Archer the exact same way she killed the drug dealer five years ago," Lucy said. "And there are going to be more deaths in her past. Exact same way. Disable, gloat, kill. She has to make sure that the people she kills know that she's smarter, *better*, than they are. That she fooled them. It's important to her to be seen as superior. To be feared and, in a sick way, admired. She's going to kill again. She's not far away, and she's not going anywhere until she's finished."

"Finish what?" Hans said.

"I don't know yet."

But they had better find out—and soon—or more people would die.

Lucy pulled Hans aside while ERT processed the scene. "I need a few minutes alone with Brad."

Hans didn't say anything at first. Lucy thought he was going to argue with her, then he asked, "Do you trust him?"

"Yes," she replied unequivocally. For a split second she thought, *Why?* Why did she trust Brad? Because he'd been a victim? Because she'd saved his life? Because he'd become a friend? Could she have been played all these months?

But she didn't pursue that thought. In her gut she trusted Brad. The same way she trusted Nate. The same way she trusted Ryan and Kenzie. Maybe it was her psychological training, or maybe it was her instincts, but if she doubted everyone she worked with, she'd never be able to work in law enforcement again.

But if he lied to her, she would have Hans take his badge. Because while there may be a legitimate reason—in Brad's head—for him to lie, she would never be able to trust him again.

Brad was squatting behind the tactical van, his back against the bumper, his head down near his knees. It couldn't be comfortable, but grief was numbing.

She stood directly in front of him. "Brad."

He looked up. His eyes were red and damp. "I want to see her."

"No," Lucy said. "Not like this."

"Damn you." But there was no venom in his voice.

"What time did you leave?" she asked.

He didn't say anything for a moment. Then, "Five forty."

"How long were you involved?"

"Since Nicole cut the plea. Sam and I watched her in the courtroom—and I was angry. She shouldn't have been allowed to make a deal. Her remorse was an act. I knew it. Sam tried to calm me down, we were drinking, and . . ." He didn't have to say anything else.

That was a little over a week ago.

"And before last week?"

"It was a long time ago. When we were working in Phoenix. She wasn't my boss then."

"Nicole knew."

Brad shrugged. "Maybe. Maybe she did. I didn't talk about it. Sam didn't talk about it. It was over long before she became my boss. I cared for her, Lucy. Sam and I—we had a history, but we were friends."

"Nicole knew," Lucy repeated. "She knew about your past relationship with Sam, and she knows you were here last night."

He slowly stood up. "How could she?"

"We'll wait for the coroner's report, but my guess is Sam was dead thirty minutes after you left."

Brad drew in a breath that sounded more like a sob.

"Why didn't she kill me, too?"

"Because she either needs you for something or wants you to suffer."

"I'm going to break her neck."

"No, you're going to do your job. And if you can't do your job, Hans is going to take your badge."

"You'd do that to me? You'd take this case away from me?" He tried to sound angry, but his voice was twisted in anguish. He stepped toward her, his hands fisted at his sides, using his height and strength to intimidate her. Maybe in the past it would have worked, but Lucy didn't flinch or step back.

"Nicole knows you, Brad. She knows that when you get emotional you make mistakes. You take risks. If you think you have any secrets from Nicole, you're wrong. What she didn't learn directly from you, she found through other means. Assume that she knows every woman you've slept with, every friend you've had and lost, every case you worked. Why was she in the DEA for fifteen years? Because it was her *life* playing both sides. She has to change gears, and that makes her mad even though she always knew this day would come."

"You don't know what the fuck you're talking about."

"You have to trust me, Brad. If you can't trust me, then I'm putting you into protective custody."

"You don't have the authority."

She raised an eyebrow and stared at him. She didn't have to say anything.

"I need air." He stepped away from her.

"I'm going to ask Ryan to take you home."

"I don't *want* to go home!"

"Take a shower, hit a wall, break a window. I don't care, but you have got to pull yourself together so you can be more help than hindrance."

"Who the hell do you think you are, telling me what to do?"

Lucy knew Nate was watching them from only a few feet away, and she felt the tension rolling off him. Nate was usually so much better at keeping his emotions in check. The last thing she needed was Nate stepping in and pushing Brad's buttons.

"You're a rookie, Kincaid. I've been a DEA agent for seventeen years. You weren't even in *high school* seventeen years ago. I know how to do the fucking job!"

"I need you to calm down," she said, her voice low but deadly serious. "I can't talk to you about Nicole until you get a grip, and when the ME arrives and takes Sam Archer's body out of that house, I don't know that I can trust you not to do something stupid."

"How dare you." But his eyes flickered to the house. "I'm not leaving." He paused. "I want to see her."

"Brad—"

"I've seen worse."

"Not someone you loved."

He turned to Lucy, surprise in his eyes. "That's the thing. I didn't love Sam. I cared for her. I was attracted to her. But maybe if I loved her like Sean loves you, I wouldn't have left this morning. I wouldn't have been worried about someone finding out we were sleeping together. I would have sensed that something was wrong and stayed. I might have been able to catch Nicole. But I let Sam kick me out, and I was okay with that. And now she's dead."

Brad took a long, deep breath, then exhaled. "I won't interfere with you. And I'm sorry for what I said."

"It's forgotten," Lucy said. She hesitated, then said quietly, "A man I had been involved with was killed. I didn't love him, but he loved me. I cared for him, like you cared for Sam. But I couldn't be for him what he wanted. And he died, partly because he loved me. The guilt wasn't something I expected, but it was there, and it ate at me for a long time. Living in the past is suicide—a slow, painful death. Don't go there. You can't change your feelings and you can't change the past.

"But I need to know everything, no matter how small, how irrelevant you think it is. Be prepared to share—no secrets. When we're done processing the scene, I need you to be in the right state of mind."

He nodded. "Can you give me a minute?"

She squeezed his forearm. "You're not in this alone."

He put his hand over hers, then sat heavily on the bumper of the truck.

Lucy walked over to where Nate and Ryan were standing next to an SAPD sedan. "I'll take him home," Ryan said. "Did you know?"

"Yes," she said. "Not because he told me, but when I walked in—I knew it was Brad who had been there. Let him stay."

"But you said—"

"He wants to see her. When the ME has her bagged, I'll walk him over."

"How are you doing, Luce? This has got to get to you."

Ryan was wrong. Right now, Lucy had no emotions. Nothing could get to her. And with Sean gone, she didn't know when she'd feel anything again.

Hans approached. "An analyst is here—Zach Charles?"

"He's one of the best tech guys we have, but he's not a field agent," Ryan said.

"He's taking Archer's computers straight to the FBI offices to determine what, if anything, was taken."

"She had a security system," Lucy said.

"The first responders said the system wasn't engaged,"

Ryan said. "The door was locked, not bolted. They kicked it in—not knowing whether she was dead or incapacitated. We have a team canvassing the neighborhood for witnesses as well as external security cameras. We might get lucky."

"We might," she said. "But Nicole doesn't care if we know the truth. She's already wanted for accessory to multiple murders. In fact, she wants us to know."

"Why?"

"To gloat. To instill fear. To prove she has the power. All of the above. Ryan—what about her phone?"

"I'll ask the ERT supervisor. Why?"

"Brad received a text message from Sam at nine this morning. She was already dead."

"You're certain she was dead by then?"

"Yes. I worked in the morgue for over a year—and based on other evidence, I'm guessing she died between six and six-thirty this morning."

"Her phone has GPS," Nate said. "All government phones can be tracked."

"I'll talk to Zach, get that going immediately," Ryan said.

Thirty minutes later the ME brought out Sam's body. Everyone stopped working and watched as the two deputy coroners pushed the gurney topped with the body bag toward the van.

"Hold up," Lucy said and walked over to the body right before it was pushed into the van. She motioned for Brad, who immediately was at her side. "Are you sure?"

He jerked his head once.

She turned to the deputy coroner. "Would you mind?"

The deputy coroner unzipped the bag only enough to reveal the victim's face. Brad stared, his body rigid. He didn't say a word. Then he turned and walked away.

Lucy looked down at Sam's body. Her head was a bloody mess, her face already bloated from the moisture in her bathroom and heat. At close inspection, she could see three points of entry on her right side. The left side of her skull wasn't even there—evidence to be collected by ERT.

"Thanks," Lucy whispered. She waited until the van drove off before she found Hans. "Hans, I need to show you something. A video that shows Nicole killing a drug dealer in the same way she killed Sam."

Ryan ran up to her, almost out of breath. "Lucy—we tracked Sam Archer's phone. It's in her house."

"Impossible," Lucy said.

"Whoever sent Brad the text message programmed it to go out at eight-fifty a.m. today. They probably accessed her calendar and saw she had the nine o'clock meeting, and wanted to buy time."

"Or mess with Brad," Lucy said.

"It's bagged as evidence. We'll know what else they got."

"Emails, addresses, phone numbers—they could have the home address of every federal agent," Lucy said.

"I'll have the director himself put out a warning," Hans said. "And Ryan—tell the ERT cyberunit that processing that phone is a priority."

CHAPTER TWENTY

Noah Armstrong was going through the box of information that Agent Logan Dunbar had sent to him prior to leaving San Antonio. It had arrived that morning, and since Noah had no leads and forensics hadn't come back with anything useful from Dunbar's townhouse, he hoped there was something here that gave him a direction.

He didn't know Dunbar well, had never worked with him except on the Reyes-Worthington investigation, but he had been a good, dedicated agent and his murder was nonsensical.

No FBI agent should be a target simply for doing their job.

There was a knock on his door and he was surprised that hours had passed since he'd sat down with the box.

"Come in," he called.

Dr. Greg van Buren, the assistant director of the FBI Laboratory Services, walked in.

"Do you have a minute, Noah?"

"Of course. Sit down." He motioned to the lone chair in his office.

Greg shut the door behind him. He was in his early fifties and had worked his way up at the lab, from lab rat to

DNA specialist to head of the DNA unit to assistant director of the lab when Rick Stockton moved from the lab to headquarters several years ago.

Greg handed Noah a folder. "I wanted to talk to you in person about Agent Dunbar's murder."

"I would have come to you."

"I have a meeting at headquarters this afternoon, and when I saw the report this morning, I wanted to share the findings in person."

That piqued Noah's interest. "Different than we thought?"

"Not the manner of death. Agent Dunbar was a healthy thirty-four-year-old with no sign of alcohol or drug abuse. There was a legal limit of alcohol in his system, likely from the two drinks he consumed on the plane for which we found receipts in his wallet. There are two important items. First is the ballistics report." He paused, nodded toward the folder. "Page four."

Noah opened the file and turned to the ballistics report. The top half of the sheet was technical comparisons; a box at the bottom listed whether the gun had been used in a commission of a crime.

"The gun that killed Agent Dunbar was used in the San Antonio shooting two weeks ago," Greg said.

"The shooting that Agent Kincaid was involved with?"

"Yes. A witness under SAPD protection was shot at outside a hospital. An SAPD detective was hit and critically injured."

"Okay," Noah said slowly, not quite sure where Greg was going with this. "Same gun. That connects Dunbar's murder to San Antonio."

"The detective was shot with two guns," Greg continued. "The initial report indicated that the witness had been the target while Agent Kincaid and Detective Mancini escorted her out. But at the request of AD Stockton, a computer analysis indicated that Agent Kincaid was the primary target. The bullet that hit her in the back—in her vest—came from the same gun that killed Agent Dunbar. I can't think this is a coincidence."

Noah didn't say anything for a long minute. He hadn't seen the analysis, and Rick hadn't told him. He'd known Lucy was there during the shooting, but had never been told she'd been targeted—or that she'd been hit.

Greg continued. "There were two shooters, two guns. Detective Mancini was hit by both shooters. Three points of entry, two serious."

"She's out of the woods, last I heard."

"Yes. I followed up with the San Antonio office before coming up here to see you. They clarified a few things from the initial report as well, which helped me put together this information."

"The shooter, unless he was a total idiot, had to have known we'd compare ballistics. That we'd make this connection. It's two federal investigations, they couldn't have even assumed local law enforcement would be slow to process evidence."

Which meant that the shooter *wanted* them to make the connection.

"The other key point is that my best ERT unit went through Agent Dunbar's town house with a fine-tooth comb. The killer was inside waiting for Agent Dunbar. No prints, but several hairs that didn't match Agent Dunbar were found on a chair in the den. We contacted the cable company and learned that a sporting event had been watched for two hours while Agent Dunbar was still on the plane."

"He knew enough to wear gloves, but may not have realized that hair sheds."

"Unfortunately, there's not enough to get a DNA sample—it was natural shedding, no bulbs attached. But the hair is like a fingerprint, so I can compare it to another sample and give you a likely match."

"So the killer arrived first—but knew that Agent Dunbar was coming home."

"That is my opinion, yes."

"Shot Dunbar with the same gun used two weeks ago in a San Antonio shooting against another federal agent. He could have driven, but Agent Dunbar didn't make his flight arrangements until Friday afternoon."

"It's possible, however unlikely, that someone could drive through from San Antonio to DC in twenty-four hours."

"Were there signs that the killer slept there? Ate there?"

"No."

Dunbar had made his flight arrangements while on a phone conversation with Noah on Friday around four in the afternoon. If the killer had known Dunbar's plans that night, he could have easily arrived on Sunday afternoon and still taken a few hours off for a nap. Still . . .

"Can you pull all travel from San Antonio, Dallas, and Houston terminating in Dulles or Reagan National from Friday evening until Sunday afternoon? And flag for individuals who checked a firearm?"

If he traveled privately, they'd never find him, but if he used a commercial airline they'd have a chance.

"Already done," Greg said. "The list is the last page of the report."

"You're good."

"My people are good. It's a long list. Three hundred and nine people traveled and checked a firearm in the forty-eight hours prior to Agent Dunbar's arrival from Texas to DC or Dulles."

It was a lot of people to sift through, but Noah would give odds that the killer flew. Airports didn't hassle people with guns if they declared them and checked them with baggage. He surmised that the killer would have taken a flight earlier than Dunbar, but the same day. He could work back from that. He had people who could split the list and give him the likeliest suspects.

"Thank you, Greg."

"There's more. Dunbar's laptop."

"Is it missing?"

"No. And it's password-protected. No one tried to break the password. However, someone copied the entire drive on Sunday night, starting at eleven thirty-six. It took about twenty minutes."

"Everything on his computer?"

"Yes. He cloned the hard drive."

"So we don't know what the killer wanted."

"I would guess that he knew he couldn't break the password, but he had to have a bit of skill to clone the hard drive—or have someone walk him through it."

"What can he do with a cloned hard drive if he doesn't have the encryption?"

"Give it to someone who has the ability to break the password or go in through a back door. Time or talent."

"I need the information from his laptop."

"I copied the hard drive to our secure server. You can access all of Agent Dunbar's data, emails, Internet searches, files, what he accessed, everything through the intranet. I gave you permission, so your login and password will get you in."

"Can the killer use the hard drive to breach our intranet?"

"No—our system doesn't allow any caching of data or passwords, though if Agent Dunbar saved any files to his laptop, those might be compromised. I have an agent dedicated to reviewing data for potential security leaks."

"What did they want so badly that they would kill for it?"

"If my people see anything, you'll be the first to know. But—to be honest—I don't think the killer knew that we'd know they copied the data."

Noah frowned. He was computer-savvy, but he didn't know what Greg was talking about.

He explained. "Dunbar's laptop was put back into its case and turned off. It appeared undisturbed. If the killer didn't care if we knew, he or she could have easily taken it or left it on the desk—just like the killer doesn't appear to care that we connected the gun to a crime in San Antonio."

"They may have known that we have GPS on all government computers."

"Plausible."

But Noah's thoughts went back to the gun used to kill Agent Dunbar. The same gun was used to shoot two law enforcement officers; more, it had been intended to kill one FBI agent and *did* kill another FBI agent. A subtle threat, but it was a threat nonetheless.

The data . . . maybe they simply wanted to know what the FBI knew about Dunbar's money-laundering investigation. Or maybe they were looking for something specific. "Thank you, Greg."

He nodded and stood. "If I can do anything, let me know."

Greg left, and Noah logged into the FBI intranet and pulled up Dunbar's cloned hard drive. This was going to take a long, long time.

But first—he needed to talk to Lucy. If the gun that had attempted to kill Lucy had been used to kill Dunbar, Noah couldn't discount that it was a deliberate threat and they planned on taking out another FBI agent.

And they very well could go after Lucy again.

Finally Tobias picked up his phone.

Nicole was furious. "Where the *hell* are you, Toby?"

"A lead."

"You idiot! Bring back my flash drive *now*."

"You're going to love me again, Nicole. I just needed to verify something, and then I'll know how to get our money back."

My money. It's MY money!

Tobias was just a front man, and if he was going to go off the rails like this when every law enforcement agency was looking for *her*, he was going to pay the price.

"What are you doing?" she asked through clenched teeth.

"I know how they took our money. The feds."

"How?"

"Just trust me for once," he said. "You always listen to Joseph, you never listen to me. I *ran* this organization while you were in prison."

"You got Elise arrested, you got your photo captured at the airport—"

"I wore a disguise. They don't have a good photo."

"It was too close, dammit! Toby. *Please*. You have to come back to base. I killed Sam Archer this morning, we need to lay low. Our people in Santiago are closing in on Kane Rogan. He'll be dead by the end of the day."

"Don't have him killed, not yet," Tobias said.

"Why?"

"Leverage."

"We don't need him as leverage. He's dangerous."

"Can't you trust me just this once?"

"Not unless you tell me what you're hiding."

"I know who stole the money."

"Who?"

"Trust me, Nicole." He hung up.

Nicole stared at the phone. Tobias had hung up on her. *How. Dare. He.*

She screamed and threw the cell phone against the wall. "I don't believe this!"

"Let me take care of him," Joseph said quietly.

Nicole was livid. She didn't know *what* to do. She paced the large room, trying to think like her cousin. Except she couldn't. Why would he do this to her? The risk he was taking . . . it was too great. He needed to tell her everything—everything he knew—so they could plan.

"Not yet," she said. "I'm going to call Uncle Jimmy."

Joseph didn't say anything. She pulled a backup phone from the drawer and turned it on. Looking at Joseph, she saw his concern. "I have to," she said. God, she sounded like a whiny child. She was reverting back twenty years to when she was scared of Uncle Jimmy and Aunt Maggie.

She was in charge now. Tobias would fuck this up if she couldn't rein him in.

"He'll never agree," Joseph said.

"I'll convince him that Tobias has fucked up. He has to know. But I can't kill Tobias without Uncle Jimmy's blessing, it'd be suicide."

Joseph took the phone from her hand. "Not if we don't pull the trigger."

"How?"

"The only reason Tobias is still alive is because you have protected him, cleaned up after him, stopped him from being the idiot we both know he is. When left to his own devices, he makes mistakes. And the one thing I know about Kane Rogan and his people? They don't play by the same rules as the feds. Let Tobias go after him."

"Do you think that's what he's doing? Trying to get Kane Rogan?"

Joseph hesitated. "Honestly, I don't know. But if this whole thing is his idea? You can be confident he'll screw it up."

She sighed and turned off the phone. "Twenty-four hours."

Joseph kissed her. "And he forgot one very important fact."

"What?"

"Lyle brought us the flash drive with all the information from Agent Dunbar's computer. But the original cloned hard drive is still with our people."

She smiled and threw her arms around Joseph. "You're brilliant. One of the many reasons I love you. Let's get it."

"You need to stay here."

"But—"

"Like you told Tobias—you killed Samantha Archer. Even if the feds don't know you pulled the trigger, everyone is looking for you. I can't risk losing you when we are so close to freedom. I'll retrieve the hard drive. I have four men on patrol. If anything happens while I'm gone, let them fight. Let them die. Take the exit route to the jeep near the dry creek bed. I've maintained the safe house outside Rock Springs. There are provisions, money, passport, and a cell phone in the jeep, plus more at the safe house."

She stared at him in awe. "You are amazing, Joseph. You always think everything through."

He caressed her cheek. "You taught me."

She shook her head, tears in her eyes. Tears because this man would do anything for her, he would die to protect her, and she loved him for it. "From the beginning, you've always been the one who thought ten steps ahead. Tobias would have screwed this up years ago if it weren't for you."

"And you." He kissed her forehead. "There was a time when Tobias did everything you said, and we succeeded. I may be able to plan for emergencies, but you had the vision from the beginning. Even Jimmy didn't have a complete plan. We're going to get through this, we'll get the money, and we'll be free to set up our own operation, under our own rules."

"We'll never be truly free from answering to Jimmy,

even if Tobias is out of the way. And what if Tobias is right about Elise? What if she does manage to get out?"

"I'm certain she will. Elise is nothing if not predictable."

Nicole laughed. Certainly he was being sarcastic.

"I'm serious," Joseph said. "What's the first thing she'll do when she gets out?"

"Make contact with Tobias."

"Exactly. And do you think that the feds are just going to let her walk?"

Her heart quickened. "She'll lead them right here."

"And hopefully, right to Tobias. But we'll be gone. Her hearing is at one p.m. tomorrow. Come hell or high water, we'll have our money and disappear, and let the feds have a standoff with Tobias and Elise. Because when it comes right down to it, without us directing traffic, those two will die in a hail of bullets they brought on themselves. They richly deserve it."

For the first time since her escape, for the first time in a long time, Nicole thought everything was going to work out just fine.

Joseph kissed her. "I won't be long, but remember what I said if our perimeter is breached. Keep your eye on the security cameras; any change, power outage, glitch, strange sounds—head to Rock Springs. Understood?"

She nodded. "But come back soon. I don't want to live without you."

The night before Nicole left for the DEA training facility at Quantico, they had a family dinner.

Uncle Jimmy stood at the head of the table at his house in Topanga Canyon. Nicole had moved from the family house as soon as she began college five years ago in order to build her cover. And she'd succeeded, in spades.

Uncle Jimmy raised a glass. It was Scotch, his pre-ferred drink, and this time he'd opened one of his special bottles, Glenlivet 21 Year Old Archive. Everyone had a glass, even those who didn't like Scotch. And while this was a family dinner, there were other people at the table. Friends, who were like family. A crime family, Nicole thought with both derision and excitement.

Because today she was the shining star. Today she'd proved that intelligence and hard work paid off.

Joseph squeezed her knee under the table. Nicole would never have been able to do this without him. In fact, she'd probably be dead.

"Nicole, you have made me proud," Jimmy said. "Your daddy and I came up with this plan years ago, but he thought your brother would be the leader. I knew, though, as soon as you walked through my door that it was you, not Chris. It was you who had the brains to see this through. Today begins a new era for the Hunt family. For years we've been relegated to working for others; today, we begin working for ourselves. In less than five years, the others will fall or work for us. What Nicole accomplished is going to make all the difference."

Uncle Jimmy raised his glass. "To Nicole."

"Nicole!" a chorus shouted from around the table. Some more enthusiastic than others.

Across from her, next to Uncle Jimmy at the head of the table, Nicole's mother slowly got to her feet. Her big stom-ach nearly knocked over her wineglass. Nicole kept her face blank, but she hated her mother and the baby she car-ried in her womb. She snuck a glance to the other end of the table, where Aunt Maggie sat smiling. Probably high as a kite. How she was willing to share her husband with her sister . . . and then not bat an eye when Tami got preg-nant? She was a forty-five-year-old flake. Uncle Jimmy was a sex addict nearing fifty. And they thought they could be parents? The kid was going to grow up a douchebag. If it grew up at all—with Jimmy's life, the kid would probably end up dead. Especially if Aunt Maggie didn't keep her happy pills locked up.

But that smile on Aunt Maggie's face wasn't all bliss. Uncle Jimmy was the face of the operation, but everyone knew—even Jimmy himself—who was the brains. Nicole supposed she'd pop a few pills if she had to share her husband with another woman.

Nicole was never getting married.

Joseph took her hand. They'd talked about this, of course. She shared everything with her lover. It had been seven years. Seven years where she'd finally had someone who was hers, all hers.

She never wanted it to end. But she didn't need a marriage certificate to prove that Joseph was hers.

"I'm so proud of you, honey," her mother said. "Your daddy would be proud of you. He died because of those people . . ." Then the tears. A flake and a wimp. Who was that baby? Her half sibling, half cousin? Just warped. Fucking warped.

Jimmy took Tami's hand. "We all know why we're here today. We all know what we need to do. For too long the Mexicans and the Koreans and the skinheads and the blacks have controlled the market. It's time for us, a real family, to be in charge. They won't know what hit them. Patience has served us well."

After dinner, Jimmy called Nicole into his office. Joseph of course came with her—she wasn't 100 percent sure she trusted Jimmy, and on the eve of her trip east to Quantico and the DEA training program, she couldn't fuck this up.

"You may have noticed Tobias wasn't at dinner tonight."

Her chest fell. "Uncle Jimmy, you have to do something about him. He's going to screw everything up!"

"I'm taking him to Mexico for a while. For his own good. I know I've failed in a small way . . . I should have found a solution for his sexual proclivities."

"You should have killed him," Joseph said.

Jimmy growled. Actually *growled* at Joseph. "Remember your place, boy."

Joseph wasn't scared of Jimmy. That worried Nicole. But Joseph wasn't stupid. He knew how to stroke her uncle's ego. "Your plan to infiltrate the DEA is fucking brilliant, but Tobias has put everyone at risk."

"He is my son," Jimmy said. "My flesh and blood. Which is far more than you."

Nicole would die if Jimmy hurt Joseph. "Uncle Jimmy, Joseph just doesn't want me or anyone else to be found out. We've painstakingly planned this, I got into the DEA! This is a long game, remember? Remember what you always taught me? That those who can see the future will win the game? Each move is a key part of the strategy, and I can't keep cleaning up Toby's messes."

At first she thought Uncle Jimmy was going to slap her, but he surprised her. "You're right, Nicole. You can't be responsible for Toby anymore. He is my son, and I will fix this. I'm taking him to my house in Mexico. Teach him control. With you in the DEA, and Joseph here to run the operation, I can take the time I couldn't before." He looked at Joseph. "I can trust you." It was a statement, but his eyes questioned.

"You know where my loyalties lie."

Jimmy looked at Nicole. "Yes, I do."

"Is there a mess to clean up?"

Jimmy nodded.

"Then I will do it. I will not risk Nicole."

"You are a good man, Joseph," Jimmy said. "And I

know, while Nicole is gone, that you'll be an example to Tobias."

Tobias would never be Joseph. He didn't have it in him. But it was clear, from Jimmy's unspoken words, that Joseph was now Tobias's keeper.

"You can't let my mom raise the kid," Nicole said, almost surprising herself.

"I won't be gone long. I'm looking forward to having a little girl around."

"It's a girl?"

"Yes."

"Keep Tobias away from her."

"He doesn't like little girls, Nicole. He's not a fucking pedophile."

Maybe not, but he was still a sick bastard.

"Actually," Jimmy said, "I think the baby will be good for Tobias. I can leverage her to keep him in line. He's very excited about being a big brother."

Big brother with a twenty-six-year age difference. Sick.

Jimmy handed Joseph an address. "Fortunately, he's gotten smarter. He picked up a prostitute this time, took her out of town."

Joseph pocketed the paper. He turned to Nicole and said, "I'll be back before you leave." He kissed her and walked out, without giving Jimmy a second look.

"You trust him," Jimmy said.

"With my life," Nicole replied.

Thirty minutes later, Nicole was cleaning up in the kitchen, worried about Joseph, anxious about reporting to Quantico tomorrow. The entire application process felt surreal. She thought for sure that someone would uncover her connection to Jimmy Hunt. But he was her aunt's husband, and she simply left her aunt off the paperwork. Small details were changed, and they had someone in the DEA to smooth things over.

So far, it had worked.

Aunt Maggie followed Nicole into the kitchen. "We're so proud of you Nicole," she said, her voice mocking.

Nicole turned to face her, keeping her expression blank. She was more scared of Maggie than Jimmy. She couldn't wait until she had the power. Then they would fear her.

"Remember, Nicole—family first. It's your job to protect Tobias. To protect all of us—including your new sister."

"Half sister," she said without thinking. She straightened her spine. She was twenty-three years old. She was about to train in the DEA. She was about to gain all the power in the family; why was she scared of this petite middle-aged woman who might weight a hundred pounds wet?

"Aunt Mags, how could you be okay with this?"

"Our plans?"

"No—with Uncle Jimmy and my mom. The baby. It's—" She bit her tongue.

"You can say it."

"It's sick."

Maggie walked over to the cabinet and took out a bottle of tequila. "I've always hated Scotch," she said. She poured a shot glass for both her and Nicole. Nicole wasn't a big drinker, but you simply did not refuse a drink from Maggie.

Maggie held up the glass, waited for Nicole to do the same. Then she said, "Family."

"Family," Nicole said and they both drained the tequila.

"Men are pliable," Aunt Mags said and put down her glass. "Make them think they have the power, make them believe it, and you can do anything you want. I like Joseph; he's a good man and he's now family. But you are the brains of your generation, just as I am the brains of

mine. Together, Nicole, we'll control the entire operation. If I didn't allow Jimmy to have his fun and games, I wouldn't have the freedom to do what needs to be done."

Nicole didn't understand what she was saying. Her expression must have conveyed that to Maggie, because her aunt continued. "It was my idea for Jimmy to take Tobias to Mexico. That gives me control over Tami and the kid. That kid is mine, not hers. I will raise her, I will train her, and she'll take after you. You'll have twenty-five years, you'll set up our organization and take it to the top. That girl will continue the legacy. We need to. It's our responsibility. Once you establish the network—I don't know how long it'll take, but this isn't a quick score. We're in this for the long haul. Once you have the network in place, you and Joseph will have your paradise, whatever it happens to be. By the time you're my age, you can retire and oversee the operation. Build the family. Build our empire. And watch it blossom."

"I know what to do." Yet Nicole couldn't imagine her aunt retiring. She liked control. It had been a while since Nicole had seen Maggie popping pills, and the woman was sharper—smarter—now. Not only were things changing, but people were changing.

"I thought for a minute that you weren't ready."

It was a veiled threat. The tone more than the words.

Nicole said, "I've been preparing for this since my dad was killed by those bastards. I am not going to fail."

CHAPTER TWENTY-ONE

"I have ten minutes, sir," Chris Rollins said over the Skype connection they'd established with him through Nate's contact at Fort Hood. Rollins was in Afghanistan and it was the middle of the night there, but he'd just gotten off duty. "Our connection isn't stable."

"Thank you for agreeing to speak with us," Hans said. Lucy and Hans were sitting in a small communications room. Zach had joined them to establish and monitor the secure Skype connection. They had good equipment on this end, but overseas it was sketchy. "I'm Assistant Director Hans Vigo with the Federal Bureau of Investigation. This is Special Agent Lucy Kincaid. Are you aware that your sister, former DEA Agent Nicole Rollins, escaped from a prison transport yesterday?"

"That's what my commanding officer told me, sir. She hasn't contacted me, and she won't."

"Did you speak with ASAC Samantha Archer three months ago, shortly after the arrest of your sister?"

"Yes, sir," Rollins replied.

"And you told her you hadn't spoken to your sister in years."

"Correct. I haven't spoken to or seen Nicole since I

enlisted in the army through the ROTC. I was eighteen, she was sixteen. We were not close growing up, and we do not speak now."

Lucy glanced at her notes. "According to Nicole's files, she asked for a transfer to Houston DEA three years ago in order to be closer to family. Specifically, you and her ailing mother."

"Agent Kincaid, my mother lives in Los Angeles. We moved to LA after my father left the service. He became an LAPD officer and was killed in the line of duty the year before I enlisted. My mother stayed because that's where her family is. Where she was born and raised."

The way he said *family* had Lucy's instincts twitching.

"And your mother didn't move to Austin when you were stationed at Fort Hood three years ago?"

"No," he said, incredulous. "I rarely speak to my mom. We don't get along."

"Is your mother dead or alive?"

"What kind of question is that?"

"Two years ago, Nicole took three weeks off to take care of her mother's estate and funeral. It was the only vacation she had taken since transferring to San Antonio."

"Agent Kincaid, I haven't seen or spoken to my mother in four or five years. If she died, no one told me."

Chris Rollins had no reason to lie, but Lucy couldn't reconcile all these falsehoods in Nicole's personnel file. "Chris, was Nicole a habitual liar while you were growing up?"

"Liar? Yeah, you could say that."

There was a lot of hostility in his voice.

"It seems we have a lot of misinformation in our file," Lucy said. "It would greatly help us if you could clear up a few things, particularly how your father's death impacted you and Nicole."

Christ stared at them, a slight delay in the video feed

freezing his disgusted expression. "Your file is a mess. I can't believe anyone let her into the DEA in the first place. I assumed all federal law enforcement agencies did extensive background checks. No one talked to me about Nicole, because I would have told them she was fucked up. Excuse me, ma'am, but it's the truth."

Lucy flipped rapidly through Nicole's file. "Sergeant Rollins, during Nicole's application process sixteen years ago, an Agent Adam Dover contacted you via phone while you were stationed in Iraq. He indicated that you had given him no reason your sister shouldn't be admitted into the DEA agent training program."

"I never spoke to any federal agent in the DEA or the FBI about my sister prior to three months ago when Agent Archer contacted me about my sister's arrest. I told her I didn't care, wasn't surprised, and I had to leave—we were in the process of breaking down camp."

"What would you have said had you been interviewed?" Hans asked.

"I would have told the truth, sir. That Nicole is ill suited for any law enforcement position because she has no respect for authority."

"Did she have a problem with your father? He was in the military and then a police officer."

"Nicole worshipped our father. I used to as well."

"Used to?"

"Until I learned that he was a bad cop. None of that will be in his file, because no one knew until he was dead. But my uncle Jimmy certainly believed it." He paused. "You don't know about Jimmy, do you?"

"No, Sergeant, we don't," Hans said.

"Jimmy Hunt. My mother's brother-in-law. Born and raised in LA. He said once, after my dad was killed, that he'd lost his best inside man. I didn't know it at the time— but I later learned that Jimmy was a narcotics dealer. My father targeted his competition and protected Jimmy's people on the street. I got out of LA as fast as I could. Army ROTC saved my life, sir."

How Hunt and John Rollins operated was almost identical to how Nicole worked both sides in the DEA.

"Can you prove any of this?" Hans asked.

"I left home twenty-two years ago and have never been back. Uncle Jimmy told me if I walked out, I was no longer part of the family. I couldn't prove anything, just talk around the dinner table. Truthfully, I didn't want to know." He paused. "Jimmy implied that if I said anything about what I thought I knew, I'd be dead. Since my dad was a corrupt cop, I figured there were others. Jimmy's charismatic, smart. I'm not surprised that Nicole fell for his line of bullshit. She has no moral code to speak of. And—" Again, he hesitated.

"Anything you can tell us will help us find her."

"I don't see how this helps, but Jimmy told us that the DEA had killed our dad. That they were so gun-happy and empowered by the war on drugs that they would kill innocent people if they could get at one of their targets. Collateral damage, he said. That was my dad. I wanted to believe it—until I found out the truth."

"There was nothing in the LAPD report on your father's death that indicated the DEA was involved in the shooting," Hans said. "It would have come out in Nicole's application process."

"I don't know what was in the report. And you know what else should have come out but didn't? Me. No one spoke to me. When I heard Nicole got into UCLA I thought that maybe she was turning her life around somehow, that she'd get out from under my uncle's thumb, but it didn't happen."

"How do you know this if you haven't spoken to her in twenty-two years?" Lucy asked.

"Fair enough. Like I said, I don't talk to my mom much, but when she calls, she blabs. Nothing incriminating, but she once said that Nicole was Jimmy's bright, shining star. I didn't ask what that meant. You should definitely look into Uncle Jimmy's record. Jimmy, not James. Jimmy Hunt. I heard on the news, or read in the paper, that he had to leave the country, he was wanted for questioning. I never talked to my mother about it—in fact, I don't think I've spoken to her since. She probably bolted with him."

Chris turned to listen to someone offscreen, then turned back to Hans and Lucy. "Agents, I really need to go. If you have more questions, contact my commanding officer."

"Thank you for your time." Hans nodded to Zach to shut down the call. "Agent Novak in LA is going to be interested in this information."

Zach said, "If you don't need me, I need to bring Juan some papers at the hospital."

Lucy reached out and touched his arm. "Is Nita okay?"

"I don't know. It was a lot worse than Juan told me this morning. They almost lost Nita and the baby. The baby is healthy, but Nita is still sick and they don't know why."

"Would Juan be up for visitors later?"

"I'll let you know."

Zach left, and Hans got on the phone. "Assistant Director Hans Vigo for Supervisory Special Agent Blair Novak."

While he waited to be connected, he said to Lucy, "What office was Dover assigned to when he allegedly interviewed Chris Rollins?"

"Los Angeles, the same office that recruited Nicole out of college."

"Your report said she moved around a lot."

"Yes. She asked for more transfers than she received, but she moved several times before landing in Houston. She didn't ask—at least not officially—to be transferred to San Antonio, but San Antonio is under Houston leadership."

"Call Noah. Tell him exactly what you told me, and then ask him to talk to Rick about any investigations into the LA or Houston DEA offices over the past fifteen years."

She was going to ask why, but Hans began talking to Agent Novak, and it was clear they had known each other for a long time.

Lucy left Hans and went to her desk. She picked up the phone, but realized she was out in the open. Anyone could listen to her call, and she remembered Kane's admonition that there was someone corrupt in her office. She didn't want to believe it was anyone on her team, but what did she really know about these people?

Zach had already left, so she went into Juan's office and closed the door. Took a deep breath, feeling out of place in her boss's office, especially without permission. But Juan had an open-door policy and she needed this conversation to be strictly confidential. Just in case. Juan's office was neat but it was obvious he'd left in the middle of work. Files were stacked on the desk, the blotter had a stack of messages, and on the short credenza behind his chair were the squad's open case files. Most information was routed through the computer system, but so much was gathered from external sources they needed to maintain paper files, which would later be digitally archived.

She picked up the phone and dialed Noah's direct line.

"Armstrong," he answered briskly.

"Noah, it's Lucy."

"I was going to call you."

"News about Agent Dunbar?"

"Not exactly. Do you have something?"

"Hans wants you to talk to Rick about past investigations into the Los Angeles or Houston DEA offices, going back fifteen years." She told him about the conversation with Chris Rollins, Agent Adam Dover's false report, and the rumor about Nicole's father possibly being a corrupt cop. "Sergeant Rollins also said he'd heard his uncle, Jimmy Hunt of Los Angeles, had fled the country to avoid arrest. Hans is working on getting information about Hunt now."

She could hear Noah writing everything down. "I'm seeing Rick in an hour, we'll talk about this. I need your help on something."

"Anything."

"Agent Dunbar's computer was cloned—his killer copied his hard drive. It was password-protected, he probably couldn't crack the code on sight, but he was able to copy all the data."

"To bring to a hacker."

"Exactly. They didn't take the laptop, and there was no sign that it was tampered with, no sign that the killer went through the house. He may not have known that there's a log generated for every action—even copying the hard drive. He must have brought his own equipment."

"What do you need me to do?"

"I have a copy of all the data on Dunbar's laptop. I'm going through the financials because I'm familiar with Dunbar's investigation, but there are hundreds of emails, memos, and reports and nothing has popped out at me as being important to Rollins or her people. Some of it is public information or soon to be made public, such as a copy of the entire report into Adeline Worthington and her real estate and money laundering partner James Everett, plus Everett's statements. Everett is already in witness protection, and nothing on Dunbar's computer relates to his whereabouts. We've contacted the other witnesses who may be in jeopardy—most of them are in DC. The marshals are taking point on protection. So far, going through these memos, there is nothing they couldn't get through a less violent approach."

"I'll take a look," she said. "I wasn't as involved in Dunbar's investigation, but I know the players."

"That's what I was hoping. There's one more thing you need to know." He paused, and Lucy sensed bad news. "The ballistics report came back—the gun that killed Agent Dunbar matches the gun used in the hospital shooting. Specifically, the gun that hit you."

Her stomach flipped. "You're sure?" Of course he was sure. "Why? It connects Dunbar to us. It proves this wasn't a random murder."

"That's what the killer wanted."

"It isn't logical."

"It is if they want to issue a direct threat to law enforcement. Specifically, a threat to you."

A chill ran through her bones. "They want us to know they can get to us. Anywhere. In the line of duty, in our own homes."

"Be extra careful, Lucy. I used to think that Sean was paranoid when it came to security, but listen to him now."

"Our house is a fortress," she said. "But—" She stopped.

"What?

"Nothing. But nothing. I'm in good hands."

"What aren't you telling me?"

She hesitated again, then said, "Sean had to go out of town."

"Sean would never leave you if your life was threatened."

"I can't go into details, but he had no choice. A friend is staying with me."

"Friend? Tell me it's one of your brother's military buddies. Because not just any friend can go up against these people. I'm not saying you're not capable, but no agent should be alone right now."

"Nate is on my squad. He graduated Quantico a year ahead of me, but he was in the army for ten years. Sean trusts him."

"Nate Dunning?"

"Why is it that everyone knows Nate Dunning but me?"

"I—okay."

"Tell me what you know. Sean instantly connected with him and when he had to leave this morning, he asked Nate to stay at the house. Even Hans knew who he was, but I didn't think much about it because Nate had gone through Quantico when Hans was there. But now I'm very curious."

"It's not my story to tell."

"Tell me," she pushed.

"I really can't. Dunning was involved in several off-book operations in Afghanistan, and I don't know the details. All I can say is that he earned the respect of people I respect. He has two Purple Hearts. Rick told me that he's up for the Congressional Medal of Honor for heroism during an ambush outside Kandahar." He paused, then said, "I'm still surprised Sean left. It must be serious."

"I don't know," she admitted.

"Is it Kane?"

She hesitated. Kane didn't like anyone knowing what he was doing or where he was. "It's complicated," she said.

"Watch yourself, Lucy. Kane Rogan is the definition of complicated."

"You never told me you knew him."

"Like you said, it's complicated." He paused. "I'm sending you log-in information to access Dunbar's files on the intranet. Let me know immediately if something jumps out at you."

Noah hung up before Lucy could ask him anything else about Kane. She sat in the silence of Juan's office and wondered why Noah had never discussed Kane with her before. Maybe he'd talked to Sean. She knew that Noah had been hostile toward Sean from the moment they met, and she thought it had something to do with Sean's brothers or RCK operations that ran afoul of one of Noah's investigations. Last year, he and Sean had worked together undercover and mended fences, but there was an underlying uneasiness when they were in the same room.

She took a deep breath. Silence. She hadn't had silence in thirty-six hours, not since Zach had come in yesterday morning, ten minutes after she arrived, and told her and Kenzie that Nicole Rollins had escaped.

Thirty-six hours working almost nonstop. Investigating. Interviews. Murder. Sam Archer was dead, Brad was losing his focus, and Kane was missing. Chaos reigned.

Exactly what Nicole wanted.

Lucy snapped her fingers. The AUSA. She needed to make sure she was on the docket to speak tomorrow at Elise Hansen's hearing. The AUSA had been working solely with Barry. He'd said he'd be back on Wednesday—but the hearing was Wednesday afternoon. It was cutting it close, especially since no one could reach him.

Again, fear clawed up her spine. Earlier, ASAC Durant had sent her a message that there was no news on Barry—he had checked into his flight from his home computer thirty minutes before he left his house. But he never boarded his plane. His car hadn't been found. He'd been missing since three thirty Friday afternoon—which meant that he was almost certainly dead.

She hoped she was wrong. She glanced at the files behind Juan's desk searching for Worthington's folder. Barry would have the AUSA contact information, but it should also be in the files on the Harper Worthington investigation. She didn't think twice about pulling the thick folder from the slot on the credenza—half of this information she and Barry had compiled anyway. Her reports, Barry's reports, memos from the AUSA on evidence—she pulled out a sticky note and wrote the name and direct phone number for the lawyer in charge of Elise Hansen's case.

And then she saw it.

She shouldn't read it. It said CONFIDENTIAL at the top. But it had her name on it, and she couldn't help herself. It was written the day she'd left for San Diego, the day before Barry's vacation started. The day before he disappeared.

> **TO: Supervisory Special Agent Juan Casilla**
> **FROM: Special Agent Barry Crawford**
> **RE: Special Agent Lucy Kincaid**
>
> *Per your request, I have evaluated and assessed Special Agent Lucy Kincaid during our investigation into the murder of Harper Worthington, CEO of Harper Worthington International. It is my opinion that Agent Kincaid should be investigated by the Office of Professional Responsibility for conduct inappropriate for a federal agent.*
>
> *I am conflicted in my recommendation, and you may want to assign another agent to evaluate Agent Kincaid, but you asked for my honest opinion.*
>
> *First, Agent Kincaid is well trained. Her instincts are sharp and she's more experienced than any rookie agent I've worked with. She's already earned the respect of local law enforcement, specifically the deputy coroner and the SAPD crime lab. In fact, she's well suited in a criminalist position and if I were going to present a positive report, Agent Kincaid should be considered for a position on our Evidence Response Team. It's clear from her background*

*that her specialty is forensics, and she proved to
have a sharp eye for forensic detail during the
investigation into Harper Worthington's murder.*

*Agent Kincaid is a diligent employee. She works
over and above the call of duty, doesn't shun
paperwork or grunt work, and puts in far more
hours than required. But she doesn't know how to
turn off the job. For example, I personally
observed her sleeping twice during the day—once
in the car while we were driving to interview a
witness, and once at her desk. Her physical
appearance indicated that she wasn't sleeping
much at night. I don't know if that was because
she was working from home or if she was simply
unable to sleep. But to be so exhausted that she
falls asleep at her desk tells me that she's unable
to discipline herself, to get proper sleep or exercise
or regular meals.*

*There is no question that Agent Kincaid is
courageous. Her actions outside the hospital likely
saved the life of Detective Tia Mancini and the
suspect, Elise Hansen, when shooters breached the
facility. And later, she risked her life to save the
Everett family. The SWAT report indicated that it
was through her actions of drawing the suspect into
their line of sight that they had a clear shot.
Yet—she clearly put herself at risk, which makes
me wonder if she's reckless. We may never know if
there was another, less risky, approach in that
situation. I would be hesitant of DEA SSA Brad
Donnelly's assessment because it is clear to me
that there is an unusual relationship between
Agent Donnelly and Agent Kincaid; therefore his
judgment may be clouded.*

As I told you previously, I am particularly

concerned about Agent Kincaid's relationship with
Sean Rogan, formerly with Rogan-Caruso-
Kincaid. Multiple times during the investigation,
Agent Kincaid gave Mr. Rogan sensitive
information about our case. While I understand
that Mr. Rogan once had high level government
clearance, he no longer is in the employ of RCK
and therefore it's questionable whether he should
be allowed access to an FBI investigation. I
requested access to Mr. Rogan's FBI file after he
came on board as a civilian consultant (to trace
the bug in Mr. Worthington's office). The request
was denied. I was informed by Assistant Director
Rick Stockton's office that the file was sealed and
if I had any questions regarding Mr. Rogan's
performance while assisting the FBI that I should
call AD Stockton directly.

As you know, this is highly unusual. I'm a
seventeen-year veteran of the Bureau and have
never come across a situation like this.

I contacted a friend of mine in the Washington,
DC, field office, a high-ranking and respected
agent who had worked with Agent Kincaid while
she was an analyst in the DC office prior to her
training. He indicated that he'd asked for her file
and was denied, and later learned that it was
sealed. This makes me question not only the
integrity of the FBI hiring process, but my ability
to trust a fellow agent.

The only information I was able to access was
her Quantico file, because you specifically gave
me access. She consistently ranked high on all
tests, graduated in the top three of her class, and is
more than qualified, intellectually and physically,
to be a federal agent. Yet she was written up by her

supervisor twice, was called before the Office of Professional Responsibility for a shooting that occurred off-campus during her free time. It was ruled justified, but the situation makes me wonder if Agent Kincaid ever takes time off—this spontaneous trip to visit her family in San Diego notwithstanding.

Perhaps, if this was all I had, I would simply report that Agent Kincaid needs to work to earn the trust of her fellow agents, because it's clear that she has a complicated background. But there were several things that happened during our investigation that make me believe that she is unfit for duty:

As I mentioned earlier, falling asleep while on duty.

Agent Kincaid resented following my orders while we were at the crime scene. She breached protocol by entering the crime scene. Though she was with the deputy coroner at the time, protocol states that if the scene is secure, we wait for the crime scene investigators.

While interviewing a known prostitute, Mona Hill, Agent Kincaid had a moment of panic over what I believe was nothing of import. Then she denied that anything happened when I questioned her.

While interviewing James Everett over his hiring an underage prostitute, later identified as Elise Hansen, Agent Kincaid spoke out of turn and jeopardized the investigation by pushing Everett far harder than was necessary to learn information we already had. It showed that she has a vendetta against those who commit sex crimes, and while her feelings may have been justified knowing the circumstances of the situation, she was unable to control her emotions or opinions.

She shared confidential information with her
live-in boyfriend, Mr. Sean Rogan.

She shared confidential information with a third
party, Kane Rogan, older brother to Sean Rogan
and part owner of the controversial security and
protection company Rogan-Caruso-Kincaid.

She shared confidential information with DEA
Agent Brad Donnelly without getting prior
approval.

She interviewed suspect Elise Hansen without
permission of the lead agent, the AUSA, or
yourself, and then she neglected to file a report of
the conversation.

It's this last point that is the most serious. After
talking at length with AUSA Christine Fallow
about the evidence we have to prosecute Elise
Hansen as an accessory to murder, kidnapping,
escaping custody, etc., it's clear that our evidence
is circumstantial or could be pled down to a
misdemeanor, and any deviation from protocol
will give Hansen's attorney more ammunition
against us. Fallow is livid, and justifiably so. I
later learned that Sean Rogan was with Agents
Quiroz and Dunning when they apprehended Elise
Hansen at the residence of Mona Hill. That
information was not in Quiroz or Dunning's
report, and later they said it was because
Mr. Rogan stayed in the vehicle and they had no
choice because he was tracking Hansen's cell
phone. If the defense gets hold of this information,
they may be able to toss any case out on a
technicality. The problem arises in that Rogan was
made an official consultant when we investigated
the bug in Worthington's office, so the defense
could argue that he was acting on the FBI's

*authority and therefore it was an illegal phone tap.
The semantics that it wasn't a "phone tap" but
that Rogan hacked into her phone to track her
GPS is going to be lost on the court in light of the
other circumstantial information.*

*I met with Agent Dunbar after the murder of
Adeline Worthington. It was clear he was angry—
he told me that Mr. Rogan had hacked into James
Everett's online banking and diverted millions of
dollars into a federal asset forfeiture account,
ostensibly with permission from the FBI. Dunbar
claimed that he complained about it—because no
one had asked for his approval, and no one
cleared the operation with me, either. But he was
told to stand down. The approval of the
operation came not from national headquarters,
but from the Sacramento FBI office—the same
office where Mr. Rogan's sister-in-law, SSA Nora
English, works. AD Stockton told Dunbar he
would discuss the operation when he's debriefed
next week, but we are both angry that we were
kept out of the loop when we are the lead
investigators in these cases.*

*I think you knew about Agent Kincaid's
background before she came to San Antonio, but
believed that she would be an asset. But I also think
you asked me to evaluate her because you are
questioning your own judgment to be impartial.*

*I am sincerely torn in my report, which is why I
delayed sending this to you. I will be back
Wednesday morning, and we can discuss this
further if you would like. I decided not to copy in
ASAC Durant. You asked me to unofficially assess
Agent Kincaid, so this report is unofficial.
However, I cannot work with an agent I don't*

trust. Barring a glaring crime, I don't believe that Agent Kincaid will be fired. She has friends in high places—based on what Agent Dunbar told me, AD Stockton is not her only advocate. And while she may be transferred when her two-year rookie probation is complete, that is still eighteen months away. Therefore, I respectfully request a transfer to another office. It's within your authority to assign me to any of the resident agencies under the SA-FBI umbrella, which would be my preference, but I would also accept assignment to another office in Texas. I would like to remain close to my brother and his family, who live in Austin. As family is as important to you as it is to me, I hope you can make that happen.

*   *   *

Sean and Blitz landed Sean's Cessna near where Kane's plane was hidden fifteen minutes before noon. Kane's plane was still there, and there was no sign that he'd returned.

Blitz took care of securing the aircraft while Sean booted up his computer and ran his custom-built GPS program. He could see where Kane had been every twelve hours since Sean reprogrammed his watch. He moved around often, rarely staying in the same place more than a day. Colorado, a lot of time in Texas—San Antonio, McAllen, Hidalgo, Dallas, Corpus Christi, all in the last two weeks. He'd also spent a substantial amount of time in the middle of nowhere in Mexico, and two days in Juarez before he arrived in Santiago.

But the trip that surprised him was that he'd been in Washington, DC, at midnight on Friday. Previously, he'd been in Dallas, and at noon the following day he was in Juarez.

Sean was certainly going to ask him about it. Neither he nor Kane was going to like the conversation. Kane was going to be livid that Sean had hacked his watch. Sean was angry because Kane had promised to keep him in the loop about anything related to Tobias.

At midnight, Kane had been within a hundred yards of the hotel where Siobhan had been staying—after Blitz had already taken her back to Hidalgo. Recon? Interviewing witnesses? Tracking someone? Sean didn't see Kane getting a room at any hotel, but there were several homes and businesses in the area.

Santiago wasn't as depressed as many Mexican towns. It wasn't large and dense like Saltillo, an hour away, and because of its location in a valley in the middle of the Monterrey mountain range, there was viable farmland here and northeast. But it could be just as dangerous as any other town in Mexico. The cartels had their fingers everywhere, and Vasco Trejo, the man who'd used Michael and the boys to cart drugs into the States, had lived in a compound only an hour from here, outside Monterrey.

"Anything?" Blitz asked a minute later.

"I'm downloading the data."

Blitz paced, continuing to scan the area. Sean was used to soldiers like Blitz. He was restless, which was probably one reason he worked with Kane. Some soldiers didn't integrate well into civilian life, and if they didn't have severe PTSD or drug problems, Kane often brought them into RCK. Duke once said that Kane wanted to save every soldier and RCK would go bankrupt if they kept hiring. At any given time they had two dozen contracted soldiers. They were paid a monthly stipend and then a bonus for every job they were assigned. The stipend would keep them housed and fed, and most had other jobs or drew a pension from the government. Blitz had been in the marines for twenty years before joining Kane five years ago. He was the oldest of the group, but the most experienced and disciplined. Kane trusted all his men, but Ranger—who originally came from Jack's unit—and Blitz were his most trusted.

"Bingo," Sean said. He zoomed in and got the exact location where Kane was now. He was an hour southeast, halfway between Linares and Galeana.

Blitz looked over his shoulder. "Well, fuck. Get in the plane. He's going to get himself killed."

Sean packed up his equipment. "Where is he? It looks like an unpopulated mountainside. A good place to lay low."

"That whole area is controlled by Felipe Juarez. He runs a small but violent gang. And he swore to Kane that if he ever saw him again, he'd get a bullet in the head."

"Kane doesn't run from bullies."

"No, but he also doesn't go into their territory alone."

"Could Juarez be working with Tobias?"

"If Tobias put a bounty on Kane like we think, then yes. Juarez isn't a drug lord. He works primarily kidnappings for hire. I'll bet my pension that he was behind Siobhan's kidnapping. He would know that Kane helps the Sisters of Mercy. He's not an idiot, and this isn't going to be easy." Blitz glanced at Sean as Sean navigated the short, rough runway and flew east. "You're stubborn like your brother, but you have to promise me, Little Rogan, do exactly what I say or none of us will get out of this alive."

"On one condition."

Blitz glared at him.

"Never call me Little Rogan again."

CHAPTER TWENTY-TWO

Lucy sat at her desk and scanned the files from Logan Dunbar's laptop. But she wasn't really seeing anything. She was heartbroken.

It was her own fault. She should never have read that memo.

That knowledge didn't diminish how she felt that Juan had asked Barry to evaluate her. Rookies were constantly being evaluated, but this was beyond routine. Worse, she'd thought she and Barry had come to an understanding, that they'd worked well together, but she must have missed his animosity.

And she'd *told* him she planned to talk to Elise Hansen. Hadn't she? Lucy rubbed her eyes and thought about what she'd done and said two weeks ago. She hadn't made an official request through Barry, but she didn't think that she'd had to since she was one of the agents of record. She'd called him the night before—she remembered it distinctly. She'd asked if he wanted to go with her. He'd said no, he didn't see the point.

Brad had gone with her instead.

But that whole week was a blur.

She needed fresh air. She needed to get out of this office.

Barry could have forgotten their conversation. Or maybe she didn't remember it the same way. Maybe when he said he didn't see the point, he hadn't expected her to follow through.

"Lucy," Hans said as he approached her desk. "Did you talk to Noah?"

She hesitated. Had that been only twenty minutes ago? It seemed like hours had passed.

"Yes. He said he's meeting with Rick Stockton shortly, and he'll find out what we need. I'm going over Logan Dunbar's files. Noah said FBI forensics determined that the killer cloned his hard drive. It was password-protected, but we have to assume that they can eventually break the code. He asked if I'd go through the information, see if anything pops out that is worth killing for."

"Is there?"

"There's a lot here. Noah said he's taking care of the financial documents that related to the money laundering and political corruption. Most of what I have here are memos to Noah and Rick Stockton about the day-to-day operations of Adeline's campaign, donor information, employee information." She hesitated. On a hunch she searched the data for Joseph Contreras. It took the computer a minute before popping out a list of documents with his name.

"Is that the assistant who may have killed the Congresswoman?" Hans pulled over a chair and sat. Lucy was surprised that it was quiet in the office; no one else in her squad was in the bullpen. She shouldn't be surprised; it was nearly six in the evening.

"We don't know anything about him. He doesn't have an FBI file, his prints aren't in the system. His Social and driver's license were legitimate, but he has a very small digital footprint. We know that his Social was issued in California."

She clicked on the file. It was a list of all Adeline Reyes-Worthington's campaign staff. Joseph Contreras had been paid out of the campaign, not a personal account. His salary was close to six figures, which seemed high for a personal assistant. His address was listed as the same as the Worthington's. Where had he lived before then?

"Kane said Contreras may have taken the hit out on him," Lucy said. "Which confirms he works for Tobias."

She quickly sent Noah an email about Contreras. After he disappeared, an arrest warrant had been issued, but there'd been no sign of him.

"So far, I haven't found any employment information prior to the Congresswoman that might give us his background," Lucy said.

She wanted to talk to Hans about the memo, but it wouldn't do her any good. He would either try to make her feel better, or remind her that the path she'd chosen wasn't going to be easy. Instead she said, "Elise Hansen's hearing is tomorrow afternoon. Last week I was told to expect to testify, but I haven't heard from the AUSA. After this morning, I'm concerned. With Barry missing . . ."

"You think he's dead," Hans said.

"Don't you? He didn't get on his plane, his car hasn't been located, no one has seen or heard from him since Friday afternoon."

Hans closed his eyes. "Yes, I think he's dead."

Her heart tightened as tears burned behind her eyes. Her first thought was about how she could redeem herself if Barry had been killed. The memo . . . she couldn't refute anything, not if Barry wasn't there to discuss it.

He would rather have been transferred than work with you.

"Lucy," Hans said, "Durant has assigned two agents

full-time to track down Agent Crawford. There's nothing more you can do."

Hans was right, but that didn't make her feel better.

Hans continued. "Dr. Oakley is wrong about Elise Hansen. I've already made a call to the AUSA in the hope that she can convince the judge to hold Elise for another seventy-two hours for a second psychiatric evaluation. Considering that Hansen is now connected—through her affiliation with Tobias—to an escaped felon who killed or had killed eight law enforcement officers, I think we have a good case."

"But there's no hard evidence that Tobias is connected to Nicole. I'm getting a very bad feeling about what's going to happen in court tomorrow. Elise will disappear if she walks."

"You're not in this alone. The FBI, the DEA, the SAPD, the US Marshals, even the Texas Rangers, are actively involved. Rollins is going to have to move at some point."

"Yet she killed Sam Archer this morning." She pulled up the video of Nicole killing the drug dealer. "I'd wanted to show you this earlier, but then we had the opportunity to talk to Chris Rollins."

Lucy watched the video with Hans as he studied it closely. Lucy said, "Forensically, Sam died the same way. Knee. Stomach. Head. What did your contact in LA say?"

"Agent Novak is one of the best I've worked with. She's going to dig around. She pulled Tamara Rollins's criminal record. Minor stuff, shortly after her husband was killed. Two drunk driving arrests and one disorderly conduct for vandalism. She did community service for the arrests, time served, and paid a fine and reparation for the other."

"And Jimmy Hunt?"

Hans nodded. "She thinks the Jimmy Hunt that Lieutenant Rollins referred to might be a known drug runner from Los Angeles. It's a common name, so she's going to confirm and get back to me. But if it's the same Jimmy Hunt, he's a wanted fugitive. I asked that Blair not go through the DEA right now. Not until we know more about Nicole's operation. Adam Dover is still an agent—he transferred from Los Angeles to the DEA office in Mexico City several years ago."

"How do we talk to him?"

"I passed the information up the chain of command. It's potentially sensitive. First, we're relying solely on Chris Rollins's statement. Verifying that he never talked to Dover fifteen years ago? That's going to be difficult. These types of background checks aren't recorded. There might be phone records, but that's going to be difficult to trace back fifteen years—possible, but we're not going to get them overnight. I suspect the DOJ will open an investigation before calling Agent Dover out on one thing from fifteen years ago. But—that said—I suspect he'll be cut off from sensitive information or put on an assignment that will keep him occupied until the DOJ can build a case against him."

"If Chris Rollins was telling the truth, that means I'm right: Nicole has been a double agent since the beginning. How does she get away with this for fifteen years?" It was a hypothetical question. She didn't think they'd find the answers until they talked to Nicole.

"Adeline Reyes-Worthington got away with money laundering and land schemes for six years before she even showed up on the FBI's radar. Patience, understanding the system, knowing how far to push and when to hold back—smart criminals without a conscience, without remorse, can fly under the radar for a long time. I suspect Rollins moved offices often in order to avoid anyone looking at her too closely."

"Until San Antonio. There's something here."

"It's a border jurisdiction. Or perhaps this was where she met Tobias and how she expanded."

"Except this was her goal. Her endgame. There's something more about San Antonio." She stared at the fuzzy image of Nicole on the video.

What's here for you? Why is San Antonio important?

Lucy said, "Kane thinks there's a mole in the FBI."

Hans cleared his throat. She put a hand to her mouth and glanced around. They were still alone. But this wasn't a subject they should talk about here.

"Do we have all personnel records for the DEA and FBI?" she asked.

"What are you thinking?"

She kept her voice low. "First, whoever Nicole has on the inside has access. But the DEA has been completely decimated since Operation Heatwave. Two out on long-term disability, then three killed in the last two days. Four, including Sam. Could one of those agents have been the corrupt agent? Tobias cleans house—that's what Kane has been saying from the beginning, and the slaughter of the Sanchez gang two weeks ago proves that. What if Nicole had the two agents killed during the escape because one or both were part of the plan and may have had information she couldn't risk getting out? They knew the route when few people did."

Hans stood. "We need to go someplace private."

"The squad is clean—they've been sweeping for bugs daily, adding layers on computer security."

Hans motioned for her to follow him into Juan's office. Reluctantly, Lucy followed. She stared at the file folder that held the memo she couldn't get out of her mind.

She had to put it aside. She couldn't keep second-guessing herself. She'd known when she went to Mexico with Kane to rescue Brad and the boys that she could lose her job. She'd done the right thing, but just because something is right doesn't make it legal. She was a sworn federal agent and had to follow the rules.

Yet it was more than that. She didn't like how Barry saw her, and that impacted how she viewed herself. She'd walked a fine line between what was protocol and what was not; she had shared information that maybe she shouldn't have shared with Sean and Kane. That wasn't the issue.

The real issue was whether her actions, such as talking to Elise Hansen after her arrest, would result in their case being tossed by the court. She didn't think so—and she wanted desperately to testify. Yet if she went under oath, she could be asked anything. That terrified her deep down—there were some things she didn't want to talk about.

"Close the door," Hans said. He settled himself into Juan's chair and rubbed his knee.

She sat across from him. "Are you okay?"

"Sore. I'm lucky I passed the physical to be cleared for duty. That had been a good day. Today isn't. I think it's the humidity. This spring has been mild in DC and that helped." Hans put his hands on the desk and stared at Lucy. "I'm here not solely because of the escape."

Her stomach dropped. Juan forwarded Barry's memo. Hans was going to ask her to resign. Or reassign her. Or . . .

"As you mentioned, there's a mole in the San Antonio FBI."

"When Tobias landed on Kane's radar, he suspected that Nicole wasn't the only corrupt agent. Do you know who it is?"

"I hadn't wanted to bring you into this," Hans said. "Noah and I don't disagree often—but this time, we did. He thought you would be in a unique position to investigate."

"A spy." She didn't mean to spit out the word, but that's how it sounded.

"I knew you would do it, but you wouldn't like it."

"It would be difficult to look at the people I like and trust and think that one of them is sharing information with a killer. When they find out I was the spy . . . they'd never trust me again." But she averted her eyes. Barry didn't trust her. Juan no longer trusted her—not after she'd violated the law and FBI protocols by going to Mexico on an unsanctioned op.

Doing the wrong thing for the right reasons.

Except she didn't think it had been wrong. It *had* been the right thing to do because Brad had been tortured and would have been killed. Rules sometimes got in the way of justice, and she was willing to risk her job when necessary.

"There are only five people—now six, with you—who know that the Bureau is investigating the San Antonio office. Myself, Rick Stockton, Rick's admin, Noah, and the FBI director himself.

"The DEA is investigating their own—sworn agents and civilian staff—and are coordinating with Rick at a high level," Hans continued. "And yes, they are looking into the two agents who were killed yesterday morning. Your theory makes sense, even more sense now that I've read all the files on Tobias. I wasn't going to tell you, but in light of Barry Crawford going missing, I feel he could be the one."

"No," she said automatically.

"His record is outstanding, but there's no sign of foul play at his house, he didn't take the vacation he was supposed to take, and no one can reach him." Hans frowned. "I can't help but put him at the top of the list."

"I worked with him. He's as by-the-book as you can get." Her heart skipped a beat. If Barry was corrupt, was that memo he gave to Juan his way of trying to take her down? Or his way of getting out of the office before he was caught? Except . . . she didn't see him as a traitor. He was smart, professional, almost too professional. "He has family. He's a seventeen-year veteran." *Nicole was a fifteen-year veteran.*

"I have no evidence pointing to anyone specifically. Is there anything that Agent Crawford knows that isn't in his reports?"

Lucy nearly froze. Barry knew a lot about *her.* And Sean. And Logan Dunbar . . .

"Once we closed the investigation into Harper Worthington's murder, Barry took over working with the AUSA and Agent Dunbar on the political corruption cases." She wondered if that's why he'd lied in the memo to Juan that she hadn't told him she was going to talk to Elise. Was he setting Elise up to be released on a technicality? But how could she say anything to Hans about it when she had read a confidential memo she wasn't supposed to see?

"And," she continued, "he would know about procedures and how we operate, who does what, strengths and weaknesses of the squad. But"—she shook her head—"I don't see Barry playing both sides. He's a good agent. Methodical, focused. I'm more concerned about his safety now that he's missing, not that he's working for Tobias."

"I don't have specific information telling me that the leak is Agent Crawford, but he's been missing since Friday evening and that was nearly three days before Rollins escaped. We can't discount that he might be involved."

"Or he's dead," she said. "Agent Dunbar was killed Sunday night, before Rollins escaped."

"And how did they know that Dunbar was going home?" Hans said quietly. "*Someone* told them. The killer was waiting for Dunbar, so he knew where he lived. He knew when he would be home. He beat him to DC. He cloned his hard drive, so there is specific information Dunbar had that they wanted . . . information that they didn't want *us* to know they wanted. Otherwise they would have taken his laptop or removed the hard drive."

Lucy felt sick to her stomach.

"Think about it, all right? If there is anything that you can think of that might lend credence to the theory."

"There's nothing," she said quietly. "But I'll go through everything I have." She paused. "Barry had his vacation planned for months and he'd be back in time, which was why I wasn't needed at the hearing. I don't understand why—I talked to her more than anyone—but I suppose her reaction this morning was an indicator of how she operates. It could be that the AUSA thought I would do more harm than good."

"I'm still trying to get in to talk to the AUSA before the hearing, but she hasn't returned my calls."

Lucy had to give something to Hans—without revealing that she'd read the letter. "It could be," she said, "that Barry and I didn't see eye-to-eye on some things." She rubbed her eyes. "I don't lie well."

"That's the reason I didn't want you going undercover on your squad."

She opened her mouth, surprised, then closed it. "I thought Barry and I worked fine together, but it was clear we had different approaches to our jobs. He called to check up on me, find out why my file was sealed. Agent Dunbar made a comment that led Barry to discover my personal relationship with Rick, and I think that's why he thought I overstepped when I didn't. If I had thought I'd done anything that would jeopardize this case, I would have said something—to Barry or Juan."

"Yet he pushed you out of the follow-up investigation on Elise?"

"I didn't know it at the time, but he didn't like that I went to interview her after the fact. It wasn't an official interview. I needed to understand her."

"Or he didn't like you attempting to gain information that could damage Hansen or Tobias."

She shook her head. "He's not a bad agent. Hans—I trust your judgment, but unless you have evidence that Barry is corrupt, I don't believe it."

Maybe you shouldn't be so emphatic. He wrote that letter against you. He told Juan you hadn't told him about talking to Elise, when you had. It could be a misunderstanding . . . but what if it's not?

"Fact: When you were shot, Crawford was not in the line of fire. Fact: When you and Donnelly went to the Everett house to check on the status of the family, Crawford stayed back and you became a hostage. Fact: Crawford didn't include you in the last two weeks of conversations with the AUSA so you don't know what's happening with Elise Hansen."

"None of that is conclusive."

"No, but it's suspicious now that he's missing."

She couldn't ignore Hans's instincts. All she could add was, "Hans, I worked with him. Not once did I suspect that he was working for the cartels."

Hans nodded. "You have good instincts, Lucy, and I hope you're right. Except if the mole isn't Barry, that means it's someone else—and we have no idea who."

Her phone vibrated and she looked at it. A text message from Ryan popped up. *Luce, where are you? Come to the conference room ASAP. Brad and I figured something out about the drug dealer Rollins killed five years ago.*

Lucy sat in the conference room with Hans, Ryan, Brad, Nate, and ASAC Abigail Durant. Lucy tried to catch a word with Brad, to see how he was doing after this morning, but he was focused on whatever he and Ryan had uncovered.

Ryan held a sheath of notes in his left hand while he wrote the name RAMON RAMOS at the top of the white board.

"Ramos is the guy Rollins killed on the video Kane Rogan's team found at Vasco Trejo's compound three months ago," Ryan began. "I vaguely remembered the case—but it was local, not federal. Two weeks ago, there was a hit on Trejo's men—Donnelly and I were part of the joint task force with SAPD and ATF. We believe that Tobias was behind the hit. The same hit that resulted in the bomb being placed in the DEA evidence locker Trojan Horse style. It's clear from Donnelly's investigation that Tobias had two goals. The first was to plant the bomb—"

Donnelly interrupted. "Because of the quantity—over twenty pounds of heroin—it was taken to the storage locker. Nicole would know we'd be in no rush to test it because there was no pending court case or even a suspect in custody."

No law enforcement agency had the time or resources to immediately process every piece of evidence that came into their possession. Most agencies prioritized evidence based on whether there was a suspect in custody, when the court hearing was set, and if there would be a trial.

Ryan nodded. "The second reason for the hit was to kill off anyone with a connection to Trejo or Sanchez. Sanchez was a midlevel San Antonio dealer who worked directly for Trejo. Trejo, also known as 'the general' though he has no known military service, used boys from foster care as mules for his drug operation. As we put together the operation, we recognized that Sanchez was the stateside boss, and Trejo was the Mexican boss."

"Agent Quiroz," Abigail said with a quick glance at her watch, "how does this relate to Ramos?"

"Lucy pointed out yesterday that Nicole was assigned to the Los Angeles office at the time she was caught on tape killing Ramos. She asked what his murder had changed; I didn't know, so I called a buddy of mine who's a retired narcotics detective from SAPD. My buddy said that Ramos worked as a courier for the Zaragosa group working the triangle—San Antonio, Houston, Dallas. A small-time transport gang moving drugs and shit for whoever paid them. The theory at the time was that Ramos was skimming from Zaragosa, so they took him out. Ramos was slimy. But my contact said something else changed after his murder. The Zaragosa group merged with Sanchez's group, effectively creating a larger network and a more stable supply chain from the border, through the triangle and beyond—into Louisiana and the Southeast."

As he spoke, Ryan drew the connections on the board.

"And why would taking out one person result in such a powerful merger?" Abigail asked.

Brad spoke. "Ramos was an informant. SAPD didn't know that, because Ramos worked with an undercover DEA agent. The DEA knew he was a scumbag but let him operate to catch the bigger fish. Right before he was killed, he fingered a man by the name of Garcia as being the new big man in town, so to speak. Garcia went down, and is currently serving twenty to life for manslaughter, drug trafficking, and conspiracy to kill a federal agent. Ryan and I think that Ramos's murder closed off all leaks to the DEA, and enabled the merger between Zaragosa and Sanchez to go through."

"Garcia," Lucy said and glanced at Brad.

"Yes, it was Pedro Garcia," Brad confirmed. "The same

Garcia who used his boys to set up the bus to be hijacked. I've already contacted the Marshals and they're preparing to transport him to an undisclosed prison and we hope to interrogate him soon."

"But Nicole wasn't in the San Antonio or Houston DEA at the time," Lucy said. "How would she know or care?"

Brad shrugged. "She killed him and things changed. The DEA thought they had a major victory, but realized a year later that a new, more dangerous machine had been created. It's one of the reasons they expanded the San Antonio office, put Sam in charge, and shortly thereafter I transferred here from Phoenix."

Ryan continued to write on the board. "Zaragosa is connected to Sanchez. Sanchez is connected to Trejo, and Trejo is connected to Tobias. However, according to information that Kane Rogan gave Brad two weeks ago, the Zaragosa group has always been run by Tobias." He connected the dots, which ended up making a circle.

Brad nodded. "I think what started five years ago, and again two weeks ago, was not just to solidify power, but to show force. To tell anyone thinking about taking over Tobias's pipeline from Mexico into the States that they'd better not think about it at all. Rogan's rescue operation south of the border severely damaged Tobias among the key players. By taking out the rest of the Trejo/Sanchez gang and firmly casting blame on them for the entire situation, they also showed force by taking out the DEA evidence warehouse."

"Where does Rollins fit in?" Abigail studied the white board with interest.

"The enforcer?" Ryan suggested.

Hans cleared his throat. "If Nicole Rollins has been working for the cartels since before she joined the DEA, she's more than an enforcer. She's a leader, and Tobias or Joseph Contreras execute her orders. I have an agent in Los

Angeles looking at her family and associates going back to her childhood. We know that her father may have been a bad cop. Her uncle is Jimmy Hunt—and if he is who we believe he is, he fled the country to avoid prosecution on a multitude of charges five years ago."

"Five years," Lucy said. "The same time Rollins came to San Antonio to kill Ramos."

"Brad," Hans asked, "is there any way to talk to Ramos's handler?"

Brad shook his head. "He was killed in a car accident three years ago."

The room fell silent.

No one had to say it was no accident. Or acknowledge that Nicole transferred to Texas at the same time.

Zach Charles rushed into the conference room. "The marshals located one of the shooters from yesterday. He's taken hostages at a bar southeast of Mission. They request assistance."

CHAPTER TWENTY-THREE

The sun hung low in the west by the time Kenzie Malone pulled into the economy parking lot of the small San Antonio International Airport. Small for her, at any rate, because she'd grown up in LA and flew out of the cumbersome and miserable LAX. They always seemed to be in the middle of construction. One perk of having seniority over Emilio was that she could pull rank and drive. She showed her badge to the sheriff's deputy who had called in the sighting of Agent Crawford's car.

Three Bexar County Sheriff patrols were parked near Barry's gold Dodge Charger. She recognized it immediately. She remembered when he'd bought it last fall. He'd had a beat-up Mustang for years and needed something more reliable. Ever practical, he waited until the new models had been released, and bought a year-old but new vehicle.

She didn't need to approach the car to know there was a dead body inside. If she couldn't tell by the smell of decomposition, the hundreds of flies circling the car did the trick.

"Shit," she said. "No one could tell there was a body in there?" She glanced around. They were on the edge of the lot, with cars parked in every third slot. She liked to park in the same place because she didn't have to search for a spot and never forgot where she parked.

"According to security," the deputy said, "earlier today a passenger notified the shuttle driver that there was a foul smell coming from this vehicle, but the driver admitted he forgot until the end of his shift. As soon as he saw the flies, he alerted security."

Julie Peters, the deputy coroner, was already on site. "I waited until you arrived, but we're all ready to open the vehicle."

"I can't believe no one noticed the flies and smell before now," Kenzie said.

Julie shrugged. "I've seen worse. People don't usually think *dead body* when they see flies. They think *rotten food*. Or they're just shitheads who don't give a damn about anyone but themselves." She walked toward the coroner's van.

Julie was difficult to read. She oozed both confidence and disdain, an odd combination. She didn't seem to have many friends, though Lucy had gotten really chummy with her. Kenzie had the distinct impression that Julie hadn't liked being asked to wait.

Julie and her assistant had on full gowns and gloves that seemed longer and thicker than the typical gloves they wore when processing a crime scene. They also put on safety goggles before breaking the lock to get into the trunk.

A powerful stench rolled out of the car that even Kenzie and Emilio, who stood a good forty feet away, could smell. She turned her head and gagged, her eyes watering.

Emilio cringed, but had more control. He'd been a paramedic for ten years before joining the FBI. And while Kenzie wasn't squeamish, she'd never gotten used to seeing a dead body. Or maybe it was the smell.

"Barry," she said.

Emilio didn't say anything.

"What are you thinking?" she said. "It has to be him. It's his car. He didn't get on a plane—any plane—this weekend."

"I don't know what to think, to be honest," Emilio said.

Kenzie walked as close as she dared. "Julie—can you ID him?"

Julie turned to Kenzie. Her mouth was a grim line, and her eyes looked bigger behind the goggles. She snapped, "A body has been in the trunk of a car for God knows how long in the middle of hot and humid Texas and you think I can take one look and ID him? I can't even tell if it's a man or a woman yet. All I see is chunky soup wrapped in clear plastic."

Bile rose in the back of her throat and she turned away. She'd never eat soup again.

Emilio squeezed her arm and steered her away from the car. "Who else would it be, Kenzie?"

She just shook her head. If she talked she would puke.

Her cell phone rang and she pulled it out. Eric. Dammit, she'd forgotten to tell him she'd be late. She stepped a couple feet away from Emilio—and farther from the car.

"Hey," she said.

"What's wrong?"

"Dead body. It's a bad one."

"I'm sorry."

"I want to see you—especially tonight. But I might be late. It's already eight o'clock, I don't know when I'll be done here, and I'll need to go home and shower."

"You can always shower at my place, babe."

Warmth rushed through her remembering the last night they'd spent together. Sunday . . . was it really only two nights ago? It seemed like it had been forever.

"But I don't have clothes at your place, *babe*." The nickname wasn't her favorite, but it had become something of a joke between them.

"Hmm, didn't we exchange keys a while back?"

"Yes, I believe we did."

"I get off duty in thirty minutes. I'll swing by the store and cook up a home-cooked meal at your place."

"You cook?"

"Not well, but I can make a few things."

"Deal. I'll text you when I have an ETA, but it won't be before ten."

"I know how it is, Kenzie. I'll see you when I see you."

She hung up and took ten seconds to enjoy falling in love. It had been a long, long time since she'd felt this way about a guy.

Emilio cleared his throat and she turned around.

Julie and her assistant had a biohazard body bag on a gurney. They were lifting what looked like a clear bag of thick bone soup from the trunk right onto the covered gurney. The plastic—thick, clear plastic that painters used—was wrapped multiple times around the body and duct-taped. Through a small hole, fluid started running out. Julie swore and quickly maneuvered the body into the body bag and zipped it up.

Emilio walked over to Julie. Kenzie followed.

"Is there anything left to make a tentative ID? Clothing? Jewelry?" Emilio asked.

"Based on the cranium, I'm comfortable saying your victim is an adult male," Julie said.

Kenzie said, "Barry wore a class ring on his right ring finger. College, I think."

"You're welcome to inspect the body, but I'd suggest we do it at the morgue."

"We'll follow," Kenzie said.

"You planning on staying with me all night? Because I'm telling you right now, I'm not doing anything other than processing and weighing the body tonight. Autopsy will be first thing in the morning. Seven a.m."

"We need an ID," Kenzie pushed. "This car belongs to an FBI agent."

Julie nodded. "I heard. I'm sorry. I can't tell you for certain that this is Barry. I know him and it sucks that this corpse isn't recognizable. Search the car, maybe you'll find something useful." She paused. "I wish I had more information for you, but the faster I get him to the morgue, the faster I can get you something."

"Thank you, Julie," Kenzie mumbled.

"The plastic leaked when we moved the body," Julie said, "but there doesn't seem to be much fluid in the trunk. I'm done here, your team can have the car."

While Julie packed up the body, Emilio said to the deputy sheriff, "We need all surveillance footage from Friday afternoon through now. Any way to tell when the car was parked here?"

"The time stamp on the ticket. There're surveillance cameras on the entrance as well, and it appears the lot is also covered. I'll grab everything from airport security."

"Stat. That's a federal agent who was murdered. Either he drove in here and someone killed him in broad daylight and stuffed him in the trunk, or someone else drove his car," Emilio said. "The FBI Evidence Response Team is on its way, they'll process the car and take it to our warehouse."

"Was there any luggage in the vehicle?" Kenzie asked.

They all looked into the trunk. A lone suitcase had been pushed back, to make room for the body.

"There's nothing in the cab," the deputy said. "We checked."

"No laptop? Cell phone?"

"We didn't go inside—but we didn't see anything through the windows."

His cell phone had either been stolen or was on his body. As the ERT truck turned into the parking lot, Kenzie pulled out her phone and dialed Abigail Durant.

"Ma'am? It's MacKenzie Malone. We found Agent Crawford's car. There's a body in the trunk. We can't be certain, but it's an adult male and most likely Barry. ERT just arrived and are going to process the car, autopsy is at seven in the morning. We're pulling security feeds."

"Shit," Abigail mumbled. Kenzie didn't think she'd ever heard the ASAC swear. "Keep me informed. We have a situation downtown. One of the shooters from yesterday is in a standoff with the marshals right now."

"Do you need us?"

"No—I already sent agents to the scene. Stay with Agent Crawford's car until ERT secures the scene. Then go home and get some sleep. Tomorrow is going to be another long day."

Mac "Big Mac" Jackson woke up this morning knowing he'd be dead by sundown.

Official sunset was eight thirty-five according to the app on his phone. At eight, he thought he might have beat out this sick feeling in the pit of his stomach that he was going to die, but of course no one can escape their fate.

He wasn't psychic or any of that other bullshit, but he could see the writing on the wall. There had been fucking *six* of them yesterday morning, but he and Dom were the only two whom witnesses had seen.

Because they were the two who dumped the fucking *car.*

Dom was in jail and he wasn't getting out anytime soon. He wouldn't talk, but he had nothing to lose. He had no wife, no girlfriend, no kids. He didn't care if Tobias put a bullet in his mother's head because Dom hated his mother. Dom was content to sit in jail and not say a word, happy as a clam to get three meals a day and work the system from the inside.

Of course, Dom was too stupid to realize that Tobias had already put a hit out on him. He was a liability.

Mac was no fucking way going back to prison. It had been hell the first time. He was a tiger, unable to be caged for any length of time. The first week he managed, but every week after messed with his head. He had panic attacks—who the fuck had panic attacks behind bars? He was six foot two of solid muscle and hyperventilated when he stepped into his ten-by-ten-foot room.

The thought of returning to prison made him sick to his stomach.

Sunset. Tonight was the night. Unlike Dom, Mac had something to lose outside of his freedom and sanity. He had a girl and a kid and he knew what Tobias did to women. He'd seen it, he'd cleaned up after the bastard, he didn't want it happening to Diana.

He knew which asshole called the cops. It was the old Indian busboy. This place was supposed to be a sanctuary, but he saw how the janitor looked at him. It was more than recognition.

But Mac had waited too long to act. He saw people starting to slip out of the bar. Half of them had guns, could take him out if they wanted to. They just didn't want to be caught by the fucking cops because they were either on parole or wanted fugitives.

Like that ever stopped him from carrying a piece.

Mac made a call. The phone was answered on the first ring.

He didn't call Tobias. Tobias wouldn't give a shit about him or his girl.

"Problem?"

"Yep."

"Don't do what Dom did."

"Don't let Tobias get to my girl."

"Be a hero, and I'll protect her. I give you my word."

"Thank you, Mr. Contreras. I'll take out as many of them as I can."

"Icing on the cake."

Mac hung up. He slipped the burner phone into his beer just in case the feds had a way of tracing the call. Yesterday, he'd considered grabbing Diana and the kid and just disappearing, but he didn't have anyplace to go. The money he'd been paid would run out fast on the run. He'd been born and raised in San Antonio. And today, he would die in San Antonio.

He stood up and stretched. Looked around. Half the bar had cleared out. The bartender eyed him warily.

"Big Mac, we don't want any trouble."

"You should have warned me."

"I didn't know! I swear, not until people started leaving."

Mac grabbed a hooker who was too high to realize what was going on.

"Hey, sugar, pay up first."

He'd never paid a whore in his life.

"Not so tight!" she whined.

He pulled out his gun. A solid .45 with a magazine of twelve rounds. But it wasn't just the power of the gun. It was the type of rounds he used, jacketed hollow-points. Might not pierce the Kevlar, but he could do some serious damage. And one of these babies in the thigh and the bastard would bleed out in minutes.

The whore stared at the gun and started shaking, but kept her mouth shut. Which was good because he might have just popped her there.

Out of the corner of his eye he saw the barkeep reaching

under the counter. Mac aimed and fired without hesitation. The bullet hit a little high—he forgot about the kick this baby had—slamming into the guy's upper right shoulder. He grabbed himself and dropped to the ground. As if Mac would waste another bullet on him.

Eleven bullets.

The whore started crying and Mac held her close, the barrel of the gun at the back of her head.

"Come in and get me, assholes," he muttered. He kept his back to the bar, where he could see the front door and the hall that led to the bathrooms. At the end of that hall was the storeroom and a back door. The cops could come in from either entrance. Or both, simultaneously.

The customers who hadn't already left cowered in the corners and at their tables. He glared at them. "Make a move, I'll kill ya," he said.

No one moved. Pussies.

He heard the boots in the hall before he saw a cop. He focused on the doorway. Saw the tip of a rifle pointed slightly down. To his right, the front door jiggled, just a little. Both entrances at once.

Sure, do it. Let's get this over.

I'm sorry, Diana. It was fun while it lasted.

As soon as he saw the cop in the hall step forward, Mac started shooting.

Ten.

Nine.

Eight bullets left . . .

The SWAT team moved in and Mac got three rounds off, all aimed at the first guy through the door, before two bullets hit him in the head.

But he didn't know it was two bullets because he was already dead.

CHAPTER TWENTY-FOUR

Supervisory Special Agent Blair Novak had been a federal agent for twenty-one years. She'd been offered an ASAC position in Omaha, Nebraska, five years ago, which she turned down because she had no burning desire to live in the Midwest, and her husband had just been promoted at Lockheed, a private defense contractor, and was beginning to make some serious money. Then three years ago she'd been offered a desk job with a 15 percent salary increase to move to Washington, DC, and work in headquarters. She and Johnny had seriously talked about that position. Not because of the money—Johnny was pulling in six figures plus even better benefits than she was—but because his mom lived in Virginia and her parents lived in Baltimore and they thought maybe they should go back home. Johnny could work at the Lockheed office in Virginia, and travel to LA as needed.

But the kids came first. JJ was a high school sophomore and Mia was a freshman. How could she just uproot her children? They'd moved from DC to LA because of her job in the first place, when JJ was starting the third grade. The move had been hardest on the kids, and she'd vowed not to do it again until they graduated. So she stayed in LA as an SSA and never regretted it. She liked her job. She liked her colleagues. She was up for a promotion to ASAC of the Long Beach Resident Agency at the end of the year when the current ASAC retired. It would be a major advance. She'd miss the fast-paced downtown office, but she'd be in charge and closer to home.

She would have helped Hans Vigo even if she didn't want the promotion, but she was more than eager to do a great job because Vigo's name carried a lot of weight in the Bureau.

Blair Novak wasn't stupid, though. If this case was as dangerous as she thought, no way was she talking to the mother of an escaped felon by herself. She tagged rookie agent Carter Nix. He was late entering the Bureau like so many recent rookies. When she was a new agent, the average age of Quantico grads was twenty-five. Now? Thirty-two. A lot had changed in twenty years. They now had more former military in their ranks and many in local law enforcement wanted to do a stint at the Bureau for either the benefits, the retirement package, or the types of crimes feds investigated.

Nix was a former marine, thirty-three, and had been assigned to Los Angeles when he graduated six months ago. He was married with two little girls, and his wife was still in the process of moving the family west. She hadn't wanted to move the girls from Denver in the middle of the school year. Blair liked Nix, liked the way he thought, but mostly she liked the fact that he was a sharpshooter with good instincts. Not that she was expecting trouble, but she preferred to have someone solid at her side.

On the way to Tamara Rollins's residence in Topanga Canyon, Blair thanked Nix for working late—it was after six, and they should have been wrapping up paperwork and heading home. While she didn't mind putting in the extra hours, she increasingly appreciated the time she had with her family.

"It's not a problem, ma'am," Nix said. "My family won't be here until the end of the month. I don't have much of a home to go home to right now."

She wanted to ask if there was anything wrong—she had a feeling that the assignment to Los Angeles hadn't gone over well with Nix's wife—but decided it was better to keep their relationship professional.

She filled Nix in on their assignment. "The property belongs jointly to both Tamara Rollins and her sister, Margaret Hunt. The only reason it wasn't seized in asset forfeiture when Jimmy Hunt fled the country was because it had been willed to Margaret and Tamara by their parents, and Jimmy Hunt isn't on the deed."

"How'd it slip by that a wanted fugitive has a niece in the DEA?" Nix asked.

"According to AD Vigo, Nicole's paperwork indicates that her mother is deceased. She also listed only her mother and brother as relatives—no aunts or uncles. We don't require employees to show a death certificate when they lose a parent, but it makes me curious as to why she lied about that. And the paperwork indicated that Tamara Rollins was living in Austin, Texas at the time." She paused a moment as she slowed for a sharp turn. "The DEA agent responsible for verifying information about Nicole Rollins's family made several mistakes. He's currently under investigation."

"Mistakes? Or intentional?"

"Don't know."

Twenty minutes later they found themselves at a gate on a private road off Old Topanga Canyon Road, nearly halfway between the Pacific Coast Highway and the 101 Freeway. Topanga itself was an interesting community, a combination of extremely wealthy homeowners wanting the privacy and seclusion of the Topanga Canyon, and longtime residents in small, crumbling houses that may have been here since the 1960s when growing pot was just to get high, not cultivate and sell. The hills and valleys that made up Topanga Canyon were surrounded by areas like Malibu and Pacific Palisades and Mulholland Highway, but the canyon itself was peaceful, a remnant of how Blair thought Los Angeles might have been sixty years ago.

Blair pressed a call button on the gate. Several minutes later a female voice said, "May I help you?"

"My name is Special Agent Blair Novak with the Federal Bureau of Investigation," Blair said. "I'm looking to speak to Ms. Tamara Rollins regarding her daughter, Nicole Rollins."

Silence. She wondered if they would even open the gate. She waited a good half minute before she said, "Ma'am? Did you hear me?"

"Tami doesn't live here anymore," the voice said.

"Are you Margaret Hunt?"

"Yes, I'm Margaret."

"Do you have a minute? It's important I talk to Mrs. Rollins."

There was a click, then nothing. Blair shook her head. "People," she muttered. She was tense, because Hans Vigo had made her tense. If Margaret Hunt was involved in her husband's illegal activity, then they had to be very careful around her.

The electric gate slowly swung open.

"I'm getting twitchy," Nix said.

"You and me both," she said. "Stay alert."

Blair drove up a very long driveway to the top of a hill. The trees and brush were dangerously dry, thanks to the drought, but had been cleared from around the large and well-maintained ranch-style home. A wide porch wrapped around the front and sides of the house.

A barn to the east had all doors closed. Two other outbuildings could be seen through scraggly oak trees that dotted the uneven land. Property records indicated that Margaret Hunt and her sister owned twenty acres, which would be worth a small fortune. The land alone was worth millions.

Margaret Hunt met them at the door. "You don't mind if we talk out here, do you?" she asked, though it didn't sound like a question. She motioned to a picnic table on the porch. "Have a seat."

"Thank you for speaking with us," Blair said and took a seat. Nix didn't. He stood behind her and watched their surroundings.

Margaret Hunt was in her sixties with long silvery-gray hair she had braided neatly down her back. She wore no makeup and her glasses made her blue eyes seem bigger and brighter. She was petite with firm, tanned skin over a layer of sinewy muscles.

"I'm going to be honest with you from the get-go. I'm not a fan. I don't trust the police, and I certainly don't trust the feds."

"Because your husband is a wanted fugitive?"

"Because of how you all treated me because my husband is a dipshit," she said.

"Fair enough," Blair said. "We're not here about your husband. We need to speak with your sister, and the DMV lists Tamara Rollins at this address."

"I haven't seen my sister in five years. I haven't seen my husband in five years. You put it together."

Okay, Blair thought. Time to change gears. "Are you aware that your niece Nicole Rollins escaped from custody yesterday morning?"

"Yep." She gestured toward the roof, though Blair couldn't see what she was pointing at. "Got satellite, saw it on the news. Nicole doesn't talk to me any more than she talks to her mother."

"We're trying to cover all the bases. Has Nicole reached out to you since she escaped?"

"Nope. She's not welcome here, and she knows it. I washed my hands of that family five years ago. I'm through. That's what I said to the feds then, and nothing has changed."

"We're trying to piece together Nicole's background. Much of the information in her record has been falsified. Were you ever contacted by a DEA agent when the agency did a background check on Nicole prior to her employment?"

Margaret stared at her. "Look, Agent Novak, I'm a recovering alcoholic. I barely remember living with my husband, let alone my sister and her family. Why? Because I was drunk and stoned and should probably be dead now. It took my husband picking my sister over me to make me realize I made my own fucking bed and needed to start clean. Good riddance. I never even knew what day it was fifteen, twenty years ago, let alone if any cop came to talk to me. And I doubt Jimmy would have let anyone talk to me. He never knew what I might say or do because I was addicted to anything that made me numb and happy." She scowled.

Blair changed tactics. "Do you remember when your sister and brother-in-law came to live with you?"

"Yeah, I wasn't so bad off then. Tami and John and their kids. At first it was good. I mean, Tami owns this property just like I do, she had a right to live here. She and John took the house up the road. Originally a barn, my daddy converted it to a house. But Jimmy and John fought all the time. You know—Jimmy ain't no saint, and John was a cop. John was killed in some gang battle or something—I never knew the details. Only that Jimmy took care of his kids, Chris and Nicole." She snorted. "And Tami. Took care of Tami a little bit too much, I tell you."

"We've been looking into the shooting that killed Officer Rollins, and there's been some information that he was a corrupt cop who may have been caught in a sting operation."

Margaret stared at her. "I never heard about that," she said flatly.

"It's not in any official records. Right now, it's an unsubstantiated rumor."

"Chris, I'm betting." Margaret shook his head. "He really had a chip on his shoulder. I guess I don't blame him much, he was seventeen when his daddy was killed, and John and Jimmy never got along. The kid knew that. He left as soon as he hit eighteen. Didn't even graduate from high school, just got his GED and joined the army. Think he might have gone through an ROTC program, you know, where you go to college and are a soldier-in-training or some such thing. I really don't remember. Tami used to keep in touch with him, but hell if I know what she does now."

"There's nothing in Nicole's file about you or her uncle. The only family members she listed was her mother, who she claimed died two years ago, and her brother."

Margaret snorted. "Well, the news said she was a fugitive, a DEA agent who was caught with her hand in the cookie jar. Why would you expect her to tell the truth about anything?"

"Did she have any close friends growing up?"

"Nope. She was a smart girl, did well in school, and fought with her mother. That's all I remember about her. She moved out when she went to college, and the last time I remember seeing her was . . ." She frowned. "I really can't say. The last time I saw her was during my fuzzy years. I think I went to her college graduation, but I'm not sure. We had a party here, I remember that."

"Do you recall ever meeting a man named Tobias? He would be a little older than Nicole."

She shrugged. "I really don't know. Nicole didn't bring men around. She had one boyfriend for a long time, don't know what happened to him. His name wasn't Tobias."

"Do you remember who this boyfriend was?"

She shrugged. "It's ancient history. Why do you care about who she dated in college?"

College. Right before she joined the DEA. "We're trying to figure out who knew Nicole at the time she joined the DEA. It might help us find her."

"Good luck with that," Margaret said. "I don't like my sister, and I'm certainly not going to lose sleep over her kid being hunted by you feds. I don't like them, I don't like you, and I just want to be left alone. My husband fucked up my life, and I'm done." She stood up. "You know, you're all the same. Come up here nosing around, playing games. Not telling me shit, because you think I'm stupid, just like Jimmy and Tami thought I was stupid and didn't know they were fucking around. Asking about Tobias and Joseph as if I know every idiot Nicole screwed. I. Am. *Done*." She walked into the house and slammed the door.

Blair could hardly contain her excitement. She walked to the car, got into the driver's seat. Nix followed around to the passenger side.

"Why didn't you call her on that slip-up?" Nix said.

"Because she would have stopped talking anyway." Blair turned the car around and started back down the long, winding gravel driveway.

"There were people in the barn. Don't know how many, but a couple. Could have been laborers." His tone suggested otherwise.

"We're going to dig around and find something so we can get a warrant and search her property and financials."

"You don't believe her?"

Blair considered as she turned onto Old Topanga Canyon Road and headed back to headquarters. "The best liars are those who mix truth with fiction. I think a lot of what she said was the truth. And a lot of what she said was a deliberate lie. Calculated so we leave thinking she's the betrayed wife of a wanted fugitive. She's still married to him even though he fled the country with her sister."

"If he left with her sister."

Blair hadn't considered that. "You think that Tami Rollins is still around?"

"Like you said, the best liars mix truth and fiction. What if she really is dead and Nicole wasn't lying about that?"

"There'd be a record of it. She didn't die in Austin, as Nicole said." Blair had that butterfly in her stomach that told her she had a juicy case in front of her. "We need to find Tami Rollins or learn what happened to her. And now we know that Joseph Contreras knew Nicole in college. Nicole went to UCLA. I worked an investigation there a couple of years back, I know the assistant dean very well. Let's swing by and see what he'll give us without a warrant. I find people are far more forthcoming chatting face-to-face." And if he wanted a warrant, she would get one.

Maggie Hunt strode through her house to the oversized country kitchen. "Are they gone?" she snapped at Tito.

"Yep," he said, pointing to the security screen. "Just turned onto the road."

Tito was slow but loyal, and had been with the family for years. He couldn't think on his feet, but he followed orders well. Maggie said, "I need everyone here in one hour for a family meeting—no excuses. Except George and Trina—send them to the vault. I want every gun and bullet we have stashed back here before dark. If the feds come back, they're not getting in. Understand?"

"Yes, ma'am." He ran out the back door to track down the half a dozen people who worked for Maggie on the property. Then he'd call in the rest. Family—which included blood as well as those they'd adopted.

With Tito on his errand, she sat down and grabbed one of the many burner phones she had. This one was international.

She stared at the wall of photos. Jimmy and his idea of *family*. He could be such a fool sometimes, but she loved him. He had the vision, she had the brains.

Jimmy answered. "Yep."

"It's me."

"Mags." His voice softened and she felt that little jolt in her stomach that reminded her why she had loved this man for forty-three years. "How are you, baby?"

She wanted to say fine, that everything was working the way it was supposed to, and she'd be down to visit him next month, as planned.

"I was great until ten minutes ago when the FBI came knocking."

"You knew they would eventually. Once they realized Nicole's file was fake they would have learned about us."

"They asked about Tobias."

"I should have told you about that."

Her hand tightened around her phone. In the calmest voice she could muster, she said, "What haven't you told me, Jimmy? Tobias can't handle himself around the feds. They'll kill him." Her voice rose. "If anything happens to my son—"

"Shh, baby, Nicole and Joseph are taking care of him, like always."

"How do they know? How did the FBI put it together so quickly?"

"They made a leap they can't prove."

"Explain," she said, fuming. The only way their organization worked was if no one knew who Tobias was. He was the unknown but powerful leader. As long as they kept up that illusion, everything worked. But if their competition found out that he was the weak link, they'd push back. That would cost time, money, and territory.

She wasn't going to lose her only child. Or her money.

"Truthfully, Mags, it's his own fault. When Nicole went to jail he started thinking on his own, and you know how he gets. When I told him to kill Harper Worthington to keep Adeline in line, he came up with an asinine plan and used Elise."

"Oh God, no." Maggie sat down heavily. Elise was a wild card. Maggie didn't trust her, not because she'd go to the cops, but because she was half crazy. Considering how crazy Tami had become over the years it was no wonder the kid was fucked up.

"Nicole's the only one who was ever able to get Tobias or Elise to do what they were supposed to, once I was forced to leave the States. Nicole was in fucking solitary confinement. What was I supposed to do?"

Grow some balls. But she didn't say that. Jimmy, living the high life down in Mexico, while *she* kept the family together.

Nicole's arrest had come before they had all the pieces of the operation set up. But it wasn't the worst thing that could have happened. Because Nicole was smart, and she had an escape plan, one that Maggie had helped her create. Everything had worked exactly as they planned . . . except the FBI should never have been able to connect Tobias to Nicole, or Joseph to Nicole.

She frowned. How had the feds found out about Joseph?

He was wanted for killing Adeline—how did they know he worked for the family? Or were they just fishing?

That was most likely. That's how the fucking feds operated.

"I'm sorry, babe," she said, "until Nicole retrieves the money we lost when Adeline went off the deep end, we're at a standstill."

"There's no more hiding in the shadows," Jimmy said. "The feds know because that bastard Kane Rogan has been feeding them information. But Joseph came up with a plan and Rogan's as good as dead."

"At least that's one piece of good news. And the feds who screwed our plans? Donnelly and Kincaid? Are they as good as dead?"

"All in good time."

"That means you don't have a fucking plan. Dammit, Jimmy!"

"Look, Mags, I know you're upset, but we have it under control. Nicole will locate our money and get it back. She's smart, you know that. And we still have a few people on the inside."

"Speaking of people on the inside—take care of Adam."

"He's already dead," Jimmy said.

"What the fuck happened?" Maggie's orderly life was spinning out of control. For *years* she'd kept this family together and now her careful, meticulous plans were unraveling.

"You just said to take care of him, who cares how it happened?"

"Tell me," she said through clenched teeth.

"We sent him to take care of Rogan. He's the one who got that redhead Rogan is hot about. We had him . . . then he went all Rambo on our men. The girl saw Dover, and he let Rogan get the girl out. I told Dover she dies or he dies. I don't know that he believed me until he was dead."

"The feds know Dover lied in Nicole's file."

"Don't matter now."

"Of course it matters! Shit, Jimmy, are you fucking stoned? They'll go through Dover's files with a fine-tooth comb. How do you know he didn't keep logs? Records? Proof?"

"He didn't."

"You're un-fucking-believable."

"He had no reason for leverage. He's been in our back pocket since he whacked John."

"We need to pull everyone out. The feds are too close and they are going to ruin everything."

"Nicole has it under control. She'll come through. She always does."

"I'm worried, Jimmy. In all these years, I've never been worried like I am right now."

"Baby, come to me."

"I can't just up and leave!"

"Pull our safety net and get your gorgeous ass down here."

She wanted to. But what if Tobias needed her? He was in over his head. She was his mother—she had to protect him. She trusted Nicole, but Joseph had always hated Tobias. She should have killed Joseph before Nicole got so attached to him.

"I've missed you, Mags."

She sighed. "I need to protect our son."

"Nicole will do it."

"Tell him to meet me at the safe house in Mexico."

"But—"

"Do it, Jimmy. I can't bear to find out the feds killed him. Tobias only listens to you."

"You're right, as always. One of the many reasons I love you, Mags."

"Call me when it's done, and I'll come down."

She hung up. Yeah, she loved him and he loved her. But she'd heard the other woman on her husband's end. She sighed and rubbed her eyes. It was her own damn fault. She'd willingly shared her husband with Tami because Maggie didn't like some of Jimmy's proclivities, and if Tami was willing to play his sick games, great—she no longer had to. But with Tami gone, and Jimmy in Mexico, Maggie couldn't expect him to remain celibate. They could only be together a few weeks of the year . . . and those weeks were spent working or keeping Tobias from doing something stupid.

And that was the biggest problem. All Maggie wanted from Jimmy was to protect their son. She knew Tobias had some problems, and she and Jimmy had tried to cure him. They managed to channel his sexual urges toward prostitutes and other whores who wouldn't go to the police, but they had to teach him not to kill the bitches. And most of the time he was able to control himself. The whores were well paid, and everyone was happy.

He slipped a time or two, but they always fixed it.

Jimmy should have seen that with Nicole in jail, he needed to leave his sanctuary in Mexico and take charge in San Antonio. If he'd done what a patriarch should do, Tobias and Elise would never have hatched such an insane plan, Adeline wouldn't have gotten so freaked, and they could have extracted their money with minimal bloodshed.

At least, no bloodshed until *after* the money was in their bank account.

But Jimmy was always more concerned about his own neck, and that weakness in her husband made her want to loathe him, even after forty-three years of loving him. Everything they'd done had been for family. *Their* family, by blood or by choice. Who was going to protect Tobias and Elise when she and Jimmy were dead? They were in their sixties, dammit, they wouldn't live forever. That they'd made it this far was nothing short of miraculous.

And a whole lot of common sense. *Her* common sense.

She made a series of calls, starting with the son.

Joseph straightened his spine when he heard the voice on the other end.

"Aunt Maggie."

Maggie wasn't his aunt, but she liked it when he pretended.

"Who took the money and when will you have it back?"

Joseph glanced at Nicole. She was going through the files—the second set of files—that he'd gotten for her earlier today when Tobias left with the original flash drive. But at the mention of Maggie's name, Nicole jerked her head up and stared at him with wide, concerned eyes.

"We have a lot of paperwork to get through. We're looking. We'll have the answers soon."

"Look faster. The feds have connected Tobias to Nicole and Nicole to me. But they don't know most of it. Yet."

He tensed. "Which feds?"

"The FBI. A bitch named Novak. They also know about you, though they haven't put your relationship with Nicole together yet. How did they do that? Why would they come here—to my *home*—asking about who Nicole was involved with in college?"

Joseph closed his eyes. He didn't see how they'd put it together . . . except all the puzzle pieces were there. Adeline's connection to Tobias and the money laundering. The fact that he'd worked for Adeline and the FBI thought (rightly) that he'd killed her. It wouldn't take much of a leap to figure that he was also working for Tobias.

And then there was Elise. Playing the victim could only go so far. Sometimes she thought she was smarter than she actually was.

"Elise is in custody."

"Tobias assures me that she'll be out tomorrow, and she's in a psychiatric hold, not federal prison."

"You know she likes to play these games—"

"She may be young, but she's not stupid. I need you to be the man here, Joseph."

It was her tone that made him tense. Hadn't he proven to her over and over again that he'd kept her family safe for years?

"I've always done what is required," he said, his voice low.

Nicole jumped up and grabbed his arm. *Don't make her mad*, she mouthed.

"I know you have," Maggie said apologetically, "but we've never been so . . . vulnerable."

"That's because Tobias put himself on Kane Rogan's radar, and that bastard doesn't stop. But we almost have him."

"Almost isn't good enough. And Kane Rogan isn't in the FBI or the DEA. So why do these damn federal agencies know so much about our operation and our people?"

"They have poured all of their resources into looking for Niki. You know that, Aunt Maggie. And Rogan has a family connection in the FBI now, here in San Antonio. We're going to take care of it, but she's not as easy to get to as the others. If we want our money, we need to be patient. It would help us tremendously if you could tell your son not do anything without talking to Nicole first."

"What? What happened?" She sounded panicked, as well she should be. But Joseph kept his voice calm and respectful.

"Tobias seems to think that *he* can find the money, and he left the safe house after I explicitly told him not to. And he's not answering his phone." Joseph needed to soften his voice. Maggie was so damn protective of her lunatic son that if she thought he was a threat to Tobias, she'd try to have *him* killed.

"Aunt Maggie," he said calmly, "Tobias went wild when Nicole was in jail, and I had my hands full putting together the escape. Everything went off perfectly. Except now Tobias is a loose cannon and he isn't sticking to the plan. The plan you helped us create," he added.

"Jimmy is recalling Tobias to Mexico immediately. By tomorrow, Tobias will be at the safe house."

Joseph would believe that when it happened. "Thank you, Aunt Maggie."

"Bring Elise home, I don't want her on her own. She's still a child."

Child? Hardly. But Joseph didn't comment.

"And get our money back!" She hung up.

He walked over to the bar and poured himself a double Scotch. Nicole put her head on his back and wrapped her arms around his body.

"I would have talked to her."

"Oil and water," he said. "Did you make any inroads?"

"I've gone through all the memos Dunbar wrote about the case. He only mentioned you a couple of times. His focus was on Adeline and the people she was helping—lobbyists, businessmen, other politicians. He knew nothing about Tobias except what the FBI told him. I'm now going through messages that other people sent him around the time that the money was moved from our accounts to the FBI. I just hope I'm faster than Tobias at figuring this out."

"Or that Maggie can get through to him," Joseph said. "Because he's *this* close to getting a bullet in his head."

CHAPTER TWENTY-FIVE

By the time Nate drove Lucy home, it was after ten and she was exhausted. No surprise there. Hans followed in an FBI pool car.

Nate checked the entire house. He also double-checked that Lucy had set the alarm.

Lucy showed Hans to the guest room upstairs, since Nate was taking the downstairs suite. Then she started pulling leftovers out of the refrigerator to warm. Someone had brought takeout to the Bureau, but it was gone before Lucy could get much of a meal, and she hadn't been that hungry at six. Then the scene at the bar—by the time the FBI had come to assist with the marshals, SAPD was on-site and their SWAT team breached the facility. The shooter was dead, one civilian seriously injured, and one cop had been shot in the arm and was in surgery—the bullet had done some serious damage, though he was expected to fully recover.

Now she was famished.

By the time she had everything reheated, both Nate and Hans had finished with showers and returned to the kitchen.

"This is a nice place, Lucy," Hans said. "You like it here?"

"I love San Antonio and the house. Sean picked it out, ordered furniture, did all the things I wouldn't have thought about. It feels like home. I told Sean the house was too big, but he expects us to have company."

Nate grabbed a water bottle from the fridge and said, "Have you heard from Sean?"

She shook her head. "I was hoping you had."

She wanted to call him, but she also didn't want to put them in danger. After going down to rescue the boys three months ago, Lucy understood, at least in part, the danger Kane faced almost every day.

And now Sean was in the middle of it, too.

The doorbell rang and Nate's hand immediately went for his weapon, though he didn't draw it.

Lucy walked to the front door, but Nate beat her there and looked at the security screen that Sean had installed in the wall.

"Jack?" Lucy said, incredulous. "That's my brother." She quickly disengaged the alarm and opened the door. She couldn't keep the grin off her face. "Jack! What on earth—why didn't you tell me you were in town?" She practically leapt into his arms as she hugged him.

He squeezed her so hard that he pulled her feet off the ground. "Luce." He kissed her forehead and put her back down.

Nate closed and locked the door, then reset the alarm. "Nate Dunning," he said and extended his hand. "Good to finally meet you, sir."

Jack took his hand and shook it. "Likewise. Call me Jack."

"What are you doing—" She stopped mid-sentence. "Oh God, no. Sean—" She started shaking.

"Lucy, don't go there." Jack draped his arm over her shoulders. "Sean is fine as far as I know. He sent a coded report a few hours ago. He and Blitz located Kane. Kane is in hiding and lost his equipment. I don't have details, but Sean and Blitz are waiting until full dark to extract him." He glanced at his watch, and Lucy suspected that whatever was happening was happening right now. "I would have been here sooner, but I flew myself out. I needed to bring some supplies that wouldn't pass through commercial airport security." He motioned toward the duffel bag he'd dropped on the floor.

She couldn't respond. The fear for Sean's safety had been sudden and very real.

Hans stepped out into the foyer. "I thought I heard a familiar voice," he said. "I gather this is a surprise visit."

"I smell food, and I could definitely eat something," Jack said. He looked around. "Sean did good," he said.

"You're the first in the family to see it," Lucy said. "Dillon and Kate were supposed to come out a few weeks ago, but they canceled on us. Patrick is busy splitting his time between DC and San Francisco." She brought out plates and utensils.

"I can hear the eye roll in your voice, Lucy," Jack said.

"Cannot."

"Can too." He pulled her hair like Patrick used to do when she was a little girl. Jack had already enlisted in the army when Lucy was born; they'd only become close over the last few years.

Lucy hadn't quite accepted Patrick's girlfriend. She knew it wasn't fair to Elle, or to Patrick, but in the six months they'd been involved, Elle had gotten into trouble half a dozen times. Patrick dropped everything to fly to San Francisco, and all Lucy wanted to ask was, *What had she done before Patrick saved her butt the first time?* "Patrick took a temporary assignment in New York a couple of weeks ago, and she went out with him. Sean wanted to meet up with them last weekend, but then Carina had the baby."

"On my way back to Sacramento I plan to swing through San Diego and see JP."

"Already gave him a nickname?" She smiled. "I like it."

"Carina hates it," Jack said, "but she'll get used to it."

They dished up leftovers and Lucy said, "I wish I had more food, but Sean and I got back yesterday morning, and then everything went to Hell." She guzzled some water. "Is that why you're here? Because Sean had to leave town? Nate's keeping an eye on things. And Hans came in from DC for the case."

"I'm here because I talked to Siobhan after Kane's team rescued her."

"Who?"

"Siobhan Walsh. She's the younger sister of Andrea Walsh, a lieutenant colonel in the marines based out of Quantico. She was Kane's commanding officers during his first tour, and a good friend. Siobhan is maybe ten, twelve years younger. They have different mothers—Siobhan's mother was a missionary. Now, Siobhan is a photojournalist who spends most of her time attached to the Sisters of Mercy taking pictures of depressed areas in Mexico and Central America to help the Sisters raise money for their work. It's dangerous, but because the Sisters of Mercy are part of a religious order and apolitical, the cartels and gangs tend to steer clear of them. There have been a few situations . . . but mostly it's contained.

"Kane called me from Santiago and said that Siobhan had been taken as bait for him, and that meant that someone must have thoroughly investigated him. It was clear that she was a means to an end."

"Is she okay?" Lucy asked.

"Yes. A couple of cracked ribs, but Padre is looking out

for her at my place in Hidalgo until this situation settles down."

"But the key point is that someone put a bounty on Kane," Nate interjected.

Jack nodded. "According to Siobhan, they want Kane alive. The only reason would be to torture him, because there are plenty of bad guys who would love to get a piece of him. Against RCK protocol—rules that Kane established years ago—Kane pursued the lone survivor without backup in the hope of obtaining information about Tobias and who hired them. Kane is obsessed with this guy."

"I've talked to him about it," Lucy said, "but he doesn't want to hear it. Especially from me."

"Actually, he does listen—he just doesn't let on that he does. He has a lot of respect for you, Lucy, and of course Sean. Kane's one of the smartest people I know, he recognizes that he's obsessed, but he also has cause to worry. In this instance, because of what happened to those boys, Kane made it his personal mission to stop Tobias. He thinks he's the only one who can, especially since I don't work south of the border anymore. I've lost my edge, my contacts are old. What he forgets is that I haven't lost my instincts, and this situation has me on edge."

"Tobias isn't in charge," Lucy said. "He's violent and vicious, and he needs to be stopped, but I would bet my badge that Nicole Rollins calls the shots." She filled Jack in on her theory about Nicole and her role in the organization, and where she saw Tobias fitting in. Jack listened as they ate.

Hans said, "We had word today that Joseph Contreras—wanted for the murder of Congresswoman Worthington—went to UCLA with Rollins. He has no record and we can't find anything on him prior to his enrollment at UCLA. No birth certificate, no family, no residence—Joseph Contreras is likely an alias."

"Kane told me about Contreras—he's technically the one who put the hit on Kane. But you knew about his connection to Tobias already."

"We suspected," Lucy said. "And that's why you're here?"

"If they put a hit on Kane, they very well could have put a hit on you, Lucy," Jack said seriously. "And you know damn well why."

She nodded. Because she'd seen Tobias.

"I'm not leaving until all three of them are dead or behind bars," Jack said.

"You may be here a long time," Lucy said, trying to make light.

Jack didn't crack a smile. "Have you kept up on your training?"

She could lie. But Jack would see through it. "I work out," she said honestly.

"First thing tomorrow, we go back to training. And I'm going to find someone local to keep you fresh."

"I'm okay, Jack."

"Let's keep it that way."

They ate and cleaned up. Neither Jack nor Nate was drinking beer, which actually worried her even more. That meant they considered themselves on duty.

Lucy took out half a gallon of chocolate ice cream and some bowls and spoons. She didn't care if no one wanted to share with her, she needed chocolate. It would calm her nerves.

"Why would she want to work for the DEA?" Lucy pondered as she ate a spoonful of double chocolate chip. "I mean, I can see the initial reasons. Find out how the DEA works, get inside knowledge of operations and processes, but for fifteen years?"

"She was the inside man, so to speak," Hans said. "For her uncle. For Tobias. Or for herself. If she is truly in charge—at least on this end—she would give orders based on what she knew. She could steer the DEA investigations toward her competition, and away from her allies."

"I've seen it before," Jack said. "You get an in, you use it to benefit your own organization. Usually bribes do the trick, but with someone more invested like Rollins? They have far more information and power. Names of informants. Operations. Undercover ops. Raids."

"She must have restrained herself," Lucy said, "otherwise someone would have figured it out."

Hans said, "Your report showed that she'd moved offices often."

"She could have cultivated an agent in every office," Jack said.

"The DEA is acutely aware," Hans said. "Had you heard of Jimmy Hunt before this?"

"No," Jack said, "and I don't think Kane has, either. Hunt doesn't operate in Kane's territory. If Kane heard of him, he didn't consider him a threat—we maintain a threat assessment we regularly update."

Lucy glanced at Nate. "You've been quiet."

He didn't say anything for a minute. He looked from Lucy to Hans then said, "I don't see how she could keep her true nature a secret for so long."

"She's a good liar."

"She worked with Brad Donnelly for three years," Nate continued. "He was her direct supervisor. Her partner. The San Antonio DEA office is small, a branch of Houston."

She knew exactly what Nate was trying to say; she didn't believe it for a minute.

"He must have suspected something," Nate said.

"We often don't know the people around us," Lucy said.

Nate didn't comment.

"Kane has worked with Brad," Lucy said, with a glance to Jack for confirmation. But Jack was listening to Nate.

"Maybe Kane gave him information to see if he leaked it," Nate said. "But you can't ask him, because he's missing."

She said to Nate, "What do you want to do?"

"Everyone I trust is in this room—or in Mexico," Nate said.

"You can't mean that."

"I do. I trust Ryan, but he has two kids. When you have kids you'll do things you don't expect to do. I trust Kenzie, but she has a new boyfriend. Do we know anything about him? All I know is he's a cop in SAPD. I trust Juan, but he's been so worried about his wife and his own family, I don't think he'd recognize a traitor even if he walked in with blood on his hands. And Barry—you said yourself, Lucy, that Tobias kills loose ends. Barry is dead right when he was supposed to leave for his vacation. We can't discount that he planned to escape before the shit hit the fan, and then Tobias iced him."

Lucy had never heard Nate speak so many words at once.

"I can't see Barry being a traitor," Lucy said. "Or Brad."

"Yet no one knew about Rollins for fifteen years," Nate countered.

"Barry could have been killed for the same reason as Agent Dunbar," Lucy said. "We'll know more after the autopsy."

Hans said, "It's clear that this situation has forced us to look at our colleagues through the lens of suspicion. Everyone is on edge. Do you have anything specific, Nate, that would cause you to doubt Agent Donnelly's loyalty?"

"I want to know how Nicole Rollins got into Sam Archer's house and killed her. Donnelly left less than thirty minutes before. ERT said there was no sign of forced entry, and the alarm wasn't engaged. I want to know why Nicole didn't kill him, too, if it was so damn easy for her to break into a trained agent's home."

Nate was angry. Maybe he had a right to be furious.

"Brad has proven himself," Lucy said. "But I can see why you're suspicious."

"We need to give him a rectal exam just like we're giving Rollins and everyone affiliated with her."

Hans said, "The FBI is running deep background checks on all DEA agents under the Houston umbrella."

"And what about our own team?" Nate said.

"I can't comment on that."

Lucy didn't say anything. Barry Crawford was dead and he was being looked at as a traitor. She didn't want to believe it of any of her team, but did she really know these people? She'd only been here for six months.

"I rest my case," Nate said. "Everyone I trust is in this room."

Lucy rinsed her ice cream bowl and tried not to think that someone she knew was involved. So many people dead. Cops—good people—killed because they were cops.

"What does she want?" Jack asked. "Her behavior is unexplainable."

"It makes sense to her," Lucy said.

Hans nodded. "Jack makes a good observation. Why is she still in town? It would be logical for an escaped felon who has every local and federal law enforcement agency searching for her twenty-four seven to get out of the country as fast as possible. I can't imagine that an escape as well planned as this didn't have an exit strategy."

"Exactly," Jack said. "That helicopter could have taken her to the border. Not over it—by the time she reached the border, it was being patrolled heavily by air and land. But there are hundreds of miles where she could have had another escape route. There are dozens of tunnels. They have resources to pay to be hidden, or bribe a border patrol agent. And with her DEA connections, she would damn well know who was for sale. Or she could have headed to Canada and disappeared there for months before trying for another country on a fake passport."

Lucy had thought the same thing.

"Yet," Jack continued, "she stayed. Why?"

"Maybe she stayed to kill Sam Archer," Nate suggested. "Revenge."

"Archer isn't the main target," Hans said. "Archer just did her job. It was Ryan Quiroz, Kane, and Lucy who uncovered her illegal activities. And Brad Donnelly who had been tortured by the cartel."

"You're thinking that she's here to kill everyone who put her away," Jack said, looking directly at Lucy.

"The same gun was used to kill Agent Dunbar in DC as was used in the attack on Lucy and an SAPD detective two weeks ago," Hans said.

Jack's face hardened. "And you didn't tell me?"

"We just learned about it this afternoon," Lucy said. "Noah called me with the ballistics report."

"It's a warning," Jack said. "You should have called me, Hans."

"It's more than a warning," Hans said quietly. "It's a promise."

"And you people aren't putting my sister into protective custody?" Jack said.

"Don't talk about me as if I'm not here," Lucy said. "And what are you and Nate? I'm safer in this house than I am anywhere."

"And you plan to walk out that door tomorrow and do your job, when you should be pulled from the investigation."

She shook her head. "I'm not running away because someone threatened me. I'm a cop, Jack, don't forget that."

"You're a target, Lucia," Jack snapped. "Don't forget *that.*"

"I get it—you're my big brother. So I'll forgive you. I'm not reckless. I'm not going to do anything to make it easy for Rollins or her people to get to me. But I'm not going to put my head in the sand and hide, any more than you would. Nicole Rollins is directly or indirectly responsible for the murders of seven cops in the last forty-eight hours. Nine if you include Barry and Agent Dunbar. She put an entire bus full of children in immediate danger so she could escape custody. Revenge is definitely in her play-book, but she's here for more than revenge. She's too smart to rush a personal vendetta if she has a chance to disappear. You're right about one thing, Jack—she's staying local because she wants or needs something. It's not solely a vendetta."

"Everyone needs sleep," Hans said when Jack was about to argue with her. "It's been a rough couple of days. But I think, Jack, that Lucy is right. Rollins is too smart to be swayed by emotion. For her, revenge is an added bonus. I suspect there is another reason each of those agents were targeted."

Lucy said, "Maybe she needs something before she can disappear. Maybe they plan to get Elise out. Hans, is there any chance I can talk to her before her hearing tomorrow?"

Hans shook his head. "No. Dr. Oakley has already filed a complaint with the Bureau against you."

"That was fast. Can you get in to talk to her? Or can we postpone the hearing altogether?"

"The hearing is mandatory because it's a forced psych hold," Hans said. "But it should be routine for an automatic extension as long as the AUSA can clearly articulate the reasons. We'll go to the hearing. You're one of the agents of record, so you should be allowed to speak."

"Elise is good," Lucy said, her voice cracking. "She knows how to work the system. You saw how she was with Oakley."

"We're doing everything possible to ensure she stays locked up, but too much is out of our hands," Hans said.

Jack rubbed her shoulders. "Go to bed. Nate and I will take turns on watch."

"Jack—"

"Don't say it. I know you're a trained agent. I know that you're smart. But two weeks ago you would have been dead if you hadn't been wearing Kevlar, and you still have that target on your back. I'm here because Sean can't be. Though—knowing what I know now, I'm not leaving Texas until that woman is stopped."

Hans nodded. "Go to bed, Lucy. We'll talk to the AUSA tomorrow morning and see what her plan is. There's nothing more we can do now."

Lucy reluctantly went upstairs, knowing that they were going to be up for much longer. She was worried about Sean, worried about the hearing, and angry. Angry that Nicole Rollins had abused the system, that she'd used her position to profit, that she was partly responsible for the proliferation of drugs in the United States. The war on drugs may be in part political, but the lives that drugs destroyed were not, and shouldn't be used as political fodder. Drugs killed everyone involved—those who sold and those who used. Everyone was at risk. So much money and violence and pain. Lives completely wasted. Hopeless. It was a cycle that seemed to be getting worse.

She showered and sat cross-legged in the middle of her big bed, acutely aware that she hadn't spoken to Sean since he'd left this morning. Over sixteen hours. His relationship with Kane was complex and she didn't fully understand it. The Rogan family was so different from the Kincaids. In some ways they were similar—two large families raised by two parents. Sean and Lucy were both the youngest. But the Rogans weren't as tight as the Kincaids. There was a lot of anger under the surface, and Lucy didn't understand why. She understood Sean—his parents had been killed when he was fourteen and his brother Duke became his guardian. There was a lot of pain and anger in what happened during those years. But why was Kane so committed to the war south of the border? Duke had been in the military for three years; why wasn't he the one Kane called on in the rare times he needed help? Why did Sean drop everything when Kane called, even though he knew next to nothing about what Kane really did? Yet when Sean needed Kane, he couldn't always get through.

She wasn't being fair. But she was scared. Truly scared about the man she loved.

She stared at her engagement ring. "Be safe, Sean," she whispered.

Then she took out her laptop and began going over the files from Logan Dunbar's computer, hoping she could find the information that Nicole thought was worth killing an FBI agent for.

CHAPTER TWENTY-SIX

It was ten minutes before midnight. Sean set up his computer again to track Kane's watch. They'd been in Mexico for twelve hours and were only marginally closer to finding Kane. He was going to go insane from waiting.

Sean and Blitz had spent the last six hours hiding from numerous patrols who were doing exactly what they were doing: looking for Kane.

Before they moved into Juarez's territory, Blitz contacted an informant to find out what was going on. It had taken four hours—four hours that Sean didn't want to waste—to learn that Felipe Juarez had accepted the bounty on Kane Rogan—dead or alive, one million US dollars. Once they moved into the region, Sean had to stay with the plane and let Blitz do recon. Blitz was right—Sean looked too much like Kane to be safe when a bounty that high had been issued. It wasn't the first time a cartel had put a bounty on Kane's head, but one million was the highest. Once night fell, it would be easier for Sean to move around.

Blitz returned with information: The gang hadn't captured or killed Kane, but they had him boxed him into a canyon. They were in the process of bringing in more people to overwhelm the area and flush him out.

He dropped a pack inside the plane.

Sean stared at the bag, anger and grief battling. "That's Kane's."

"He either lost it or used it as a diversion. He has a day's supply of food and water on his person, but his radio is completely busted." He dumped it out on the ground. It was destroyed, shot with multiple bullets.

Blitz pulled out Kane's sat phone and put it in his own pack. "You also need to know that Kane's been shot."

"How do you know?" He kept staring at the broken radio. *Dammit, Kane.*

"That's the word, that he's injured and holed up. They'll find him if we don't find him first. Or he'll die."

"Kane is too stubborn."

"And he has a knife, two sidearms, and an M5. Enough ammo to hold off a small force, but I don't know how many rounds he may have used earlier, or if he was able to procure more. And that won't help if they have grenades. Which I assume they do. Good news is that he had the wherewithal to keep his first-aid kit with him." Blitz looked at him quizzically. "Are you really ready for this?"

Sean nodded. No, he wasn't. He didn't want to die out here. But he didn't want Kane to die out there, either. If anyone could make it out of this trap, it was Kane—but even Kane wasn't invincible. Kane was injured, he needed help, and there was no way in hell that Sean would let him die if he could do something to stop it.

The first bounty on Kane was to grab him alive. Kane didn't know that the bounty had been changed to a kill order. It was much easier to kill someone than capture him still breathing.

Blitz pulled down his mask. He'd already darkened his

face with cosmetics for camouflage. Sean quickly covered his face, then pulled down his own mask.

Blitz had a good idea where Kane was hiding. Partly because the gang had already covered much of the area, and partly because Blitz knew Kane's methodology. He'd want to be near water because of his injury and not knowing how long he would be stuck there. He also would want a good vantage point to identify potential threats.

"How fast can you get this plane out of here dark?" Blitz said.

"Fast."

"We might not have more than a few minutes."

They were not on a real runway, which was the single greatest problem. Sean had spent the hours Blitz was gone going up and down the clearing to get rid of anything that might damage the plane—rocks, tree branches, filling in holes—and prevent them from getting into the air. The other problem was they didn't have much distance to gain speed for takeoff. If he couldn't get the plane up, they'd go down a steep rock face and crash into trees and boulders on their way to the bottom of the canyon. Survivable? Maybe. While being pursued by gunmen? Probably not.

He didn't want to crash his plane. He liked it, he'd made many special modifications, and he didn't want to break in another. But this was the one time he wished he could fly a helicopter.

He was going to take lessons as soon as he got back to San Antonio.

"I'll get us up," he told Blitz. He looked at his watch. 12:05. He turned to his computer and motioned for Blitz.

The soldier came over and looked over Sean's shoulder. "That's almost exactly where I thought he'd be," Blitz said. "Couldn't trust my instincts?"

"We have the tech, we damn well are going to use it,"

Sean snapped. He shut down his laptop and stowed it in the plane.

They had a two-mile trek down into the canyon. Sean had never truly feared for his life before. He'd been in harrowing situations. He'd flown under fire for Kane. He'd fallen down a mine shaft and hadn't known if anyone would find him. He'd been shot at, barely escaped a forest fire, and once long ago had nearly died in the plane crash that claimed the lives of his parents.

He'd taken his life in his hands many times. He loved street racing and had crashed twice, once resulting in a broken leg. He'd been fifteen and legally not allowed to drive. He'd been reckless in his youth, not only with his plane and cars and speedboats, but in putting himself into dangerous situations. Maybe he'd had a death wish for a while after his parents died. He'd gotten out of the crash with minor injuries; his parents were dead. He'd buried their bodies. He never talked about it. He hadn't even told Lucy everything. He really didn't want to dig too deep in his psyche.

That was sixteen years ago, more than half his life, and now he had so much more to live for. He wasn't going to hurt Lucy by getting himself killed.

"Let's go," Sean said, edgy.

"I'm waiting for someone."

Sean froze. "Who?"

"Ranger."

"You didn't tell me."

"Because I didn't know if he'd make it in time."

"Yet we're waiting for him."

"You have to trust me."

Sean didn't say anything. He did—and he didn't. He didn't trust many people. Not anymore. There'd been a time when he trusted the wrong people.

"He knows where we are. He parachuted in on the other

side of the mountain, to avoid being detected. I'm giving him fifteen more minutes, then we go with or without him."

"Don't leave without me," a voice said behind them.

Sean whirled around, gun in hand. Blitz didn't.

"You're edgy, Little Rogan," Blitz said.

Ranger came out of the shrubs. That a man as large as Ranger—six foot three and two-hundred-some pounds of solid muscle—could be so stealthy was almost unnerving.

"It's my brother who's been shot."

"And our commander," Blitz said.

"And my best friend," Ranger said. "Kane Rogan is not going to die today. But we'd better go, because they're getting close. They're going to find this plane at the first crack of light."

"I don't plan on being around at sunrise," Sean said.

"Good." Ranger slapped him on the back. It hurt, but Sean didn't show a response. "Don't get yourself killed, kid."

At least he didn't call him "Little Rogan."

Sean turned on his cell phone. On the top of the mountain he had a signal, one bar, and that's all he needed to get out a text message.

Going dark. I love you.

He watched the message clear, then he turned off his phone and followed Ranger and Blitz down the mountain.

CHAPTER TWENTY-SEVEN

Lucy was dozing off when her phone vibrated. She reached over and grabbed it. She'd been up here for an hour going over the files. Maybe she'd slept for ten minutes.

It was a message from an unfamiliar number.

Going dark. I love you.

No signature, nothing to tell her it was from Sean, but she knew it was him.

She shifted her papers around and her laptop woke itself up when she bumped it. She'd been reading a long legal document that the AUSA had sent to Logan Dunbar. That's what had put her to sleep.

She was about to shut off the computer and go find Jack—he needed to know about this message from Sean. He might know what it meant. Maybe he'd heard something else. But a phrase on the screen caught her eye.

Civilian consultant CC474, authorized by ASAC DEAN S HOOPER, Sacramento Division, FBI, the former director of the White Collar Crimes Division out of Washington, piggybacked a

program on the wire transfers in order to prevent
EVERETT from transferring the full amount of the
laundered money to the account controlled by
TOBIAS.

Civilian consultant.
Sean.
Undercover agents, informants, and anyone else the
AUSA or FBI didn't want to publicly identify were given a
coded number. Access to that list was severely restricted,
and she didn't know if even Nicole would have someone
that far up the ladder working for her.

Except . . . she'd read something that afternoon about a
civilian consultant. What was it?

The memo from Barry.

She searched Dunbar's documents for anything from
Barry Crawford. She found a memo, not from Barry but
from Dunbar to Rick Stockton. He'd written it after Sean
had found the bug in Worthington's office, when he was
still angry that the investigation into Worthington's murder might impact his investigation into political corruption.
This was before Adeline Worthington had been killed and
before they'd connected her money laundering to Tobias
and, by extension, Nicole Rollins.

She skimmed most of it because it was a rehash of the
conversation they'd had in Ritz Naygrow's office at the
time. Most of it was accurate, though slanted from Dunbar's point of view. Until near the end when he wrote:

I hesitate to mention this because I know that
you have a professional and personal relationship
with Rogan-Caruso-Kincaid Protective Services. I
respect much of the work that they've done over
the years as consultants to the FBI and other law
enforcement agencies. However, I was told that

*Sean Rogan resigned from RCK. He has no
contract with the FBI or any other government
agency, and I am concerned that using him as a
civilian consultant on the Harper Worthington
murder investigation could come back to bite us in
court. While I was told by SSA Casilla that Rogan
was hired by Worthington's company to run the
security audit, it's clear that he assisted the FBI
in identifying and tracking the legal wiretap on
Worthington's office phone.*

*I feel compelled to mention this because the
case I am building against Congresswoman
Reyes-Worthington is solid, but her attorneys will
exploit any hole, jeopardizing a year-long
investigation. It's one of the reasons that I have
been vocal in my opposition to using civilian
consultants in many of our white-collar
investigations. The risk may be slight, but it exists
and cannot be overlooked.*

*I understand that Sean Rogan has unique
skills and was instrumental in infiltrating the
hacker organization known as NET, resulting in
saving an untold number of lives, but the potential
conflict with his involvement with a federal agent
and involvement in a major investigation remains.
I look forward to discussing this further with you
when I return to DC after this case is put to bed.
I apologize if I have overstepped, but felt it was
important to let you know that there could be a
problem in the prosecution of our case if we don't
restrain our use of civilian consultants.*

She jumped up and ran from her room. She found
Jack and Nate in the dining room talking quietly. Jack
had moved Sean's security iPad to the table in front of him

and was monitoring all the cameras Sean had set up around the property. Hans wasn't there.

"I know why Nicole is still in town."

"I thought you were asleep," Jack said.

"I dozed off, just for a few minutes." She showed him the message from Sean. "He sent this about fifteen minutes ago."

"Good."

That momentarily sidetracked her.

"Good?"

"I suspected Sean would break protocol and contact you before they went to retrieve Kane."

"What do you know about it?"

"Not much. Ranger parachuted in to assist in the rescue operation."

"Rescue?" She was repeating Jack, but she was confused.

"I don't know specifics," he said. "The Juarez gang has been dispatched to a region southeast of Santiago because of the increased bounty for Kane. That's why Ranger decided to go down. Ranger was part of my unit before I retired. He's one of the very best. You have to let this go for now. Go back to sleep."

She sat down at the table. "I can't," she said. "I know why Nicole wanted Dunbar's files."

She rubbed her head. Maybe she was blowing it out of proportion.

Nate slid over a water bottle. She drank, then said, "There was no reason for Rollins to kill Dunbar. And why in DC and not in San Antonio where it would have been easier to get to him? Because they needed something from him. His laptop. Logically, he would travel with his laptop, and that laptop has all the information about Congresswoman Worthington's case."

"But none of that is private. He would have sent memos

and reports to everyone else involved. If they destroyed the laptop, the information is still out there."

"They didn't want to destroy it, they only wanted to see it. They need information. For Nicole to escape and have a chance to survive on the run, she needs money. The money that Sean siphoned off into the FBI asset forfeiture accounts."

"Did Dunbar have access to that information?" Jack asked.

"I don't know—but in the hundred-and-ninety-page court brief, it clearly states that a civilian consultant was responsible for hijacking the money transfer under the authorization of Dean Hooper. It doesn't name Sean, but it has a UC code."

"That doesn't mean they'll know it was Sean," Jack said.

She shook her head. "The brief isn't the problem, it's everything together. First the brief clearly states *how* their money was seized. Then a memo that Dunbar wrote to Rick Stockton after Sean found the bug in Worthington's phone identified Sean as the one who found the bug, and he explicitly said that Sean was acting as a civilian consultant. Dunbar also referenced Sean's involvement in going undercover with a hacker group in New York. It wouldn't take a genius to realize that the civilian consultant in the brief is Sean. Hooper is in Sacramento; Sean was born in Sacramento. Sean graduated from M.I.T. They know Kane Rogan was in town two weeks ago, they know Kane and Sean are brothers, and they know that I'm living with Sean."

She looked from Nate to Jack. "We have to find a way to warn him!" Her voice cracked. "He needs to know that he's as much a target as Kane."

"He's always been a target, because he's Kane's brother and he was in Mexico when Kane raided Trejo's complex."

Why didn't they see what she saw? "Rollins wants Sean to get their money. It's the only reason she would stay local when every cop in every agency is looking for her. We're talking about over ten million dollars. Money that she would consider *hers* and that Sean has the skills to retrieve. I think this whole bounty on Kane was initially because she thought Kane took the money. Sean told me"—she glanced at Nate, then continued—"that there were some operations where he hacked into a cartel's account at the behest of Kane."

"I'm aware. That's long in the past. RCK doesn't sanction those actions anymore. We can't, not with our relationship with federal law enforcement."

"But *Sean* did it, not Kane—yet they might think it was Kane because he took responsibility for the theft. He's the face behind the Trejo raid. So they wanted him to get their money thinking *he's* the one who took it. Now they have discovered that it was a quasi-sanctioned federal operation, and that Kane *didn't* do it. Sean did."

Jack didn't say anything for a minute. He and Nate exchanged looks and Lucy wanted to scream. Did they think she was paranoid? She knew she was right. Deep down she knew that as soon as Nicole hacked into Dunbar's hard drive, she would realize it was Sean who took her money.

Jack said, "I'll call Padre. He's the contact for the team. The first place they'll go is Hidalgo."

"Okay. Okay." She took a deep breath, let it out. "Thank you."

Jack took her hand. "I'm not going to let anything happen to Sean."

She didn't say anything. Jack couldn't make a promise like that. Hundreds of cops were looking for Nicole, combing through her contacts, her family, her cases. Everyone wanted her caught. Lucy believed in the system. There were more good cops than bad. No one was going to stop looking until they found her and put her in prison for life.

But between now and then? Sam Archer was dead. Barry Crawford was dead. How many people did Nicole hate enough to kill? No one Lucy cared about would be safe as long as Nicole was alive.

Prison hadn't stopped Nicole before; it wouldn't stop her now.

In the deep darkness, Blitz set a fast, steady pace down the mountain. The three of them wore night-vision goggles. The air was warm, there was no breeze, and every footfall sounded like a cannon, but they moved as quietly as possible. Blitz took the lead, Ranger the rear.

Sean realized that he was ill suited for this kind of work. His specialty was computers and electronics. Give him a security system, he could hack it. Give him an airplane, he could fly it from anywhere. He'd even go so far as to say he could survive in the wilderness if he had to. But military-style operations weren't his strength, and he could count on one hand the number of ops—outside of being the getaway pilot—he'd done with Kane. And that included the raid of Trejo's compound three months ago after rescuing the boys.

He trusted Blitz and Ranger because Kane did, but he recognized that Kane's men had formed this line with him in the middle because Sean wasn't a soldier.

Stop second-guessing yourself, Rogan. Kane is your brother. You can do this.

It was the fear that they would find Kane dead that terrified Sean most of all. He didn't want to fly his brother's corpse back to Texas. Kane was a loner with many friends. Friends like Ranger and Padre and Blitz and Jack, who were soldiers and comrades. But Kane still had an aura of loneliness. He kept the family at arm's length, and while

Sean knew some of the reasons, he didn't completely understand. He wanted to. He admired Kane, respected him, was frustrated with him, but mostly he didn't want to lose him. It bothered Sean greatly that he was closer to Lucy's brother Patrick than to any of his own brothers. He was closer to Jack than he was to Kane, and Jack and Kane were two of a kind. Except—Jack didn't keep his family at arm's length. Jack recognized that family mattered, that family made life better.

There was nothing Sean wanted to do more than marry Lucy. Getting Jack and Patrick and the others as his brothers was icing on the cake.

He had a lot to ask Kane. Things he'd tried to get him to talk about before, but Kane refused. Like about their parents' plane crash sixteen years ago. About their older sister Molly's overdose even farther back. About what had happened to make Kane hate their brother Liam, and if that event had forced Liam into what was essentially an exile in Europe. Sean wanted to understand some of the choices Kane had made and why. Kane never talked about himself, but Sean had to change that.

Blitz put his hand up. Sean stopped walking. No one moved for a long minute. In the distance Sean could hear vehicles, but he saw no lights and no people. Then Blitz motioned to move forward, but at a slower pace.

They stopped several more times. Sean's nighttime hearing sharpened—he heard voices in the distance, two or three men talking. A distant sound of a jeep. Sound carried faintly in the still night. He began to sense the same movements that Blitz did, as if his dormant instincts had kicked into high gear.

It took them seventeen minutes to reach a ditch next to a road not much better than the old dirt road Sean had used as a runway earlier. This road wound across the mountain, from the base to the top, but parts of it were extremely steep and narrow with areas barely the width of a vehicle. They didn't use the road coming down to avoid being seen, but in a pinch they could use it going back up. They were nearly two miles from the plane, shorter as the crow flew.

Blitz motioned for them to drop. There was movement in the canyon in front of them, then the headlights of a vehicle swooped right over where they'd been standing. Soon Sean couldn't hear anything but the whine of a jeep that hadn't been well maintained. The sick fumes of exhaust as it passed them made Sean's eyes water. The jeep stopped twenty yards away and three men got out. They left the lights on but turned the jeep off.

The three were talking and smoking. Sean didn't understand everything they said—they spoke in rapid Spanish. But Blitz listened intently. A radio buzzed and one of the men responded with an affirmative, then all three started down the other side of the embankment and into a dense grouping of trees.

Blitz spoke so low Sean almost couldn't hear him.

"They've narrowed the search to this ravine. They're close, we have to go now."

He turned to Sean. "Stay here."

Sean opened his mouth to argue. Blitz said, "You can hot-wire that jeep, can't you?"

"Yes."

"Be alert. No guns unless absolutely necessary. Radio silence. We need fifteen minutes, max. I'll signal you on the radio when we're one minute out. That's how long you have to hot-wire our transport. Don't approach the jeep until my signal."

Sean nodded his agreement. Sean understood the reasoning—Sean was the expert on cars and planes. But he didn't have to like it.

"Rogan, I need to know that you can protect yourself if necessary."

Sean knew exactly what he meant. He dipped his head once.

"If we're not back in twenty minutes, leave the jeep, get back to the plane, and go."

"I'm not leaving without Kane," Sean whispered.

"Do as you're told," Ranger said. "We'll get Kane out."

Thirty seconds later Blitz and Ranger were gone, thirty degrees south of where the three men had headed.

Sean waited.

He didn't wait well.

But he waited.

Five minutes later a burst of gunfire came from the direction Blitz and Ranger had gone. Sean had his gun in hand and scurried out of the ditch toward the jeep, staying low to the ground. There was no signal to hot-wire the jeep, and if he turned it on too soon it might alert a patrol. That's when he noticed that one of the three men who'd gotten out of the jeep was standing by a tree on the other side of the embankment, smoking. An AK-47 was strapped over his shoulder. Sean couldn't see if he also had a side-arm. He was frozen in place by the gunfire, which stopped as quickly as it started. The trail of cigarette smoke moved slowly in Sean's direction. There were shouts in the distance, but Sean couldn't hear what they were saying. He couldn't even tell if they were speaking Spanish or English.

Sean remained flat on the road. If he stood up, the movement might startle the guard. He quietly holstered his gun and unsheathed his knife, remembering Blitz's admonition. Sean didn't know what was happening in the ravine. He didn't want to think about being the last man standing. He didn't want to think about fucking this up and risking all their lives.

His heart pounded so hard that all he heard was blood rushing through his veins. He willed himself to calm down. Focused on the guard across the road. Focused on what he had to do as soon as Blitz gave him the signal.

He looked at his watch. Only eight minutes had passed. Fifteen minutes, Blitz had said. Did he know exactly where Kane was? He'd done recon, and they verified with Sean's GPS, but what if Kane had moved in the last hour? What if he'd lost his watch? What if he was dead?

Had Blitz told Sean everything he knew?

Sean pushed his doubts aside and focused on the guard. By concentrating on the immediate threat he slowed his heart rate enough that he didn't feel the pressure of his own fear.

The guard's radio transmitted static, then a voice.

The guard answered. Sean made out a few words.

Gone.

The marine.

Camp.

At least that's what he thought, his Spanish was very rough.

Then he heard an order, didn't know what it meant until the guard tossed his cigarette after crushing it against a tree and started toward the jeep.

Sean's radio beeped twice in his pocket.

The guard pulled keys from his pocket and was about to hop into the jeep.

Sean crawled closer, staying low. But his movement caught the attention of the guard. He shined a light into the ravine. "Jose?"

Sean jumped to his feet as soon as he reached the jeep.

The guard jumped, whirled around and fumbled with the gun that was strapped to his back.

If you hesitate, you're dead.

Kane had beaten that message into Sean's head during training. Sean didn't hesitate. He used his momentum to grab the bar of the jeep and swing his legs around to kick the guard in the chest. The guard spun around and fell to his hands and knees.

Don't hesitate.

Sean let go of the bar as the guard shouted once for José. Sean tackled the guard, pushing him fully to the ground, facedown. The guard swung his hand around, holding a switchblade. He stabbed at Sean, slicing his arm. Sean reached forward and slit the guard's throat. Warm blood shot out, soaking the ground, the coppery stench burning Sean's nose. He was breathing hard, feeling disconnected from his body. His arm burned from where the guard had cut him. Sean jumped up and heard more gunfire, this time much closer.

He was about to hot-wire the jeep but saw the keys in the dirt. He picked them up and stuck the key in the ignition. It turned on the first try.

Sean dropped his knife between the seats and pulled his gun, expecting trouble to burst onto the road.

A voice came through his radio. It was Blitz.

"Now, kid."

Ten seconds later Blitz came through the trees. He didn't have his mask on, and his eyes were wild but determined. Right behind him was Ranger half carrying, half dragging Kane. Sean put the jeep in gear and started rolling forward as Blitz helped Ranger put Kane in the back. Ranger jumped in next to Kane and Blitz ran around to the passenger side. Before he was even in, he ordered Sean, "Go, go, go!"

Sean drove. He didn't spare a glance at Kane. He thought his brother was alive, but he couldn't tell. The road ahead was treacherous and he could easily flip the jeep, killing them all. Or drive off one of the sheer drops. Or worse, not kill them—and then the cartel would catch up to them and torture them before putting a bullet in their brain.

Stop. Focus.

Driving always calmed Sean, even driving through

difficult terrain. He went faster than he should, getting a feel for the jeep and what it could do, how it could take the turns. The dirt road was deeply rutted and strewn with rocks and branches and shrubs growing out of shallow holes.

A ping on the metal of the back reminded Sean that people were after them.

"They're everywhere," Blitz said, his voice grim.

"Kane?" Sean asked.

"Alive."

That was it. Blitz was focused on the surroundings. He fired a couple of times and Sean didn't know if he hit anything or was trying to chase their attackers into the shadows.

Another ping and Sean felt something hit his face. Shit, that hurt. Blood dripped into his eye and he absently wiped it off. He didn't think he'd been shot; it was a ricochet off metal.

He dared to speed up.

"Slow down," Blitz said.

"I got it."

"There's a ninety-degree turn ahead, sheer drop to the left. Slow down!"

Sean eased up and shifted gears. The jeep whined.

Then he saw the curve.

"Shit!"

The road was so narrow the jeep could barely pass. To the left was the drop, to the right a ravine. The road was at an angle, and the jeep was top-heavy.

Sean speeded up just a bit. He was close to the edge and didn't dare look down.

Blitz was swearing under his breath, and Sean could have sworn he heard Ranger recite some Bible verse in the back.

Sean became one with the jeep. He understood its limitations and its strengths. He leaned away from the curve as the rear tire dipped off the edge. If he slowed, they'd be stuck or worse, spinning and slipping down the mountainside.

"Downshift!" Blitz said.

Sean ignored him. If he downshifted, he'd slow for a second and they'd be toast. Instead he pressed on the gas and their momentum propelled them forward and out of danger.

And then it was over.

"Fuck," Blitz said.

Sean continued to speed up and almost immediately they were at the top of the small mountain. He prayed his plane hadn't been discovered. There was no way to get to Kane's plane except by going back the way they came—directly through enemy territory.

He floored it once they hit the clearing. The moon was rising and he would be able to see better—but that also meant their enemy would be able to see them.

He stopped the jeep next to the plane. As soon as he turned off the ignition, he heard their pursuers.

It sounded like a fucking army was after them.

There were shouts and orders in the distance, and at least one vehicle though it seemed that most of the gang was on foot, but Sean didn't see anyone. Yet.

Blitz opened the doors, and he and Ranger slid Kane onto the floor of the plane where Sean had taken out the extra two seats. Sean's little Cessna 185 had little comfort, but many unseen bells and whistles. Sean climbed in and turned the ignition. He needed to get this baby warmed up fast. He'd long ago upgraded the engine with more horsepower, but planes weren't like cars. They couldn't go from zero to sixty in six seconds.

He slowly started to roll.

"You gotta be faster, kid," Ranger said.

"Close the door," Sean ordered.

"I need line of sight," Blitz said, his gun out and ready to fire on anyone who emerged from the mountain.

"I need to fucking get us off the ground! Close the damn door!"

Blitz complied. Sean pushed his plane, knowing what it was capable of, but needing more out of it than he'd ever asked. He couldn't see directly in front of him because his nose was up, the two front tundra tires much larger than the small tail wheel in the back. He glanced behind him, trying to catch a glimpse of Kane, but Blitz was sitting in the rear-facing seat, blocking Sean's view.

Sean glanced out the side window and saw headlights among the trees. Shit. He'd have to pop the plane off the ground and try to build more speed by flying several feet from the surface. It was dangerous, but at this point if he didn't do something the men coming up the mountain would open fire. He'd reinforced his plane and windows, but weight was always an issue and Sean couldn't put in all the safety features he wanted. With enough firepower, Juarez's men could take out the engine and crash the plane.

"Hold on," Sean said through clenched teeth.

He'd only done this once before, but he could hear his first flight instructor Deborah in his ear.

"Be the plane, Sean. You're a natural."

He wished Deborah were here now. She was the only person he'd admit was a better pilot than he was.

A bullet hit Sean's window and it cracked. One more direct hit and it would be gone. If he hadn't swapped the cheap plexi-glass with sturdier material, he'd be dead.

Sean didn't think anymore, he acted on instinct. Another bullet hit the plane, but he blocked out the danger and concentrated on the push and pull of the yoke to pop off the ground. He had to get the wheels up to minimize the drag and gain more speed.

It worked. Only five or so feet off the ground, but he already felt the engine respond. The thin air wasn't doing him any favors, but the cooler evening helped. He wouldn't have been able to do this at high noon. All the lights in the cockpit were good. His controls looked good. He could do this.

The Cessna straightened and leveled off. Sean's heart raced as a jeep and two men popped into view, only fifty feet in front of him. He didn't have time to think; he immediately pulled back on the yoke. If his wheels hit the vehicle, they were toast.

That he cleared the jeep and didn't crash was a miracle in itself, but they weren't clear yet. The two men now behind them sprayed bullets at the plane and Sean felt every hit as if it were his own body. The plane dipped and he compensated. But something was off. The controls felt mushy. The plane dropped again and hit ground, bouncing all of them hard. Kane grunted from the back. Sean almost had enough speed.

Get the damn plane in the air.

He pulled up on the yoke and this time, the plane didn't dip down. Suddenly there was no ground at all. He was off the mountain. He felt another ping of a bullet and the plane suddenly yawed to the left.

"Shit!"

"What?" Blitz demanded.

"Left tire is blown." That would make landing a load of fun. Sean straightened the plane and gained altitude.

He looked at his controls and gauges. Only one system was completely down—the one system he'd installed himself. Communications.

But the plane still felt mushy. He couldn't see the wings, but he suspected there were some holes in them. He banked slowly south. The plane wasn't responding well, he wouldn't be performing any tricks. They needed to circumvent Monterrey because traveling over the Mexican city would alert authorities.

"How is he?" Sean asked.

"I can hear you," Kane said. His voice was weak. Sean heard Ranger tearing open Kane's clothes.

"Shit, boss."

"Just get me to Padre."

"Padre can't fix this," Ranger said quietly. "You need a hospital. You've lost a lot of blood."

"Did you stop the bleeding?" Blitz asked.

"I'm trying."

The plane tilted from the sudden movement as Blitz and Ranger worked on Kane.

"Don't move any more than you have to," Sean said. His jaw was clenched so tight his head ached.

"How long, Little Rogan?" Blitz asked.

"Hour." Though he wasn't sure the plane was going to make it. "I lost communications. I can't alert Padre or air traffic control."

"Cell communications?"

"There are places where we might pick up a signal, but I lost my transmitter. My left wheel is flapping rubber and there're holes in the wing."

"Are we going to reach Hidalgo?"

"Yes." *I hope.*

"He needs blood," Ranger said.

"My satchel," Kane said.

"That can wait, boss."

Silence, then there was movement in the back. Sean winced and compensated. His maneuverability sucked. He had to continue to work the rudders to counter the yaw of the blown tire. He'd be tense until they landed.

Kane said, "I tracked the bastard who kidnapped Siobhan. He's a fed. Dover, agent out of Mexico City."

Kane shifted and groaned.

"Boss, I stopped the bleeding, but you still have a bullet in you."

"Get it out."

"No."

"It's an order."

"Fuck that, I open up the wound and you'll bleed to death."

"Kane and I have the same blood type," Sean said. "Can you do a field transfusion?"

"Too risky," Ranger said. "And you need to fly this bucket of bolts."

"I'm not going to let my brother bleed to death. Where's he hit?"

"Thigh and back. Near his kidneys. I stopped the bleeding. As long as we get him to the hospital—then we'll take your blood. But I'm not going to fucking do surgery in a plane that's falling apart around us."

Blitz came forward and sat in the copilot's seat. The plane tilted again and Sean swore. "Shit, Blitz. Buckle up." It had seemed to take forever to get the damn plane to turn. He had to take it slow and wide. But he was finally heading in the right direction.

"You're bleeding," Blitz said to Sean.

"A guard at the jeep. He was given orders to leave. I stopped him."

Blitz looked at Sean's arm under a penlight. "Knife. Deep. We need to clean it up, kid. You'll need stitches."

"Do it and don't tell me."

He winced as Blitz sprayed antiseptic on his arm. "It ain't gonna be pretty, but it'll be better than nothing."

Sean withstood the pain of the needle as Blitz put several stitches in his arm. He glued the edges to seal the cut, then taped on a loose bandage.

Blitz handed two horse-sized pills to Sean. "We don't know where that knife has been. Take these."

Sean did as he was told and guzzled an entire water bottle.

"Well, that was fun." Blitz leaned back in the copilot's seat and closed his eyes.

Sean wasn't certain he was being sarcastic.

CHAPTER TWENTY-EIGHT

Nicole woke up to Joseph talking on the phone. She'd fallen asleep on the couch reading stupid, boring emails to and from Logan Dunbar. Sure, there was some information in here that might be beneficial to them later, but nothing that pointed at who stole her money.

She stretched and her back cracked. She walked over to the coffeepot on the bar and poured herself a cup of hot black coffee. Joseph squeezed her hand and continued his conversation.

Or rather, continued listening. The expression on his face was rigid. Something bad had happened.

"Send me everything you have," Joseph said. "Don't argue, just do it. To me, understand?"

He hung up and rubbed his eyes.

"You need sleep," she said.

"Rogan got away. Those bastards shot him, had him cornered, and he fucking got out."

"This is like a bad joke. We set the trap and he avoids damage like the Road Runner cartoon."

"His days of running will soon be over. The report says he was seriously injured."

"We can't assume anything."

"They had dozens of people on his tail, and somehow his men found and extracted him. No one knows how the fuck they found him, but they know how he got away. Two men, one black and one white, carried him out under gunfire. Then—get this—Sean Rogan flew the plane out of Mexico."

"You're right. I don't believe it."

"Juarez is sending us photos, but he recognized the Rogan brothers on sight. Jimmy had Adam Dover killed when he let the redhead and Kane slip away the first time—if he was ID'd, his time was up anyway. But Rogan grabbed his wallet and phone and knows who he is."

Nicole sat heavily on a bar stool. "Okay—we can adjust. We knew that Dover could be made if the feds looked deep into my file. I'm surprised it took them three months to uncover it."

"I spoke to Maggie again. The feds she spoke to were from the FBI, and our contact learned late last night that our favorite bitch is the one who put it together. She spoke to your brother, dissected your entire personnel file." He slid over a thin packet. "This is your profile, darling. I didn't know Kincaid was a profiler."

Nicole grabbed the papers and flipped through them. Words and phrases jumped out at her.

Rollins is in charge; Tobias is a figurehead . . .

Rollins is ruthless . . .

. . . money is her primary reason for staying local . . .

. . . narcissistic . . .

. . . resents the DEA, blames the DEA for her father's death . . .

. . . the murder of John Rollins should be reopened . . .

. . . her uncle is Jimmy Hunt, a wanted fugitive who fled five years ago . . .

"How the *hell* does she know all this?"

"Your brother was *very* chatty."

"I should have killed him long ago."

"He's never been a problem until someone asked the right questions."

Nicole screamed and crumbled the papers in her fist. "That *bitch*! What gives her the right to psychoanalyze me? Like she can possibly know me?" She took a deep breath. "At least they haven't made all the connections. But if Elise opens her mouth again—"

"My concern is that Kincaid knows your house in San Antonio was a cover. We dismantled the safe house in the city, but if they're looking for safe houses, it's only a matter of time before they find this place."

"How?"

"I'm good, Niki. Very good. But there are property records. It'll take someone very sharp to connect the company that owns this property to us, but we need to leave the country. You're not safe." He put his hands on her shoulders. "I can't lose you, Niki. I would rather die."

She wrapped her arms tightly around his neck. "I don't deserve you, Joseph."

"It's the other way around," he whispered.

The door opened and both Nicole and Joseph pulled their weapons.

Tobias.

Nicole feared for a minute that Joseph would shoot him, but he slowly lowered his gun.

"You fucking idiot," Joseph said.

"Screw you."

"Stop," Nicole said. "We don't have the time to argue."

Tobias glared at them. "You talked to my dad? He wants me in Mexico *now*. That's fucked."

"It's for your own good, Toby. We need to lay low until we get the money."

Tobias handed her his phone. "Look at the pictures."

She did. Lucy Kincaid. Going into her house. Leaving

her house. Never alone. She recognized Nate Dunning from the FBI, but not the old guy, and not the half-Hispanic guy who came in late last night. "You went to her *house*?"

"I didn't do anything, just watched. Too many people are keeping tabs on her, but I thought if I could grab her we'd have leverage."

"Do not touch her! Fuck, Toby! The wrath of God will come down on us, and we don't have time for it before we get the money. Remember the bigger plan. We'll take care of her when it's time."

"No one is that well protected," Tobias said.

You are, she wanted to say, but didn't.

Tobias tossed her the flash drive he'd taken. "Lyle and I went through the files, made a list of every name in every email over the last two weeks. Some high-up fed named Dean Hooper authorized the operation to take our money, but he's in Sacramento."

She wanted to strangle him and kiss him—the names! Whoever did it would be on record. She'd read the legal briefs, but they didn't name anyone specifically. Just a *civilian consultant*.

"Let me see it," she said.

"Go to the notes app on my phone."

She did and scrolled through.

"Did you know that Kane Rogan is in surgery in Hidalgo?" Tobias continued. "He slipped away. *Again.*" He glared at Joseph.

Joseph tensed and Nicole put her hand on his arm. "Stop it," Nicole said. "We're in this together, Tobias. Don't bait Joseph. We know what happened with Rogan, Juarez, and Dover."

Joseph showed Tobias the photo that Juarez sent of the four men climbing into the plane. "Recognize them?"

"Rogan, his brother, the black guy—I know him. He stole my helicopter at Trejo's place. Bastard."

"They're all going to be dead when we're done here."

"Good," Tobias said.

"Wait—wait!" Nicole tossed Tobias his phone and ran to the couch where all the papers she'd printed from Dunbar's hard drive were strewn about. She rifled through them until she found the memo she was looking for. She waved it around, giddy. "Rogan! He took our money."

"You said he didn't have the skill," Tobias countered.

"Not Kane, the soldier. *Sean Rogan.* His brother. Did you know that he used to be a hacker? Then he made millions designing computer games when he got out of college. He worked undercover for the FBI to take down another hacker organization. And he's living with that bitch Kincaid. It's all here—I just didn't see it. *He's* the civilian consultant who worked with the FBI to siphon off our money. He has the skill, Kincaid must have given him information."

"Okay," Joseph said, "if it is Sean Rogan, how do we force him to give it back? Kane is under guard at a hospital, Kincaid is being watched by military types, who else can we grab for leverage?"

"Sean Rogan himself. And believe me, when I'm through with him, he'll retrieve all our money and then some. Because he'll know if he doesn't, everyone he cares about—Kincaid, his brother, and those fucking boys in the fucking *boys' home* he set up—will die."

She turned to her cousin. "Toby, how did you get so close to Kincaid without being seen?"

"Her neighbors are on vacation. I'm not stupid, Nicole. I know how to do recon. Lyle disabled the alarm and we hung there for the night. Nice place. Perfect view of Kincaid's house."

"Lyle," she said to the man who might still die for picking Tobias over her, "go back there. I'm going to try to grab Rogan on his way back from Hidalgo—I'll bet once his brother is in the clear, he'll hightail it home to check on his precious girlfriend. But if we miss him, I want to know when he gets home and who else is there. Keep me notified of every change, every movement, every person— I don't want to be surprised."

Lyle left, and Nicole kissed Joseph. "Today is the day. We'll have our money and leave Texas for good. And every one of those pricks who thought they were smarter than us will be dead by sundown."

CHAPTER TWENTY-NINE

Lucy woke up to a quiet voice in the dining room. She sat up. The lights were dim and at first she didn't know who was talking; then she recognized her brother's voice. He was on the phone. It was barely five in the morning; she didn't think she'd fallen asleep until three, and she'd stayed on the couch, feeling somehow safer here than alone in her bed without Sean by her side. The scent of rich coffee had her mouth watering. She stretched then walked gingerly to the kitchen, the tile floors cold on her feet. She doctored her coffee with cream and sugar and walked back to the dining room.

"ETA?" Jack said into the phone. "I would come down, but—yeah. Yeah—well, tell him he's used eight of his nine lives and he's getting too old for this shit. Put Sean on the phone."

A huge weight lifted from her chest. They were okay. They were all okay.

Jack said, "Good work, Sean . . . She's right here."

She took the phone Jack offered her.

"Hey," she said softly.

"Hey yourself, princess," Sean said. At the sound of his voice her eyes watered. She sipped her coffee, letting the emotions wash over her. Relief. Nerves. The remnants of fear.

"You're okay."

"A couple bumps and bruises. Nothing that won't work itself out in the hot tub."

She smiled and rubbed her eyes. He was alive. That was all that mattered.

"Kane? The others?"

"Kane will be fine. Jack has the details. I need to get on the road. We had an issue with my plane, so I'm driving up."

"Not alone."

He didn't say anything for a second. "I'd planned on it. Why?"

She told him about the information in Dunbar's computer. It came spilling out in one long run-on sentence. She paused, but before Sean could say anything, she said, "I have no proof, but we know the reason Tobias had Harper Worthington killed was because Adeline kept the money she was supposed to launder for him. Why, we don't know, but that's really not important at this point. What's important is that you're the one responsible for Tobias—and Nicole Rollins—not getting their money back. Rollins knows that."

"It's a stretch," he said.

"It's not!" she exclaimed. Why didn't he see that he was in danger? Why was everything about her? He wasn't an idiot; he had to see the truth. "I've taken every precaution I can because I agreed with you that there is a threat on my life since I helped take that bitch down in the first place. I know, in my gut, that she's still here because she wants *her* money. It's all about Rollins, and if we don't remember that we're going to regret it. She blames you as much as me—but she knows that you're the only one good enough to get it back."

"I won't drive alone, Lucy."

She let out a long sigh. "Thank you."

"I'll let you know when we leave and when to expect us home, okay?"

"Thank you," she repeated.

"Sweetheart," he said softly, "it's going to be okay. I promise. Kane found information that's going to help the feds take them down. I have to go, Rick is calling."

"Stockton?"

"I don't trust a lot of feds, and neither does Kane. We're only giving the information to Rick, and he can decide what to do with it. I love you, Luce."

"I love you, too, Sean. Please be careful."

But he'd already hung up.

She handed Jack's phone back to him. "What really happened?" she asked.

"Kane is in surgery. He was shot twice. He's probably going to lose a kidney, but fortunately he has two of them." Jack gave her a half smile.

"That's not funny."

"Lucy, he's going to be okay."

"I can handle the truth, Jack."

He took her hands. "I know you can. I'll tell you everything I know, I'm not trying to sugarcoat it. Blitz learned that Tobias—through the man we believe is his intermediary, Joseph Contreras—doubled the bounty and changed it to a kill order. One million dollars if they recorded Kane's execution. Kane didn't know about that, and after they rescued Siobhan Walsh, he followed the lone survivor into hostile territory."

"Define *hostile*."

"It's a region southeast of Santiago near the Tamaulipas border where Kane has made enemies with a particular small but violent guerrilla gang run by a hood named Felipe Juarez. The problems down there are primarily rival criminal organizations." He paused. "Sometimes, when a criminal group gets taken out or stymied, they pass the blame to Kane even when he had nothing to do with their downfall. It can both help our cause and hurt it. But with Juarez, it's definitely a personal vendetta against Kane."

She nodded that she understood and motioned for Jack to continue.

"The fact that they used Siobhan as bait made Kane uncomfortable that these people knew more about how he operated and who he protected than he was comfortable with anyone knowing. He was also concerned about the Sisters of Mercy, a religious order that works throughout Mexico. Retribution is always a threat with these people. What he learned, however, was that there's a major deal going down—a collaborative effort uniting factions and giving Tobias—and Rollins—more power and control. This deal is costly, and may be why Rollins and Tobias are so desperate for the money Sean siphoned. It explains why they went to such great lengths to get the money—the murder of the congresswoman's husband, the kidnapping of her partner, and finally breaking Rollins out of prison."

"Because she's the leader," Lucy said. "Everything fell apart for them three months ago when Kane confiscated part of their gun shipment, and we stopped their use of the boys as couriers. Rollins went to prison and Tobias was left floundering. For fifteen years Rollins has been building to something . . . everything she's done has led her to San Antonio, to enact a Big Plan. Capital *P* Plan because my psych training tells me that Rollins does nothing without this *Plan* in the mirror. Fifteen years and no one knew anything about Rollins . . . and in three months, with her out of the picture, everything comes crashing down. Any sane criminal would have left the country with the three million she had, but she's still here. Because the bigger picture—the big Plan—is more important than her free-dom."

Jack listened carefully. "When did you grow up?" he said under his breath.

"If Kane got this information, how did he get shot?"

"That I don't know, but the gang called in reinforce-ments and surrounded him. He was shot at some point in the standoff, yet still managed to outwit them and find a hiding place. He lost his equipment during the attack, but apparently your boyfriend tracked him through his watch."

"His watch?"

Jack smiled. "When Kane realizes that Sean repro-grammed his watch so that he could track Kane's move-ments, Kane will go ballistic. But it saved his life."

"What happened to Sean's plane?"

"During the escape, it was shot multiple times. It's a testament to Sean's piloting capabilities that he was able to even get it off the ground, let alone fly it back to the bor-der. Ranger thinks it's scrap."

Her heart skipped a beat.

"And," Jack said, "Sean gave two pints of his blood for Kane's surgery. But Sean and Kane are both O negative, and there's not a lot of that blood type to go around. The hospital won't let him leave for another hour, at least."

"Universal donors," Lucy said, "but they can only re-ceive O negative."

"Exactly. Lucy, it could have been a lot worse. Blitz was shot, but it's not serious. Sean has a few stitches."

"But they're alive."

"Yes."

She closed her eyes and thanked God. "Okay." She looked at her brother. She was relieved, so why did her eyes feel so damp? "Thank you for being honest with me."

"Always, Lucy."

Nate came from down the hall. He'd showered, his short brown hair still wet, and was fully dressed. "I'm making breakfast," he announced. "Doc Vigo is on some big conference call in Sean's office. Durant sent us all a message to be in at oh-seven-hundred. Huge briefing."

"You don't have to cook for me, too," Lucy said.

"Sean told me to."

"You do everything Sean says?"

Nate just smiled and walked down the hall to the kitchen.

Jack said, "You can't cook."

"Of course I can."

"I suppose you *can* cook, but it's not edible." Jack smiled. "Mom tried with you, but it didn't stick."

"You're all just mean. My cooking isn't that bad."

"With enough salsa, anything is edible."

She glared at him.

He kissed her forehead, then pulled her into a tight hug. "I'm proud of you, Lucy. You have Dillon's brains and my instincts."

She didn't understand what he meant. "I've done nothing. And apparently I can't cook, either."

He smiled. "Shower, get dressed, we leave here in forty-five minutes."

Jack borrowed Sean's favorite car—his beefed-up Mustang—and followed her, Nate, and Hans to FBI headquarters. Lucy understood his precaution, but thought it was overkill. As soon as Nate drove through the gate, Jack peeled off going who knew where.

Hans was quiet on the drive over, spending time on his phone—not talking, but texting and reading emails. He was tense, and Lucy wanted to know what his earlier conversation had been about, but didn't ask. He'd tell her if she needed to know, and *wanting* to know didn't qualify.

As soon as they stepped into the FBI building, Hans detoured toward the SAC's office. Then he turned around and said, "Lucy?"

"You need me for something?"

"No—just call Noah and tell him about what you learned in Dunbar's files."

"I sent him an email."

"Call him."

And then he was gone.

Lucy and Nate walked down to the VCMO Squad wing. Juan's light was on and his door open. He sat at his desk, not in his customary suit, but in slacks and a polo shirt. He looked like he hadn't slept in days.

"Juan," she said. "How are you? Nita?"

"Nita is still struggling, but she's out of the woods. Micah is fine—better than fine, considering."

"Zach didn't have his name."

"I didn't—couldn't name him without Nita's input. We never picked names for the other kids until they were born. You look at them and then you just know . . ." His voice trailed off. "Nita had a rough time. But last night she woke up, was talking. The doctors don't know exactly what's wrong. They just know what it *isn't*." He shook his head. "They're keeping her for at least another day, and she's still very weak, but she told me to check in. Just for a couple hours. I'm taking maternity leave for at least three months." He smiled, but it didn't reach his tired eyes. "Seems odd, Nita did all the work, but I get to take time off."

"I'm sure you'll be doing more than your fair share over the next few weeks," Lucy said.

He nodded, looked at a point on the wall but she suspected his mind was still with his wife. Then he shook his head and said, "Abigail told me about Barry."

"The autopsy is being done this morning. Julie Peters is handling it. She's the best."

Juan was quiet.

"We'll find the people who did this."

Again, silence.

"Juan?" Lucy closed the door and sat down. "There are some people who have wondered if Barry was a traitor. I don't. He was a solid agent who did an outstanding job. Anything I can do to prove that, I will."

Now Juan looked at her. "You mean that."

"Of course I do. I learned a lot working with Barry on the Worthington homicide. We have different styles, but never—not once—did I think he was anything but a professional agent. I hate that anyone would question his loyalty."

She half hoped and half feared Juan would mention the letter Barry had written. Instead he said, "Be careful, Lucy. I've lived in San Antonio my entire life, except for the months I was at Quantico and the two years I was a rookie in Colorado. I've never seen a level of violence like I have over the last two weeks, starting with the Worthington murder."

"I'm being careful." She stood, because it was clear Juan's mind was elsewhere. "Please give Nita my love. If it's okay, I'd like to stop by the hospital or the house later this week."

He looked at her and shook his head. "Lucy—I care about you. But my family is my number one priority right now. Until . . . until the situation with Rollins is resolved and everyone involved is behind bars, stay away from my family."

Lucy had nothing to say. What could she say? Juan was essentially telling her that she was too dangerous to have around.

Could she blame him? After what had happened these last few weeks? She'd put herself in the sights of a ruthless killer. Anyone she was around was in danger as well.

She could argue that she was just doing her job; that it wasn't her fault Tobias and Nicole had targeted her and her family. Except that this was only partly true. Even if she could argue that she'd done everything by-the-book when investigating the Harper Worthington murder two weeks ago, the real issue was the off-book operation three months ago when she, Kane and Sean rescued the boys and Brad Donnelly. That event had started this chain reaction of violence and murder.

But could she have done anything else? Let all them all die?

She walked out. She half expected Juan to say something, to apologize, to tell her he didn't mean it the way it sounded.

But he didn't.

The squad room was empty. Lucy checked the conference room, but the briefing hadn't started. Only the chief analyst sat at the front sorting through documents. "Ten minutes," he told her.

She went back to her desk and called Noah on his cell phone. DC was an hour ahead of Texas, but it was still only eight in the morning on the East Coast.

Noah answered immediately. "I talked to Hans about the memo you sent last night. You should have called me."

"It was three in the morning in DC."

"I wasn't sleeping anyway. I discussed it with Rick, then we were on a conference call with Sean, Hans, Hooper, and one of Kane's men. Have you heard if Kane is out of surgery?"

"An hour ago he was still in," she said.

"How confident are you that your profile of Nicole Rollins is accurate?"

That seemed to come out of left field.

"Hans and I have been working on it together, I think we have a good understanding of her motivation. I wish I knew more about her background, but it's clear that she entered the DEA for the purpose of infiltrating the organization in order to expand her family's criminal enterprise. I suspect, based on Agent Novak's assessment in Los Angeles, that her uncle Jimmy Hunt steered her in that direction. He's a fugitive, and I have no information on whether he's still active."

"He is," Noah said, "but he's been a fugitive for five years. We have no idea where he is or how he's operating. At least, not until now. It's clear that Rollins has been protecting him, using her access and contacts to uncover any potential threat to Hunt. We suspect that she informed him of the DEA raid five years ago—he slipped away only hours before and fled the country to avoid arrest."

"So Nicole is de facto in charge."

"Where does that leave Tobias? Because for the last three months, Kane Rogan was confident that Tobias was a criminal mastermind behind the murder of six marines, stealing US military supplies and weapons, and building a pipeline up through Mexico all the way to Louisiana."

"Tobias is involved," Lucy said. "Partners, most likely, but even if they are equals, Nicole is the brains. It's clear that he took over when Nicole went to prison and that's when their master plan started to fall apart. He made mistakes. His actions jump-started our investigation. We know far more now about their organization than we learned even after Rollins was arrested. He's more the public face, someone who does what he's told. An important player, but it takes someone smarter—shrewd, patient—like Rollins to manage. When she wasn't around to tell him what to do, he followed his piss-poor instincts. With time, I will prove it." She hesitated, then added, "My guess is that this

Joseph Contreras is the same Joseph that Nicole went to college with and that would suggest that Joseph might be her lover. Definitely a confidant and extremely dangerous."

"I trust your judgment. But you're still guessing at this point."

"An educated guess."

"And they want their money. That's why Rollins is still here."

"It's the only logical reason—aside from revenge—that she would stay in Texas. According to Jack, Kane figured out why they need the money right now. That's what your conference call was about, right?" She was fishing, but it was logical to assume that.

"In part," Noah said. "Hans concurs with your assessment, that revenge is only one motive and that it may be more important to Tobias than to Rollins. Archer, Crawford were both tortured. Dunbar was executed, he died immediately. That hit was solely for information."

"Noah, I'm worried about Sean," she admitted. "Everyone here is watching me, Brad Donnelly, and Ryan Quiroz. We're covered. My brother Jack flew in from Sacramento to stay with me. But Sean is traveling from Hidalgo to San Antonio practically on his own. And we can't assume that Rollins doesn't have people down there. She'll know by now that Kane got out of Mexico, and she has enough people, between her and Tobias, to learn that Sean was with him."

"But they don't want to kill Sean. They want him to hack into the FBI to retrieve their money."

"That's what I said in my memo," she said. Something was wrong with this conversation and she didn't know what it was. "But he won't do it. You can't think he'd work for them."

"That's not what I meant. I meant they're not going to shoot him on sight, because they need his skill."

"If they get to him and he refuses, they'll kill him. If they find a way to manipulate him into doing it, they'll kill him when they're done. Noah—if Nicole wants to hurt me, and she does, the best way would be to k-kill Sean." Her voice cracked and she wished Sean were here, right now. Or that Kane wasn't hurt, because Kane would know how to protect his brother.

In a soft voice, Noah said, "Rick is well aware of the threat to Sean. He concurs with your analysis."

She was relieved, but Noah still seemed to be holding something back.

"Rick just called me into his office," Noah said. "I have to go. Watch yourself, Lucy. I mean it."

Then he hung up. And Lucy didn't feel relieved that he agreed with her.

Because Lucy had been talking to Noah, she was late to the briefing in the main conference room. But there was hardly anyone there—only Durant, Hans, Brad, Nate and the Houston DEA director Edward Moody.

"I'm so sorry," she said. "I had a call—"

Abigail shook off her apology. "Hans explained. We were just making sure everyone was up to speed. Nate can fill you in on the details, but the one thing you should know is that we've loaned Agents Proctor and Quiroz to the DEA until they get their office back up to fully staffed."

Moody said, "Both Brad and Abigail have told me how diligent you've been on not only this investigation, Agent Kincaid, but working with our office during Operation Heatwave and other cases. I sincerely appreciate your help and insight. I also appointed Brad as the Acting Director of the San Antonio office."

That appointment was well deserved, but had to be difficult for him

Moody continued. "We've also employed an outside

security assessment company to ensure we have no more rotten apples."

Lucy straightened and glanced at Brad. He winked at her. They hired RCK? That had to be it.

Abigail said, "Of the six men we know assisted Rollins in her escape, two are dead—the shooter at the bar and the first suspect we arrested, who was killed in prison. Two others are in custody and under tight protection in another jurisdiction—we can't risk someone getting to them like the first suspect. The DOJ is offering a deal to whoever talks first, but so far they have remained silent. The other two are still at large."

"What about Agent Crawford?" Lucy asked.

"Agents Malone and Figueroa are working with ERT on processing the evidence from Agent Crawford's murder. Ritz has been in contact with Crawford's brother, and there will be a service at the family's church next week. I will send out the details as soon as they're settled, but the FBI director has already indicated that he will be traveling here for the funeral. Juan Casilla has taken maternity leave. In light of his absence, I'll be running the day-to-day operations in the VCMO Squad until we are fully staffed." She turned to Hans. "You had something, Dr. Vigo?"

"Agent Kincaid and I have a preliminary profile on Nicole Rollins and her people." He slid hard copies over to everyone at the table. "The highlights are in a packet that was distributed via email last night to everyone involved in this investigation. None of the key points has changed, even with the additional information we learned this morning."

Had Hans even slept last night? Lucy glanced through the information and realized that most of it was from the reports she'd been sending to Abigail and Hans. Her profile, her assessment of Nicole, Joseph, Elise . . . everything was here in a slightly different format.

"I had a report from our legal attaché in Mexico City—
we attempted to take Dover into custody late last night. He
hadn't gone into work this week and wasn't at his apartment. According to his supervisor he was working with
local authorities to track a fugitive, but the case he created
was pure fiction. A source saw Dover outside of Santiago
two days ago where we believe he was sent by Tobias or
Rollins to kidnap an American citizen. He slipped away
and we believe someone tipped him off that he was wanted
for questioning. He's considered a fugitive and likely still
in Mexico."

Hans continued, "The information coming out of Los
Angeles is that Margaret Hunt, Rollins's aunt, slipped up
during her initial interview. She may not have realized it,
and SSA Novak didn't tip our hand. We're in the process
of getting a search warrant for the property. But this information, coupled with the profile that Agent Kincaid
wrote, gives us valuable insight. More details are in the
packets."

Hans looked at the few people at the table. "Wear your
vests on and off duty. Be prepared at all times. And don't
go anywhere alone."

CHAPTER THIRTY

Lucy wanted to talk to Hans, but Hans went into a meeting with Juan in Juan's office with the door closed. While she waited, she and Nate went over Logan Dunbar's computer files more carefully. While she was confident she'd found what Nicole was looking for, it was vital that they make sure there was nothing else she might be interested in that could jeopardize an agent or a current operation. The case against Adeline Worthington was detailed, but most of the information was either public record or would be made public record as soon as the indictments were complete. Noah and the AUSA were reviewing that part more carefully because he was privy to information about the other defendants and witnesses.

"Did you know that the DEA hired Rogan-Caruso?" Lucy asked Nate quietly.

"No. I thought something might be up when your brother followed us here. Your brother is tight-lipped. Still, Moody didn't say it was RCK."

"Brad knew."

"He bounced back quickly," Nate muttered.

"Nate, you're not being fair."

"I don't like this. I don't like not trusting people. Don't repeat what your friend said, I get it. I can *think* one thing; *knowing* something doesn't mean ignore my instincts."

"What do your instincts say?"

"That there's a reason Rollins is one step ahead of every law enforcement agency in Texas."

"Who's running property searches?"

"Um—" Nate glanced at notes that he'd been taking. "Texas Rangers. They have state jurisdiction, can access records quickly, and have a good working relationship with local cops. Durant is working directly with them."

"But do they have all the possible names? The property isn't going to be listed under Nicole Rollins; we would have found it after her arrest three months ago. And Joseph Contreras has been wanted by the FBI for the last two weeks, so anything under his name would have popped by now. But there's Margaret Hunt, Tamara Hunt, any number of entities that one or all of them may control. Even Elise Hansen might be used."

"Durant is feeding the Rangers everything we have, but if it makes you feel better, send her a message."

It would, so Lucy did. She added at the bottom:

Because I'm going through Agent Dunbar's files, I'm pulling out all names and entities that were part of Adeline Worthington's land scheme, because she may have set up Nicole's escape plan, whether she knew it or not. James Everett may know something as well—is there any way the marshals can arrange a conversation with him? Or ask him about land transactions? It could have been set up five years ago, when Joseph Contreras started working for Adeline, or as recently as two or three months ago, if Joseph wanted a safe house

after Nicole's arrest. It would be remote and
secluded, with multiple access points, including
the ability to land a small plane.

Nate read over her shoulder. "Good thoughts, all of them."

"I'll need your help—it'll take all day."

"Or longer," he said.

"Wait—" She scrolled through the attachments to the original indictment that Dunbar had planned to file prior to Adeline Worthington's murder. "Agent Dunbar, you are a saint."

She hit PRINT and ran over to the printer.

"What did you find?" Nate asked.

"Attachment D—a six-page list of every entity or individual that was involved in a land deal with Texas Holding Company, the front company for Everett and Adeline's money laundering."

"You just saved us hours of work."

"Maybe—but there are no transaction dates, it'll need to be cross-referenced to the original files."

She sent the attachment to Noah Armstrong in DC and copied in Abigail Durant, along with her theory about why she felt the safe house property was on the list.

She couldn't wait. She half walked, half ran through the office to Durant's suite. She was in a closed-door meeting, so Lucy sat and waited. She read the list carefully—nothing jumped out at her as suspicious. That didn't mean there wasn't something here. She just didn't have all the information she needed to make the assessment.

While she waited, she logged into a computer at an empty desk and forwarded Agent Blair Novak in Los Angeles the same information that she'd just sent Noah. She cc'd Hans, Brad and Nate. In a case like this it was better to make sure that everyone was in the loop, because it would be too easy for something to slip through the cracks.

She responded to some of her emails, waiting for Abigail to be done with her meeting because Lucy knew—in her gut, her heart, her head—that the property was on that list. Abigail could make things happen. If the Texas Rangers could prioritize their search with the list from the Texas Holding Company, they'd find Nicole faster.

Durant's office door swung open. Brad and Moody stepped out. "Whoever you need," Durant was saying.

"Kincaid," Brad said when he saw her.

Durant frowned. "Agent Kincaid is a target, I don't want her in the field today."

"What happened?" Lucy asked.

"The agents the FBI has at Saint Catherine's spotted the mother and boys we've been looking for, the boys who missed the bus on Monday when the hijackers boarded."

"They're at Saint Catherine's?"

"I just got the call," Abigail said.

"Ma'am, that's my church."

"And they could have been sent there lure you out."

"Nicole knows where I live. If she really wanted to get at me, she knows where to find me. Ma'am, one of the boys at the home is in danger. Sean hired a private guard for the house, but we know these people will do anything to get the results they want."

"There are no children at Saint Catherine's—Father Flannigan informed us that he canceled the summer school program for the week."

"Not students—I'm talking about the foster kids who live in the group home across the street. Their legal guardian is the diocese and Father Flannigan," Lucy said, itching to leave. "I know the boys. I need to go. I'm not going to be rash."

"Ma'am," Brad said, "as I told Mr. Moody, we can't let these people change the way we work. We can't let them scare us into not doing our jobs."

Abigail looked torn for a moment, then she nodded. "Bring Dunning with you," she said. "And call in Quiroz and Proctor for backup."

Moody nodded. "I'll be at the DEA office." He looked at Lucy oddly. "Kincaid?"

"Yes, sir."

"Jack Kincaid—he's not your husband, is he?"

"My brother."

"We hired RCK, as I mentioned in the meeting. I didn't make the connection until now. The other one, Patrick, is also a brother?"

"Correct," she said.

"They come highly recommended. Thank you." He walked out.

Thank you for what?

"Brad," Abigail said, "I'm trusting you not to go off half-cocked. You lost not only your boss, but a friend."

"I'm good, ma'am. I assure you, I'm not going to risk the lives of any other agent. But this is our best lead right now."

"Then go."

Hans was still in Juan's office with the door closed. Lucy asked Zach to tell him what they were doing, then Lucy, Brad, and Nate left.

St. Catherine's wasn't far, and Lucy called Father Mateo as soon as they drove off while Brad got on the phone with the agents in the field.

"He's not answering," Lucy said. She dialed the house line for the boys' home.

Sister Ruth answered on the second ring.

"Ruth, it's Lucy Kincaid. Is Father Mateo there?"

"No, he's at the church."

"Is the security team that Sean hired inside or outside?"

"They're inside. They said two FBI agents are outside the church. Is everything okay? You're scaring me, Lucy."

"I'm sure everything is fine, but let me talk to one of them."

A moment later a deep voice came on the line. "Pete Toscano here."

"Pete, this is Lucy Kincaid." She didn't know Pete or his partner, but Sean would have brought in the best.

"Yes, ma'am, Agent Kincaid."

"There may be a situation at the church. We have a team outside and more on the way. I'm hoping it's nothing, but we're not taking any chances. Please keep all the boys in the house, in direct line of sight, until you hear from me, and if you can, do a head count right now. Call me back if there are any problems or you're missing anyone."

"We're on it." He hung up.

"Father Mateo is at the church," she told Brad and Nate. "He may have canceled school, but he would never cancel Mass." She looked at her watch. "Mass would have ended about fifteen minutes ago. There are two full-time employees for the church. The school has a separate staff, but they're in a different building on the campus end of the property."

Nate got off the phone with the agents. "The agents said Garcia went with her boys into the church after Mass ended and the parishioners left. No one has come out. They want to know if they should go in."

"No," Brad said. "We need information and if we spook her she may not cooperate."

"It could be a trap," Nate said, glancing at Lucy.

Brad looked at his phone. "Quiroz and Proctor are at the church. They're doing recon but won't enter unless there's an immediate threat."

Two minutes later Brad pulled into the church lot and parked next to the other agents. Through their open car windows, Ryan said, "I circled around and looked in through the vestibule door. The boys are sitting in a pew near the front. I couldn't see their mother."

"Father Mateo?"

"He's not in the rectory. The secretary said he was in the church, but I didn't see him. I told her to lock the doors."

"We get the boys out if we can," Proctor said. "We don't know if the woman is a threat or a victim."

"I'll get the boys," Lucy said. "They're six and seven years old. You'll terrify them with your gear. They're likely very distrustful of law enforcement. Their father is in prison, and their mother is still involved with him."

Ryan concurred. "Bring them out and I'll take them to the rectory."

Proctor said, "Donnelly, Dunning, go through the side door and secure it. We'll go through the main doors. Kincaid, you'll approach the boys. If you see any threat, give the signal. Check coms." They sounded off to make sure all communication units were working and then approached the church on foot.

The boys watched with wide eyes as the five law enforcement officers came into the church. The men stood back while Lucy approached the children and said, "Do you speak English?"

The boys both nodded in unison

She smiled. "You're Matthew and you're Lucas, right? I'm Lucy. This is my church, just like it's your church. Father Mateo is a very good friend of mine. I also work for the FBI, and I know your grandmother. She's been very worried about you."

The boys didn't move, but the older boy tilted his head in surprise.

"Do you know where Father Mateo is? It's important I talk to him."

The older boy looked over to the confessional in the far rear corner of the church. A light was on over the door, indicating that someone was inside.

"Do you see that man?" She gestured toward Ryan. "I know he looks kind of scary, but he has two little boys, just like you. He's going to take you to the rectory to see Mrs. Seewig. Okay?" She reached out and hoped they took her hands. A sign of trust.

The older boy moved toward her, but the younger boy didn't budge.

"What's wrong, Lucas?" she asked.

"Mama said do not move or else."

"You are such a good boy for listening to your mother. But my job is to protect people." She showed him her badge. "That's what this means. And I especially protect children like you. Ryan"—she pointed—"he has a badge, too, and he's going to make sure nothing happens to you. I will explain it to your mother. I promise, you will not get into any trouble. It's really, really important that you go with Ryan."

The older boy, Matthew, said, "Is Mama in trouble? Because we didn't go to school?"

"No, she is not in any trouble. I need to talk to her, though."

"She's been crying," Matthew said. "All the time. I don't like it when she's sad."

"Let me try to fix it, okay?"

He nodded. "Come on, Lucas." He held out his hand to his brother. "Mama needs us to be brave."

The younger boy was reluctant, but took Lucy's hand. She walked them over to Ryan, put their small, sticky hands into his large palms. Then she watched him leave with the boys, Proctor backing him up.

Lucy walked up the aisle and stood in the back, right outside the confessional. She couldn't hear anything through the soundproofing. Five minutes later the door opened on the confessor's side. Elena Garcia stepped out, her face puffy from tears, her eyes rimmed red. She looked around the church for the boys, panic in her eyes.

"Elena, Matthew and Lucas are safe," Lucy said.

She whirled around and said to Lucy, "What did you do with my boys? Where are they?" Her voice was as panicked as her eyes.

"I'm Special Agent Lucy Kincaid with the FBI. My partner took your boys to the rectory for their own safety."

"No, no! I need my boys with me. You don't understand!"

"Let's talk somewhere—"

Mateo stepped out of the confessional and said, "Elena, you can trust Lucy. She's a friend."

Elena burst into tears and Mateo put his arm around her. He looked at Lucy with sad eyes. "Let's go to my office," he said.

They walked across the courtyard to the rectory and into Father Mateo's office. Nate followed and, after clearing Father's office, he stepped outside the door but kept it open.

"Elena," Father Mateo said, "I trust Lucy. She is a parishioner, she is a good person. What you told me is sacred, but as I told you, God had forgiven you, you need to forgive yourself. Sometimes unburdening our hearts to those who can help is the only answer."

Elena took the tissue that Mateo offered her and nodded. "I don't want to go to jail," she said in English tinged with an accent. "My boys—my mother is old, she can't watch them all the time, and I worry—"

"Elena," Lucy said, "if you tell me the truth, I will do

everything in my power to help you. No one wants you to be separated from your boys."

"My husband—he called me Monday morning from prison. It surprised me, because it was early, and he doesn't call early. I thought something was wrong. He said, 'Lena, don't let the boys go to school. Don't let them on the bus.' I ask why, he tells me nothing. I beg him, he repeats himself and then—he says a threat, that I can't let the boys on the bus but I can't tell anyone or they will be hurt. My boys—" She shivered. "I took them to my mother, because I had to go to work. But I kept thinking why would Pedro do this? Why would he call me like this? So I asked a friend to pick them up. A . . . a man I have been seeing." She looked at Father Mateo. "I haven't done anything, I am married, but he has been kind to me."

"Elena, I told you that Pedro broke the sacrament of marriage by killing a man."

"I know you say that, but he says I go to Hell if I divorce him."

Mateo's face hardened just a fraction, but Lucy didn't miss it.

Lucy said, "What happened then, Elena?"

"I heard about the explosion and left work, met up with Tim—and he was scared. I told him everything, and he'd read an article in the newspaper about how boys of prisoners were being used by the drug cartels." She crossed herself. "So Tim and I went to his parents' house with the boys. I thought—I thought maybe Pedro was going to have someone take Matthew and Lucas. I thought he found out I was thinking about the annulment, I don't know how, but he scares me. If he knew . . ."

"He can't hurt you from prison," Lucy said.

"He has friends," Elena said.

Mateo cleared his throat. "Elena, did you know about what would happen on the bus before the explosion?"

Lucy was surprised that Mateo asked the hard question, until Elena shook her head. "No, Father, like I told you, I didn't know—I just did what Pedro said. And then I ran, and I know I should have come to you first, told you what happened, but I was scared."

Lucy said, "Elena, you've done nothing wrong. You couldn't have known that the children were going to be taken hostage. Your husband set you up. Maybe he was trying to protect your sons, but most likely he was paid for information about the bus route."

"Dear Lord," Elena said and crossed herself again. "This was all his idea! Pedro told me Saint Catherine's had a summer school, that it wouldn't cost much, and he sent me money for the enrollment. I thought it was so good of him to think about our boys and their education, and now that they're older, my mother can't keep up with them."

"Did you question where he got the money in prison?"

She looked stunned. "No—should I have? I—I didn't think. It wasn't much, just enough to cover the first month's tuition. My mother and I were going to save for the second month. Sometimes I get tips at the hotel. I put tips in the bank for college. I wanted to go to college, but I got pregnant." She blushed and averted her eyes. "I want my boys to have an education, to be smarter than me, to have good, honest jobs."

"Where's Tim now?" Lucy asked.

"He didn't want me to come, but I told him I had to go to confession. I haven't been able to sleep or eat and I called my mama last night and she said the police were looking for me. I didn't know what to do. He's waiting for me down the street."

Mateo said, "You did the right thing, Elena." He turned to Lucy. "You can protect the family."

Lucy didn't have the authority to offer protection, but if she couldn't get the FBI to do it, she would ask Sean.

He'd hired the two men watching the boys in the group home; he must know of someone else who could protect Elena and her sons until they found Rollins.

"I'll find a way," she said. "In the meantime, can they stay at the boys' home? There are two private security guards inside, and it's the only place I can think of until I can arrange something through my office."

"Of course," Mateo said. "As long as you need a place, Elena, you have one."

Lucy and Nate escorted Elena and her children to the boys' home across the street, and Lucy explained the situation to Pete and Sister Ruth. By the time she walked back across the street, Ryan, Brad, and Leo Proctor had returned from talking to Elena's boyfriend.

"He's clean," Ryan said. "We ran him, no warrants, no record. Works as custodial staff for the public school district, been with them for eight years, right out of high school. I have his contact info, license, address—all checks. Scared shitless, but more concerned about Elena. I told him she was in protective custody and would call him when she could, but I don't want him or anyone knowing where she is."

"That was a bust," Brad said as the five of them gathered around the two SUVs. "We didn't learn anything."

"At least we know how it started," Lucy said. "And one other important fact—her husband, the one in prison, must have talked to someone recently so he knew when to make the call. Can we get his records?"

"We already requested them," Brad said.

"I'll have Zach follow up," Nate said.

"Nicole would know that we would eventually learn this information," Brad said. "She isn't going to let her people slip up by going on record."

"With all the violence? The explosion? The multiple agencies? Yes—we'd get the records, but if we weren't specifically looking for something, we wouldn't necessarily know it when we saw it," Lucy said. "Nate, ask Zach not just for the phone records, but for the visitor logs as well, going back a full month."

Nate sent Zach a message.

"It's nearly time for me to be in court," she said. "Elise Hansen's hearing." She called Hans. He picked up the phone, rushed. "Hans, I'm heading to the courthouse. We can pick you up."

"Where did you go?"

"Saint Catherine's." She told him what they'd learned. "Sort of a bust, but we have another small lead that Zach is checking out."

"I'll meet you at the courthouse." He hung up.

She stared at the phone. "I have a feeling that everyone is avoiding me today."

"Not me," Nate said. "I'm sticking to you like glue. Is everything okay?"

"Hans will meet us at the courthouse."

Ryan said, "Leo and I will follow up on the prison records, compare this Pedro Garcia with any names that might be associated with Rollins or Tobias. Donnelly, you're with us."

He looked like he was going to argue. "One minute." He turned to Lucy. "Don't worry about Elise. I know you're concerned because of the circumstances, but this isn't a trial. You'll have more leeway to talk to the judge, give him your opinion."

"That's not the problem—it's the psychiatrist. She's bought Elise's story and believes she's the victim. I don't have the credentials to tell the court that Elise is a sociopath and manipulated the system. She hasn't denied injecting Worthington, but she convinced Dr. Oakley that she's been abused and manipulated and she didn't know she'd killed him. I have nothing to connect her to Rollins, except through Tobias. Yet . . . I have nothing solid to connect Tobias to Rollins. We *know* that they're working together, but proving it . . . even circumstantially? We're not there yet."

"The AUSA will most likely ask the court for more time to evaluate," Brad said. "They like to delay when they can, and because Elise is a minor with no family in the area, and the only family she's claimed is a brother who is a wanted fugitive, I don't see how they'll let her walk. If the AUSA can't keep her in the psych ward, she'll be in juvie."

Ryan nodded. "Donnelly's right. With Tobias linked to the murders of several cops, the court isn't going to be lenient. Holding her for another two weeks is a reasonable precaution."

"I hope you're both right," Lucy said.

Her phone rang. It was Kenzie.

"What's up?" Lucy asked.

"Lucy, I wish you were here."

"What happened?"

"I'm at the morgue. Julie Peters just finished the autopsy on Barry. It was—awful."

"You didn't have to watch," she said.

"I know—and I feel like shit that I walked out in the middle of it. Emilio stayed. I've never felt like this before."

Lucy had worked at the DC morgue for over a year; she was used to the sights and sounds and smells. But it was always different when you knew the victim. And considering the state his body had been in, this autopsy must have been one of the worst.

"Julie got a positive ID?"

"No—that's how bad it was. His body was so decomposed we can't tell by looking at him. She sent blood, teeth, and tissue samples to the FBI lab at Quantico. They have the capability here, but Durant wants our people on it. Everything is already on a plane."

"Come over tonight. You shouldn't be alone."

"Maybe I will. Eric's staying with me—he knows how hard this week has been."

"Eric—Eric Butcher? Your boyfriend?"

"He's been so great. Last night—it would have been worse without him."

"I'm glad you have someone." Lucy knew exactly how Kenzie felt. Sean made everything better. She missed him. Even having a houseful of people, even having her brother in town, wasn't the same as having Sean by her side.

"I just spoke with Abigail, and Emilio is writing up the report. Barry was tortured before they killed him."

Lucy's stomach flipped. "How?"

"Because of . . . the state of his body, Julie couldn't determine much, but every finger had been broken while he was still alive. His jaw was cracked. The cause of death was a bullet in the head."

Lucy closed her eyes and pushed aside all the emotions that threatened to escape. She took a deep breath, then said to Kenzie, "Where?"

"Where what?"

"If they tortured him, they had to have taken him someplace. What time did airport security show Barry's car arriving?"

"Uh—just before midnight on Friday."

"Do they have a decent image of the driver?"

"Not from the parking lot, but they know it's a man with dark hair over six feet tall. He left the lot on foot heading toward the departure gates. Zach has a team going through all the footage there to see if we can get him on camera, boarding a flight, something."

"Have them specifically check flights with a stop in

DC, as well as the external feeds at the pickup and drop-off zones."

Kenzie didn't say anything for a moment.

"Is there something else?"

"I—I couldn't process all this so fast. How do you do that?"

"Do what?" But Lucy knew exactly what she meant.

"Never mind, I'll double-check with Zach. I'm sure he knows what he's doing."

"He does, but it never hurts to run through the checklist with a fresh set of eyes." She pinched her nose and wished she could better learn to balance her analytical side with her compassionate side. Kenzie had called her because she needed to commiserate about watching the autopsy of a friend and colleague. She hadn't needed the questions and orders. "I'll let you know when I get home."

"Thanks, but I think I'll make it a quiet night with my boyfriend." Kenzie hung up.

Lucy felt miserable.

CHAPTER THIRTY-ONE

Hans wasn't waiting for them when Nate and Lucy arrived at the courthouse. She sent him a text message, and he responded that he'd been held up but was trying to make it before the hearing.

Once Nate and Lucy went through security and checked their weapons, they went to the third floor where AUSA Christina Fallow paced in the hallway on blood-red stiletto heels.

"Agent Kincaid," Fallow snapped and approached them. She glanced at Nate with narrowed eyes.

"Special Agent Nate Dunning," he said.

"Where's Agent Crawford?" she demanded.

"He was killed Friday afternoon," Lucy said.

Fallow paled. "Killed? No one told me."

"We found his body last night."

"Oh God." She sat down heavily on a bench. "What happened?"

"We believe Nicole Rollins sent someone to kill him," Lucy said. "We can't prove it yet—but we will."

"Rollins? I'm going to be sick." She looked at Nate. "Are you replacing Agent Crawford?"

"No, ma'am. Agent Kincaid is the agent of record."

Fallow shook her head and buried her face in her hands. A moment later she looked up and said, "Why didn't you tell me that you spoke to the defendant?"

"It wasn't about her case, it was about Nicole Rollins's escape."

"I don't care if you wanted the name of her hairdresser! Her lawyer is up in arms. And I only found out twenty minutes ago when I got here."

"I talked to her yesterday morning for fifteen minutes. You can watch the recording."

Fallow sighed. "That's not the only reason I'm upset. The case is fucked. We have nothing on her."

"She killed a man."

"Manslaughter. Extenuating circumstances. Her lawyer wants a plea—ten months in a minimum-security facility until her seventeenth birthday and then emancipation after a court hearing. Her mother is dead, she doesn't know who her father is."

"But we don't know if any of that is true," Lucy said. "She can't prove who she is. She's given us nothing to verify her identity. She held James Everett at gunpoint and forced him to transfer millions of dollars to accounts controlled by Tobias."

"She says she was acting under duress."

"We can produce two witnesses who will testify that she was not acting under duress," Lucy said. Sean would testify, and she hoped Kane would as well.

"She's a minor. She doesn't have to prove anything. She gave us her name and she doesn't have or doesn't know her Social Security number. Her mother always went by the name Sue Hansen, but we can't confirm that—Sue? Suzanne? Susan? Elise was raised practically on the streets, she thinks her mother is dead, and she told the shrink that Tobias was her foster brother in Las Vegas, Nevada."

"There has to be a record in the foster system."

"We've been trying to get it, but it's going to take more time."

"Don't they print foster kids?"

"Some jurisdictions do, but not the jurisdiction she claims to be from. And even if we did have it, because they're minors the prints aren't uploaded into the criminal database. If they're a missing person, the prints will be in the missing persons system; her prints haven't shown up. No one has reported her missing. But the system isn't perfect."

"Elise is a sociopath," Lucy said. "She can't be released into minimum security anything. She has to be closely monitored."

"The court-appointed shrink doesn't believe she's a sociopath," Fallow said.

"Her shrink has been played," Lucy said. "Just like Nicole Rollins played the DEA for fifteen years."

Fallow looked at Lucy oddly. "What does she have to do with this?"

Before Lucy could answer, the bailiff opened the door. "The judge is ready."

Lucy followed Fallow into the small courtroom. Elise was already inside with Dr. Oakley and her attorney. She wore a modest pale-blue dress with shell sleeves. Her hair was clean, brushed, and pulled back on the sides. She wore no makeup and looked like a twelve-year-old cherub.

Elise turned and looked at Lucy. She smiled. Then she winked. She turned to her doctor and grabbed her arm. Lucy could see her shaking from twenty feet away. Oakley looked over at Lucy and narrowed her eyes, then patted Elise on the arm and whispered in her ear.

Lucy's mouth dropped open. She couldn't believe that she was the only one who'd seen what had happened.

Nate cleared his throat. She caught his eye—he'd seen

it, too. But that wasn't going to help them in front of the judge.

There was no one else in the room ready to testify. Elise with her two people; Fallow and Lucy; the bailiff and a court reporter.

Lucy leaned over to Fallow. "What's going on? We should have other witnesses here—"

"This isn't a trial, it's a hearing," Fallow said in a low voice as she sat down in the front. Lucy sat next to her. "We aren't presenting evidence, we're making a case to keep Hansen in a criminal psychiatric care unit. But Kincaid, this isn't going to be pretty—I was expecting Agent Crawford. He's good with the court. He knows what to expect. And he knows this case."

"I know this case, too. And I know Elise Hansen better than you can imagine."

"I hope so, because I need to give the court a damn good reason not to accept the offer of ten months in juvie."

"Reason number one? She'll walk away." How could Lucy make Fallow see the truth?

"Listen, Kincaid—I had prepared with Barry, and he was supposed to be back from his vacation this morning. I wish I'd prepared you as well."

"Why didn't you?"

Fallow stared at her as if she didn't understand the question. "Because . . . Barry was the lead agent. You're a rookie. Not everything was by the book—I would have called you if there was a trial because if I didn't, the defense certainly would, but I'd really hoped this wouldn't go to trial." She leaned closer and whispered, "I already offered two years, maximum-security juvenile detention. They declined."

Lucy hadn't known—she was stunned. In an equally

low voice she said, "Elise Hansen is a cold-blooded, sociopathic killer. She should be tried as an adult."

"There's not enough evidence," Fallow hissed.

"Keep her in lockup for two more weeks. I'll get evidence."

"After talking to Naygrow this morning, that's my goal, and I think the Judge will at least give me the time. I'm going to ask for two weeks at first, then seventy-two hours."

"All rise for Judge Eleanor Axelrod."

Fallow looked stunned. She waited until the judge was seated before she said, "I was under the impression Judge Goodman was presiding over this case."

"Judge Goodman's trial has taken longer than expected and instead of postponing, I agreed to sit in on this hearing." Axelrod looked at Fallow pointedly. "Is that a problem, counselor?"

"No, Your Honor. But if you need more time to become familiar with the case, I would be happy to postpone the hearing until Monday."

The judge looked at the defense. "Mr. Johnson?"

He rose. "Your Honor, we believe that justice would not be served by keeping my client locked up. My client's court-appointed psychiatrist agrees. In fact, continued incarceration with violent, mentally disturbed felons would be extremely detrimental to my client's emotional and physical well-being."

Lucy couldn't move. Eleanor Axelrod—she was the judge the cops on Operation Heatwave dubbed "Easy Axe." She was the judge who'd released Jaime Sanchez—who then skipped bail and ended up kidnapping his niece and Brad. Could she be one of Nicole Rollins's inside people?

"Ms. Fallow?" the judge asked. "Do you have a problem with me presiding over this hearing?"

"No, Your Honor."

"Then let's proceed."

Christine glanced at Lucy and in her expression, Lucy saw that they'd already lost.

The judge looked over the sheets in front of her. "It's my understanding that no official charges have been filed against the defendant?"

"Not yet, Your Honor," Christine said. "She was remanded into mandatory fourteen-day psych evaluation. Dr. Oakley was appointed as her psychiatrist. However, we have charges we're on the verge of filing. We have three days after this hearing to file."

"I'm aware of the law," the judge said. "What charges do you plan to file?"

"Your Honor, the lead FBI agent, Barry Crawford, was tragically murdered this weekend and he was instrumental in the development of this case. His partner in the matter is a rookie FBI agent and I need time to bring her up to speed."

"Is this the rookie?" the judge asked and looked at Lucy. "Name?"

"FBI Special Agent Lucy Kincaid," Christine said.

"I see a reprimand on file by the defense related to Agent Kincaid."

"Your Honor, if I may be allowed to go through our case and why the government believes that the defendant should remain in custody—"

"First I'd like to know why Agent Kincaid was reprimanded by the defense." She turned to the defense table. "Mr. Johnson?"

"Two weeks ago as well as yesterday, Agent Kincaid spoke to my client without counsel present and without informing Dr. Oakley. Yesterday, Agent Kincaid threatened my client with unwarranted jail time if she didn't confess to knowledge of a crime of which she has no information."

"Your Honor," Lucy began.

"You'll have your turn, Agent Kincaid. Because you are a rookie, I will say this only once: I will not tolerate any interruption in my court."

Lucy bit her lip. The tape would prove that was not what happened during yesterday's conversation with Elise.

"Mr. Johnson, continue."

"You have Dr. Oakley's report in the file, and it's clear that my client is not a threat to anyone but, in fact, is the target of a known fugitive. She has been abused and threatened by both this fugitive and by officers of this court— namely, agents with the FBI."

"I've read Dr. Oakley's report, and you'll have your chance to expand on it." She turned to the prosecution. "Ms. Fallow, what charges do you plan on filing? I understand that Agent Crawford isn't here to assist you, but don't you have some idea at this point what you believe the defendant did that was a crime?"

"My office intends to file charges of manslaughter, kidnapping, and extortion," she said.

"On a sixteen-year-old girl?"

"Yes, Your Honor."

"You'll have to give me more information. Do you have any evidence?"

"Yes, Your Honor, but this hearing isn't about evidence, it's—"

"I know exactly what this hearing is for," Axelrod said.

"Normally, I would have the FBI agent of record go through the investigation, but with Agent Crawford—"

The judge interrupted Christine. "Agent Kincaid, were you part of the investigation that resulted in the arrest of Elise Hansen?"

"Yes, Your Honor."

"Then share with the court what you believe Ms. Hansen did."

Lucy stood. "On Friday, May twenty-ninth, Harper Worthington—the husband of Congresswoman Adeline Reyes-Worthington—was murdered in a motel. The coroner's office determined that he'd been poisoned with curare, a lethal neuromuscular blocker. The poison had been injected into his neck, and he died within thirty minutes. During that time, he would have been incapacitated from the drug.

"A witness placed a woman of Elise Hansen's description leaving the scene shortly after the time of death as determined by the Bexar County Medical Examiner's Office. With the assistance of SAPD Detective Tia Mancini, we tracked the unknown female subject to another hotel, and eventually to the employment of Mona Hill, a woman known to—"

The judge interrupted. "I know all this, Agent Kincaid. I've read the file and the AUSA report. Do you have anything new to add?"

Lucy was momentarily flustered, but she continued. "I—I think it's important to understand how Agent Crawford and I came to believe that Ms. Hansen was complicit in murder. For example, evidence collected at the motel and subsequently in the office of Congresswoman Worthington proved that Ms. Hansen knew that Mr. Worthington was dead and yet still took photos of him. She also engaged in oral sex on his corpse with the purpose, I believe, of ensuring that the FBI would have enough evidence to find her."

"Stop," Judge Axelrod said.

"I'm not finished."

"Your story is ridiculous."

"It's true, Your Honor."

"Why would someone intentionally leave evidence in order to be arrested?"

"The plan, we believe, was for Elise to be seen as the victim in order to get close to the investigation and set up an assassination attempt that would appear to be an attempt on her life, when in fact it was an attempt on a federal agent."

"And a sixteen-year-old prostitute created this elaborate scheme."

The judge's tone was complete disbelief, but Lucy pressed on. "I cannot say whether she came up with the plan, but she was aware of it. She also kidnapped James Everett, a real estate developer who had helped Congresswoman Worthington launder money for a known drug cartel run by a man known to authorities as Tobias. Elise threatened Mr. Everett at gunpoint, then fled before the authorities arrived. She was arrested by Agents Dunning—" Lucy gestured to Nate in the back—" and Quiroz of the FBI while on the run."

She had far more to say, and because the judge was silent, Lucy decided to push. "While I'm not a psychiatrist, I have a master's in criminal psychology from Georgetown University and advanced training in criminal profiling. It's my opinion that Elise Hansen is a narcissistic sociopath who has no remorse for her actions—she's incapable of remorse. If this court releases her to any facility other than a maximum-security facility like the one she's been in for the last fourteen days, she will soon reconnect with Tobias and continue to commit felonies. Tobias is a known associate of former DEA Agent Nicole Rollins, who escaped from custody Monday morning. Tobias, Rollins and several other individuals are guilty, all told, of the cold-blooded murders of nine federal agents and corrections personnel."

No one said a word.

"At a minimum," Lucy said, "if the court believes that Elise Hansen is a victim, she should be kept in a secure facility for her own protection until Rollins and Tobias are apprehended."

Lucy could say more. She *wanted* to say more, but she knew that if she went beyond the facts she would get herself into trouble. She'd already strayed too far off course, but she thought she made it clear that Elise was complicit in the murder of Harper Worthington.

The judge turned to the defense. "Mr. Johnson?"

"Thank you, Your Honor. Dr. Oakley would like to address the court."

"Of course, Doctor."

Barbara Oakley stood. She was shaking. But it was from anger, not fear, Lucy realized as soon as the woman opened her mouth.

"Your Honor, Agent Kincaid may have a master's degree, but she is not a licensed or trained psychiatrist. She's a rookie FBI agent who has been brought up in front of the FBI's Office of Professional Responsibility *twice* in less than a year. She was suspended for two weeks less than three months ago because she violated FBI protocol. I would request that you completely ignore her ignorant claims that she can diagnose my patient with armchair psychology."

How the hell did she know that Lucy had been suspended? That was a private personnel matter and not public information. Agents in her office knew, but that was it. Juan hadn't filed the suspension with OPR—at least, he'd told her he hadn't.

The realization that there was a leak in the FBI was driven home in that moment.

"Elise Hansen is barely sixteen years old," Oakley said. "She doesn't know who her father is. Her mother was a prostitute and a drug addict who, when she went to prison, turned Elise over to foster care. Elise has been in and out of foster homes half of her life. Three years ago, when she was thirteen, she was raped by one of her foster parents, and the one person who stood up for her was Tobias. I am not disputing anything the government has claimed this man has done, but it's vitally important that you understand that to Elise, he saved her life. She saw him as the only one who could protect her from a system that had failed her. Tobias used her, manipulated her, threatened her—and it was because she had seen him hurt other people that she believed he would hurt her if she didn't do what he said.

"Elise admits to meeting Harper Worthington and injecting him, but she believed it was ketamine, not a deadly poison. She was ordered to seduce Harper Worthington and take incriminating pictures. She didn't ask why, because she did what she was told out of fear of punishment. I have addressed each of Agent Kincaid's preposterous allegations in my report to the court."

"Your Honor," AUSA Fallow said, rising, "this is a hearing, not a trial."

The judge glared at Fallow. "And you think I don't know what's going on in my own court, Ms. Fallow? Do not interrupt again." She turned to Dr. Oakley. "I read your report in chambers this morning," she said. "You indicated that Ms. Hansen lived in fear of this Tobias."

Dr. Oakley nodded. "Yes, you Honor. Elise is terrified of what Tobias will do to her. What Agent Kincaid claims is a dark and twisted fairy tale. Elise is a victim, not a criminal. For more than twenty years, I have worked with hundreds of teenage prostitutes and abuse survivors. It's clear that Agent Kincaid has no understanding or sympathy for girls who have been grossly and systematically abused. Elise has made many mistakes, but everything she did was to survive in a world where no one ever showed kindness—except for, perhaps, the most dangerous man wanted by the FBI.

"It's my opinion that Elise suffers from extremely low self-esteem, abuse, and that she devalues herself as a human being. She needs our help, not our punishment. There is a group home in Austin that has a place for her. The house is fully certified and run by one of my colleagues who has helped hundreds of sexually abused teenage prostitutes go on to lead normal, productive lives. This court can and should monitor her progress for the duration of the program."

She sat down and patted Elise on the arm.

Lucy wanted to scream.

"Ms. Fallow, does your office oppose putting Ms. Hansen in the Austin Group Home?"

"Yes, Your Honor. We absolutely oppose a group home option. If we could simply have three more days—we will be filing charges."

"And you have evidence to support those charges?"

"Yes, Your Honor."

The judge sighed and rubbed her eyes. "Why is it that incarceration is always the answer with the government? This girl is hardly more than a child. The system has failed her. The least we can do is give her hope. You haven't filed charges yet because, I believe, you're still trying to build a case where none exists."

"No, Your Honor, we were waiting for this hearing—"

"Sounds like an excuse to me, Ms. Fallow. I'm granting the defense petition to place Elise Hansen into the Austin Group Home for Girls for a period of twelve months. At that time, this court will reevaluate the order. Ms. Hansen, you will be required to abide by all the rules of the group home, to meet with your court-appointed psychiatrist weekly, and to appear before this court when requested.

You are officially a ward of the court. Ms. Fallow, if you have charges you wish to bring against the defendant, I would suggest you get your ducks in a row soon, because delay is not your friend. Court adjourned."

Lucy jumped up. She couldn't believe what had just happened. "Your Honor! You can't do this! Elise Hansen is a cold-blooded killer!"

"One more word, Agent Kincaid, and I will hold you in contempt. I don't think you would fare well in jail for twenty-four hours."

She opened her mouth but someone grabbed her from behind. She whirled around, almost in full panic, then saw Nate's face. He shook his head once, his mouth set in a thin line.

She stared into his dark eyes. He was angry but calm. She took a deep breath. Then another.

Nate was right. If she went to jail, she would be vulnerable.

She turned and walked out of the court.

Where was Hans? He was supposed to be here. He was a trained forensic psychiatrist. He could have countered everything that Dr. Oakley said and the judge would have to listen. Wouldn't she?

Nate grabbed her elbow. "Let's go." He led her out of the courtroom as soon as the judge left.

"I—"

"Lucy, this isn't helping. This was set up from the beginning. Everyone suspects Axelrod is on the take. This proves it. Christine Fallow will put together the charges."

"Elise will disappear before then."

"I know."

"Dammit!"

They collected their weapons and went outside. Lucy first tried Sean, but his cell phone went to voice mail. Then she called Hans as soon as Nate pulled out of the parking structure and headed toward FBI headquarters.

"Elise was sent to a group home in Austin," she said. "You said you'd meet us at the courthouse. She's going to run. The judge didn't listen to me or the AUSA."

"Where are you?"

"Heading back to headquarters."

"I'll explain when you get here."

He hung up—again—without giving her anything else.

"Something's wrong," she said to Nate.

She tried Sean again. And again, his phone went to voice mail.

CHAPTER THIRTY-TWO

Agent Blair Novak was the team leader, but she deferred to SWAT for an operation like this. She hoped Margaret Hunt would open the gates and let them conduct their search peacefully and without incident, but she trusted her instincts, and her instincts told her this would be anything but easy. That's why she'd taken the time this morning after securing the warrant to put together a large, experienced team to serve the warrant and conduct the search.

The Hunt property was fenced on all sides. They could approach from the other side of the hill if necessary, and her SWAT team leader had a team of four on the easternmost boundary waiting to cut through the fence if Blair ordered it. The north side was difficult to bypass, but the south bordered another property, and they'd already talked to those property owners and had evacuated them just in case.

Once everyone was in position, Blair approached the gate in a lone SUV with Carter Nix in the passenger seat and two other agents in the back.

She pressed the button.

It took a long time before someone answered. Blair didn't recognize the voice.

"Blair Novak with the FBI. We have a federal warrant to search this property. Please open the gate."

Silence.

"This is the Federal Bureau of Investigation," Blair repeated. "We have a warrant. Open the gate immediately or we'll be forced to disable it."

A female voice came over the staticky intercom. "You have no rights here, Agent Novak. I've done nothing wrong."

"We have a search warrant, Mrs. Hunt."

"I don't believe you."

"If you open the gate, we can show you the warrant."

"I'm sending a boy down to fetch it."

Was she stalling? Why? It was within her rights to read the warrant.

"I'll give you five minutes."

It didn't take that long. A tall, lean young kid came down the driveway. He said, "Stick it through the gate, then back away."

Blair did exactly what he said. He picked up the papers and walked back to the house.

Five minutes later, Blair rang the buzzer again.

Hunt answered immediately.

"Please open the gates," Blair said.

"Over my dead body."

A rifle blast echoed in the canyon, and Blair and her team took cover.

"Well, shit," Blair said and called for more backup.

Elise hugged Barbara Oakley tightly with her good arm. The other was still in a sling. It hurt a little, but she thought she could dump the sling when she got out of here. The doctor had taken off the cast yesterday and put on a thick black brace. But the sling made her look more innocent, and she needed all the sympathy she could get. "Thank you, thank you," she whispered, bringing tears to her eyes. They were tears of laughter, but the do-good doc didn't know that.

"Everyone deserves a second chance, Elise, especially you," Oakley said. "One reason I picked Austin is because it's an hour away. You'll be safe there."

"Do you really think so?" She made her eyes wide. Toby always said she looked innocent when her eyes were big.

"Yes. The people who run it are wonderful and trained to handle any situation. They will make sure you are protected. But you need to do your part. Don't contact Tobias. I know you feel like you owe him something. He may have helped you when you were thirteen, but he's not helping you now. He used you. Do you understand that?"

Elise nodded and forced her lips down. She bit her bottom lip because after practicing in the mirror for hours she knew that made her look nervous and vulnerable.

"I will see you every week, we'll talk, you can tell me how school is going. You're a smart girl, Elise. You deserve the chance to go to high school, to go to college. To grow up."

Oakley had no idea just *how* smart she really was. "Do you really think my past doesn't matter?"

"Only the present matters. You are not the same girl you were at thirteen; you're not the same girl you were two weeks ago. The girls you will be living with have similar stories. They were hurt by people who should have protected them. They will help you; I will help you. All I want is for you to grow into the amazing young woman I know you can be. Confident. Smart. Someone with a future."

Her attorney Johnson approached them. He looked a bit nervous, and Elise winked at him when Oakley turned her head to greet a colleague. That flustered him, and she almost smiled.

"Dr. Oakley," Johnson said, "I can arrange for San Antonio PD to escort Elise to Austin."

Elise grabbed Oakley's arm and squeezed, her eyes wide with fear. She didn't say anything. She didn't want to oversell it.

Oakley patted her hand. "Mr. Johnson, Elise is extremely distrustful of law enforcement, and with good cause."

"I'll have a female officer take her," Johnson said, "and you can of course come."

"I've already been approved to transport Elise to Austin this afternoon. The group home is waiting for her, and I'll be able to get her settled."

"Um, Doctor, for your safety maybe—"

Elise said, "Dr. Oakley, maybe Mr. Johnson is right. What if Tobias is looking for me? What if he knows that the hearing was today? What if he is waiting for me outside? What if he hurts you? I would just *die* if the only person who has ever been nice to me was hurt. I can do it. I can go with the p-p-police."

"Honey, Tobias has no idea about this hearing. It's not public information. The transcript is sealed because you're a minor. We'll be safe. If you really would feel safer with the police, I can ride with you."

Elise forced herself to look confused and torn. "I would rather go with you, but I'll do whatever you think is best."

Dr. Oakley smiled and squeezed her hand. "I need to contact my office and let them know, and then we'll gather your belongings and leave. All right?"

"If you think so," she said. Elise watched Oakley walk down the hall and get on her cell phone. She let out a long sigh. "Spill," she said to Johnson. "She won't be gone long."

"He said to be alert as you merge onto the freeway."

"Good." She wagged her finger at him. "You were a naughty boy, Mr. Johnson. Trying to get the good doc not to take me. Trying to bring the police into my business."

"Th-That's not what it was. I had to go through the motions. Make it look legit."

"It *is* legit. Another fuckup like that and your wife will get the pictures and know what you are *really* doing when you're working late."

He paled and swallowed and she thought he was going to have a heart attack right in front of her.

When Elise was still incognito and hiding out at Mona Hill's place, she'd accessed some of the bitch's blackmail files. But then Mona Hill abandoned Elise when she needed help the most and when Elise went back for the dirt, it was gone.

But she did get the scoop on her lawyer. After all, how else could she afford a top lawyer like Johnson? And Oakley bought his explanation that he was doing this pro bono.

Right. If *pro bono* meant defending her so his wife didn't find out what a slimy, hypocritical, horny gay fuck he really was.

Oakley came over and smiled. "It's all settled. Are you ready, Elise?"

"I think so. I have butterflies in my stomach."

"That's normal. And healthy. Are you hungry? Would you like to get a late lunch before we hit the road?"

"I think I'm too nervous to eat. I don't want to get carsick."

"There is nothing to be nervous about, but I understand." She took Elise's left hand and they walked down the hall.

Elise looked over her shoulder and said, "Thank you, Mr. Johnson. I couldn't have done this without you."

* * *

Sean pulled into his driveway just after one p.m. Tired. Sore. But the adrenaline was still pumping through him.

He'd just gotten off the phone with Blitz. Kane was out of surgery. His left kidney had to be removed, but miraculously that was the only serious damage. He'd need to be in the hospital for a minimum of forty-eight hours, and then Blitz would take him to Jack's house to recuperate. Sean said, "Call me first. We have the space here, and I want to keep an eye on him."

"He won't like that."

"Do I care?"

"I hear ya, Little Rogan."

"Knock it off." He hung up.

He pressed the button he'd programmed on his phone to open the garage.

Nothing happened.

A windowless white van pulled up right behind him. Four hooded men with guns jumped out of the side door and rushed his car.

He pressed the EMERGENCY button on his phone.

He could get to his gun. He might be able to kill one of them before he was dead.

But like Lucy said, they didn't want him dead. They wanted him to give them their money.

"Open the door right now and you live."

Still, self-preservation instincts had Sean hesitating. They had to believe that he wouldn't cooperate. They had to know about him, that he wouldn't go down without a fight. A threat to his life wouldn't get him to help, and they damn well knew that.

"Your girlfriend is at the federal courthouse right now. When she leaves, we will be following her. We know that she has a protective detail with her. We know that her brother Jack Kincaid is following her around like a damn dog. And if you think we won't take them all out, you are mistaken. Get out of the fucking car *now*!"

Sean opened the door. "If you touch her I will kill you."

The bastard laughed at him and Sean hit him hard in the jaw.

Instantly, two pairs of hands grabbed him, ripping open the stitches on his arm. He winced as they pushed him to the pavement, zip-tied his hands behind his back, and searched him for weapons. They tossed everything they found back into his car, including his cell phone. Then they pulled a black bag over his head and dragged him to the van. He fought until they hit him and he saw stars.

The van peeled out of the neighborhood and they were gone.

CHAPTER THIRTY-THREE

Lucy practically ran into FBI headquarters. Everyone had been acting odd, but she was so focused on the Elise Hansen hearing that she barely noticed what was going on around her. The closed-door meetings. Jack coming to town. Sean not answering his phone.

"Lucy," Nate called after her.

She ran down the hall to her squad room. No one was there.

"Stop," Nate said.

She turned around. "Tell me what's going on. Now. Something happened—I feel it. Was Sean injured in Mexico? Is that what you're not telling me? Did something happen to Kane in surgery? Dammit!"

Nate said, "Hans is in Abigail's office. He's waiting for you."

"Tell me!"

Nate didn't say a word, and he avoided looking at her. She walked briskly back down the hall and toward the administrative wing. Abigail's door was open. They were all waiting for her—Hans, Brad, Abigail, Ryan. Nate followed her in and closed the door.

"Sit down, Agent Kincaid," Abigail said formally.

Lucy sat, her back straight, her hands in her lap. "What happened?" she asked, forcing her voice to remain calm. She didn't feel calm, and she sounded even worse.

"Sean is alive," Abigail said. "Okay? Know that."

"What. Happened." Lucy repeated the words slowly, calmly.

Hans said, "This morning I was on a conference call with Sean, Rick, Noah, and Kate."

"My sister-in-law Kate?" Kate taught cybercrime at Quantico and was as good with computers as Sean.

Hans nodded. "We discussed what you found in Agent Dunbar's files, and concurred with your assessment. Kane Rogan also found information in Mexico—I mentioned the corrupt DEA agent, Adam Dover, in the meeting this morning. What I didn't say was that Dover was tasked with luring Kane to Santiago because Tobias believed that Kane stole his money. When Kane escaped the first time, the order was changed to a kill order. That is likely because Tobias and his people were able to decrypt Dunbar's files and they figured out what you did—that Sean was the civilian consultant who siphoned their laundered money into the FBI asset forfeiture account."

"I already know what you're going to say, and no. I will *not* support this plan. You want Sean to go undercover. Last time he did that, he almost got killed. And that's why Sean is not returning my calls—he knows I can talk him out of this ludicrous idea."

"Yes, Sean knew that if he spoke to you first, you wouldn't agree."

Her stomach twisted in knots. "What? What does that mean?"

Brad shook his head. "He's already done it, hasn't he?"

Lucy jumped up. "You—you exposed Sean to these people?" She stared at the group in the room. Hans. Nate. Brad. Abigail. Ryan. By their expressions, Brad

was the only one who hadn't known about the plan. Yet—
he didn't seem to be upset about it. "Tobias? *Rollins*?
They're killers! Rollins killed Sam Archer in cold blood.
They kidnapped an innocent woman in order to lure Kane
into a trap. They tortured and murdered Barry Crawford!"

She wanted to be a strong agent, she wanted to shut
down her feelings and accept that this was a good plan,
that Sean was smart and capable. Except it wasn't a good
plan. It was risky and dangerous and . . . and . . . Tobias
killed everyone who got in his way.

And they knew that she'd see him. This was their way
to punish her. To force Sean to steal for them, then they
would kill him.

"Jack is tracking Sean," Hans said. "He's not going to
let anything happen to him."

"Jack knew?" she said. Her brother kept something like
this from her?

"It was Sean's idea," Hans said. "He talked it through
first with Jack, then Sean called me. I brought in Rick,
Noah, and Kate and we put together the plan with Sean."

"They're all in DC. What good are they going to be at
finding Sean in Texas?"

"Kate is one of best cyber experts in the FBI, and she
is working in her lab at Quantico with state-of-the-art
equipment. Equipment even Sean would be impressed
with."

Hans was trying to make light of the situation, but Lucy
shook her head. "You all did this behind my back because
you knew that it was a bad idea. Don't you understand that
as soon as he does what they want they will put a bullet in
his head?"

"Kate and Sean worked together on the technical end
of the plan—"

"They'll use him as a hostage! You haven't thought this
through. No one has! Sean gets their money, they kill

him, it doesn't matter if we find them, *Sean will still be dead!*"

"Lucy," Hans said firmly, "Agent Adam Dover was murdered yesterday morning. *Before* we learned that he falsified Nicole's reports. Dover was sent by Tobias's organization to trap Kane in Mexico; we know he was killed by his own people. Between your reports, what Kane learned from Dover, and what Blair Novak learned in Los Angeles, we have a clearer picture of what is going on. Jimmy Hunt is the patriarch of his family. Nicole Rollins is his niece. Rollins's mother and Hunt's wife Margaret are sisters. Jimmy Hunt has been a fugitive for five years, and we believe that was when Rollins stepped up her game. She killed Ramos, transferred to Houston, then San Antonio. She'd been helping her uncle for years, until he could no longer operate in the States. We believe that Joseph Contreras is Rollins's lover, that they met in college and together with Jimmy Hunt control a large segment of the drug trade into the Southwest.

"But this goes beyond drugs. Criminals and cartels pay them for safe transport of whatever they need moved— drugs, guns, human beings. What we don't know is how Tobias fits in. Is he partners with Hunt? What's his real name? How does he know Elise Hansen, and where does she fit in?"

Hans caught her eye, but Lucy didn't know what to say. She didn't know what to do—the man she loved was in immediate danger.

Hans said, "One hour ago, Blair Novak took a search team back to the Hunt property with a federal warrant, and they are now in the middle of a standoff. Margaret Hunt and her people have fired on federal agents and the entire canyon has been sealed off by law enforcement." He paused. "We're doing everything we can to resolve the situation peacefully, but we suspect this was their plan all along, to go down in a bloodbath."

"And now Sean is in the middle of it," she said. Why would Sean do this? Why would he risk himself? Not just put himself at risk—it was suicide. It was a damn suicide mission, because Lucy couldn't see a way out.

She looked pointedly at Hans. "Do you know exactly where Sean is right now?"

Hans said, "Sean rigged the GPS in his watch to give off intermittent bursts of data, in case they have high-tech scanning equipment."

"I can see a million ways this can go wrong and no way that this can go right."

"Agent Kincaid," Abigail Durant said with both a firm but understanding voice, "through extensive police work and hundreds of man-hours, we've narrowed down the area where we believe Rollins is hiding. We seized the electronics from the two men we arrested this morning. We have the phone from the bar shooting last night, and though it was damaged our tech team is working on it. The documents that Kane Rogan retrieved from Agent Dover in Mexico give us far more information than we had before. We have pooled information, resources and evidence from every federal and local law enforcement agency in the state. Zach has been working with Quantico around the clock putting together all the data and coming up with an actionable plan. The information you found in Agent Dunbar's records related to the property that Texas Holding bought and sold is so far our single best exclusionary data—we've already input the data and excluded where Rollins *cannot* be, thereby narrowing our search. We have six separate SWAT units ready to recon possible locations, and as soon as we have a confirmed location, we'll be there. No one wants your fiancé harmed in any way."

"They'll see you coming. Nicole is a meticulous planner. She'll kill Sean just because she can." Lucy glared at Hans. "How do you know exactly what happened to him? How do you know he's not dead? Did someone just *watch* him get abducted?" Her voice hitched. This couldn't be happening. It couldn't.

Hans hesitated, then nodded to Nate. Nate showed Lucy footage from her own house, the security system that Sean had put together. He was sitting in the driveway for a long minute in a car she didn't recognize. A van pulled in behind him and four men with semi-automatic rifles surrounded him. Thirty seconds later Sean got out of the car, hands up, then hit one of the men and two others threw him to the ground. Hit him. Cuffed him. Put a bag over his head and dragged him to the van. Seconds later they were gone.

Gone.

"Nate? You knew?"

"I'm sorry, Lucy."

"No. No!" She jumped up. She couldn't do *nothing*. "They will kill him. Even if he does what they want, they'll kill him. You all knew about this idiotic plan this morning. And you didn't tell me!"

"Lucy, you're a good agent, but Sean's your blind spot. You never would have let it happen."

"Damn right I wouldn't! And Noah—he knew. That's why he was asking me all those questions—oh my God, oh my God, I'm the one who said they wouldn't kill him right away. You did this because of my profile. What if I'm wrong? Dammit, Hans! What if I got it wrong and he's already dead?" She could scarcely breathe.

"We did this because we all agreed that the money is the single most important thing to Rollins and Tobias."

"I will never forgive you." She felt sick to her stomach. Sick with loss. "I need air."

Nate followed her out. "Go away!" she screamed at him.

He didn't. He stayed several feet back as she left the building, walking around the path that circled to the FBI garage. She was hysterical, she needed to control herself. She needed to get it *under control*! She was a trained agent, why was she acting like a hysterical lover?

Because she would never see Sean again. In her heart, she knew this stupid, stupid plan was going to get the man she loved killed. And everyone was in on it except her. Everyone was involved. Her closest friends. Her own brother. Maybe she wasn't cut out for this work anymore—not after all she'd learned in these last three months: that these criminals abused children, used them, killed them; that they had no respect for human life; that they killed federal agents just because they were in the way, just because they were doing their job trying to keep the streets safer. People safer. Kids safer.

And for what? To lose everything? Kane was nearly killed in Mexico because he saved a woman who had never done anything to anyone, but had simply been easy bait to lure Kane in. Sam Archer was killed in her own home. Barry Crawford was tortured for hours before he was killed. And now Sean was a hostage.

They had Sean. They wouldn't let him live. Especially since they knew that he'd been the one that caused this chain of events in the first place. If he hadn't worked with the FBI and siphoned off their money two weeks ago, Nicole would have escaped and disappeared because they would have already had everything they needed to complete their plan.

Nicole would kill Sean out of revenge, but she would also do it to punish Lucy. That bitch knew that the best way to hurt Lucy—and to punish Kane Rogan—was to kill the person they both loved best.

Lucy stopped pacing, bent over with her hands on her

knees, and took several deep breaths. They'd never let her be part of this if she couldn't control her emotions. Wasn't that what she excelled at? Keeping her emotions in check? Wasn't that what happened earlier today when Kenzie called her, wanting a friend to talk to, not an agent to discuss case details? Her ability to control her feelings made her a good agent, a good investigator. It was only with Sean that she let her emotions ooze over into everything else.

Her heart rate slowed. She took another deep breath. Her thoughts came into focus. She put herself in Sean's shoes. What had he been thinking?

Time. They'd run out of time. Whatever Kane had learned in Mexico meant that time was against them, and more people would die in order for Nicole to get her money, unless Sean stepped up and allowed himself to be taken. All the legwork would have landed them at their hideout . . . except it was taking too long.

Lucy knew Sean better than anyone. If he believed that he could help, that he could stop innocent people from being hurt, then he would step up and risk himself to save others. Because he could. Because he had the skill. Because he was smart . . . and ruthless.

She pulled out her cell phone. She didn't expect Jack to answer, but he did.

"I know," she said.

"I'm not going to let him die."

Hearing Jack say it gave her a small nugget of hope. "What's happening?"

"I'm monitoring Sean's GPS signal and putting together a map. As he moves, I'm positioning myself as close as possible without being spotted."

"Where are you?"

He didn't say anything.

"You're not going to tell me."

"You do your job, I'll do mine." He hung up.

Lucy pocketed her phone and walked back into the building. She ignored everyone else, but went to Zach. "Where's the map? I want to know how close we are to finding them."

"We have a command post set up in the main conference room. All data is being fed into there."

She went to the conference room. The map of southern Texas, everything within a three-hour radius of San Antonio, had been posted on one wall. Large areas had been blacked out. Multiple computers were being used to process data and eliminate properties one by one. One computer monitored Sean's GPS every fifteen minutes.

She was about to sit down and go through more property records when Hans said, "Lucy, we have something you need to see."

Her heart skipped a beat, then she said calmly, "What?"

He handed her a printout. "We informed Agent Dover's supervisor that he was missing and presumed dead and was under investigation for kidnapping and corruption. His office searched his apartment and found a safe with evidence that will put Jimmy Hunt away for life. Plus, a letter. It answers some of our questions. I just sent a copy to Blair Novak in LA; she might be able to use the information to get Margaret Hunt to stand down."

Lucy read the letter. It was dated three months ago, the day after Nicole was arrested.

To whom it may concern:

If you're reading this, I'm dead. If I was killed in the line of duty or in a seeming accident, most likely Margaret Hunt put a hit out on me.

Twenty-three years ago I was approached by Jimmy Hunt, a low-level drug dealer seeking to expand his base. He'd known I'd looked the other

*way on some cases in order to earn a little extra
money. At the time, I didn't think much about it.
They were minor cases and no one was getting
hurt. This time, he had a job for me that would
change everything.*

*His brother-in-law, John Rollins, was a cop
with LAPD who initially was helping Jimmy with
his dealing. But according to Jimmy, Rollins made
a pact with a rival dealer. Family does not betray
family. We set up an operation, called in Rollins's
team as part of LAPD backup, and in the course of
a firefight Rollins ended up dead. It was a hit, pure
and simple, and Rollins could go out a hero while
Jimmy was able to regain and expand his own
enterprise.*

*I helped Nicole Rollins obtain a job in the DEA
as an agent. She was recruited on her own, but
I taught her how to make herself appealing to
the DEA so they would recruit her. I falsified
interviews and reports in order to ensure that the
DEA wouldn't easily be able to find out she was
related to the Hunts.*

*Five years ago when I could no longer protect
Jimmy Hunt from his illegal activities—
documentation and my diary are enclosed in this
file—I alerted them that my office was getting a
warrant. Jimmy fled the country and Margaret
destroyed all evidence at their ranch in Topanga
Canyon. She's a terrific actress and fooled everyone
into thinking that her husband ran off with her
sister. While it's true that they had an open
marriage, Tamara Rollins did not leave with
Jimmy. Margaret killed Tamara when she learned
that her sister had given the DEA anonymous*

information about Jimmy that led to his exile. Tamara's body is buried in a barrel somewhere on Margaret's property. I blame myself for her death; I'm the one who told Margaret that Tamara was the only one who could have leaked the information. Now I'm not so sure. It might have been Nicole herself, in an attempt to take over her uncle's operation completely. It's clear that Nicole is smarter than Margaret and Jimmy think.

I grew up in a dysfunctional family, and being with the Hunts was a roller-coaster ride that at times was amusing, in a dark and creepy way. Margaret and Jimmy have a son, Tobias Hunt, who is a sociopathic killer. For years, the family has been cleaning up his messes, which usually involve rough sex with prostitutes or drug addicts he picks up—girls he doesn't think will report the abuse or are willing to do anything for a fix. There have been times when the violence resulted in murder. When Nicole left for DEA training, Jimmy took Tobias to Mexico to teach him how to control his sexual urges. But after Jimmy's daughter was born, Jimmy told Nicole that Tobias was her responsibility.

To Nicole's credit, she came up with a plan that both kept Tobias under control and gave her more power than she'd ever had on her own. Tobias is a formidable opponent. He's rash and violent and puts the fear of God into people. He hides his violence behind a soft face and he enjoys the contradiction. He makes friends easily, and kills them just as easily. He enjoys the role Nicole created for him because he gets what he wants— fear—while being able to protect the family.

Nicole keeps him in women, keeps him in Mexico on one of six properties she owns through a shell company, and she gives him specific assignments.

Five years ago something changed. I don't know exactly what happened, but Nicole killed Ramon Ramos in San Antonio claiming he was a DEA informant. I think—but can't prove—that it was really Nicole who set Jimmy up, framed her own mother, and killed Ramos as a cover from her own family so they wouldn't know she orchestrated the entire thing. Tamara was flaky and weird, and after she had the baby she went a bit crazy. I would, too, if my kid was a sociopath who gutted cats and drowned dogs for fun.

Once Nicole transferred to Houston and I transferred to Mexico City, there was a peace in the family that I appreciated. Without Jimmy mucking things up, Margaret ran the organization with military precision. The details of how she brokered deals with cartels throughout Mexico are enclosed in the documents, including individuals she bribed or threatened. With Margaret in LA and Nicole in San Antonio, they controlled two important pipelines from Mexico into the US. And they did it while staying under the radar and using Tobias as the go-between.

I can't discount the importance of Nicole's longtime lover, Joseph Contreras, in the success of this operation. He found an ingenious way to launder money and continue to fund the very expensive organization. The expression that you have to spend money to make money is very true—and the reason they were successful was because they had enough money to make them successful. I don't have details on how the money-laundering operation worked; all I know is that Joseph works for a congresswoman who is on the take. How she's able to use her position to launder for Nicole, I have no idea, and asking questions can get you killed.

However, I'm writing this letter now because Nicole Rollins was arrested yesterday. The word is they have sufficient evidence to keep her locked up. While I don't believe she will turn on her family—she has an almost religious obsession with protecting her cousin Tobias from his own stupidity—I fear that with her in prison, Tobias will put everything at risk. The only person who seems to understand this is Margaret, and in our last conversation she told me that she and Nicole already had a plan should Nicole ever be arrested.

Still, a series of events has led me to believe that I am no longer safe from the Hunt family. If the investigation into Nicole shows that I was the one who falsified her records, the Hunts will kill me before they allow me to talk about their operation. That is why I'm putting together this file. Seeking forgiveness, maybe.

No, not forgiveness. I probably wouldn't have done anything different. It was truly fun while it lasted. More, I want to stick it to the Hunts because while they preach loyalty until they're blue in the face, they'll stab you in the back if they think they can get away with it.

Fuck you all.

Adam Dover

Lucy read the letter twice. Her hands were shaking.

"Are you okay?" Hans asked.

"If he'd only named her," Lucy said.

"Excuse me?"

"Elise Hansen. Elise is in fact Tobias's half sister. Jimmy Hunt and Tamara Rollins. It's all here. We can use this with the AUSA to put Elise in maximum security. And it explains so much about Nicole—and Tobias."

She looked at Hans. "Do we have the files? Do they include Nicole's plans? Did Dover know where she's hiding out?"

"Yes, no, and no," Hans said. "Dover's boss said the files are documents of drug transactions and shipments, mostly into Los Angeles. There's very little about Nicole in there."

"Okay," she said, shifting gears. "We need to use Elise as bait."

The room grew quiet around her.

"What do you mean?" Hans said.

"This whole time we knew that Elise was somehow involved with Tobias and, by extension, Nicole. But we didn't know why or how they were connected. She's half sister to both of them. If Nicole has been protecting Tobias for years, because he's family, she'll do the same for Elise."

"What do you have in mind?" Abigail said.

"Tobias gave his sixteen-year-old sister a lot of freedom. Power. He had her kill Harper Worthington. He had her screw James Everett and attempt to blackmail him with a sex tape to keep him in line. She set up her own attack— she let herself be shot—to get to the hospital to find out exactly what we know and to set me up because I helped take down her brother's operation in Operation Heatwave." It was really because Tobias knew she'd seen him. In her gut, she knew that was the reason. "Through any of this,

Tobias could have made Elise disappear—either get her to safety, or kill her. But he didn't. She's smart and ruthless and a survivor—but he didn't kill her because she's family."

Lucy turned to Hans and held up Adam Dover's letter. "Who knows we have this?"

"Only the team that raided his apartment. Everyone in this room. Noah and Rick Stockton have copies, Edward Moody, and the DOJ."

That was a lot of people, but it hadn't been released publicly. "What if we have a press conference and release some of this information, but imply that it's coming from Elise."

"You'd put a target on her back," Abigail said.

Lucy refrained from saying that Elise had, in fact, set up Lucy to be shot in the back. Instead she said, "This afternoon, the court placed Elise in a group home in Austin. There's no doubt in my mind that she'll walk away at the first available opportunity. But there's a chance she could still be at court, or at the detention center before she's transported. We have cause to put her into protective custody, don't we? Cut her off from everyone, even her lawyer if we say her life is in danger. Have the AUSA read an indictment, we make it up as we go along. Maybe we list charges even if we can't prove them."

"There are so many legal problems—"

"Nicole is an escaped fugitive. She killed cops and she will kill Sean. And if she finds out that Sean is scamming her, she'll kill him now. She has no rights," Lucy said.

"There is precedent," Hans said, "if we word the statement right."

"Wouldn't Nicole pick up on that?" Brad said. "She understands how the DOJ operates, the lines we can cross and those we can't."

"We have to take the risk," Lucy said. "We have information in this letter that Nicole and Tobias don't know we have. And some, we can extrapolate based on what we know. We issue a statement and imply that a member of the family is turning state's evidence—then detail things that Dover revealed, but they'll think that Elise gave us the information."

"And then what?" Brad said. "They come in and try to kill her?"

Lucy wasn't sure. She wanted to put them on edge, force them to make a mistake.

"No, I think that Tobias will try to rescue her. How certain are you, Brad, that there's still a mole in the DEA?"

"We're transferring everybody. They don't have access to any information, and if they did, they'd know we were setting them up. But we're waiting for the independent review."

Hans said, "What if we stated that our witness is under sedation and suicide watch? Then release—internally— the location?"

"There is no guarantee anyone will come for her," Abigail said.

"No, there isn't," Lucy said. "There's no guarantee that Nicole hasn't already killed Sean. If we can draw Tobias out, we can arrest him on sight. Until we find Nicole's safe house we can't just sit around and wait for information!" She forced herself to calm down. Emotion was her enemy. "Also, if we let Elise watch the press conference, I have a feeling she'll get so angry, she'll tell me anything I want to know. She'll be livid that her plan didn't work exactly like she wanted. I suspect that's the only way we'll get her to trip herself up."

Zach said, "I'll call the detention center and find out when she's being transported."

Abigail said, "I need to clear this with Ritz and Edward."

Hans said, "I'll approve the operation and notify DC.

Inform Ritz and Edward what we're doing, but it's need-to-know. We'll release the information selectively to the list."

Abigail nodded and left the room.

"List?" Lucy asked.

Hans glanced around. The only people left in the conference room were her, Brad, Nate, and Hans. And Zach, in the corner on the phone.

Hans said, "I've already set a trap for the mole in the briefing papers I distributed this morning. I emailed documents the night before to a list of people who had access to specific information that we have reason to believe has been leaked to the drug cartels. Because the FBI only assists the DEA in these operations, the list was surprisingly small—a dozen people, including civilians. Each document was slightly different. Kate wrote a virus program so if any document is shared electronically, we can trace it. So far, no one has forwarded the email to anyone else. However, to minimize being discovered, Kate said the traitor would most likely print it out and share it. That's harder to track—unless we can reclaim the physical document. Each one is slightly different."

"And you want to release what? Different locations to this list?"

"We'll only have one shot. We'll need to make each location look like it's real, which means lots of resources. We're spread thin now."

Lucy didn't want to do it—but she realized that she might have information important to the case that she didn't realize was important. "May I look at the list?"

"Are you sure? We talked about this yesterday—"

"I'm sure."

Hans nodded. "Let's go to Juan's office."

Zach jumped up from his workstation in the corner. "Uh, Dr. Vigo?"

"Yes?"

"Elise Hansen was processed out of the detention center by Dr. Barbara Oakley. They left ten minutes ago. They're currently on their way to Austin."

"Ten minutes ago?" Brad asked. "That was fast."

"They?" Lucy asked. "Dr. Oakley is in the transport van?"

"Dr. Oakley is driving, there is no transport," Zach said.

"Get Oakley on the phone, stat," Hans said. "I'll convince her to turn around."

Zach immediately pulled up her numbers.

"The judge gave the defense everything they wanted," Lucy said. "I tried my best, but the judge wouldn't accept what I had to say."

"Judge Axelrod almost tossed Lucy in jail for contempt," Nate added.

"Axelrod?" Brad said. "The judge was supposed to be Goodman. I know Goodman well, he would have given Christine Fallow nearly anything she wanted, within reason."

"We asked for three days to prepare charges because our lead agent had been killed," Lucy said.

"And she didn't give it? Un-fucking-believable."

"Dr. Vigo?" Zach said. "Dr. Oakley's not answering her cell phone."

"Trace it."

"Sir, we need a warrant."

"Do it," Hans said. "Her life is in immediate danger."

This was the one time that Lucy wished she hadn't been right. She'd warned Oakley, she'd told the court the truth. And now the woman was in danger . . . and Elise was going to hook up with Tobias. And with Nicole.

No one spoke while Zach went through the tedious process. They had the capability to trace cell phones, but legally they were in a gray area.

Lucy walked around to the map on the wall that outlined every parcel of property in a hundred-fifty-mile radius.

Where are you, Sean?

She turned to look at the computer. Every fifteen minutes, Sean's watch uploaded his location.

He hadn't moved in thirty minutes.

"Nate," she said, motioning him over. "Look."

Sean had spent the last thirty minutes on the far side of Canyon Lake, an hour north of San Antonio. She called Jack and his phone went directly to voice mail.

"Hans—" she said.

Zach interrupted. "Dr. Oakley's phone is not moving. It's at the parking lot of the Alamodome."

"That's less than a mile from the courthouse," Brad said.

Hans told Zach, "Call SAPD, emergency channels. We're too far away to get there quickly. Ryan, find Proctor and head there now. Proceed with caution. Stay in contact with SAPD and call in regularly. No one is to go off the grid, understood? Zach is coordinating all agents—where they are, who they're with, what they're doing. We're not losing another agent to these assholes."

When they left, Hans said, "I know you wanted to go, but—"

"No. Look." She pointed to the computer-generated map with Sean's GPS. "I called Jack; he didn't answer."

"Dunning," Hans said, "you're driving. Donnelly, you're with us."

"Sir—" Nate began.

"It wasn't a request."

Sean's internal sense of time was well developed, as was his acute sense of direction. Even with the bag over his head, based on the road surface, speed, and traffic sounds he sensed they were heading out of the city. They didn't stop for nearly an hour, then they parked in a remote area. For a minute he thought they would kill him and dump his body, but when they ordered him to strip and put on what looked like hospital scrubs, he realized they were being extra cautious. Smart. Too smart. He had to dump his watch as well, which meant Jack couldn't track him.

Jack was likely ten minutes behind them, but because of the delay in the GPS—for security in case they swept him for any transmitting device—it would be at least fifteen minutes before Jack knew he wasn't moving. By the time he got here, he'd only find the watch. Sean suspected they were nowhere near Rollins's safe house.

The watch had recorded everything since he'd been taken, but he couldn't upload the data to the server with his hands zip-tied. The kidnappers had talked almost the entire way, some of which Sean caught—such as, they were meeting Contreras by a lake—and some that was muffled because of the bag over his head. FBI technology could separate the voices from the ambient sound and hopefully there were more clues in the data.

Sean was angry—though this was his idea and he knew it was the best chance of catching Rollins and Tobias, he was furious that he'd been grabbed. If he hadn't planned to be submissive, he would have fought back. Four against one . . . not great odds. But he would have fought. He hated being passive.

He was standing in the heat, though anything was better than the black bag over his head. He wasn't claustrophobic, but the discomfort was real, the unknown keeping his heart rate elevated and his adrenaline pumping.

There were four kidnappers, and two walked away under the shade and drank water. He wanted water, but didn't ask. They retied his hands. Sean could break the zip-ties, but that would defeat the purpose of being taken to Rollins.

He glared at the kidnappers. They were guns for hire, not too bright, but they obviously did what they were told. Forced him to change then restrained him again. Obviously Rollins came up with the plan. Anyone who could run an international drug operation while working as an agent for the DEA was no idiot.

Another car drove up only minutes after Sean had changed. It was a two-door pickup truck like thousands of other nondescript trucks. He recognized the man who got out of the driver's seat.

Joseph Contreras.

He hadn't seen him before, but Lucy's description had been right on, including the scar on his face, his complexion, and his build. But it was more his manner, the way the others deferred to him, the way he took charge.

"Sean Rogan," he said.

Sean remained silent.

"You and your family have caused us a lot of problems. That will end today. I will make one thing clear. I am a man of my word. You and your brother are already dead men. I'm sure you've figured that out—from what I've heard you're quite the genius." He stepped closer. Sean itched to hit him. His wrists chaffed under the zip-ties.

"But I give you this promise. If you retrieve our money without games, I will spare your girlfriend."

"I don't believe you."

"I'm being honest here, it's your problem if you can't see that. I could lie and say you'll walk away free and clear after this is over, but you would know I was lying, so that doesn't benefit us. You'll die knowing that Lucy is alive—provided she doesn't come after us. We'll have what we want—our money and freedom; your dead body; and even more important, taking from Lucy what she loves the most." He paused. "Consider this, Mr. Rogan. If the situation was reversed and you survived but Lucy did not, how would that make you feel?"

Sean didn't—couldn't—respond.

I'm going to kill you when this is over.

Joseph smiled, but there was no humor, no friendship. His ruthless grin cut Sean to the quick. "Exactly. Agonizing pain. Rage. Dear little Lucy will be gutted without shedding a single drop of blood. And that makes Niki very happy. And what makes Niki happy, makes me happy."

Joseph nodded and the kidnappers put the bag over Sean's head again, then picked him up as he struggled, partly out of survival instinct, partly because he was so angry he couldn't remain still. They maneuvered him into the pickup, onto the floor behind the bench seat. There was barely enough room for his six-foot-one frame, and the metal on the back of the seat dug into his back.

Joseph put the truck in gear, then said, "And Sean, if you fuck with us, I will turn Lucy over to Tobias. You may not be aware, but Tobias has a particularly sick sexual fetish that I'm sure he would be happy to satisfy with Lucy. So not only will you be dead, but she will be, too—after serving Tobias's needs for as long as she can stay alive." He paused. "I've been told that the stronger girls last weeks. To me, Lucy seems to be very strong, in both body and spirit. But you won't be around to save her from a fate that is far, far worse than death. I've seen some of the women when Tobias is done with them. Even I pity them."

CHAPTER THIRTY-FOUR

Nate was nearly to Canyon Lake when Jack called Lucy.

"There's nothing here," he said.

"Sean's GPS says he hasn't moved in nearly an hour."

Jack was silent a moment. "The van is here."

"And Sean?"

"His watch."

Lucy's vision darkened. She closed her eyes, willed her heart rate to slow.

"We'll be there in ten minutes."

"Stay at headquarters. I'm working with Kate on this. Let us do our job, Lucy."

"This *is* my job." She hung up. She couldn't think straight. But she had to.

Focus, Lucy. Do what you do best.

"They either knew or suspected that Sean was wired or had a tracker," she said to the men in the car. "Jack said the van is at Canyon Lake as well as Sean's watch. Ten to one they had Sean strip. They researched him. After they read Dunbar's memo, I'll bet they researched Sean and learned about the technology he patented or worked with. They may even think there's a subcutaneous chip and scanned him, which is dumb. He doesn't trust the government enough to implant a tracker that he couldn't easily remove."

"They knew," Brad said. "Or they suspected he was wired."

"Not necessarily," Hans said.

"We have a mole in the FBI—of course they knew!" Lucy exclaimed.

"If you were Nicole and you didn't have a mole," Hans said calmly, "would you run a search on Sean? Would you strip him and change vehicles?"

"Of course, but—" She paused. "I see what you mean. She's smart and cautious."

"She knows he's a tech genius," Hans said. "Maybe it went too easy at the house. Maybe they think he had a weapon or another cell phone on him that they didn't find when they searched him initially. Whatever it is, it doesn't mean they know he's working with us."

"But now we don't know where he is," she said. Bile burned her throat; she swallowed and squeezed back threatening tears. "He could be anywhere."

"Not anywhere," Nate said.

"Nate's right," Hans said. "They'll take him to their safe house because once they get the money, they don't need to hide anymore. They'll attempt to flee."

"They also won't need Sean," Lucy reminded him. She called Kate and prayed her sister-in-law would answer.

"I'm on the phone with Jack," Kate said in lieu of *hello*. "I have no news." Lucy heard Kate's fingers working rapidly on a keyboard.

"Kate, do not lie to me and do not handle me. How much time does Sean have to hack into the FBI and transfer the money?"

"I don't understand what you mean. How fast can he do it?"

"I thought you had a plan! How long can he stall? How long before they kill him?"

"Lucy, stop. You're going to make yourself sick thinking about the worst."

"Just give me a fucking answer!"

No one said a word. Lucy breathed deeply. Why couldn't she tap into her icy calm when she needed it the most?

"Sean is the smartest guy I know," Kate said. "And I don't say that to make you feel better. As soon as he starts moving money, I'll see it, and we'll be able to communicate. He needs the Internet to transfer, and he knows how to send coded messages. We've already worked out those details this morning, and we have a backup plan. You're forgetting one very important thing: These people are desperate for that money. And none of them, not even that bitch Rollins, knows what Sean is capable of. They don't have tech skills, not like me and certainly not like Sean. As soon as he's online, I'll pinpoint his location. They can route the feed through any security or country, it doesn't matter. I will find him."

That actually made Lucy feel better. Kate was no slouch, but she'd once told Lucy that if she were ten years younger she would have been raised on tech like Sean had been and would have been as good. Lucy didn't doubt it.

"I'm counting on it," she said and hung up.

Hans said, "Ryan sent me a message. They have Oakley. She'd been locked in the trunk of her car."

"In this heat? She could have died."

"She's injured, sick and disoriented. There's damage to her car, as if someone rear-ended her. The Astrodome is near the on-ramp toward Austin, so it's likely her car was hit, she pulled over, and then was forced to drive into the parking lot where she was knocked out, tied up, and put in the trunk. It bought them time."

"Did she say anything?"

"She is adamant that Elise was kidnapped."

"You don't believe that. Because *I* certainly don't believe it."

"Elise may have played the part," Hans said.

Lucy nodded. "Yes, she would. If they'd killed Dr. Oakley, she would have gloated and admitted to everything because she enjoys proving to people that she's smart. But since they didn't kill her, pretending to be taken against her will would keep her in the role of victim."

"Why?" Brad asked.

"She thinks that if their plan goes south, she can still walk away. She thinks about herself first. Her self-preservation instincts are better than anyone I've met."

"Fucking psychopath," Nate mumbled.

"There's Jack," Lucy said when they approached the white van that she recognized from outside her house. She climbed out of the backseat as soon as Nate stopped the SUV.

Jack approached immediately. She didn't know where he'd parked Sean's Mustang.

"I told you there's nothing to see," Jack said. He stared at Nate as if blaming him.

"We were already on our way," Lucy said. "I spoke to Kate. Fill me in."

"Sean hasn't gone online."

Lucy walked over to the van and looked in the back. Tossed in a pile were all of Sean's clothes, including his boxers, socks, and shoes. His watch had been tossed on top. Other than that, the cargo van was empty.

"Did you search the front? Compartments?"

"Yes, and it's clean. Zach traced the plates—it was reported stolen this morning."

"Security footage?"

Jack raised an eyebrow. "You're not the only one who knows how to do their job."

"Sometimes I think I am, because I knew as soon as I heard about this plan that it wouldn't work."

Jack's jaw tightened. Lucy supposed she was essentially saying *I told you so*, but if Jack's wife Megan were in Sean's situation and Jack knew it was a bad idea, he would be saying the same thing, and he knew it. "What is your plan now, Jack?"

"Go back to headquarters."

"You're not my boss, you're my brother."

"Same thing."

She would have laughed if she weren't so angry. And heartbroken. She shouldn't have come here. What had she been thinking? That Jack would lie to her? He never had—until the lie of omission this morning when he didn't tell her about Sean's plan. And that, ultimately, was what hurt. She trusted Jack more than anyone except Sean. He'd never lied to her, he'd always been blunt, he'd always called her on her own fears. He'd helped her in ways he could only guess: She would never have been capable of loving Sean if Jack hadn't helped her grow strong—physically and emotionally—after she'd been kidnapped and raped eight years ago.

She became acutely aware of the silence. That Hans, Nate, and Brad were watching her and Jack while standing around the SUV.

She didn't have all the answers. She didn't know what to do now, but it wasn't going back to headquarters and waiting for word as to whether Sean was dead or alive. She turned to Hans.

"What now?"

She could feel Jack's surprise that she didn't address him. But he hadn't had an answer that involved her.

"Get the watch," Hans said.

Lucy and Jack both looked at the pile of clothes in the back of the van. Lucy reached out and picked up the watch. She'd never seen it before. "You think he left us information. I should have thought of that."

"We'll take it to Zach," Hans said. "I've heard he's good."

"He is," Lucy said. "Sean has a lot of respect for him."

"And we call Blair Novak and tell her we need information from Margaret Hunt sooner rather than later."

"How much time do we have, Hans? Truthfully—I need to know."

"They're not going straight to the safe house on the chance that they were followed, and they also don't want Sean to know where they are on the chance he gets away," Brad said.

"Why do you say that?" Hans said. "They want their money now, not later."

"Nicole played me for a long time, but there are some things she couldn't hide. She's meticulous, she's organized, she will not leave anything to chance."

Lucy nodded. "Brad's right. It's why she gloated to Sam, then killed her when she could have left her to bleed out. Because there was no guarantee that she *would* bleed out before help arrived, or before Sam could get to a phone."

"Then I'd give them an hour or two to get to the safe house. Beyond that—I don't know how long it takes a competent hacker to break into a government bank account and transfer money."

"Three to four hours, tops," Jack said. "I'm sure Sean could do it faster."

"They don't care if he's caught," Lucy said, "they will move their money again as soon as he transfers it."

"Is Sean really capable of hacking into a government account?" Brad asked, partly in awe.

"Yes," Lucy and Jack said simultaneously.

"You're not letting him do it, though, right?" Brad said. "If it all goes sideways—I'm sorry, Lucy, but there is the chance—then Nicole will have tens of millions of dollars and she can easily disappear."

"The only way the plan works is if they see the money in their account, and we don't have that information until Sean gives it to us," Hans said. "Then it's up to Kate to hack it on her end and get the money back."

"That's a lot of what-ifs and maybes."

"We hope it doesn't get that far," Hans said.

Lucy said, "So do I, because as soon as they see the money in their account, Sean is dead."

Blair Novak hung up the phone.

Hans wanted information now. She couldn't promise him anything, but they both knew that the longer the stand-off, the worse the outcome.

Still, she wasn't going to risk the lives of her people because the assistant director of the FBI needed information she didn't even know if she could get. The assistant special agent in charge was on his way along with the county sheriff's elite SWAT unit and assistance from the LAPD. The hostage negotiator had been trying unsuccessfully for thirty minutes to get someone to pick up a phone.

The SWAT team leader quickly approached her. "Something's wrong, Agent Novak."

"Define *something*." She hated vague comments.

"When my team first got into place, we identified a minimum of seven hostiles inside the property. No one has moved for thirty minutes. No gunshots have been fired. We have no line-of-sight on any individual. The helicopter reports that five hostiles went into the barn on the northwest side of the property and haven't left. There is no movement inside."

"Any children?"

"Not that we have seen."

Margaret Hunt was in her sixties, but if she had some sort of cult working out here there could be children or innocents. Blair didn't have a solid understanding of what the Hunts were up to, and the lack of information disturbed her. In a perfect world, she would have had weeks—or at least a couple of days—to pull together everything on Margaret and Jimmy Hunt and Tamara Rollins, down to their childhood pediatrician and favorite movie.

"Do we have eyes?"

"We have one radar unit, but we're too far away to use it on the house. I can get a team close enough to the barn—there's natural cover on the backside."

"Do it. I want to know how many are in the barn and what they're doing."

"Suggestion?"

"I'm all ears. Until the ASAC gets here and takes over."

"There are six outbuildings—the barn is the largest." He unfolded a piece of paper from his pocket and drew out rough boxes. "The barn is here—northwest corner. Three buildings less than one thousand square feet are between the barn and the main house. On the south side of the property there appear to be several cottages. No movement has been seen on the south side except for one of the houses. This area, we might be seeing a meth lab or another chemically or explosively dangerous situation. What I'd like to do as soon as the sheriff's SWAT team arrives is split up—we'll clear and secure the barn and three buildings north of the house; the sheriff will clear and secure the three small houses. That leaves the main house and we can surround it."

"Set it up," she said.

Blair waited, not something she enjoyed. She trusted her SWAT team—they had the best-trained SWAT in Southern California, hands down. They worked well with the LA County sheriff because they often cross-trained together. With shrinking resources, they needed to help each other as much as possible.

Ten minutes passed before Blair heard from SWAT that they were in position and would be going in after scanning the barn with the radar unit.

Chatter was minimal on the SWAT communications channel—mostly reports and check-ins and all-clears. Then she heard something that chilled her.

"Delta Team reports no movement in the barn. Repeat, five suspects, no movement."

"This is Alpha One, where are the suspects?"

"Prone on the ground. No movement. No signs of life. How would you like us to proceed?"

"Proceed with caution. Go, go, go!"

Blair listened from the safety of the tactical station set up just outside the Hunt property gates. A minute later a command was issued, "Barn is wired. I repeat, barn is wired to explode. Do not breach any building!"

"Are the suspects moving?" another voice asked.

"Negative, we have line-of-sight, five suspects are immobile in the center of the barn. Main barn door has trip wire. We're backing off. Everyone proceed with extreme caution. Bomb unit is on the scene. Stand down."

A suicide pact. Either they were already dead and planned to take out as many cops as they could, or they were planning to die in the process.

But setting up explosives took both skill and time. When had they done it? After her visit yesterday? Was this the plan all along? Did Margaret Hunt plan to kill herself rather than go to prison?

Or maybe Margaret Hunt wasn't here. She hadn't seen the woman. She'd heard a female voice over the intercom . . . it could have been anyone. Blair had assumed it was Margaret.

She called Hans Vigo. "Hans, the property is wired to explode if we breach the buildings. The bomb squad is working on it now, but there have been no shots and no sightings for forty minutes. Five suspects down and presumed dead—possible suicide or murder-suicide. I can't get to the house until it's cleared, but my gut tells me that Hunt is not here."

Elise laughed as she bounced in the passenger seat. "You were amazing, as always, big brother." She leaned over and gave him a wet kiss on the cheek.

"Stop that," Toby said. But he, too, was smiling. "You did well, kid. Everyone doubted you, except me. I knew you'd do it."

"You've always had faith in me. That's why I love you best."

Love was a relative word. What did it really mean? She'd read all the definitions and she wasn't feeling it. What did an "intense feeling of deep affection" mean, anyway?

But Toby *loved* that she liked him the most. And she did—because he was fun and smart and let her have fun when she wanted to. He'd played the part that Nicole created *so* well, he should win an award. Big, bad Tobias, the man no one knew but everyone feared. Elise had called him the Dread Pirate Robert, but Nicole didn't like that. It wasn't *serious* enough. Nicole, the definition of a wet blanket.

But Nicole was smart—super smart. She thought ten steps ahead of everyone else, and Elise could listen to her for hours telling stories about how she set up this informant or took out that competition or pulled another one over on the DEA.

"I didn't want to hit you," Toby said as he drove up the highway. He exited on a frontage road just outside the city.

"I *told* you we had to make it look good."

"You think we're going to fail."

"No—I think we're going to win *big* but it'll fuck with that bitch fed who reads minds."

"She doesn't read minds."

"Like hell. But no one will believe her. She was slapped down good. Almost got contempt of court and jail."

"I wish she had—I could have taken care of her in jail."

"Guess what? She's *engaged*. Saw a big fat diamond ring on her finger."

He didn't say anything.

"What?" Elise said.

"Maybe this is going to be more interesting than I thought."

"It's all interesting. Nicole is on the FBI's most wanted list! I'll bet she's excited *and* pissed off."

"Don't push her today, little girl."

She stuck her tongue out at him.

"I'm serious. She's on edge and Joseph is being a prick."

"Big surprise there." She rolled her eyes. Joseph was less fun than Nicole.

Toby parked behind a Cadillac Escalade in a remote area. No one was around. "Oh, I like it!" Elise exclaimed and jumped out of the car.

"I knew you would."

They climbed in and Toby cranked up the air-conditioning as he sped off. "What did you mean about this getting interesting?" Elise said, remembering that she'd digressed.

"We have Sean Rogan."

"Get outta here."

"Seriously. Grabbed him outside his house. He's the one who stole our money. Hacked in and siphoned most of it off before Everett could put it in our accounts."

"I *knew* it!"

"What did you know?"

"He was there—somewhere close—when I was with horny old Everett. The bitch Kincaid said something in court today—about how I forced Everett to transfer the money. *Forced*. Really. It was *our* money to begin with." She frowned. There was something else she needed to remember . . . what was it?

"What?"

"I don't know."

"Don't bullshit me."

"I'm not, I just—" Then she remembered. "Mona."

"That fucking bitch. I'll snap her neck the minute I see her."

"She said something to me when she picked me up. I wanted the rest of her files—she had everything on everyone. She said everything was gone, all she had left was what she'd already given us. Someone destroyed her life's work and she was going to rebuild somewhere else."

"And you didn't think to tell me?"

"When the fuck could I have done that? I wasn't exactly allowed to have visitors in the loony bin!"

"You know how."

"Johnson is a prick and I don't like him. He almost screwed up our plans today. You should kill him. You should let me kill him. We can kill him together! That would be fun."

"Elise—"

"Well, you know now, and that's what's important. I'll bet Sean Rogan is the one who did it. If he's all that good and shit."

"Why would he? How would he have known that

Mona had blackmail files? Do you think the feds ordered him to?"

"I don't know. But it'll be fun to find out, won't it?" She paused. "How long until we get there?"

"An hour or two."

"Why that long?" she said.

"We have to go the long way. Be careful."

She shrugged. "No one's following us."

"I have to make sure. I have to do everything right—Nicole is edgy. I have to prove to her that she can trust me."

"Whatever."

"Don't make her mad."

"What's she going to do? We're family."

"I have a surprise."

"I love surprises." She paused. "A better surprise than grabbing Sean Rogan?" She laughed. "Oh, I wish I could see Lucy's face when she finds out!"

"Or when she finds him dead."

"Exactly. What else? Tell me!"

"Joseph isn't as bad as I thought."

"You hate him."

"He hates me," Toby pouted. "I don't know why. I never did anything to him."

"He's just jealous." She kissed his cheek again. "So what did he do that impressed you?"

"He grabbed a fed."

"Who?"

"That's for me to know and you to find out."

"Asshole."

Toby laughed. He turned off the freeway toward a small, private airport.

"Who are we picking up?" Elise asked, half excited and half apprehensive. "Daddy? Is Daddy here?"

"He won't come back to the States. He's paranoid," Toby said.

She frowned. She missed Jimmy. She had so much fun with him and he taught her the most important lesson *ever*: Never let anyone know your exit strategy.

Ten minutes later they were at a small airstrip. But there wasn't a plane in sight. Tobias said, "Wait here," in his serious voice, the one he used when he really wanted Elise to do exactly what he said.

Elise considered following him, but she wasn't quite sure what was going on.

Then she saw the bitch.

"Well, shit," she muttered. "Just when I thought it was going to be a good day."

CHAPTER THIRTY-FIVE

Joseph drove Sean around for over two hours. Sean was numb by the time the truck stopped. He suspected the journey was the most roundabout way to get to where Nicole was holed up. And it worked—at first he tried to keep track of turns and changes in speed, the quality of the roads and the sounds of traffic, but with the dull roar of the undercarriage coupled with the bounce and being restrained, Sean couldn't figure out where they might be.

There was one interesting event—a phone call that seemed to anger Joseph. All Sean heard was a few words, but Joseph was furious, speeding up after he threw his phone on the dashboard. At least, that's what it sounded like.

But the last fifteen minutes were the bumpiest, and Sean knew they were on an unpaved road. As the truck slowed, Sean heard nothing but the truck and gravel.

Joseph got out, leaving the truck idling. A minute later he got back in, rolled the truck forward a hundred feet, then got out. A gate. He wasn't surprised. Texas was a huge state with large chunks of property, vast spaces, private roads.

He wished he had his watch. It would be much easier if

he didn't have to write code on the fly. He could do it—but it would make the entire situation more difficult and he'd risk getting caught. Fortunately, Kate was monitoring the FBI's asset forfeiture account. As soon as she saw him go in—as soon as he attempted to get in—she'd be all over it.

It would almost be funny—if his life weren't in danger. Ten years ago when he was hacking into a bank he did everything in his power *not* to be caught by the feds. Now he needed to make sure they could not only trace his computer, but do it in real time.

They drove another five minutes—a long, gravel road that twisted around and slightly down. By the time the truck stopped and Joseph cut the ignition, Sean's body was covered in bruises and he had a splitting headache.

Joseph got out of the truck and spoke to someone. Sean couldn't hear what they were saying, his ears were still ringing. A minute later, the door opened, the bench seat was pushed up, and two sets of hands reached in and pulled Sean out. His hands bent awkwardly and he grunted in pain.

He was dropped to the rocky ground and someone cut the zip-ties.

"Get up," Joseph said.

Sean reached up and took the bag off his head. His eyes slammed shut in the brightness. He had little feeling in his hands and feet. He tried to stand, staggered, and fell.

Joseph swore under his breath and said, "Lyle, grab one arm, I'll get the other."

They roughly dragged Sean across the gravel road. He tried to kick himself into a standing position, but his legs were like noodles, the pins and pricks burning inside. His arm that had been cut during Kane's rescue throbbed and dripped blood as the remaining stitches tore.

He cried out when a sharp rock hit the small of his back. "Stop!"

They dropped him and Sean rolled over to his knees. He took a couple of deep breaths and saw a railing and porch stairs. He crawled to the stairs, pulled himself up, and used the railing as a crutch. His numb muscles slowly stretched as the blood circulated. He surveyed his surroundings. The terrain and hills told him he was west or northwest of San Antonio. Because they were in a valley, he couldn't see much around him, but to the northwest there were scraggly peaks. He didn't know the geography of Texas well enough to figure out exactly where he was, but he'd guess between fifty and eighty miles outside the city.

He spotted two armed guards on the porch—they weren't trying to stay hidden—but there were others moving just outside his vision. How many people did Rollins have working for her? Four who kidnapped him, Joseph, Lyle, who else? The two on the porch had the same look as the gangbangers at Vasco Trejo's compound three months ago. Young men with angry, dead eyes.

If this place was anything like Trejo's compound, then there would be a minimum of eight roaming guards. Inside, it would only be the inner circle. The elite. Joseph Contreras. Nicole Rollins. Tobias.

Joseph whispered something to Lyle, who ran over to the truck and drove off. Joseph pushed Sean into the house.

Sean realized he was in over his head when he stepped inside the large, sparsely furnished house. It was a sprawling two-story cabin-like home with two staircases and large windows showcasing the vast, dry landscape. He wasn't getting out of here without help.

And he had no idea if he could clue Kate into where he was—or if he did, whether reinforcements would get here in time.

Escape might be his only option to survive. And in this unknown terrain, escape wasn't really an option.

Nicole Rollins ran into the room. She stopped when she saw him.

"Sean Rogan." She smirked and looked him up and down. "Agent Kincaid did pretty good for herself, didn't she?" She sauntered over to Joseph and gave him a kiss.

Nicole looked different from her photos—her hair was shorter and she'd lost weight. But Sean would have recognized her though they'd never actually met.

"You did it," she said to Joseph with a smile. "We're almost done."

He glanced at Sean, then pulled Nicole to the side. Sean couldn't hear what he told her, but Sean suspected it was about the phone call he'd received.

"We'll be gone by sunset," Nicole said.

That meant she expected Sean would need about three hours. He could work with that. It was more time than he thought he would have.

Nicole walked over to Sean and smiled, but her pale-blue eyes remained cold. "You have work to do," she said, "and not a lot of time to do it. Follow me."

He did, because he didn't have a choice. Joseph trailed behind, close enough that Sean could feel his breath on the back of his neck. Nicole led Sean to a great room, complete with a bar along one wall, a pool table to the side, and a desk with three state-of-the-art laptops open and waiting.

"Sit," she said.

Sean complied.

"Obedient, aren't you?" she said. "And quiet. No wonder Lucy loves you so much."

Sean wanted to break her neck.

While he and Kane had been running around trying to find Tobias, all along it was Nicole who was in charge.

Lucy had started thinking about that possibility two weeks ago, but it wasn't until the escape that it became clear. Tobias was part of this operation, no doubt, but Nicole Rollins was in charge and Sean would not forget it.

She pulled up a chair and sat next to him. "Let me tell you how this is going to work. Adeline Worthington, may she burn in Hell, stole twenty-three million dollars from me. I don't need to explain to you how she did it—you already know she was laundering money for my operation. But what you don't know is *why* she stole from me."

He didn't say a word.

That seemed to irritate Nicole. "She stole it because of you. You and your fucking brother and your bleeding-heart girlfriend. Those guns Kane took from us? They were bought and paid for. And then they were gone. How do you think that made me look to my suppliers? To my people? Weak! But worse—I was arrested. I could have fixed it . . . I'm good at that . . . but not from behind bars.

"James Everett, the prick, only got back three point three million. I want *all* my money."

Sean cleared his throat. His mouth was dry, but he said in a gruff voice, "There wasn't twenty-million in those accounts."

"Because *you* interfered."

He finally looked her in the eye. For a moment, she said nothing and he just stared. Then he said, "I was in the next room. I cloned Everett's computer and siphoned off half the money. At most, there was nine, ten million. So either you're lying to me and want me to steal more than you lost, or Everett cheated you. But either way, there's only six million, take or leave, in the FBI asset forfeiture account that I slipped the money into."

She leaned forward. "You're going to get me twenty million dollars before eight p.m. tonight, and I don't give a fuck how you do it or who you steal it from. But if it's not in my account, not only are you and Kane dead, but I'll enjoy torturing your girlfriend and watching her beg for her life."

"If you think the Rogan family is ruthless, you have never met the Kincaids," he said in a low voice.

For a split second a glimmer of fear drifted in and out of Nicole's expression. Then she said, "I'll take my chances."

"Where exactly do you expect me to get twenty million dollars?"

"You're the hacker, Mr. Rogan. The FBI has multiple asset forfeiture accounts. I don't care which ones you steal it from, I want twenty million, and you'd better get started."

He put his fingers on the keyboard of the largest laptop. "Wait," Nicole said. She nodded to Joseph, who then left the room. "You didn't think I trusted you, did you?" she said.

A minute later Joseph walked back in with FBI Agent Barry Crawford.

Barry looked like shit. He'd been severely beaten and Joseph had to hold him upright. One eye was completely swollen shut and the other was bloodshot. His clothes were filthy and torn, he stank of vomit and blood, and his right hand was bandaged but hanging limp at his side.

Everyone thought he was dead. And he would be soon if he didn't get medical attention.

"Barry," Sean said.

Barry stared at him blankly. Had he been drugged? He gave no indication that he recognized Sean.

Sean turned to Nicole. "Who was in Barry's car?"

"No one important to you," she said. "Barry has been extremely helpful over the last few days. I knew he would be. Joseph didn't believe him when he said he had no idea who stole our money, but once I got out of jail I explained to Joseph that Barry was too law-and-order. I knew immediately that this wasn't a sanctioned operation—the FBI, *no* federal law enforcement agency moves that fast. But I didn't realize it was you until we finally cracked open Agent Dunbar's files. Then everything became clear."

She walked over to Barry. The fed straightened, then staggered as if he was in pain. Joseph let go of his arm and Barry sank to the floor. He was dying.

"Poor Barry didn't even know that his own partner was responsible for everything, including the pain and suffering he had to endure before we figured out he knew shit." Nicole turned to Sean. "Make no mistake about it, your little fuck-buddy started all of this. If she hadn't gotten her panties in a wad about Michael Rodriguez, if she hadn't played the hero by going down to Mexico to save Brad, if she hadn't seen my cousin and nearly blown *everything* . . . Barry would have made it to his high school reunion in Seattle. Lucy started it, and you, jackass, finished it. You stole my money with no sanction from the FBI. I don't know who you know or what you have on them. But it's clear you did whatever you damn well pleased and found someone in the FBI to cover for you."

Sean stared at her. He maintained complete control. He had to, or he might blow this whole operation. He said coolly, "You have no idea what you're talking about."

She ignored his comment. "Here's the deal. Barry isn't going to last much longer. He knows nothing—obviously," she said, waving a hand toward his swollen face, "so he's not much use to me. I can, however, still make him suffer, so you fuck with me, I'll fuck with him, and you'll know it's all your fault from beginning to end." She grinned. "I'm a poet."

She sat down next to Sean. "I know a lot about computers," she said, "and I'm watching."

Sean didn't move.

"Starting hacking, Rogan. Time is ticking."

He knew what to do, but to do it while Nicole was watching . . . he would have to be extremely careful. That meant hacking not only the FBI asset forfeiture account, but rewriting the computer's code to send an electronic beacon to Kate so she could find him.

And he would have to rewrite it so Nicole couldn't tell that's what he was doing.

Sean's headache grew worse.

Ten minutes later a commotion in the front of the house startled Nicole and she jumped up. But she didn't leave Sean's side. "Joseph!" she said.

He ran out and a minute later returned.

"We have company," he said flatly.

Sean couldn't read Joseph's expression, but Nicole tensed. A minute later a skinny woman of sixty with a long dark-gray braid down her back walked in. Nicole was obviously surprised, but she ran over and gave the woman a hug. "I thought you were going to Mexico," she said.

"Change of plans," the woman snapped. "When this much money is at stake, do you think I'm going to trust just anyone?"

She walked over to Sean and stared at him. "So you're Kane Rogan's brother. Spitting image." She slapped him so hard Sean almost fell from the chair because he wasn't expecting it. It was all he could do not to grab the woman's wrist and twist it.

"We haven't been formally introduced," Sean said through clenched teeth.

"Call me Maggie."

"Niki!" a voice cried out.

As Sean watched, Elise Hansen—the teenage prostitute who had killed Harper Worthington—ran into the room and hugged Nicole. That was when he saw the resemblance. For a second he wondered if Elise was Nicole's daughter . . . the thought sickened him, especially since he knew how Elise lived her life and what she'd done. What she did for fun as well as survival.

Then an older man walked in. Nice looking—not too tall, a little big around the middle, and balding. Everyone's-favorite-uncle type . . . except Sean realized that this was Tobias.

The man for whom his brother had been searching for months.

"So did he give us our money back?"

"We'd just started when you came in," Nicole said.

"Seems like he's still working without supervision," Maggie said.

Nicole strode back over to Sean and looked at his screen. "What are you doing?"

"Breaking into a secure bank. Isn't that what you wanted?" His heart was beating too fast. He prayed Nicole didn't have any more computer skills than the average competent federal agent.

"Don't move a muscle," she growled. Then she turned to the group. "I need to watch this bad boy to make sure we get all twenty million back into our account. Get changed, do whatever, but we leave tonight. The feds aren't close, but they're pushing, and I'm not going to wait around for them to find us."

Sean immediately thought: *How the hell does she know what's going on?* Hans had told him the need-to-know list was small. Was it a guess on Nicole's part or was there someone Sean trusted who had betrayed them?

Kenzie walked into her cozy house just after five Wednesday evening. She was exhausted and felt like shit.

Everyone else was still working, but Abigail told her to go home. She had barely slept last night and she'd arrived at the morgue at six thirty this morning. Watching the autopsy—as much as she could stomach—had been harder than anything she'd done on this job. Or in the army.

"Eric?" she called. His car was in the driveway. She'd been so relieved when she saw it, because she didn't want to be alone. Not after today.

She heard the shower running and considered jumping in with him, but truthfully, she wasn't in the mood for fun and games. She just wanted to be hugged.

Her house was small, a little two-bedroom two-bath in a borderline area, but not too far from headquarters. She owned it, the first time anyone in her family had ever owned a house. She'd also been the only one to go to college. Her mom had been a single mom, her dad an asshole who left when she was two. Her mom raised her on her own, no help from anyone else, and Kenzie never once doubted that she was loved. She almost called her mom, just to say hi, but decided her mom would worry too much. Kenzie had to get the grief out of her system or her mom would know that she was upset, and then her mom would worry. She never wanted her mom to worry.

She sat down at her desk, in the dining room. She didn't need a formal dining table, and the breakfast nook off the kitchen was large enough to seat six. The dining room had a lot of light and space, and better, she could watch football on Sundays while sitting at her computer writing reports.

Kenzie pulled up her email and started skimming for anything that might be important, but she couldn't get Barry out of her head.

She and Emilio had searched Barry's house. ERT had already gone through last night to process it for blood and trace evidence, but they'd come back with nothing. The house was clean. Kenzie and Emilio were searching for any clue, no matter how small, but also found nothing. They interviewed Barry's neighbors, and his elderly next-door neighbor was the only one with information—Barry had talked to him Friday afternoon before he left on his long weekend to tell him he was going.

The hardest part—after the autopsy itself—was going through Barry's things. Pictures of him with his brother and brother's family. Pictures of him coaching his nephew's Little League team. Barry had played baseball in college, had been pretty good Kenzie heard, but she'd never once asked him why he hadn't gone into the big leagues. Was it by choice? Had he always wanted to be a cop? Or had he wanted to do something else? He'd been a friend, a colleague, an all-around good guy—yet she didn't know much about him. He didn't share a lot of personal information because he believed work was for work. The few times they'd gone out for drinks with the squad Barry had loosened up a bit. She wished she'd had more opportunities like that.

Dammit. She had tears in her eyes. Barry was a good agent. He didn't deserve to be tortured and murdered and left to turn into soup in the trunk of his own car.

She saw an email from Hans Vigo that had been read. She didn't remember reading it, but she was so exhausted last night she might have forgotten. She opened it again. It was a profile of Nicole Rollins along with some other information about the case, Tobias, and the young prostitute Elise Hansen.

She definitely hadn't read this email. She would have remembered. She thought back to last night . . . she hadn't checked her email, and this morning she'd skimmed through her messages on her phone only looking for emails that hadn't been read.

She tensed, straightened, and listened. The shower was still going. She brought up her computer log and scanned it. She'd arrived home last night at nine ten. Her email had been accessed at seven thirty. She'd been asleep from one

a.m. until five . . . her email had been accessed at two in
the morning. The email from Hans Vigo came in late last
night. It had been opened at two ten a.m. and then printed.
The computer log showed her that several other emails had
been read, yet those had been marked unread in her email
program.

The bastard forgot to mark this email as unread so she
wouldn't know that it had been accessed.

And he'd done it again just one hour ago.

That bastard had made love to her, watched her fall to
sleep, then snuck out and spied on her.

No—he wasn't spying on her, he was spying on the
case . . . and the only one he could be spying for was
Nicole Rollins.

"Hey, babe," Eric said behind her.

She whirled around and realized too late that she should
have put on a poker face. Eric immediately saw the truth.

The shift in his handsome face had her reeling, from
affection to fear to anger. "It's not what you think," he said.
He wore nothing but a towel around his waist.

"Really? So you're not helping Nicole Rollins?"

"I didn't have a choice. I'm sorry, I didn't want to hurt
you. I like you, Kenzie."

"Bullshit. You used me. You're a fucking *cop*! She
killed your friends. People we know. Barry Crawford!"

He made a move toward her and she grabbed her gun
from the desk and pointed it at him. "Don't move, Eric."

He kept his hands up. "Kenzie, I'm a dead man in
prison. You know that."

"You should have thought about that before you jumped
in bed with the cartels. Before you helped a cop killer."

She glanced at her phone on the desk. She needed to
get backup. She needed to subdue Eric first.

"Sit down," she ordered, motioning toward the closest
chair. "Now."

He stepped toward the chair, then suddenly turned and rushed her.

She fired her gun. The bullet hit him in the abdomen. His momentum had him falling into her. She kicked him away and kept the gun on him.

"You shot me!" he said. He held his stomach and blood poured through his fingers.

With her gun still trained on him, Kenzie called 911 for an ambulance . . . then she called Abigail Durant.

CHAPTER THIRTY-SIX

Lucy and Nate rushed to the hospital and found Kenzie in the waiting room, pacing, her arms wrapped tightly around her body. Lucy had already spoken to Hans and there was a team going through SAPD Officer Eric Butcher's apartment, finances, computers, and phones. This was their first viable lead—they had the inside man.

"Kenzie," Lucy said.

Kenzie turned and stared at her. Her eyes were swollen from crying. Lucy stepped forward to hug her, but Kenzie turned away. "I told Abigail everything I know."

"I'm here for you."

That was partly true. She wanted to make sure Kenzie was okay, but she also hoped that she had information about Rollins's location. Sean had been gone for five hours. They didn't have much time.

"Kenzie," Nate began.

"Stop. Just stop," she said. "I'm an idiot. I was sleeping with him for three months. Practically since our first date. I liked him. I more than liked him. He was funny and cute and I—I—" She took a deep breath. "He used me."

Lucy wanted to tell her that wasn't true, but she couldn't. So she said, "He used a lot of people, Kenzie. Ryan was

the one who introduced you to him after Operation Heatwave. Ryan feels like shit, too. But it's not his fault, and
it's not your fault."

"Tell that to Barry Crawford and Samantha Archer."

Emilio ran into the waiting room and immediately
hugged Kenzie. She accepted momentarily, then pushed
him away. "I'll be okay, Emilio. I wish I'd killed him. He'll
probably survive. What does that make me?"

"Human," Emilio said. "But I have some good news.
The body in Barry's car? It's not Barry."

Kenzie blinked at him. "I can't believe the lab processed
the DNA that fast. They only got it an hour or two ago."

"Julie Peters just called me. She called in a bone expert
from the university—and he's positive that the body is that
of an adult male under the age of twenty-five. She then
called the FBI lab and got Barry's blood type from his
employment records. Barry was A positive. The victim
was B positive."

Kenzie stared at him. "He's alive?" Then her face
clouded. "If he's alive, then where is he? Is he a traitor?
Did he turn on us, too?"

"We don't know that," Emilio said.

But Lucy had thought the same thing as soon as Emilio
said the body wasn't Barry's. If the body in the trunk
wasn't Barry, where was he? Who had stolen his car? Why
had they left it at the airport? To throw them off? To keep
them from looking? To delay them?

Delay. If the FBI thought that Barry was dead or missing
before Nicole's escape, everything could have changed.
There was no guarantee that the schedule would remain
the same. So hide Barry's car in plain sight—he was supposed to be on vacation for his twenty-fifth high school
reunion. A long weekend. No one would miss him.

If Barry was involved, he would have simply driven off,
and no one would have thought anything about it because

he wasn't expected to be back until Wednesday morning. But if he wasn't involved, if he was grabbed between his house and the airport, why would Nicole's people put his car at the airport, but keep him alive? There were other places to dump a car. To mess with the FBI? To confuse them? To implicate Barry?

Or maybe Nicole had nothing to do with it, and it was Tobias, playing games again like he'd done with Elise and Harper Worthington. Create an elaborate plan to kill Worthington, but one that ultimately tripped him up.

"Barry is a victim, not a suspect," Lucy said.

"You can't know that!" Kenzie said.

"I know Barry."

Kenzie shook her head. "How? You worked with him on one case. You've been in San Antonio for only six months. How can you say with any certainty who anyone is or what they're capable of?" She tossed her hands in the air. "None of this shit happened until you got here. Barry said something the other week and I didn't get it, but now I do."

"What?" Lucy asked quietly.

"Where Lucy Kincaid goes, trouble follows."

"Hey," Nate said, frowning. "That's not fair."

"And what is it with you, Nate?" Kenzie asked. "Following her around like a lovesick puppy? You haven't left her side since Monday. And Ryan said you're staying at her house while her boyfriend is out of the country?"

"Stop," Nate said. Maybe it was his tone or his posture, but Kenzie took a step back. "You're out of line, Kenzie. I know you're upset, I don't blame you, but you're wrong about everything. Rollins kidnapped Sean Rogan this afternoon. He's been missing for nearly six hours and we have no idea where he is. We came here hoping you might have some information from Butcher, a clue—something you don't even know is important—and you decide to use this opportunity to slam Lucy? To make insinuations? That's not like you. Snap out of it and help us, or we'll go back to headquarters."

Kenzie stared at Nate. "I—" She turned to Lucy. "I didn't know."

"It's okay."

"No, it's not." Kenzie rubbed her face with both hands. "If I knew anything, I'd tell you. He fooled me. He practically moved in with me these last two weeks and now I know why."

Emilio said, "I'll stay here with Kenzie and talk to Butcher as soon as he's out of surgery."

"Thanks, buddy," Nate said.

Lucy was nearly paralyzed. Six hours and counting. Every passing minute was bringing Sean closer to death.

"Luce," Nate said quietly, "we'll find him. Let's go."

Kate Donovan nearly jumped when she saw the message pop up on her screen. It had to be from Sean, though it was a long string of computer code that he must have written on the fly. She studied it for a minute, then realized he was giving her access to the computer he was using, a back door.

She immediately copied and pasted the code into her programming system and her screen went blank.

"What the fuck?"

Then a new desktop came on. It was a back-end portal into the US Treasury.

"Holy shit, he's hacking the US Treasury."

The Secret Service protected the nation's money, and this was going to show up on their radar, if it hadn't already.

She immediately called Zach Charles in San Antonio. He answered on the first ring. "Zach, it's Kate. Are you in the conference room?"

"Yes."

"Put me on speaker. Sean just contacted me. I'm getting into his computer now, working on his location." She split her screen and scrolled through the files until she found what she wanted. "WestNet is the provider," she said.

"Roger that," Zach said. "Pulling up their territory."

In the background she heard voices, then Hans said, "Kate? What's the status?"

"He's hacked the Treasury."

"How long does he have?"

"I don't know. He could do it faster, I'm sure, but he knows it's going to take us time to reach him."

"We don't have time. Where is he?"

"I'm working on it!" She and Sean had come up with the technical end of this plan, and when he lost his watch she feared their backup plan wouldn't work.

Zach said, "I have the map of WestNet. I'm overlaying it on the Texas Holdings map."

Kate said, "I have the ISP, am pinging it now. Shit."

"What's going on?"

"Security issues. Sean tripped a silent alarm, so to speak."

"By accident?"

"I doubt it. I've read his files, I know what he's capable of."

Hans said, "So does Nicole Rollins. If she thinks he's delaying—"

"Look, I'm doing the best I can! If Sean tripped the alarm, there's a reason."

In the background Zach said, "Two Texas Holding properties overlay with WestNet. One sixty miles northwest of the city, one seventy miles directly west of the city. Both over one hundred acres."

Hans ordered two teams to head toward each property.

"Backup will be coming. Stay off the coms. Cell phones only. Go."

"I got something," Kate said. "Sean sent me a note. Damn, I got it. I'm sending you the coordinates now and I'm sending them to Jack. The compound is west of your location. It's going to take you an hour or more to get there."

"We have alternative transportation. Good work, Kate."

"It's only good work if you get him out alive."

CHAPTER THIRTY-SEVEN

Hans stayed at FBI headquarters to coordinate the teams. Lucy, Nate, Ryan, and Brad were in a Bexar County Sheriff's helicopter heading to a landing point ten minutes from the compound. They couldn't get any closer by air if they wanted the element of surprise.

Jack was on the ground already, and field teams were en route, but it would take time to bring in enough people to swarm the compound.

As soon as they landed, Lucy called Kate. "Status."

"Sean's taking his time. He's sifting through accounts. He's transferred five million dollars so far. He's given me the access information for their accounts, but I wasn't fast enough the first time and they moved it almost immediately into another offshore account. This isn't easy, Lucy."

"I need to know that he's alive."

"He's stalling, but working methodically. Giving them just enough so they know he's following through."

"How much time?"

She paused. "Twenty minutes, tops. Fifteen, to be safe. Be careful, Lucy."

Lucy hung up and Nate said, "Jack's already in position. Backup will be here in twenty."

"Sean doesn't have twenty minutes. He can't stall forever."

Ryan said, "Proctor is with the marshals and they're en route. Proctor is coordinating from the tactical truck, but they're still fifteen minutes out. The sheriff's departments from Bexar, Kerr, and Bandera Counties are putting up roadblocks on every highway. The Rangers are moving into every area in between—the terrain is difficult, lots of back roads, dirt roads, creeks, vast open spaces. We'll have two helicopters up and circling an outer loop to avoid being spotted, but they can come in fast when needed. Two more on the ground waiting for orders. Every county surrounding the compound is on alert."

Ryan pulled out his phone. "Zach just sent us an aerial map of the compound. Check your email."

They all pulled out their phones. There were several outbuildings, but the main house took up the center of the property. "Nate, you've talked to Kincaid?"

Nate nodded. "Jack is set up here," he said and pointed to a ridge with a direct line-of-sight to the house. "He said there are four men patrolling outside the house, and there are at least two roaming patrols of two men each."

"Eight on the outside and how many inside?"

"No word on who's inside, but there's an Escalade in the drive. We ran the plates; it's owned by a company in San Antonio that has no employees."

"Another shell," Brad said.

Nate nodded. "There's a security camera at every corner of the house." He pointed to another building on his phone. "A barn here may have other vehicles or ATVs. There's at least three good escape routes that we can close off, and three more that are only accessible on foot or ATV."

"They'll use the alternate routes," Ryan said. "If they know we're coming, they'll know we have the roads blocked."

"That's what Jack said. But our primary goal is hostage rescue."

Sean. *The hostage.* Lucy nodded. "Let's go."

Nate looked at her.

"I'm not staying behind," she said.

"We'll get into position and wait for Jack's signal."

"We have to take out the cameras," Lucy said.

"How?"

"Kate. She's into their network, she can find them." Lucy called Kate.

"Status is unchanged, Lucy." Kate spoke fast.

"There are four security cameras outside the house. Can you kill them?"

She didn't respond right away. Lucy heard her fingers flying over the keyboard. "Yes," she finally said. "When?"

"Timing," Lucy asked Nate.

"Five minutes until we're in position, then we're just waiting for Jack to give us the all-clear—meaning the roaming patrols aren't between us and the house. We'll need to take out the four guards."

"Eight minutes," Lucy said to Kate. "And give Sean the heads-up."

"I'll try—but that's going to be tricky. Be careful, Lucy."

Lucy hung up. "Tell Jack," she told Nate.

"Eight minutes might be cutting it close."

"We're already cutting it close."

Barry was dying in front of Sean and he could do nothing to help him.

Elise danced around Sean's workstation, touching him at every opportunity, and Nicole kept pushing her back. "What's that?" Elise asked. "Is that how you did it two weeks ago? I *knew* the network couldn't be that slow. How did you get the passwords? Or do you just know all the back doors? What—"

"Knock it off, Elise," Joseph said.

"Is this how you destroyed Mona's files? Do you have the blackmail files? I want them back. Can you show me how?"

"Elise, stop!"

She pouted. "I wanna learn to do what he does."

"You don't have the patience," Joseph said.

"Leave her alone," Tobias said. He was sitting at the bar watching the security screens and eating.

Sean had never witnessed such a dysfunctional family. They'd been arguing and bickering from the minute Tobias and the others arrived. He'd finally pieced it all together, how they were connected and how they operated. They were all a different kind of crazy. Joseph, however, was the one he had to watch out for. He was the only one who seemed to have a clear head for planning. Nicole might have . . . except she had gone from being in total control when Sean first arrived to being fidgety and restless. Because of Maggie.

It took Sean a bit longer to put together the clues that Maggie was Tobias's mother and Nicole's aunt. Elise was the product of Tobias's father and Nicole's mother. Making her a half sister to both Nicole and Tobias. It was enough to make Sean's head spin, and he wondered what family dinners had been like. But Elise was much younger, and Nicole was already in the DEA by the time she was born.

Sean had stalled longer than he thought he could get away with because the five of them were arguing, but Maggie was becoming suspicious.

"It shouldn't take this long," Maggie finally said.

"We have eighteen million in our primary account," Joseph said. He was monitoring the banking information. "Five more and we're done."

"Why stop at twenty-three million?" Tobias said from

across the room. "He's hacked the fucking *Treasury*. We can take a hundred million. More!"

"We stop at twenty-three because we need to leave Texas," Margaret said. "It's no longer safe. I can't believe how you all have fucked this up."

Nicole glanced over at her aunt. "It wasn't me, Aunt Mags."

"You were arrested."

"Because of your son."

"You always blame him."

"Because it's always his damn fault!"

"You're right about that, Nicole," Sean couldn't stop himself from saying.

Elise hit him so hard when he wasn't expecting it that he fell out of his chair. "I don't like you," she said and kicked him in the stomach.

The feeling is mutual.

Joseph grabbed Elise by the arm and half dragged her over to the bar. "Sit."

She stuck her tongue out at him.

Sean climbed back into his chair, ignoring the bruises and throbbing in his arm. He spared a glance at Barry, who lay on the floor, eyes closed. He was breathing, but there was no way that Sean could escape with him. The poor guy wouldn't be able to walk a hundred yards let alone miles.

"The plane leaves at midnight," Maggie said. "That's our only window of opportunity."

"Midnight?" Tobias said. "That doesn't give me enough time to get to Kane Rogan."

"You should have killed him the first three times you had the opportunity," Maggie snapped. "What have I taught you, Tobias? From the very beginning, act swiftly. If you'd given the kill order in Mexico he would have been dead."

"Hey, that was all Joseph," Tobias said.

Joseph glared at him. "I'm warning you," he said in a low voice.

The computer screen flickered for a brief second and Sean almost missed it. Then it came again.

Kate had written a message on the computer notepad.

He had to look at it without drawing suspicion, and if Kate had risked his life to get it to him, it had to be important.

Nicole was ignoring the fighting behind her. "Wrap it up, Rogan." She was getting weary, but her eyes were glued to his screen. "One more transfer."

"You know," Sean said conversationally, "if you'd all just listened to Joseph from the beginning none of this would have happened. He seems to be the only one with an ounce of real strategic planning in his bones."

Maggie came at him with a gun out. That, Sean wasn't expecting.

Nicole pushed Maggie's arm up. "Stop it! He's baiting you, can't you see that?"

While Nicole was distracted, Sean opened the notepad through the DOS function that he was writing code in. Less of a chance that he'd be caught.

843 EXT SEC OUT ALERT

He immediately wiped the screen.

"What was that?" Elise said. "He just did something."

Nicole whirled around. "Why is the screen blank?"

"I didn't do anything. It's from the other end."

"It's here," Joseph said. "The money is all here."

Sean hadn't released the last five million. Kate must have done something . . . cloned his bank account? Sent false data? Whatever she did, it was going to save his life or cost him his life. They had originally planned to mirror the account information, but it would be extremely difficult and risky, and the chances of success—without knowing the account number and bank beforehand—was next to impossible. But maybe Kate had found a way while he was messing around in the Treasury back-end, stalling.

Tobias was still at the bar. The cameras. External security. A SWAT team was outside and the cameras were going down in—he glanced at the clock on the computer—one minute.

Maggie said, "Once he's dead, he won't be of use to us."

That was kind of obvious, wasn't it?

Sean looked down at Barry. His one good eye was open and watching Sean. Sean put up one finger. If Barry understood, he didn't say anything. But his eye was focused. That was a good sign, wasn't it?

Joseph showed his phone to Maggie. She stared and it was clear she didn't quite understand what she was seeing. Sean wondered if Joseph and Nicole had another endgame, because they were both surprised—and none too happy—when Tobias brought his mother into the house.

"Good," Maggie said. "Now split it."

"Let's do that from the road. I'm getting a bad feeling about this. Too many people know too much," Joseph said.

"From the road, huh?" Maggie said. "What's your plan? You thinking of stabbing the family in the back?"

Nicole said, "No, Aunt Maggie. Joseph is the most loyal person in the world. You know that."

"He's not family."

"He's been more a family to me than any of you," she snapped.

"He turned you. Against your own family."

"I don't know what you're talking about. I've been working to *save* this family for *years*. Tobias has risked us more times than I can count, and you just are too blind to see it!"

The security screens went blank. Tobias didn't notice because he'd come around from the back of the bar to defend his mother. Elise sat there sucking a lollipop, watching with wide eyes and a shit-eating grin, as if she'd seen this all before and she always enjoyed the show.

Sean stood up and immediately eyes—and guns—were on him. "I have a plane," he said. "You want it, it's yours. Just let Barry live. None of this was his fault."

"Right. He was just unlucky enough to get your girlfriend as a partner," Nicole said.

"Fiancée," Elise corrected from across the room. "He popped the question and she said yes. She has a big-ass ring on her finger."

Shit, eyes turned toward Elise, and the security screens behind her.

Joseph saw the blank screens first.

He turned to Sean, gun aimed at Sean's head.

A gun went off and Sean thought he was dead. But it was Joseph's brains that were blown out of the side of his head. His expression didn't change as he collapsed to the floor.

Nicole screamed. "No! No, no, no!"

"FBI, freeze!" a commanding voice said.

Nicole knelt by Joseph. "Joseph! Please, get up!"

Maggie Hunt turned her gun on the four FBI SWAT team members that stormed the room. She was dead before she could fire a round. Nate and Ryan moved cautiously toward where Nicole was shaking Joseph.

"Put your hands up, Rollins. Slowly—let me see your hands!" Nate commanded.

Jack Kincaid came in from the back, pushing Elise Hansen—or, rather, Elise *Hunt*—in front of him. "She ran out the back door."

"He kidnapped me! He hurt Dr. Oakley! Thank God you're here."

"Save it," a familiar voice said.

Lucy.

She took off her helmet and glanced around the room until her eyes caught Sean's. She smiled, just a little, but the love and relief in her eyes gave Sean all the peace he needed.

Then she saw Barry on the floor. "Oh my God! Barry?"

"He needs help."

Lucy knelt next to him. "Barry, it's Lucy Kincaid. We're going to get you to a hospital."

Nicole screamed and Sean turned to where she knelt sobbing and bloody next to her lover. She had a knife and threw it at Sean at the same moment the fourth SWAT member—Brad Donnelly—shot her three times in the chest.

Sean reacted quickly, but Nicole had been aiming center mass, and the knife embedded itself in his arm—the same arm that had been sliced open while rescuing Kane. Lucy rushed over, horror crossing her face.

"I'm okay." He winced as he pulled the knife out.

Lucy grabbed a bandage from her belt and wrapped his arm. "I thought—"

"I'll be fine." With his good arm, he touched her. He kissed her forehead. He was alive. He had Lucy. It was all he needed.

Leo Proctor walked in and said, "We've secured the immediate grounds."

Jack said, "Where's Tobias Hunt?"

"He was here until—" Sean remembered seeing Elise bolt, but not Tobias. Which meant he'd gone the other direction. "He ran that way, the way you all came in, not the way Jack came in."

"We didn't pass him."

Proctor said, "Search the house, top-to-bottom, on your toes!"

Lucy and Sean stayed with Barry while the rest of the SWAT team searched the house and the grounds completely twice.

Tobias Hunt was nowhere to be found.

An hour later, after Barry had been airlifted to the hospital and Elise arrested, Leo Proctor came back to the staging area and said, "We believe he went on foot to a dry creek bed. We found tracks there. It was rough terrain, but he stayed off the main roads. The Rangers are in place, and we have helicopters out with search lights. We'll find him."

Lucy shook her head. She didn't want to assume anything, not where these people were concerned. "Out of all of them, he was the dumbest, yet he got away? Is this ever going to be over?"

"I know where he's going," Sean said, wrapping his good arm around her shoulders. "He's in for a very big surprise."

Kane Rogan hated hospitals. He hated people taking care of him, he hated feeling helpless. He hated the antiseptic smell covering up the sick, the way nurses fawned over him like benevolent dictators, and not being able to leave. Like a prison.

But mostly, he hated being injured.

He'd been shot, stabbed, beaten, and left for dead, but he'd always managed to heal and come out on top. Now he was forty-three and his age was a factor. He felt older than his years for the first time in his life. The surgery had been successful, he'd been moved from recovery to a private room a few hours ago. He was supposed to be sleeping, but he was in too much pain. If the nurse saw that he'd palmed his pain pill, she would have put something in his IV.

Kane could tolerate the pain. He would take the antibiotic drip, but he wasn't going to get doped up on pain meds.

Blitz had come to see him earlier and bring him supplies that the hospital couldn't provide. Kane had questions that Blitz refused to answer. His men couldn't lie to him—Blitz just told him everything was under control. But he wouldn't give him details, he wouldn't tell him where Sean was, and he wouldn't tell him if the FBI had a plan to capture Nicole Rollins.

Kane wanted to be free, to be mobile. He had ideas on how to find her, but he couldn't do it from a hospital bed. And he needed Sean's help. He didn't like bringing his little brother into his messes, he didn't like asking for help from anyone except his team, but Sean had proven himself time and time again.

"I knew you wouldn't be sleeping."

He turned his head toward the door, his hand under the sheet. Then he relaxed.

"Siobhan."

She smiled and for a moment, for one short minute, his heart felt lighter. She walked over to his bed. "Blitz said you were already going stir crazy. You lost a kidney. You always take care of everyone, you need to let someone take care of you for a while."

She was the most beautiful woman Kane had ever laid eyes on. The most compassionate, frustrating, loyal, stubborn, talented, beautiful creature on earth. From day one, when he'd first seen her, he'd been haunted by her. Haunted, maybe, because his life couldn't include romantic entanglements. It wasn't fair to Siobhan. Not just because of his life, but because he would put her in danger. Just being friends with him had put her in danger.

"You're thinking dark thoughts," she said and sat down on the edge of his mattress.

"You shouldn't be here," he said.

"Maybe not, but you're really not in a position to do much about it, are you?"

He scowled.

She frowned and felt around his sheets. He grabbed her wrist. "Don't," he said.

"Kane." The lines creased on her smooth forehead. Her red curls had escaped from her braid. She brushed them out of her eyes, but couldn't hide the worry he saw in their bright-blue depths. Another reason why he couldn't love her. He never wanted to see her sad. He never wanted to see her in pain, or in danger, or in fear.

He wasn't ignorant. They'd both felt this attraction from that first day, when she risked her life to save a child and he came in to save them both.

But it couldn't be.

She leaned over and kissed him. "I've always loved you, Kane," she whispered.

"No," he said.

"I can't turn my feelings on and off. But this week—I had to tell you the truth. You have to know how I feel. You're the most arrogant, annoying, impossible man I've ever met. And you're the bravest, most dedicated, most loyal man I know."

"I can't change, Siobhan." His voice cracked. The pain, not the emotions. Because he couldn't afford to have emotions.

"I've never asked you to change," she whispered. "You never wanted to be a hero, but it's what you are. And if you think I'm going to walk away after this week?"

"You have to."

"Don't tell me what to do."

A faint footstep sounded out of place. With all the hospital sounds, the one thing Kane had noticed was that nurses tread silently.

This footfall wasn't silent.

"Drop to the floor," he ordered Siobhan.

She dropped.

Tobias stepped into Kane's hospital room. Kane had never seen him, but he had Lucy's description, and it was right on the money.

Tobias had a gun in his hand.

"Isn't this fun?" Tobias said. "You survived a fucking army in Mexico, but will be taken out by one man. And how about it—I'll get the girl after all."

Kane pulled the trigger of his gun—the gun Blitz had brought him earlier. He pulled the trigger five times, though the first bullet had been fatal.

Hospital staff and security rushed into the room. Someone helped Siobhan up. Kane watched the heart monitor beep. His heart rate had barely elevated when he killed Tobias.

He was no man for Siobhan.

There were questions and someone took his gun, but he didn't need it anymore; Tobias was dead. Siobhan refused to leave, but she was crying.

"Don't look at me like that Kane. Don't—I know you, dammit!"

Kane was in a fog. Maybe they'd stuck some pain meds in his IV when he wasn't looking.

Blitz came in, arguing with security. But he must have told them something they wanted to hear, because they let him enter.

"I'm sorry," he said.

"It wasn't your fault, Blitz."

"I had the entrances covered. I'd never have let her in here if I thought he was in the building."

"Take her to Andie's."

"No!" Siobhan said. "I'm not leaving."

Kane stared at her. His heart broke. But his life wasn't the life for Siobhan. "You're not staying."

"This isn't over, Kane. I'm not letting you do this to yourself. To us."

"There is no us, Siobhan."

She shook her head. "I meant what I said, Kane. All of it."

She walked out.

"Boss, you should—"

"Shut up," he told Blitz. They really had put something in his IV. "Make sure she gets home safely. Understood?"

Blitz nodded and left.

Kane finally slept. And dreamt of Siobhan.

CHAPTER THIRTY-EIGHT

Saturday

Lucy stared out the window at the pool, but she didn't really see anything. She was numb.

She should be celebrating. She should be *happy* that the events that had started three months ago were over. Almost everyone involved was dead, except for Elise Hansen. She was in jail. She would not be getting out, regardless of what Dr. Oakley said. She was being transferred to a maximum-security federal prison while awaiting trial, and that suited Lucy just fine.

She should be celebrating that she'd helped take down a violent drug cartel. Jimmy Hunt had been apprehended by the DEA in Mexico City based on the information obtained from the traitorous DEA agent Adam Dover. They had searched the Hunt property in Los Angeles and found the remains of Tamara Rollins, killed five years ago for what reason, they still didn't know. Considering what Sean revealed about how the family fought, it wasn't surprising that one of them had killed her . . . though it was surprising that not one of them seemed to care. Kane survived surgery and the loss of a kidney, and Barry Crawford was slowly recovering in the hospital. He may not regain sight in one of his eyes, and he had additional surgeries in his future, but he would live. All of that was good news.

And mostly, she should celebrate that she and Sean were alive. That they'd lost no one in the raid on the compound, and that finally, things might get back to normal.

But she couldn't smile. She could muster up no relief or joy or emotion. She was in a daze, and all she could think about was how much she almost lost.

Sean stepped into the living room, moving slowly. He had a cracked rib, his arm had been stitched up at the hospital and he wore a sling to protect it, and the only remnants of his ordeal were bruises all over his body from being tied up and stuffed behind the seat in Joseph Contreras's truck. She ached for him. But he was alive.

"Lucy."

"I'm okay."

Sean put his good hand on her shoulder and didn't say anything.

"No, I'm not," she said. "I'm not okay. I almost lost you. I—I can't. I can't stop thinking about it. When I close my eyes, I see you dead."

"I'm not dead, Lucy."

"I know! But—dammit, I'm so mad at you."

She turned into him, buried her face in his chest, afraid if she touched him too hard she'd hurt him.

He wrapped his arm around her and drew her in. It was so gentle, so tender, the tears started falling. "I'm not mad at you," she said.

"I know."

"When it was just me, I didn't care. Because what I did was my choice. My decision. If I was hurt, it didn't matter because no one cared."

"Your family cared."

"That's not the same."

"I know."

"I love you so much, Sean. I was so angry with you, with Hans, with Nate, with Jack—all of you conspiring to risk *your life*. It's not just your life anymore."

"It was the best plan we could come up with. They put a million-dollar bounty on Kane's head, Lucy. If we didn't stop them—"

"I'm selfish."

"God, no, Lucy. Don't."

"All I thought when I saw that video of those bastards dragging you to the van was that you let it happen. You risked your life—*your life that you promised to me!*—for the greater good."

"I did it, in part, so you wouldn't be in danger."

"Don't you get it? My life would be over without you. I had no life before you. I will have no life after you."

"That's not true, princess. That's just not true."

"Don't do it again. Not without me. Everyone plotted against me—"

"Lucy, it wasn't that." He hesitated.

She looked up at him through her tears. "Tell me."

He touched her face, his eyes full of both worry and love. "Jack said that if you knew, you'd be in danger."

"That's crazy. You're the one who put your *life* on the line."

"If you knew before we enacted the plan, you would have gone to the house. I couldn't risk that. I couldn't risk you, not with these people. Not with what they've done."

"They could have killed you."

"But you knew they wouldn't, not without their money."

She whispered, "But what if I was wrong?"

"You weren't. Is that what this is? That you're doubting yourself? You were right, Lucy."

"Psychology is not a hard science. It's part science, part experience, part *guessing*."

"But you were right," he repeated.

"But I could have been wrong!"

"But you weren't."

She stepped away. "You're impossible."

"I love you, Lucy. I hate seeing you in pain."

"You're the one with a cracked rib and bruises over half your body."

He reached out and touched her. "Set a date."

"What?"

"Our wedding. I love you, you love me, and dammit, I want to be married. Living together is fun, but I'm yours. You're mine. I never thought I'd want that stupid piece of paper, but I want it. I want to see you in a white dress holding colorful flowers. I want your family, and my family, to sit in the pews of Saint Catherine's and watch me tell the world how I feel about you. About us. About the better man you have made me."

How could he be so . . . happy? She'd almost lost him. She was struggling to forgive him, to forgive everyone who did this behind her back. She couldn't lose him. Didn't he know that she would be completely destroyed? She could lose her job, she could lose this house, but she would be nothing if she lost Sean.

"It can't be tomorrow," Sean continued, "unless we fly to Vegas. And you deserve a better wedding than Vegas. Not to mention, your father would probably kill me."

She almost smiled. "I think we should wait at least until your bruises disappear." Then she turned away from him because she just couldn't bear to look at his swollen face anymore. It hurt.

"Lucy—please. I'm okay."

"You almost weren't."

"But I am. I know you're mad—"

"Yes, I'm mad, Sean. Do you know what it would do to me if you—you had died?"

"Yes. Because I think about it all the time, about what would happen to me if you died. Two weeks ago you were shot in the back, Lucy. If you hadn't been wearing a vest, you would have died, or been paralyzed. I close my eyes and watch that bullet hit you over and over again."

She faced him and squeezed his hand. "Sean—"

"I've almost lost you so many times. When you nearly fell down the mine shaft in the Adirondacks. When you were run off the road by that psycho in DC. When you went to Mexico to rescue Brad and the boys. You risk yourself because that's what you do—I can't ask you not to do it. Kane risks himself because that's what he does. I don't think I ever really understood why Kane does what he does, not until these last few days. Now, I do. If not us, who?" He gently hugged her. "This was something I could do. I had no intention of dying, I didn't even consider it an option. And I'm really sorry I didn't tell you about the plan."

"Don't do it again."

"Okay."

"I mean it. We both put ourselves at risk. It's our job— our vocation, I guess. Just like Kane and Jack and Father Mateo, we do it because we couldn't do anything else. But I can't be kept in the dark. If I think you're not telling me something because it'll hurt me or because I'll try and stop you, then we'll never truly trust each other. I didn't like the idea for a lot of different reasons, but I trust *you* and I trust my brother, and I knew Jack would move Heaven and earth to save you. But I can't be coddled or protected, Sean."

"I am sorry. And the reverse goes, too." He kissed her.

She sighed. The anger was gone. The fear was beginning to fade away. "That's fair." She smiled. "So where are we going for our honeymoon?"

"Honeymoon? I don't think we've had a vacation that didn't end up with trouble."

"Trouble finds us, Sean. That doesn't mean we shouldn't go away. Hawaii, maybe. What's the homicide rate in Hawaii? Probably low. It's too pretty for people to be violent. Let's find a place on a small island where there are no murders, no kidnappings, no gunrunning or drug cartels. We'll go and just relax."

He laughed. "I don't know if you understand the meaning of the word *relax*."

"But you do, and you'll teach me."

"I'll enjoy every minute."

"October."

"Okay. Why October?"

"Because everyone says that October is beautiful here in San Antonio. And we deserve a beautiful wedding day."

"That isn't one hundred percent humidity."

"That too."

"Okay. October it is. Four months should be enough time to plan a wedding."

"Small wedding."

He raised his eyebrow. "The Kincaids and the Rogans are both quite large families. And we have friends."

"Medium wedding."

"Okay. What day?"

"I'll call Father Mateo and ask him what he has available." She paused. "Is that okay with you? Saint Catherine's?"

"I told you it was."

"But I know how you feel about churches."

"Lucy, I have a hard time with religion, but I love you, and I love your faith. I like Mateo. He's everything that I think a man of God should be. If they were all like him and Padre, the world would be a much better place. And it matters to you."

"I would marry you anywhere."

"I love you for that, Lucy, but the sacrament means something to you. And because it means so much to you, it means something to me. I want the boys all there, I want my family, your family, our friends. I want a party. I want lots of champagne and the best Scotch and great food. And then we're going on a honeymoon. You get to plan the wedding, I'll do anything you want. But I get to plan the honeymoon. Keeping your low-homicide-rate criterion in mind."

She smiled slyly. "Should I be scared?"

"Never."

There was a beep at the front door, and Sean tensed. The door opened and Jack walked in with Kane. Sean relaxed when Jack reset the alarm. Lucy wondered if he would ever truly relax again, and that made her sad. Sean had always loved fun, loved playing games and doing things that gave him pleasure. Sailing. Skiing. Racing. Sitting by the pool under a blue sky. Picnics in a meadow of wildflowers. He loved living so much . . . and yet, so much had happened, so much had they suffered. And she didn't know if it would be easy to forget. If they would ever forget. If they could, at any time, relax.

She watched as Kane eased himself into the oversized chair. Kane wasn't a man who relaxed, ever. She'd only met him three months ago, but the only time she'd seen him even marginally relax was here, in their house. Whether it was because he was with his brother, or because he felt safe, she didn't know.

"Thanks for bringing him up here," Sean said to Jack.

Jack didn't dignify the thanks with a comment. "Megan is flying in tomorrow morning," he said.

Lucy realized that Jack had given his entire week for her. For Sean. The anger she felt over his part in keeping

Sean's plan from her disappeared. She walked over to him and hugged him tightly. "I love you, Jack."

He hugged her, kissed the top of her head, and said, "I love you, too, kid."

"I didn't mean what I said."

"I know."

She took a deep breath and stepped back. "If you need to go home, I understand."

He looked at her as if she were speaking a foreign language. "Luce, I want to be here. Megan wants to be here, too. Unless you both need some time, I could get another place. I'll be in San Antonio for at least two more weeks. I'm the point person for Operation Cleanup."

Sean laughed, then winced. "Is that what you're calling it?"

"Seemed appropriate. Patrick will be here next week, as soon he's done with that job you referred to him in New York. He'll be going over all electronics and computers." Jack put his hand up. "I know what you're going to say, Sean. But you can't be involved in this one."

"That's not what I was going to say."

Jack snorted, and Lucy almost laughed. "I think Sean was going to say he told me so."

"About?"

"The house. I told him it was too big for us, and he said we both had large families who needed a place to stay when they visited."

Sean kissed her. "Exactly. You're all staying here. That's why I picked the place. For family."

"You won't feel crowded?" Jack said.

"No," Lucy said. "There is nothing I would want more than having my family here, in our home." She squeezed Sean's hand and sat down on the couch across from Kane and Jack. "I didn't realize how good I had it."

"What the hell are you talking about?" Jack said.

She didn't feel comfortable talking about this, but she had to. She had to accept the past before she could live in the future. "You. Dillon. Patrick. Everyone else. Mom and Dad. Especially Mom and Dad. I shut you all out. Even you, Jack, when you were training me after what happened . . ." She still had a hard time talking out loud about her kidnapping and rape. "I didn't think of you as my brother. My *family*. You were my instructor, my coach, my drill sergeant, but not my brother. And Kane—you saved my life two weeks ago."

Kane shook his head.

"Yes. Because of you, I put on the Kevlar. I don't wear it all the time, there isn't a need, but that day, because of something you said, because you cared, I wore it. I was terrified when Sean went down to Mexico to look for you, but not for a minute did I want him to stay home. Because we—all of us—are here for each other. And I never appreciated it, truly appreciated my family, like I do now."

Kane looked at Sean. "Blitz told me how you found me."

"I don't think either of us is in a fighting mood," Sean said. "Give me a week or two for my ribs to heal."

"Thank you."

Sean smiled. "I knew you'd forgive me."

"Never do it again."

"I'm not going to lie to you."

"What does that mean?"

"It means, I'm not making promises I can't keep."

Kane grunted. "We'll talk later."

The four of them sat back and relaxed. There was no need to talk, no need to further rehash what had happened this past week. "The pool house is all yours, Kane," Lucy said with a yawn. "As long as you want it. Jack, both the guest rooms downstairs have their own bathroom, so you and Megan will have privacy when Patrick gets here. And if Dillon and Kate decide to visit, we have two guest rooms upstairs."

"One is empty," Sean said. "I'll order some furniture. And maybe I'll look into finding an architect to convert the space above the garage into an apartment."

"I don't think you two are going to want people here all the time," Jack said. "You'll get sick of it."

"No," Lucy said. "I don't think so."

She hugged her future brother-in-law Kane. There was something in his eyes—something had changed. She wouldn't say it was a softening, but it was a shift. Affection? Relief? She didn't know.

"I'm glad you're here, Kane."

She hugged Jack. "I can't wait to see Megan. I never really got to talk to her at Christmas."

"I'll call Dillon. Order him and Kate to take a weekend and visit."

She smiled. "I'd like that." She took Sean's hand and helped him up. "Time for bed," she said. "It's been a long week."

October. Five months . . . and then the Rogans and the Kincaids would be united permanently.

And until then, it looked like they would have a full house.

ACKNOWLEDGMENTS

I am always grateful to those who help make my books the best they can be. First and foremost, the amazing people at Minotaur/St. Martin's Press, from art to marketing to production, but especially my editor, Kelley Ragland. She makes me a better writer. Research is also an important part of my writing process, and I couldn't do that without the selfless group of experts at Crime Scene Writers, specifically Wally Lind, Lee Lofland, D.P. Lyle, and Robin Burcell. They've helped me with the details more times than I can count. Coroner Chris Herndon from Colorado was absolutely critical with some information for this book. If I got the death scene wrong, I'm solely to blame. This time around, I needed help understanding how land records were maintained in Texas, and Hadassah Schloss from the Texas General Land Office was extremely helpful.

Writers are so generous with their time to help other writers, and I owe a huge debt of gratitude to my friend Deborah Coonts who is a pilot and a flight instructor (as well as a lawyer and a writer!). She helped make my rescue scene ten times better than the original. Again—if I made a mistake translating her expertise, blame me.

And always, my family keeps me sane and caffeinated. I love you all.

POISONOUS

Available in April 2016 in hardcover
from Minotaur Books

Dear Ms. Revere:

My name is Tommy Wallace and I live in Corte Madera, California. Last summer my stepsister, Ivy Lake, was killed and no one knows who did it.

I talked to the detective and she said she can't talk to me about what happened. She was nice and everything, but told me to talk to my dad. I thought she couldn't talk to me because I was too young, so when I turned eighteen last week, I went back to the police station and Detective Martin still wouldn't talk to me about what happened to Ivy.

I am writing to you because you help people. I've been watching your show and you find out what happened to people who died. I went to your website and read the article about how you found out what happened to an architect who was killed last year. That was in Atherton, which is not far from me at all! You said you wanted to find out what happened to him because his family deserved to know the truth and have closure. I don't really understand what closure means, but if it means knowing who hurt Ivy, that's what I want.

No one is like they were before Ivy died. My dad says that the police don't know who killed her or why. My stepmother gets mad all the time because the police haven't arrested anyone. My dad thinks that Ivy's boyfriend killed her. My sister thinks that Ivy's best friend killed her. My stepmother thinks that I killed her.

I would never, ever hurt anyone even if they were really mean to me. But now Paula won't let me come to the house to visit unless my dad is there, and he works so much he isn't home hardly at all. Austin says she's scared of me. He called her stupid. (I told him it wasn't nice to call people stupid. I don't like being called stupid.) I miss Bella and Austin so much sometimes I cry. (My mom says it's okay if boys cry sometimes, but my dad says I'm too old to cry.) I don't know why Paula thinks I would hurt Ivy. She wouldn't let me come to Bella's birthday party because my dad was out of town. I don't want Bella to think I don't like her anymore. My mom tried to make me feel better by taking me for an ice cream cone. I love ice cream more than any other food. I thought she was mad at me, but when my dad came back from his trip he came over and my mom yelled at him the same way she yelled at him when they were getting the divorce. My dad left and didn't say good-bye to me. I think he's mad at me, too.

I want everything to go back to the way it was before Ivy died, but Austin says that can't happen. He told me the only thing that will fix everything is if the police find out who really killed Ivy, and then Paula will know I didn't do it. But the police don't seem to be trying anymore. My dad says that we pay their salaries and they should be working harder.

I don't have a job so I don't pay their salaries, is that why Detective Martin won't talk to me?

I don't want anyone to think I hurt Ivy. I don't want Austin to get in trouble for coming to see me when he's not supposed to. I want to go to Bella's birthday party in April when she turns six and give her a present. If you can just tell my stepmother I didn't do anything wrong, she'll have to believe you.

Thank you for reading my letter.
Sincerely, Tommy
Thomas Andrew Wallace

CHAPTER ONE

Monday

Maxine Revere and her right hand everything, David Kane, flew into SFO on Labor Day. Max didn't like traveling on holidays, but she didn't have much of a choice with her hectic schedule. They took a shuttle to the car rental lot and David handled the paperwork while Max scanned her email for anything she needed to address immediately. A dozen messages down the inbox was an email from her lover, Detective Nick Santini.

I know you're angry that I cancelled our plans this weekend. I'll find time later this week to come up for a day. Let me know when you land.

Max didn't know why she was still so irritated at Nick. She'd planned on flying in a few days before her scheduled meeting with the detective in charge of the Ivy Lake homicide—thus avoiding flying on a holiday. But Nick called her Thursday night and cancelled. He said he had to swap shifts at the last minute. Something about his excuse didn't ring true, so she pressed him for the reason. Maybe what bothered Max the most was that she had to push him before he told her the truth. His ex-wife was fighting for sole custody of their son and he had a critical meeting with his lawyer. Max hadn't met Nancy Santini, but she doubted she'd like the woman who was attempting to prevent a good father like Nick from spending time with his own child. She was manipulative and vindictive, and why Nick couldn't see it, Max didn't know.

She dropped her smartphone into her purse without actually responding to Nick's message. What could she say? That she understood? She didn't, and she wasn't going to lie to Nick about how she felt. He didn't want her opinion on the matter, and she certainly wasn't going to tell him she would be waiting with intense anticipation for his unconfirmed arrival. If he drove the hour to Sausalito to see her, great. If not . . . well, she really didn't have much say in what he did or didn't do. He'd made that perfectly clear when she started asking questions about his custody battle.

David approached her, rental keys in hand. "Whose head did you bite off?"

She looked at David and raised an eyebrow. When she wore heels, she and David were eye-to-eye. "Excuse me?"

"When you're mad at someone, your eyes narrow and the lines in your forehead crease."

"You're telling me I have wrinkles. Terrific."

"It's Nick."

"If you know, why did you ask?"

David led the way to the rental car without responding. It was a rhetorical question, but Max wished David wouldn't act as if she were on the verge of dumping Nick. She was the first to admit she didn't do long-term—or long-distance—relationships well.

Nick was different. She wasn't being a romantic to think so; she wasn't a romantic at heart. Yet when he'd cancelled their weekend plans, her gut had twisted uncomfortably. She didn't want it to be over so soon.

David popped the trunk of the luxury sedan and maneuvered his lone suitcase into the trunk alongside Max's two large bags. Her laptop and overnight bag went into the backseat. She sat in the passenger seat and slid the seat back for comfort. After five and a half hours on a plane, she wanted to stretch her long legs.

She could travel light if she had to, but she didn't know how long she'd be investigating this case. She'd told Ben she wanted ten days for the Ivy Lake investigation. He scowled at her—it was the only word that fit his irritated-with-Maxine expression. Then she told Laura, his admin, not to schedule anything for two weeks. She'd almost skipped town before Ben found out she'd blocked off so much time, but he'd called her on the way to the airport and whined at her. She'd already recorded the October show—early, she reminded him—it wasn't like she had to rush back. If she needed to do any re-takes, they had a sister studio in San Francisco.

"You took a week off in Lake Tahoe, and now an investigation that shouldn't take more than a few days you're taking two weeks?"

"Good-bye, Ben." She'd hung up on him. She wasn't going to explain herself. She knew what needed to be done to keep her show running smoothly, and she'd do it.

David pulled out of the parking space and merged into the dense traffic that would take them through San Francisco and across the Golden Gate Bridge. Max stared out the window. She liked San Francisco, but didn't have the love affair with it like she did New York City. She'd never once considered living here, though she grew up only forty minutes south of the city. She couldn't put her finger on why—maybe it was simply that San Francisco was too close to her family.

"Why does he let her get away with it?" Max asked after several minutes of silence.

"What are you talking about?"

"Nick's ex. The games she's playing."

"He's not letting her get away with anything," David said. "There's a process."

"She's trying to deny Nick the right to see his own son."

"No," David corrected, "she's seeking full custody so she can leave the state without violating the joint custody agreement."

"Why do you know more about this than I do?" She had mixed feelings about David's relationship with Nick. While it made her life easier that her closest friend actually liked the man she was sleeping with, she didn't particularly appreciate that Nick and David had conversations that she wasn't privy to. Lately, Nick had been talking to David more than her.

"This is an area I have more experience in than you," David said.

"Maybe I should have been a judge," she said.

David's spontaneous laughter didn't improve her mood.

"I would make a good judge," she added defensively. "I'm exceptionally good at weeding through fact and fiction."

"Perhaps in criminal court," he said and cleared his throat. "Not so in family court."

"I'd certainly put a stop to her blatant manipulation tactics. She's changed her mind three times about where she and her boyfriend are moving. And who is this boyfriend, anyway? First they're getting married, then they aren't, but are planning on moving in together? With Tyler in the house? How can Nick put up with it? Doesn't he have a say in who his minor son shares a house with? This whole situation stinks, and it's not going to end well for anyone."

"You need to stay out of this, Max. Nick knows what he's doing, but it's sensitive."

"I don't understand."

"That's a first."

Max didn't respond. It was David's tone—what wasn't he telling her? Was there something else going on with Nick and his ex that David knew about but she didn't? Why would Nick hold back from her? They'd had a wonderful vacation together in Lake Tahoe six weeks ago—until it was cut short by Nick's ex-wife. Still, she'd been understanding. Mostly. Sort of.

Okay, she'd been a bitch after the fourth call from Nancy Santini demanding that Nick bring Tyler back to town. Nick never told Max what their argument was about, but something Nancy said had Nick leaving the same day. Max detested these sorts of games, especially when children were involved.

Max had no children of her own and doubted she ever would. But she'd interviewed enough kids over the years and learned one important fact: kids picked up on lies faster than most adults. They knew what was going on in their family even if their parents tried to shelter them. How did that help them deal with the world? How did that help them grow into honest citizens? Never had Max found a lie better than the truth. Lies were expedient. They solved an immediate problem but created more problems in the future. And the only way to fix the situation was to keep telling lies until they exploded and everyone was stained from the deception.

Nick refused to say a negative word about Nancy in front of his son, and while Max could respect his position on the one hand, telling the truth was not being negative. The truth was neither good nor bad, it simply *was*, and Tyler was smart enough to come to his own conclusions. What would he think about his father who remained silent in the face of Nancy's manipulations? How could he respect him? How would he handle his own relationships when he grew up if all he saw was Nancy's bad behavior, for which Nick remained silent—at least around his son?

"You're thinking quite loudly," David said.

"I haven't said a word."

"Sometimes you don't need to."

"Speaking of kids, will you be *allowed* to see Emma?" She winced at her tone. David didn't deserve her anger, though he seemed to be trying to irritate her. "I didn't mean it like that."

"Yes you did," David said. "I'm going to Brittany's tonight. She said we'd play it by ear."

"Another manipulative bitch," Max said under her breath.

"She is," David concurred, "but I want to see my daughter, so I deal with it. I have fewer rights than Nick because Brittany and I never married. I will not risk my time with Emma." He paused, then added, "Stay away from Brittany, Max."

David's tone had gone from normal to threatening in one sentence. A few months ago, Max would have pushed the conversation, but she'd realized over this last summer how deeply she valued David's friendship. She wasn't going to risk her relationship with her best friend and business partner by arguing with him about the mother of his daughter. So, as difficult as it was for her to remain silent, she kept her mouth shut.

Brittany treated David like garbage. She insulted him in front of Emma and refused to let David have more time with his daughter than the court mandated. The only consolation was that Emma was a smart kid. She'd be thirteen next week and adored her father. She was surprisingly well-adjusted considering her parents didn't get along. Brittany might be a bitch, but David got along with Brittany's parents and apparently they had a lot of clout over Brittany. If it weren't for them, David said, he'd never have been part of Emma's life.

Max put David and Nick and their respective children

out of her mind and spent the remainder of the drive responding to messages from her producer, Ben Lawson, and staff. Ben had wanted to send a small crew with Max because he sensed this case was going to be good—for Ben, "good" meant good for *Maximum Exposure* ratings. Max axed the idea of traveling with anyone but David. She needed time in the field without a cameraman or support staff. The interpersonal connections she made were important, but the nuances in tone, expression, and body language were lost when a camera was involved. Max had been a freelance reporter for years before agreeing to host *Maximum Exposure* for the cable network NET, and she still preferred to work a case alone, asking questions, pushing people to be truthful, proving or disproving evidence.

Though she'd be the first to admit she was happy to let the competent NET research team take over much of the grunt work. They'd compiled all the public information on the Ivy Lake investigation, including news clippings, profiles of Ivy's friends and family, and television coverage.

After going back and forth with Ben on the news crew until her irritation overflowed, she sent back a message:

I'll call in the crew when I see fit, but if I see a camera in Corte Madera before I'm ready I'll quit.

Ben just didn't know when to drop a subject, or how to give up control.

She could relate.

While Ivy's stepbrother's letter had affected her and prompted her to act, she'd grown even more curious after speaking to Tommy Wallace on the phone. He barely spoke. She tried to get him to talk about Ivy, about why he wrote the letter, and his responses were simple and brief. Any other case and she would have been suspicious and likely dropped the matter altogether, but after reading the files her staff put together, she realized from the media reports that Tommy might be mentally handicapped.

Which made her wonder if he wrote the letter himself or if someone helped him. And if so, why?

Max had spoken to Grace Martin, the detective in charge of the Ivy Lake death investigation, when she received the letter from Tommy Wallace two weeks ago. First to feel out whether law enforcement was inclined to help or hinder her investigation, and then specifically to ask about Tommy.

"I spoke to Tommy Wallace several times," Grace had said. *"He's slow, not stupid."*

Grace seemed amenable to Max's involvement when they spoke on the phone—the case was fourteen months cold with no leads. She agreed to meet with Max in person, which was a big win for Max—too often she had to fight with the local police for access.

Max had read Tommy's letter multiple times. Her stomach twisted each time. There was an honesty of expression that surprised her, but what really hit her was the lack of anger or grief. Maybe Tommy's "slowness" made him less emotional. When people wrote to her, there was always pain and anger. Rage on the page, Ben had once said. Parents wanted answers about the murder of their child. A spouse fighting with the police for more time and resources because their betrothed had been murdered or disappeared and there were no answers. But Tommy's letter was unlike any she'd read before. And while he might have had help writing the letter, there was no doubt the sentiments were true.

While Tommy's letter had her looking at Ivy Lake's death, it was the circumstances themselves that propelled Max to action. Ivy Lake had been seventeen when she'd been killed—pushed off a cliff, according to the forensics report. According to the police department, they had interviewed dozens of individuals, mostly minors, many who had reason to hate Ivy.

If the pen is mightier than the sword, the keyboard is mightier than the pen. And Ivy used her keyboard to expose the secrets of her schoolmates through social media—including one girl who'd committed suicide after bearing the brunt of Ivy's attacks. Ivy's murder had spun a web of stories in the local media about cyber-bullying, but in the end, the stories stopped, the investigation hit a dead end, and life went on. Without a killer in custody. Without answers for the family. Without justice for Ivy.